Andrew MacAllan lives with his wife in Wiltshire. His previous novels, *Succession*, *Generation*, *Diamond Hard*, *Fanfare* and *Speculator*, are all available from Headline.

Also by Andrew MacAllan

Traders

Andrew MacAllan

HEADLINE

First published in 1994
by HEADLINE BOOK PUBLISHING

First published in paperback in 1994
by HEADLINE BOOK PUBLISHING

10 9 8 7 6 5 4 3 2 1

ISBN 0 7472 4587 8

Typeset by CBS, Felixstowe, Suffolk

Printed and bound in Great Britain by
Cox & Wyman Ltd, Reading, Berkshire

HEADLINE BOOK PUBLISHING
A division of Hodder Headline PLC
338 Euston Road
London NW1 3BH

Traders

One

Afterwards, long afterwards, when all the fuss had died down, and people would ask Anna when it had all begun, what had really marked the start of everything, she would always wait for a moment before replying.

This gave the impression that there might have been several starting points, all of which she remembered well. But, of course, whatever answer she gave could never alter the fact that there had only been one. Her moment of departure from a life of total routine and dull predictability was etched in her mind and memory with the sharpness of a steel pen.

In those days, she had worked at the big house. This was one of the largest in Perthshire and stood on top of a hill. It still did, but now each floor was divided into flats for the elderly, and the building was somehow diminished, no longer a domineering, frowning castle whose owners controlled the land as far as they could see from the topmost turret. Now, others owned this land, split up between several farmers. The laird and his lady had gone long since. Then, things had been different.

On the eve of Anna Ballater's seventeenth birthday, one year after the end of what politicians and writers in newspapers were already calling the Great War, she was hurrying home from the big house. She had been kept late – the laird had guests arriving – and so dusk had already darkened the land when she set out. A faint evening mist rose like steam from fields near the river. Because Anna was in a hurry, she took a short cut by the side of Soldier's Wood to her parents' cottage on the edge of the estate.

Her father, a wartime sergeant in the Camerons, was carpenter for Mr MacTavish, the Laird of Long Glen, and Anna worked in the main house polishing silver under the watchful and usually friendly eye of the housekeeper, Mrs Deakin.

Anna did not particularly like her job, but there was little choice in the village for girls of her age; her mother, sensing Anna's opinions, would frequently remind her how fortunate she was to get what she called 'a place'. Anna agreed, but privately she did not intend to grow old in other people's service, like Mrs Deakin and the cook. She thought she could do better than this – but how? She felt optimistic that one day, somehow, and somewhere, an opportunity would arise and then she would take it; but what this might be she had no idea.

Once, a travelling fair came to Perth and she won the prize of a leather travelling bag for shooting at a sideshow. She was a good shot; her father still had his army service revolver and boxes of cartridges and Anna practised, shooting rats that came in hundreds out of the fields after harvest.

The owner of the sideshow had not wanted to give her the prize for scoring what he had hoped was an impossible number of bull's-eyes, but Anna insisted. She had won the prize and she wanted it. A crowd gathered to hear the argument, and reluctantly the man handed the bag to her.

Anna had a strong will and was always reluctant to agree to whatever she felt was an unfair decision.

'Right's right,' her father would often tell her. 'Be your

2

own person, follow your own star, and if you ever want a helping hand remember there's one on your own right arm.'

Fine, brave words, she thought now, but how would she help herself to seize an opportunity when it came?

She was thinking about this as she reached the wood. The moon was already riding above the highest branches of the trees. They waved nakedly, like strands of hair drifting in the wind. Anna did not like Soldier's Wood. Indeed, everyone in the village of Long Glen agreed that it was a place to be avoided after dark. And even on a hot day, in the heat of summer, when she would walk through it with friends, she was always struck by the fact that here no birds sang. Horses would shy and throw back their heads in fear if riders, ignorant of the wood's reputation, attempted to ride into it. Dogs would cringe and crawl and make water in their terror if any owner tried to drag them past the outer trees.

To one side of the wood lay a small, deep loch. Here, on hot summer days, during the school holidays, Anna had learned to swim. She and her friends then went on to practise swimming under water, seeing how long they could last before they needed to come up for air. Anna discovered a way that the others copied. She would cut a reed from the bank of the lake, put one end in her mouth and let the other stick up out of the water and breathe through this.

Anna tried to focus her thoughts on those summer days in the past, to take her mind off how sinister the wood looked now, at evening. Carefully skirting the wood, she heard a faint cry from the darkness within. She paused, suddenly conscious of the frightening speed with which her heart had begun to beat. Was this a human cry or an animal caught in a snare, a trap? Or could it be something else altogether? She listened. Again she heard the cry of a creature in an extremity of pain, and the sound of anguished weeping.

'Is there anyone in there?' she called nervously, hoping there would be no answer, and that, however improbably, the sound was caused by wind in the trees, maybe by one branch rubbing against another.

'Aye, me,' a woman's voice answered her from within the wood. 'Who are you?'

'Anna Ballater.'

'Where are you going?'

'Home. From the big house.'

'You're the carpenter's girl. Please come and help me. In God's name, help me, child.'

'Who are you?' Anna asked nervously.

'Jeannie Moore,' the woman replied.

The name meant nothing to Anna, who was reluctant to go into the wood in the dusk. There were local stories of odd lights flashing at night, of strange cries and shouts and worse things that honest, God-fearing people did not care to name. The most they would say was that the wood was haunted.

The belief grew because the name, Soldier's Wood, recalled a long past tragedy. Over a hundred and fifty years earlier, at the time of the last pitched battle of Scots against the English on Scottish soil, an English soldier had somehow become separated from his company. Wounded, bewildered, half blinded, so the story went, he fled like a hunted animal into the wood for shelter. But villagers sought him out and killed him, not quickly, not kindly, not easily, but slowly. They cut off his fingers, his nose, his testicles. And then, with ropes round his ankles and his wrists, the strongest

4

men in the village – who each summer would toss the caber or putt the shot at the Highland Games – deliberately pulled him to pieces. Afterwards, ashamed, they buried the soldier's shattered corpse under the trees. That is why the locals still called the place Soldier's Wood. Some said it was haunted by his spirit; others, by the spirits of those who had murdered him, when they could so easily have spared his life, for the war was already over.

'Help me. Please help me,' the woman called again, more urgently this time.

'Where are you?' Anna asked her, hoping she was not too far inside the darkening forest.

'Just here, off the track. Please. Come.'

Anna pulled her skirts round her, took a deep breath and went into the wood. Only yards from the track she reached a small clearing. In the centre of this open space, twenty or thirty feet across, a woman was kneeling. In the pale light of the moon Anna could see the long spring blades and polished, sharpened saw-teeth of a mantrap. A boy was lying with one leg caught between the teeth just above his ankle. His were the cries she had heard. The woman, wrapping her shawl round the jagged teeth to save her hands, was desperately trying to lever the blades apart.

'If we don't get him out, he'll die,' the woman said tersely. 'He's bleeding badly now. Help me, I beg you.'

'But how?' Anna asked her. It was impossible for the two of them to pull those wicked spring blades apart; they were far too strong.

'I'm holding the teeth off his bone as much as I can, but I can't keep on,' said the woman. 'Get a log, a piece of wood – anything – and put it between the blades and then we can both lever them apart.'

In the gloom, Anna could not see anything except some bits of rotten twig, a few broken branches. She walked to the edge of the clearing. Here she found a few strands of rusty wire, once used to fence some animal and still threaded through a metal upright. She gripped this with both hands. It was raw and scabby with rust. She pulled. The wires, weakened by the cold rain of unnumbered winters, fell away. She pulled out the spike, ran with it to the woman. She pushed it between the blades and together they put their weight against the jaws. The rusty metal bent, but it did not break, and gradually the blades drew apart by half an inch, then an inch.

'More!' the woman cried. '*More!*'

Anna closed her eyes and felt her head almost burst with the strain of her effort as she put all her force on the stake. The jaws opened another fraction of an inch, and the woman pulled out the boy's foot.

'Now you can let go,' she said.

Thankfully, Anna threw away the stake. The spring blades of the trap clanged together with a boom like an enormous gong.

'Have you a handkerchief, child?' Jeannie Moore asked her.

'No,' said Anna. 'I haven't.'

'Give us a strip off your slip, then.'

Anna pulled up her skirt, tore a strip from her cotton slip. The woman wound this round the boy's leg, picked him up.

'Where are you taking him?' Anna asked.

'Home.'

'Where's that?'

'In the wood.'

'He needs a doctor. Shall I call Dr Bailey?'

'I've no money for a doctor, girl. I'll cure him myself. He's alive, that's the main thing. Thank you. You've saved his life. He's my only bairn.'

'What about his father? Will he go for the doctor?'

The woman smiled. 'Not him,' she replied shortly. 'He doesn't live here with me in any case. Now, I must be away. I want to get the lad to bed.'

As she turned, Anna saw her face for the first time. Until then it had been obscured by her long hair. Now she tossed this back, and the moon shone on a face scarred and marked by streaks of thickened flesh. It was more like a mask than a human face and Anna recoiled from the repulsive sight.

'You're not the first,' said Jeannie Moore bitterly. 'Dogs did that to me. Wild dogs.' She paused suddenly, as though she had intended to say more, to explain whose dogs they were and why they had attacked her, but at the last moment thought better of it.

Then, with a swish of her long skirts, Jeannie Moore was gone and Anna was alone in the clearing in Soldier's Wood, wondering whether she had really seen those deformed features or whether she had only imagined them. She hurried out of the wood and on to her home. Her mother was waiting at the front door for her.

'You're late, child,' she said chidingly. 'Were you kept long by that Mrs Deakin?'

'A bit long. Mr MacTavish had company, and then something happened on the way that delayed me.'

'Oh? What?' Suspicion, worry, concern clouded her mother's voice. Anna told her.

'Did the woman give you her name?'

'Yes. Jeannie Moore.'

'I've heard tell of her. A gypsy or a witch. An ugly one,

too, by all accounts. Tell your fortune for a copper, they say. Was the boy badly hurt?'

'I think so. But it was really too dark to see.'

Anna's father, Graham Ballater, joined them in the doorway, puffing at his clay pipe.

'The bailiff told me yesterday that the laird was putting out mantraps to stop poachers. That's against the law, of course. Has been for fifty-odd years and more, so when the bailiff asked the blacksmith to sharpen the blades on an old trap, he refused. But the bailiff got someone else to do it for him soon enough. When you've enough clout you can always find someone who'll do anything to keep in your good books. That boy will be lucky if he doesn't lose his leg. Those blades are rusty. He could easily get blood poisoning.'

'I told his mother she should see a doctor, but she said she's no money.'

'That's like enough. Well, now you're home, we have a treat for you, Anna. A rabbit pie, and then apple crumble. I know you like that.'

'I do indeed,' Anna agreed warmly and came into the homely kitchen. An old black dog lay stretched out in front of the stove. He thumped his tail on the floor in welcome. She bent over, and stroked his head. A black dog, a black wood, trees black against the moon, a face scarred beyond recognition, a boy terribly injured. She shuddered at the memory.

'I didn't like Soldier's Wood,' she said suddenly, almost thinking aloud.

'I don't blame you, child,' her mother agreed. 'No God-fearing person likes that place after dark.'

'You really think it's haunted? It doesn't seem possible. That English soldier was killed years and years ago.'

Her mother shrugged. 'Maybe. But you know what it says in the hymn about time. As far as the Lord is concerned, a thousand ages in His sight are like an evening gone. So maybe it's the same with Old Nick. I don't know. Some people say one thing about that wood, and some another. But when I've had to come through late, walking with your father, he'll tell you how we've seen odd lights in there, and heard a sort of singing. Odd things it's not nice to talk about, even to think about. Now tuck into your supper, girl, and get the chill out of your bones.'

Anna did as her mother suggested. But as she ate, and afterwards sat by the fireside, hearing the hiss of flames, seeing pictures of palaces in the heat of the red-hot coals, she thought of the lonely woman and the boy and wondered how they were.

Next morning Anna was up as usual at six, and hurried across the fields to the big house. As she passed Soldier's Wood, she stepped off the path into the clearing. The rusty stake was still there. So was the mantrap, stained with blood, the boy's blood. She walked on quickly, wishing she had not seen that. Surely no one could bleed so much and still live.

Dr Bailey, a bachelor, and set in his ways, had been in practice for several years. He often rode on his rounds with his little black leather bag strapped like a pannier on the side of the saddle. In the summer he went by dogcart with a groom holding the reins. Motor cars were coming into fashion for doctors, but mostly in towns. He didn't altogether trust them, although he owned a Singer.

He was riding now along the track that led to the village when a woman stepped out of the thick bushes on one side of the way. Her face was wrapped in a plaid shawl, which she pulled off her head as he approached. Her hair was black as a raven's wing and well-combed. She wore gold earrings. She had been pretty once, he guessed, but now, in her mid-forties, her face seemed grotesque with its repulsive scars. He had seen her about before many times; a gypsy woman of some kind. He nodded a greeting to her, and made to ride past. She reached out a hand and gripped his horse's bridle. The animal stopped.

'Doctor,' she told him urgently. 'I need your help. I'm desperate for it, but I've no money for your fee. My bairn's sore ill.'

'What's wrong with him?'

'He had his foot caught in a mantrap.'

'A mantrap? Round here? Are you sure?'

'I know. I helped to free him.'

'Where is he?'

She nodded towards the bushes. 'In here. Would you have a look at him? Please. But I can't pay you. I haven't a bawbee.'

'Of course I will have a look at him,' Dr Bailey assured her. 'Don't worry about my bill. I'm like Robin Hood. My richer patients pay more so I can treat others free.'

Jeannie nodded. She had no idea who Robin Hood was. All she wanted was the doctor's help, and quickly. He followed her between bushes and came across a hut, more like an animal's shelter than a human habitation, made of boughs plaited together, with flattened reeds and rags on the roof. The doorway was simply a hole amid this dried vegetation. He followed the woman through. On a bed of rushes lay a boy, aged perhaps twelve or thirteen. Dr Bailey could see he was running a high temperature; his skin was flushed and dry.

The child was covered by a rough blanket. Dr Bailey

10

lifted it off his foot gently to examine the gash, and shook his head.

'We'll be lucky if he doesn't get blood poisoning,' he said gravely.

'That's what I'm afeared of. Would he die then, Doctor?'

'Not necessarily.'

'Would he lose his leg?'

'He might. But we'll try and save that.'

'Can you?'

'I'll do my best,' said the doctor. 'It's lucky you saw me. Hours make all the difference in a case like this. Now, no more talk. Boil me some water, quick as you can.'

Jeannie poured water from a stone flagon into a soot-blackened pan, hung this from a hook on a tripod outside the hovel. She collected some small twigs, lit a piece of paper and coaxed the fire into white heat by blowing through a hollow reed.

The doctor watched her, then cleaned the wound, soaked a square of lint with the strongest disinfectant he carried, and bound up the leg. With the mother's help, he raised the boy's head, gave him a sleeping draught with a tincture to help reduce his temperature.

'Is he taking any food?' he asked Jeannie.

'A little broth, that's all.'

'Give him plenty to drink. Boiled water, not straight from the burn. I'll be back to see him in the morning.'

His temperature was down then, not completely, but encouragingly lower. By the end of the week the boy was sitting up and cheerful. The festering and the red, puffy, suppurating flesh around the wound had almost disappeared.

'You can deal with him yourself now,' Dr Bailey announced with satisfaction. 'I've done all I can. Now all he needs is nursing and any nourishing broth you can manage – rabbit, onions, carrots – and he'll be fine directly. What's his name, by the way?'

'Davey. Davey Moore.'

'And you're Mrs Moore?'

'Jeannie Moore,' she corrected him carefully.

He nodded. Many of these gypsy women were not married, but they remained faithful to men they loved or thought they had once loved, and took their names without any benefit of clergy or clerk. Out in the Scottish countryside people's lives were far more complicated than he had ever imagined as a medical student at St Andrews. He wondered what had caused the fearful injuries to her face. He knew she had only recently moved into Soldier's Wood. Some said she had been with a travelling fair, telling fortunes. She'd probably been in a fight over some man and her opponent had scarred her face. Well, that was none of his business; what was done was done. He had long since given up trying to understand the convoluted relationships of some of his patients.

'Every morning, take off the bandage,' he told Jeannie now. 'I'll leave you another one so you can use them turn about. Put plenty of salt in the water, and boil it for ten minutes. Let the bandage cool, and when it's dry, replace it. Keep on like that every day until the wound has healed.'

'And it will heal, Doctor?' Jeannie Moore asked him anxiously.

'It certainly should now.'

'I don't know how to repay you.'

'There's no need. I told you that when I first arrived. I get my real payment in seeing a patient cured. When I first saw the lad, I wasn't too sure he would come through, even with an amputation. Now I am. You're looking after him

12

well and he's got a strong constitution. He'll be all right.'

'God bless you, Doctor.'

'Thank you. And God bless you, too.'

Dr Bailey walked out through the bushes, unhitched his horse. As he was about to ride away, he heard the woman call to him. He turned. Jeannie Moore was running towards him.

'I told you I can't pay you in money,' she said. 'But I can tell you something. You're going to be a rich man, Doctor.'

'A rich man? Me? No. Whatever makes you say that?'

'I cannot say. I simply know it,' she told him.

'You have second sight, then?'

She shrugged. 'I know what I know. Sometimes I see what will happen, sometimes not. The gift is not in my control. God is never in any man's debt, Doctor. You are going to be rich.'

Dr Bailey laughed and rode away. The woman meant well, no doubt, but she was talking nonsense. These gypsy folk often did when they thought it would please. He felt vaguely disappointed; somehow, he had expected better of Jeannie Moore than rubbishy talk of this kind.

When he reached home, his housekeeper was waiting for him in the porch. She handed him a long envelope with red seals on the back.

'Who's this from?' he asked her.

It did not bear a stamp and so could not have been brought by the postie. In any case, posted letters usually arrived in cheap brown envelopes and were bills or notes from patients asking for some pills or medicine.

'It came by special messenger, from Perth,' his housekeeper told him in awed tones. 'He told me he works for Mr Cameron, a Writer to the Signet.'

'A lawyer?' said the doctor, surprised. Perhaps someone

was suing him. He could not recall any action of his that would cause anyone to go to law. Better find out, he thought, and slit open the envelope.

Inside was a letter with a heavily embossed heading. The Writer to the Signet begged to inform the doctor that the writer's client, the Honourable Miss Cecilia Ogilvy, had died recently. Her will had just been proved and she had left a legacy of twenty thousand pounds to Dr Bailey.

The doctor reread the letter several times. Was this a hoax, someone's idea of a joke? The address seemed genuine. He handed the letter to his housekeeper.

'Does the name mean anything to you?'

'Aye. I remember Miss Ogilvy. A maiden lady of advanced age. You helped her years back, just before the war.'

'How? She wasn't a patient of mine.'

'Her car overturned. The driver had been drinking, I think. She broke a leg. You set it for her by the roadside.'

'You're right. I remember now. She paid me half a guinea there and then. But this fortune for that? I only did my job.'

'Aye. But many wouldn't. And maybe she's no friends. And you've heard the minister speak often enough about entertaining an angel unawares, Doctor. He preached on that text last Sunday.'

'But I never thought this could happen in real life – and to me! A Bible text is one thing. Living here is another. Well, well. I'd better write off to this lawyer fellow straight away.' As he spoke, he remembered the gypsy woman's prophecy, 'You're going to be rich.' And now he was, just as she had told him. But how the devil could she have known?

Months passed. The memory of that evening in Soldier's

Wood gradually faded from Anna's mind. She had almost forgotten about it when, quite unexpectedly, she heard Jeannie Moore's voice at the back door of the big house.

Anna was in the boot room at one side of the door. It contained a heavy table her father had made for dirty boots and shoes, with brushes to clean them and tins of polish, black, brown and dubbin. Anna climbed up on the table, to see over the top of the frosted window panes. The laird had fitted this glass into the downstairs windows of the servants' part of the house to stop them looking out instead of getting on with their work. Jeannie was talking to the housekeeper, Mrs Deakin.

'Sorry to disturb you, ma'am, indeed. But I've a boy here who's hungry and I havena eaten this day myself. In the name of mercy, have you a crust you could spare?'

'The master is very strict on these things,' the housekeeper replied primly. 'He does not give to beggars at the door.'

'I'm not a beggar.'

'But you're begging for bread.'

'Not by my choice, ma'am. I'll do what you wish to earn it, willingly. I can polish silver. I can pick herbs for you, bring you lavender, sprigs of heather.'

'We've no call for them here. The gardeners look after that sort of thing.'

As Mrs Deakin spoke, the laird, Mr MacTavish, approached from the stables. He had been out riding; he was a tall, fat man with thick black hair and sideburns. He usually came into the house from the stable entrance, but on hearing voices he had decided to see who was gossiping at the back door at this hour. When servants were talking they weren't working, and he paid them to work, not to chatter.

'What do you want, woman?' he asked Jeannie. She had

15

pulled a shawl across her face. She was not proud of its mutilations.

'I was asking, sir, for a slice of bread for my bairn.'

'As the housekeeper's told you, we don't give to beggars here. There's plenty of work for those who want it. Be on your way!'

'I'm willing to work at any job I can, sir.'

'I don't want your kind of work. As like as not you'll cast an eye over things, see where the silver is kept, what you can lift, what you can steal. You lot are all the same. You're out poaching if you're a man, and the women go picking clothes off a washing line. Now, get on your way! I'll not tell you again.'

'I am different, sir,' said Jeannie Moore quietly.

'In what way different?'

Jeannie Moore did not reply. Instead, she lifted the shawl from her face. Anna saw her look directly into the laird's eyes. He flushed, took a step back towards the house. He's frightened of her, Anna thought. Has her face shocked him or is there another reason? It was almost as though he recognised Jeannie, despite her disfigurement, but how could he possibly know her?

'My bairn had his leg badly damaged in one of your traps, sir,' Jeannie Moore went on.

'Rubbish, woman,' said Mr MacTavish more briskly. He had quickly recovered his composure.

'I have a witness. A young girl. And also the doctor who cured him.'

'Ah, Dr Bailey, eh? He's a wealthy man now, so I heard. Just come into money. We won't be seeing him around here much longer, I expect. He'll be off to the town to lead the gay life. You'll have to prove what you say, woman, and I'll deny we have any traps out at all. So I warn you to watch your tongue, or the provost will put you behind bars.'

'For speaking the truth, sir?'

'For making a totally false accusation. For hanging about my back door when you're told to leave. Now get off this property or I'll put the dogs on you.'

'You have a young son, sir,' said Jeannie Moore.

'So I do. And what's that to you, woman?'

'He's two years old, I understand.'

'You understand correctly. Now be on your way. You've wasted too much of my time already.'

'I have something to say to you, sir, before I go. Your son is two, but he will never see his third birthday.'

'What the devil do you mean? Are you putting a curse on him?'

'This next Thursday, at this hour, eleven o'clock, he will drown.'

'Drown? Where? We are not at sea in a sailing ship. Are you trying to frighten me? I'll have you know, your sort of talk cuts no ice with me.' He turned to Mrs Deakin. 'Call the butler and make sure she is seen off my property and stays off.'

The laird's voice was now thick with anger – and was there something else that distorted his speech? Could it be fear that perhaps this wretched woman did possess a power greater than his – or knew some secret he did not wish revealed? He strode past both women into the house. His polished spurs jingled on the hard flagstones.

'You heard what the master said,' the housekeeper told Jeannie nervously. 'You'd best be on your way. He has a nasty temper when he's roused.'

'I do not need you to tell me that,' Jeannie Moore replied. 'I heard what he said. And you heard what I said. So forget his threats and remember the day. Next Thursday.

A week today. Dead. By drowning.'

Jeannie Moore walked away out of the cobbled yard. She did not look back. Anna climbed down from her perch and went into the bread store, where half-loaves of old bread, crusty ends, and bits of toast left from the family's breakfast were kept to be fed to the chickens. She felt among the stale loaves, took one that still seemed soft, and ran out across the cobbles to the gate.

Jeannie was about a hundred yards away, walking down the dusty road. She looked defeated, old; her shoulders sagged. Anna ran after her, caught up with her. The woman turned, anger and fear on her ravaged face. Then she relaxed as she recognised Anna.

'I thought you'd come to set the dogs on me,' she admitted. 'What have you got there? Bread?'

'Yes. I can't get you any more, and I'm sorry, I can't wait. I have to get back.'

'So there is someone with a kind heart in the house,' said Jeannie thankfully. She put the loaf in her apron, folded it over carefully to conceal it.

'Goodbye,' said Anna. Then, 'How's your son?'

'He's doing well, but he's hungry. He's growing fast, you see.'

Anna would like to have spoken longer but she did not dare; she could not afford to have her absence noticed.

The following Wednesday, early in the morning, Mrs Deakin asked to see her in her room, next to the butler's pantry.

'I've a special job for you tomorrow, Anna,' she explained. 'The master wants young Hamish to be taken up the hill right after breakfast, and to stay there all day. His nurse is going with him, and two of the maids. I want you to go too.'

'With them?'

18

'No. I want you to see which path they take, and then keep to one side. See but don't be seen. I want you to stay there all day, and when they come back, you come back too, and tell me if anything unusual happens up there. But no one must know I sent you if you are discovered. Promise?'

'I promise. But what do you expect to happen?'

'Oh, nothing really. But last week a gypsy woman at the back door said something nasty to the master about the boy. He fears he might come to some harm near water.'

'There's no water up the hill.'

'Exactly. The only water is in the loch down here and in the burn. I want you to keep an eye on things. But do not be seen, and don't tell anyone except me what you are doing.'

'But what about the other maids? They'll wonder where I am.'

'Let them wonder. I will share your work out between them, and it's only for one day. You're a country girl. You know how to follow a stag without the animal ever guessing you're watching him, don't you?'

'I've done that with my father, yes.'

'Well then, follow these, but don't let them see you.'

At seven o'clock next morning Anna arrived at the house. A pram – a big basket with large spindly wheels – stood in the front hall, while the nursemaid fussed over Master Hamish. She strapped him into the pram with a leather harness so that he could not fall out. Two maids appeared. One was carrying a small hamper, the other, some rugs. Mr MacTavish came out of his study. This surprised them all; the laird and his wife were never early risers.

'Be on your way, then,' he told them briskly. 'And look

after the boy especially. When you let him out for a walk, two of you go with him. And whatever you do, don't let him wander off on his own for a single moment. I'll see you back here late in the afternoon.'

'Very good, sir.'

The three women curtseyed. The nursemaid pushed the pram and the two others followed behind. Anna noticed that one maid was carrying a thick ash walking stick. She went into the kitchen premises.

'Have they gone yet?' Mrs Deakin asked her.

'Yes, ma'am. Just now.'

'You be on your way too, then. Here's something to eat.' She passed Anna a small tin with a handle, which she tied to the belt of her dress and set off, up the hill. It was quite easy to keep out of sight of the other women, who walked slowly, taking it in turns to push the pram. The farther away they went from the house, the slower they walked and the more they giggled.

They had taken a steep path up the hill that was used by labourers, no one else. It had been raining and parts were muddy. Anna followed in the heather about fifty yards away, well to one side. Every now and then she would crouch down and let them go ahead and then follow. She kept them in sight till they reached the peak.

She saw the nursemaid put on the brake with her foot. This acted on one of the wheels. The little boy, bouncing about cheerfully inside the pram, was straining against his harness. One of the maids spread out a rug on a soft patch of grass and all three sat down. Anna moved so that she could see and hear them.

The second maid said, 'I've brought some whisky. We'll have a dram.'

'How did you get that?' asked the nursemaid, impressed.

'Took it. The old butler wanted a feel. I said he could have a feel if he'd let me have the whisky. He steals a bottle a day. Dirty old sod.'

She poured an inch of whisky into three metal beakers, added water. They toasted each other, then had another. It was very hot up here. There were no trees, and so no shade from the sun. One maid took out some sandwiches, passed them round. The other passed the bottle for the third time.

'That's strong stuff,' said the nursemaid appreciatively. 'I've never drunk so much in the middle of the day. Just to sniff it makes me feel squiffy.'

'Best to drink it, then fall asleep, forget what time it is,' said the maid who had brought the bottle. 'Let's finish the bottle. We may never get another chance like this.'

'Good idea. We don't want to take an empty back. It's not as if we could get tuppence for it from the shop.'

She poured a fourth round, a fifth. Then she lay back on the short grass, holding up a hand to shield her eyes from the sun. Within minutes she was asleep.

'Look at her,' said the second maid enviously. 'Think I'll have forty winks myself, if you don't mind.'

'Feel free,' said the nursemaid. 'I'll watch till you wake up.' She crossed to the pram, rocked it gently on its curved springs.

'All right, are you?' she asked the baby.

Hamish chortled happily.

'Sunshine will do you good,' she told him. 'Though the gentry don't like it. They say it spoils their complexion.'

She was talking to herself now, a little drunk. She came back and sat down with the other two. Within a minute she, too, was asleep, snoring. Now the boy began to cry out and jump more vigorously against the harness. The pram was rocking. Suddenly, it tipped on its side. One of the wheels spun uselessly in the air.

Anna got up, ran towards the pram, eyes on the baby struggling now and screaming. She did not see a hidden root, and tripped, falling on her face in the warm heather. When she got up, the wheel had stopped spinning, and Hamish had stopped crying.

She ran on to the pram. He was half in, half out, tied by his leather harness. The pram had capsized. The baby's face was in two inches of water in the rut left by the wheel of a farm cart. She righted the pram, undid the harness, shook Hamish vigorously, felt his pulse. There was no beat. The boy was dead. She shook the nursemaid awake.

'The boy's ill,' she said, not wishing to tell her the terrible truth.

'What do you mean, ill? He was all right a moment ago.'

'Well, he isn't now. See for yourself.'

The nursemaid stood up shakily, eyes half closed against the sun. She saw mud on the side of the pram, and Hamish lying back on the pillow, his face streaked with muddy water.

'What happened?'

'The pram tipped up.'

'How?'

'The baby was jumping about so much, it tipped over.'

'What are you doing here?'

'I was out walking.'

The nursemaid picked up the baby, smoothed his face. His head lolled like the head of a broken china doll.

'My God, he's dead!' she cried. 'He must have hit his head.'

'No. He drowned.'

'How could he? There's no water here.'

'There is. In that cart track. He drowned in it.'

'Oh, my God.' The nursemaid kicked the two maids awake. 'He's dead, he's dead!' she screamed, and her screams echoed round the hill. 'What can we tell the laird?'

They stared at each other in horror, their faces still puffy with sleep and whisky.

'Say the pram ran away and overturned,' suggested the nursemaid. Then she remembered that Anna had seen what had happened.

'You won't tell on us, will you? she asked beseechingly. 'We'll lose our jobs if you do.'

'The little boy lost much more,' Anna replied coldly. 'He lost his life.'

That evening Anna told the housekeeper what she had seen, but did not say the other three had been drunk.

'I must tell the master,' said Mrs Deakin. 'The nursemaid has a different story.'

Within minutes the laird sent for Anna.

'I have heard your account of events from Mrs Deakin,' he said. 'What were you doing up there?'

'Taking a walk, sir.'

'A walk? It's not your day off, Mrs Deakin told me. Your story does not agree with what the nursemaid and her two companions say. How do you account for that?'

Anna said nothing.

'It is three to one,' said the laird. 'But nothing will bring back my son. His death was foretold by a gypsy woman at the back door only last week. I didn't believe her, but sent the boy up the hill with three women to look after him, away from any chance of falling into the burn or the loch, just in case anything happened. And now . . .'

The laird's voice tailed off, his emotions almost

overcoming him. He seemed to forget Anna was still there. His face was haggard, the flesh drawn tightly over his skull. He looked shrunken and old. Anna had never liked him because of his cruel tongue, but now she felt sorry for him.

Then the laird remembered why he had called her in; not just because her account of the accident differed from what the other women said, but for another reason.

'I understand you have been seen with that gypsy woman?'

'I was walking past Soldier's Wood some months ago. She was there with her son, who had been caught in a mantrap.'

'She mentioned that. But I didn't believe her. They'll say anything, these people, if they have a mind to. And that's the only time you've seen her?'

'No, sir. I saw her after she called here. I gave her a piece of bread.'

'Ah, so you did, eh? Why?'

'She was hungry, sir.'

'You mean you stole a piece of bread? She had just put a curse on my son. Did you know that?'

'I heard what she said, sir. But it was a prophecy, not a curse.'

'Was it? She killed my son, in effect, whatever it was. She told me he would drown. So I sent him away from the house where there would be no water. But he drowned all the same, just as she said. In a couple of inches of water. And you were there. You knew this?'

Anna said nothing.

'You knew this,' he repeated.

'I heard what the woman said, sir.'

'What were you doing up on the hill?'

'I was taking a walk, sir.'

24

'So just by chance you walked up the hill? But not with the others. They didn't see you until –' his voice broke '– until afterwards. And why go walking when it's not your free day?'

Anna did not reply. She had promised Mrs Deakin she would not reveal her part in this, that it was at her direct instruction she had followed them.

'Nothing to say, have you? Well, I have. The housekeeper tells me she had no idea where you were. She had to get another maid to do your work. And then suddenly you come back with the others. No explanation as to why you went off on your own. No apology, nothing. You've nothing to say, but I have. You are dismissed. Now. I think you are somehow in league with that gypsy woman. So you are free now to spend all the time you wish in her company. Now get out. And never let me see your face again.'

He turned away.

'But how the devil did that woman know my son would die?' he asked himself wretchedly. 'How? *How?*'

Two

Graham Ballater, the estate carpenter, was a stocky, prematurely grey-haired man in his early forties. He lived with his wife and Anna in a cottage at the far end of the estate. He was thankful to be back in his previous job after four years in the army. The Ballaters were proud of their only daughter; there had been two other younger children, but both had died in infancy. Anna, her parents felt quite certain, would one day rise from her present job in the big house and perhaps be promoted to housekeeper. Then she might marry a butler and 'better herself' in their description and so leave domestic service altogether. Butlers had the habit of abstracting quantities of their masters' wine and spirits, a custom either unseen or condoned by their employers, and it was not uncommon for them to retire young and take the licence of a public house. If Anna was anything like her mother, she'd be a good cook. Altogether, her parents believed that a very pleasant future awaited her.

On this particular morning, Graham Ballater was not thinking about the future, but about an event of the immediate past; something most extraordinary had happened on the previous evening. He was friendly with the farrier Donald Coupar, a widower about the same age, who lived in the cottage next door. Coupar liked a dram as often as he could get one, which was pretty regularly. He had been greatly shocked and saddened by the death of his wife Mary from a wasting disease only four weeks previously.

The local minister had tried to comfort him, saying that the Lord gave and the Lord took away in His own time, and there must be a reason for everything the Lord did, even if it was known only to Himself. To grieve too long or too much for the death of anyone was therefore in a sense querying the wisdom of the Lord. The minister was saddened that, despite repeated visits to him, Donald Coupar still seemed unable to come to terms with his loss. Worse than this, he had told the minister that he intended to try and get into contact with his wife beyond the grave. He had sought Ballater's opinion on this.

'How do you propose to do it?' asked Ballater, a practical man. 'No one can cross the border from the grave.'

'Even so, I want to try. I read a book when I was a boy at school – about the only book I ever did read – about the time long ago when people thought the world was flat, but various old voyagers thought it must be round. They said that when they looked out to sea, watching for an approaching ship, they'd first see the tip of its mast, then gradually the top of its sails, then the whole deck, as though the ship was coming uphill, up a slope. All kinds of much cleverer men told them that the world could not possibly be round. If it were, people would drop off the other side. But it is round. The seafarers – practical men – proved their point.'

'And you mean to prove yours?'

'I mean to try.'

'How?'

'There's a gypsy woman, Jeannie Moore, lives rough on the edge of Soldier's Wood. Got a terribly scarred face. I went to see her when Mary was first took bad. She wanted her palm crossed with silver before she'd tell me anything, even the time of day. I had no silver, so I gave her tuppence.

It was all I had. I think she knew that, for then she told me Mary would not live.'

'Did she tell you when she'd die?'

'She did,' Coupar replied. 'To the very day. I saw the doctor on the morning of that day, not mentioning what I'd been told, and he said Mary was sinking fast. By sundown the dear poor soul was gone. Just as the gypsy said.'

'So how's this gypsy going to help you?'

'Every so often she, and others of her kind, meet in a copse in the wood.'

'What do you mean, others of her kind? Is she a witch – like some folk around here say?'

'I don't know. I just want to go and ask her at one of those meetings.'

'You may come to harm, interfering with people like that.'

'I can take care of myself.'

'Against another man, maybe. But not against the forces of Satan.'

'They may not be the forces of Satan, though the minister seems to think they are.'

'If they weren't, if there was any goodness in them, they wouldn't meet in the dark in the middle of a wood, would they? I've heard terrible things go on in Soldier's Wood. But what exactly, I don't know.'

'That's why I want you to come with me.'

'I'll do no such thing, man.'

The farrier sighed. 'I can understand how you feel, Graham, but I'm asking you as a friend, as a neighbour who needs your help.'

'If I did come with you and this woman couldn't do anything to help you, then will you give up trying to contact Mary?'

'I'll have to.'

'All right. I'll come with you this once, if you promise to stop meddling in things that don't concern any of us. If educated men can't get in touch with the dead, how do you think you can?'

'I don't know. I just want to try and speak to Mary one last time.'

'When is the next meeting or whatever they call it?'

'Tonight. At ten o'clock. The woman told me.'

'Does she know you'll be there?'

'No. I've told no one but you.'

'Are you taking anything to protect yourself with?'

'A stout stick.'

'I've a revolver,' said Ballater. 'I'll take that. It's a good weapon to have to threaten anyone who gets nasty. Gives you confidence. I learned that in France. Besides, I've heard there's men at these gatherings as well as women. They may not want strangers to see whatever it is they get up to. I'm not taking any money with me, of course.'

'I have no money to take,' Coupar replied with a sad smile. 'I'll take my hope.'

'Actually, it's not a very good night for me to come,' said Ballater doubtfully. 'I've just remembered. My wife's seeing her mother in Perth tonight. I'm on my own. I said I'd wait in for her.'

'She'll understand, I'm sure,' said Coupar. 'Have supper with me. I'm used to fending for myself now I'm on my own. Nothing special – a couple of eggs, half a dozen rashers of bacon, some mushrooms.'

'Well, I suppose it will be all right.'

At about eight o'clock that evening Ballater called at Coupar's back door. The smell of frying permeated the cottage. They sat down at his kitchen table, started to eat.

'You certainly cook well,' said Ballater. 'I had no idea you were such a dab hand at it. These mushrooms are great. Very soft.'

'I know. There's only one place they grow, too. On the edge of Soldier's Wood.'

'I usually pick mine in fields nearer here.'

'Aye, so do I. But when I was down seeing Jeannie Moore in the wood I saw quite a lot growing there. So I picked them. Anyhow, tuck in. Plenty more where they came from.'

The two men set off just before ten o'clock. Graham Ballater had told his wife that quite unexpectedly he had to check a fence he had mended earlier in the day with a young helper. He had left a farm lad to hammer on some of the rails, and he should have checked them earlier. He was going out to do it now. The farrier was coming with him. His wife nodded. Her husband often went out at night for such checking; he would be back before she returned.

The two men set off across the fields and joined the track that ran alongside Soldier's Wood. They had both served in the army and walked in step. The thick leather soles of their boots made no sound on the soft earth. Every now and then, Ballater's right hand strayed to the pocket of his rough tweed trousers to feel the comforting, serrated outline of his revolver.

When they reached the wood, they walked more slowly for about fifty yards till they saw a narrow path leading to the left among the trees. This was no wider, no more significant than a badger's track, but they recognised it easily enough. The moon was full now, riding high above the dark thin branches. There was no wind. An owl called, and as they bent to go beneath some of the lower branches, bats' wings fluttered nervously in the silvery evening air.

31

They paused, not so much because they were tired or did not know where they were going, but because suddenly they felt uneasy. They sensed something alien in the wood. If they had been on their own, they would probably have turned and run. But each feared that the other might call him a coward, so they stood for a moment and then began to move forward together, slowly, carefully, half prepared for flight.

Within a dozen paces they came to an open space. They paused again on its perimeter, concealed in the bushes. Ahead of them, they saw thirteen people standing in a circle. They were not sure whether they were men or women because they wore cowls and cloaks that reached down to the ground. The moon moved behind a cloud and the light faded, became foggy.

Then across the circle, on the far side, they saw a great goat standing on his hind legs. He was tall as a very tall man. His horns were up in the air, and his front legs drooped like broken arms. He stood as though he was human, head and shoulders towering above the others. His eyes were green, and glowed in the semi-darkness. And he was staring straight at the two men, not moving, not blinking, just watching them.

Both men knew fear then as they had never felt fear before, either in the trenches or here in the Scottish countryside. Sometimes they had been frightened when a bull was loose in a field or when roughs from a travelling fair had come with staves and sticks to try and flush out the laird's pheasants, and they had faced them on their own and unarmed. But that was fear of a physical kind. This was fear of a mental sort they had never experienced before, never even imagined, because it was unimaginable.

Their mouths dried, their tongues felt like leather, and

they breathed with difficulty. The hairs on the backs of their necks rose like prickles. They felt they were in the presence of some power greater than anything they had ever encountered, and in a basic animal way they sensed this was a power to harm, a power of evil.

Several black cats now came into the ring of people. They were plump female cats and they moved slowly, not purring but inquisitively sniffing the hems of the garments of the thirteen people standing there. Like the goat, the cats were of enormous size, large as collie dogs. And then, as though on a signal the two men could not comprehend, could not even hear, they leapt into the air.

The cats literally flew, round and above the heads of all the people. One came towards Ballater, so close that it brushed the side of his face. He felt fur on his flesh and horror gripped him in an iron vice.

He staggered back, and pulled his revolver from his back pocket. He stood, panting for breath as though he had been running a long way uphill with a weight on his back, as though there was not enough air left in all the world for him to breathe. The cat flew at him for a second time. Ballater raised his revolver in an instinctive reaction and fired. The bullet hit the right side of the cat's face.

The sound of the explosion echoed and re-echoed throughout the wood like a cannon shot. Ballater saw the goat start back, drop his front legs. People turned hooded faces towards him – and he fled.

Donald Coupar fled with him. They ran until they reached the track beyond the wood and then on to their cottages. They ran without speaking, without stopping, exhausted physically and mentally. Finally, they paused outside their front doors.

'You hit it,' said Coupar thickly. 'That cat.'

'I know,' admitted Ballater. 'And you didn't get a chance to talk to your witch.'

'I don't even know if she was there. They all looked alike. I'm going to have a large whisky and forget all about it.'

'You'll not be trying to talk to your wife on the other side then?'

'No,' said Coupar firmly. 'I'll not.'

He went into his house. Ballater heard the rattle of bolts. He stood outside his own front door breathing more deeply, slowly, steadily, until the racing panic of his heart slowed. Then he went in. He poured himself half a glass of whisky and sat by the fire trying to forget what he had seen and what he had done.

After her dismissal, Anna arrived home late from the big house. She did not want to tell her parents she had been summarily sacked, but eventually she would have to do so. However, the end of the day seemed a bad time to pass on ill news. Morning would be better, if only because she thought it could not be worse.

But breakfast – porridge cooked in the overnight stove and served with milk and honey – also seemed the wrong time to tell them. Her father looked tired, worn, worried. How could she possibly tell him now that she had no job? But she must tell someone, or at least ask for advice as to what she should do now, but not her parents. She sensed that they simply would not understand, but who did she know who might? She could think of no one – until she remembered Jeannie Moore. She had known grief and hunger; disappointment would be no stranger to her. She would ask her advice.

Anna left home at her usual hour, but instead of going to the big house, she turned off from the track into Soldier's

Wood, walked on until she came to the little hutment where Jeannie Moore lived. She paused outside.

'Are you in there?' she asked brightly, and on the instant suddenly wished there would be no answer, that no one was here and she could go away. Something about this wood made her uneasy, made her flesh crawl. Then she heard a groan from inside the hut. She bent down and went through the opening.

Jeannie Moore was lying, fully clothed, on a mattress of rags and dried leaves.

'What's the matter?' Anna asked her.

Jeannie did not answer. Anna was not certain she had even heard her. She lay with her eyes closed, her legs drawn up, hands clenched in pain. Anna's eyes had grown accustomed to the gloom, and she saw with horror that Jeannie was terribly wounded. One ear had been shot or cut away. Blood had congealed like dark red jam where her ear had been. She had tried to bandage the wound with a strip of cloth which was soaked with blood.

'What's happened to you?' Anna asked in a hushed whisper.

Jeannie opened her eyes. 'I can't tell you, child,' she said weakly. 'But I know that my time has come. I am dying.'

'Where is your son?'

'With a relation.'

'Does he know about you being ill?'

'Not yet. But he will be told.'

'Can I help in any way? Can I tell him?'

'No, he is being looked after.'

'What has happened to your ear?'

'I cannot tell you now, girl. But, believe me, I am dying.'

'Don't die,' Anna pleaded. 'Please don't die.'

In her shock at finding Jeannie Moore in this condition,

she had forgotten why she was here at all: to ask her advice, her help. Now, that was impossible.

'You're a kind child,' Jeannie Moore replied, speaking slowly. Her voice sounded as though it came through thick cloth hangings. Each word, each syllable, was slurred. 'We are all living on borrowed time,' she said. 'One day our loan is called in. Then we can do nothing but pay. Now my debt is being demanded of me.' She paused. 'I'd like to give you something to remember me by,' she said at last.

'Please, I don't want anything,' Anna assured her. 'And you're not dying. Let me call Dr Bailey. He'll help you. You must have treatment. You can't just lie here.'

Jeannie Moore sat up very slowly. 'No,' she said weakly. 'I do not want the doctor. He has been kind to me already in treating my son. But it is too late now for him or anyone else to help me.'

As she moved, her terrible wound began to bleed. Clotted drops of blood leaked onto her shoulder. She did not seem to notice.

'I can't give you anything, child, except one gift that was given to me. The gift to tell the future – or parts of it. Not everything, but a vision seen as through a glass.'

'I don't want *anything*. I told you. Except for you to get well. I'm going to fetch the doctor, whatever you say.'

'You'll do no such thing,' Jeannie retorted, her voice suddenly firm and forceful. 'I tell you, he can do nothing to help me now. But I may be able to help you, just a little, with this.'

She moved a hand under the rags, picked out a round wooden box, the size of a pill box. She lifted the lid. Inside, Anna saw several small slices that appeared to have been cut from the dried stem of a plant.

'What are they?' she asked.

'Some folk would call them magic. I don't know why or how they work, but they can help you to look into the future. My mother gave me the secret, where they grow and what they are. I would like to hand them on to you. When you have a decision to make, or if you want to help someone with advice as to what will happen maybe weeks or months ahead, chew one of these pieces. If it is too hard and tough to chew, put a match to it. Burn it and then swallow the ash. You will then see what others cannot know. Not all the future, mind you, and not always, but some of it. You will see pictures, people, places you may never have been to, but when you go you will recognise them at once. You have to work out for yourself just what these pictures mean – if you can. A bit like a jigsaw or a candle that gives enough light to see your way around a darkened room, but not enough to read by.' She sank back, exhausted.

'What are they?' Anna asked her, examining the thin wafers.

'Pieces of a sacred root. They grow in several places, but few people know their strength. Now you will also discover it.'

'Is it really magic?' Anna asked her nervously. She shook the little box, sniffed the contents carefully. Jeannie Moore smiled wanly.

'Of a sort, it is, yes.' Her voice was trailing away, fading.

'How long will they last?' Anna asked her.

'I cannot say. You have enough there for four or five glances into the future. So don't waste them. Guard them. Only use them when something very important is involved. When they are gone, you will be on your own. Goodbye, child. And may this gift guide you well.' Jeannie Moore's voice faded to a weak whisper. Then her whole body arched like a bow when the archer pulls the string, and she fell back on the crude bed.

Anna felt her pulse, but as with the baby Hamish, she knew she was in the presence of death. She picked up the box, stood for a moment looking down at Jeannie, wondering how she had been wounded so grievously. Then she ran out of the hut, out to the edge of the wood. As she ran, she held the box tightly, thinking about what she had been told. If Jeannie Moore really could foretell the future, why hadn't she known that someone would wound her and she would die? Couldn't she have avoided this – if she knew it would happen?

But then Anna answered her own questions. Of course Jeannie Moore could not alter her future. Being able to foresee it was quite a different matter. And maybe she had indeed seen that she was about to die. She had been adamant that the doctor could not help her.

Anna did not stop running until she reached her cottage. Unusually, the front door was open. Anna went inside. Her mother was seated in the kitchen, her head in her hands on the kitchen table. She was weeping. Graham Ballater stood behind his wife, one hand awkwardly on her shoulder, trying to comfort her.

'What's the matter?' Anna asked, looking from one to the other, her own problem temporarily forgotten at the sight of her mother's distress.

'You should tell me,' said her father stonily. 'You've been dismissed. When?'

'Yesterday.'

'Why didn't you tell us then?'

'I didn't know how to. I was ashamed. It was nothing I'd done, nothing at all. There was no reason.'

'The laird's a man of uncertain temper, I give you that. But he usually has a reason for what he does, even if it's sometimes difficult to understand. Anyhow, his bailiff has just been here. He's putting us out of our house. All of us.'

'But why? Because of me?'

'So he says. Because of you.'

'What did he say I'd done to bring this on all of us?'

'You know what happened to young Hamish, drowned yesterday? Apparently, you've been seen consorting with a woman they say is a witch. The laird's certain she put a curse on the boy, told him he'd drown. He purposely sent him away from any possible risk of water and then the wee laddie drowned in two inches of muddy water in a cart track. Did you know that?'

'Yes. I was there.' Anna explained how the housekeeper had asked her to go and report back to her, but not to mention this to anyone; and how Mrs Deakin now claimed she had taken time off without any authority.

'I see,' said Graham. His voice was more conciliatory. 'She's a bitch, that one. But where've you been now, girl? You've been running.'

'Yes. I went out to see that woman again.'

'You mean Jeannie Moore?'

'Yes.'

'Why?'

'I thought if she did have second sight, she might help me, tell me what I could do, where to go to find work. There's none round here if I haven't a character.'

'And there are no cottages round here, either,' said her father grimly. 'We're all in this together, you know, as a family. What advice did she give you?'

'None. She was dying. She died when I was with her.'

'*Died?* How?'

'She'd been shot in the side of her head.'

'What do you mean, shot?' asked her father, and his

voice sounded hoarse and dry.

'There was a terrible wound to her ear. I asked her what had happened, who had done it. She wouldn't say. Or maybe she couldn't.'

'I see.'

Mrs Ballater was sitting up now. She looked from one to the other. 'Your father's very shocked, girl,' she said. 'Not just about losing our home and you being dismissed, but about something else that happened last night.'

'What was that?'

'I went out with Donald Coupar, the farrier,' Ballater explained. 'He'd got some tomfool idea that Jeannie Moore could help him speak to his wife, who's been dead these four weeks. I tried to talk him out of it, and so did the minister. But he wanted to see the woman, for she had given him the exact date his wife would die. He believed she might help him now. But, to be blunt, he feared to go into Soldier's Wood on his own to meet her in the dark. So I went with him.'

'And what happened?'

'We saw a lot of figures standing in a circle in a clearing. There was a goat up on its hind legs. And suddenly wild black cats appeared. One flew through the air and attacked me. Donald had taken a stick and I had my revolver. I never meant to use it, but I thought the cat would have my eyes if I didn't. So I fired, and hit it on the side of its head.'

'And then?'

'We ran off as fast as we could. I counted thirteen people there and these animals. Something very odd was going on. I don't know what, but I admit to you both, I've never felt so frightened in all my life.' He paused. 'Tell me, on which side of the head was Jeannie Moore hit?'

'The right side.'

'My God,' said her father weakly. He sat down. His face was very white. He was trembling.

'Why? What's the matter?' Anna asked him. And then she began to realise what had frightened him.

'You think Jeannie was the cat? She was turned into a cat, or maybe a cat turned into a human? Her?'

'I don't know what I think,' said her father. 'I've never believed these sort of stories. They usually come from people who've had a dram too many. But now I'm not sure about anything.' He stood up. 'Well,' he said with an attempt at brightness, 'It's no good sitting here discussing things we don't understand. We'd better get packed.'

'What about that poor gypsy woman, dead in the wood?' Mrs Ballater asked him.

'I'll tell the doctor,' said Anna.

'That's no use if she's dead.'

'Who else can I tell? The policeman? The laird's a magistrate, remember.'

Before her father could reply, they heard the sound of a car approaching. It stopped outside their cottage. Dr Bailey came towards them.

'Can we help you, Doctor?' Ballater asked him.

'No. But maybe I can help you. I have just heard from the bailiff that the laird is putting you out of your home.'

'That is true, sir,' said Ballater. 'And for no fault or misbehaviour on our part.'

'So I understand. I have tried to persuade him to change his mind but I need not tell you, he's a stubborn man. Once he has an idea in his head, it's very difficult to dislodge. However, I know your reputation as a craftsman, and I have a cottage on my property which has not been lived in for some time. If you would care to renovate it, make it a home, it is yours for as long as you wish.'

'I appreciate your kind offer, Doctor, but I've no job now and I cannot pay you a rent,' said Ballater.

'I'm not asking for rent. As you may have heard, I have received a totally unexpected legacy. In the circumstances, I feel I should share my good fortune. You can live there without rent. You have your tools, and no doubt you could do any carpentering jobs I need, and others may want. You could also make chairs or tables and sell them. I would be prepared to advance you some money to buy wood in the first place. That would not be a gift, of course, but a loan. A business investment, if you like.'

'You're very kind, sir,' said Mrs Ballater. 'Very kind indeed. May the good Lord reward you for your generosity.'

'We should help each other while we can,' the doctor replied. He turned to Anna. 'The laird's of the opinion that you are somehow in league with the woman Jeannie Moore who he claims bewitched his son,' he told her. 'What is your version of this?'

Anna told him.

The doctor nodded. 'It's as I thought. I must say, this woman did have a rare gift of second sight. She prophesied something that was going to happen to me and it happened that same day, something about which she could have had no knowledge whatever, no inkling of any kind. I could find no explanation for it, except that she had this gift. The laird has just sent some keepers into Soldier's Wood to look for her. They found her, dead. Shot in the head, apparently. She will be buried as early as possible, probably tomorrow. She has a son, you know. He is being cared for by friends or relations for the time being. What will happen to him later, I have no idea.

'Anyway, I intend to go to her funeral. The saying is, you give a dog a bad name and you hang him. I don't know exactly how or why this poor woman died but I wondered if you would come to her funeral, Anna? Together we'll show that, whatever happened to her in her life, Jeannie Moore should be honoured at the leaving of it. Will you come?'

'Yes,' said Anna, 'I will come.'

Dr Bailey nodded his approval. 'There's one thing I should add, Ballater,' he said, as though just remembering it. 'There's only one small bedroom in this little cottage of mine. Barely room for a double bed. You're far better off here with two rooms. So I don't know what you're going to do with your daughter.'

'She can sleep downstairs,' said Mrs Ballater quickly.

'I don't think that would be possible – or advisable. She's of an age to have a room of her own. Perhaps she could find a job in one of the big houses here.'

'Not without a character from Mrs Deakin,' Anna pointed out.

'Well, there is one opportunity of employment I think I could offer her, but it would mean going abroad. I have a younger sister Eileen, married to Captain Johnson, an officer in the army, due to be posted to India. They have two small children. One, the elder, is a boy, and I am sorry to say he is what they call in the modern way mentally retarded, what you and I would call not quite right in the head. However, they are devoted to him, but they need someone to look after him and his sister. I would give you a reference myself, Anna, if you would care to accompany them. That would be a way out of the immediate problem.'

'How long would that be for, Doctor?'

'The voyage to Bombay probably lasts five or six weeks, according to the number of stops the ship makes. It'll be a trooper, which is pretty slow. The army posting would be a matter of years, of course.'

'Would I be out in India for years?'

'Not necessarily. You might get a job as a nursemaid for an English army family coming home, and so be back here in a short time. If you wanted to, that is.'

'And then what would my future be if I didn't and stayed in India?'

'What you make of it yourself. You're seventeen and good-looking, personable. You might marry out there. It's very difficult to look ahead more than a week, or even a day nowadays.'

'We'll talk it over,' said Anna's mother. 'And thank you very much, Doctor, for your kind offer of accommodation for us.'

'Move in whenever you like. I understand that may be pretty soon because the bailiff tells me a new carpenter has already been engaged and he will need this cottage. Goodbye to you both. I look forward to hearing your decision, Anna. But again, sooner rather than later. My sister and her husband are due to sail in a matter of weeks.'

That night, in the doctor's cottage which, as he said, was very cramped, the three of them discussed Anna's future. In the meantime, they had made up a temporary bed for her down in the kitchen. There were only two rooms, a kitchen with chairs and a table, and a bedroom upstairs. A stone privy stood behind the cottage, and a wooden-handled pump to draw up water from a well.

'I'll have to go,' said Anna without enthusiasm.

'I don't like to see it. You're so young,' said her mother. 'What have we done to deserve this? We were a happy family. It's all the fault of that woman who's dead. She's willed it on us.'

'No, no,' said Anna. 'She did nothing of the kind. She

was just a poor, unhappy soul.'

'She was a witch, more like,' retorted her father. 'How else do you account for the shot in the head? She was that cat. Must have been.'

'Rubbish,' said Anna firmly. 'I can't believe that.'

'You don't have to,' her mother replied. 'But there are all manner of things in this world we know no reason for and can't explain, but they happen. Then we *have* to believe them. I'm not the only one to have my doubts about that woman. Your father agrees with me, though maybe he would not admit it to you. And the laird may be a stubborn body, but he's not a fool. He's got his own thoughts about her too.'

For the next few days Mrs Ballater tried desperately to find employment locally for her daughter. She did not like the prospect of Anna going so far away for an unknown time, perhaps even for ever. She visited housekeepers in all the big houses round about, but they all explained politely that they were suited, and in any case no one would take on a new girl who did not have a character. And why had the Ballaters been put out of their cottage? No smoke without fire, thought the housekeepers, and rattled the keys on their belts, thankful they were not in Mrs Ballater's predicament, or Anna's.

So, finally and reluctantly, Anna decided to accept Dr Bailey's offer. Her mother helped her to pack, putting in sprigs of lavender to keep the linen fresh.

'You might as well take your Christmas present, for it's no likely you'll be back home by then,' she told Anna, and handed her a small parcel, wrapped in brown paper.

'I must open it now, then,' said Anna, tearing off the paper. She held up a black, one-piece bathing costume with a white belt.

'It's lovely,' she said enthusiastically, kissing her mother. 'And I should have lots more use for it in India than here. The sea's bound to be far warmer than the loch.'

Anna folded up the costume carefully and put it in her bag. Neither she nor her mother could possibly imagine the circumstances in which she would wear it for the first time.

Anna said goodbye to her parents and, with a one-pound note given to her by Dr Bailey, travelled to Liverpool to meet his sister. She was a plump, rather vague woman in her mid-thirties. Sometimes she had a look of worry and concern, as though events were too much for her, and life was proceeding at too fast a pace. And then her mood would change, and she would be smiling and cheerful. Her children were five and six. The elder was clearly an imbecile, incontinent, incapable of feeding himself, a creature who lived and breathed but could not communicate, apart from making animal grunts and groans. Anna doubted whether he understood the simplest remark addressed to him.

She was surprised that Mrs Johnson asked her so few questions about her upbringing and why she wanted this job so urgently. She assumed that Dr Bailey must have told her and therefore Mrs Johnson did not wish to refer to the reasons in case she embarrassed Anna.

Anna embarked on the trooper *Pride of the Regiment* with all her belongings in the bag she had won at the fair. The Johnsons travelled first class; Anna shared a very small cabin with two other nursemaids, Lucy and Dorothy, both some years older, in third class. The cabin had a single porthole with a circular glass pane that could be locked open. There was no other ventilation. Anna unpacked her few belongings on the first evening as the ship moved slowly out to sea.

46

The last thing Anna took from her bag was the small wooden box Jeannie Moore had given to her. The two other nursemaids were up on deck; already, they felt queasy although the sea was calm. They had never been to sea before, and the thought of a long voyage in this cramped cabin brought on sickness as much as the movement of the ship.

Anna removed the lid of the box, examined the contents. On the impulse, with the knife she had brought with her – all third-class passengers had to supply their own knives, forks and spoons – she cut one of the root slices in half. Then she closed the box, wrapped it in a red flannel nightgown, pushed it right down to the bottom of her bag. She put the piece of root in a metal ashtray chained to a small table which was bolted to the wall to stop it moving in rough weather. She struck a match, held it to the pale splinter.

It immediately caught fire and then glowed as she had seen twigs glow in a bonfire when they were too damp to take flame. She blew over the ash to cool it, then chewed the dry grey dust. The smoke had a certain piquant smell, not quite like wood smoke, but with a strange aroma she could not place; something alien, but not at all disagreeable. As Anna chewed, she felt increasingly relaxed and more confident of her future.

She lay back, put up her feet, and closed her eyes. Between wakefulness and sleep she could see another ship upon another sea. She heard a voice, metallic, disembodied, like someone calling down a well: 'You will be rich. You *will* be rich – one day.'

'And then?' she asked. Her voice echoed the question, almost ironically. And then? And then? . . .

The ship in her mind sailed closer, so that she could

see the funnel and decks, not white but grey and dark, like a ship of stone. Then she saw a smaller vessel close to the first. Two men were standing on the deck and, with a spasm of surprise, she saw she was swimming in a sea blue as cobalt. Then she was somehow on deck with them. The picture gradually became blurred and suddenly erupted in a flash of fire and a blaze of flame, bright as the summer sun. Anna sat up, screaming, as though she had just experienced a nightmare. The other two girls had returned to the cabin and stood staring at her in amazement.

'You all right, ducks?' asked Lucy.

'I must have dozed off.'

'Gave us a fright, you did. Having a bad dream, were you?'

'I suppose so. I can't really remember.'

'Hell of a pong in here,' said Dorothy, wrinkling her nose. 'Got some special scent you're using? New stuff to attract men, eh?'

'No. Nothing like that.'

'Well, there is something,' Lucy agreed. 'Pooh! Thank goodness the porthole's open. We'd be smoked out otherwise. I'm going back on deck. Air's fresher there. Coming up to say goodbye to old England?'

'No. I think I'll stay here for the moment. We've got three weeks to pop up on deck until Cape Town.'

'Two,' Lucy corrected her. 'I know. A sailor told me. We go round the Cape of Good Hope, up the other side of Africa, call in at one of these islands with fancy names, like Mamora or Zanzibar, and on to India. Then do you know what I'm going to do? I'm going to marry a sergeant, a dashing white sergeant. It'll be *wonderful*. Might even have the regimental band to play at our wedding. Think of that.

What have you got in mind, ducks?'

'I don't know,' Anna admitted. 'Depends really on what the future has in mind for me.'

And as she spoke she heard the voice again, familiar now but from far away, as though someone was calling against the wind, against all probabilities, 'You will be rich, one day.'

And then? And then?

Mr MacTavish, the Laird of Long Glen, sat in a leather armchair on one side of the fire in his study. The local minister, Mr Mansfield, wearing his customary dark suit with four-buttoned jacket, and highly polished black boots, sat uncomfortably on the edge of a chair facing him. Between them on a table stood a bottle of whisky, two glasses and a siphon of soda water. The laird had already taken three drams. The minister sipped at a small measure in a large glass of water. He did not care for alcoholic drinks, but equally he did not wish to offend his host.

They had returned from the funeral of the laird's young son, Hamish. The laird and his lady had organised sandwiches, pots of tea, with whisky for those who wanted something stronger. The mourners – all local people, conscious of their social position in relation to the man who owned their houses and controlled their jobs – had not stayed for long. Mr MacTavish was not a popular or a generous man. They would rather be in their own homes than here in his.

He gave a deep sigh, held up the bottle of whisky to Mr Mansfield, raising his eyebrows questioningly.

'No more, thank you. I have enough,' said the minister quickly.

The laird nodded. 'I'll just have another wee one,' he

said, and poured himself two inches. 'I'm glad you could stay behind, minister,' he went on. 'You conducted a fine service for my dear boy. My lady wife and I are greatly in your debt.'

'I was very sorry to have to do it, I can tell you,' said the minister sincerely. He was a homely, simple man, without guile or sophistication. 'It's one thing when we have to lay to rest an old body who has lived his life's allotted span, three score years and ten, maybe more. It's quite another when a young lad or lassie whose life, one would have thought, lay all before them, is being buried. But the ways of the Almighty are inscrutable, sir. I can only offer the comfort that has been mine when I have lost a loved one. There must be a reason for it.'

'Maybe. But if so I can't see it,' MacTavish replied shortly. 'You also buried that woman Moore who put a curse on him, so I heard.'

'Aye, I buried that poor soul. But from what you have told me, it was no curse or blight of the evil eye she laid upon your laddie. She simply foretold what would happen. She did not *make* it happen.'

'I understand what you mean. But you did not see the terrible face of that woman, scarred and hideous and full of venom and hatred. She came begging at the back door for her child. So she said. But I've had a lot of trouble from these gypsies. So have many other householders round here. They thieve like jackdaws. They'll wheedle their way into the house on some specious pretext just to pick up what they can. Outside, they steal fruit, vegetables, kill grouse, pheasants, deer. Not a salmon's safe in the river, in or out of season.'

'They're probably hungry. I'm sure they don't do it to sell.'

'Maybe. But this thieving must be stopped before it leads on to worse things.'

'Oh, I agree,' said the minister quickly. 'I agree. I'm not defending them at all. I'm just trying to find a reason for their behaviour. It's very difficult when you live in a big house with servants and money in the bank to understand what it's like when you have nothing at all. When you're out there, cold and hungry, you think: the laird'll never miss one bird or a teaspoon. He'll never miss one wee salmon.'

'You have to take that view, minister. I understand that entirely. Our Lord was always on the side of the underdog, if I read the scriptures correctly. But He wasn't on the side of evil-doers. And that woman was evil. I'm surprised you could bury her.'

'I was sorry you put Ballater, the carpenter, and his wife and their daughter Anna out of their cottage,' said the minister to change the subject.

MacTavish shrugged. 'That girl Anna was involved in some way. I'm sure of that. Hiding in the heather, up on the hillside, watching the maids with my son. Why, I am by no means clear.'

'She told me before she left – as you may know, sir, she's gone as a nursemaid to India with the doctor's sister, looking after their two bairns – she told me your housekeeper had asked her to go.'

'That has been totally denied.'

'By the housekeeper, of course?'

'Of course.'

'Well, it's one woman's word against another. And the housekeeper has much more to lose if the girl's account is believed. Anna has already lost everything because she's gone. I was very sad to see the Ballaters put out. They are a decent, God-fearing family.'

'You think I acted harshly?'

'Since you ask my opinion, sir, I do. I think that, on reflection, you would not have done what you did. After all, Ballater has been a loyal servant to you for years, and he served his country bravely right through the war. Whatever their daughter may or may not have done – and personally I would take her word on anything – her father and mother did not know what happened to your son until your bailiff told them.'

'I was overwrought. My son dead, cursed to death. The doctor had already told me my wife could not bear another child. I am in the position, as you remind me, of having a big house, a large income, all kinds of benefits except the one I want most – an heir. Denied me by that bloody woman.'

'Do not speak ill of the dead. That does not do other than demean you, sir.'

'Possibly. But you have not suffered as I have suffered. It is easy for an outsider to say what should or should not be said or done. For my boy to drown in a couple of inches of water in a cart track! No one but a witch could make that happen. Do you believe in such creatures as witches, Mr Mansfield?'

'I believe that there are many things, as Shakespeare says, in heaven and earth, that are not dreamed of in our philosophies and are quite beyond our knowledge. Years ago, when I was a young man, if anyone had told me that if I poured some spirit into a machine it would vaporise and with a series of small explosions would drive a car along the road quicker than any horse, I would have laughed at the idea. But what would once have been magic is now commonplace.'

'That doesn't answer my question. Do you believe in witches?'

'I do not disbelieve in them. Maybe the powers some claim for them will be explained by science one day. I have seen people in this parish who have been sick unto death and someone who you might call a witch has visited them. Once, the woman Moore lit a bowl of dried herbs by the bed, told the patient to breathe in the smoke, and he recovered.

'One man, now moved from the parish, had a septic ulcer on his leg for years. The chemist dressed it every week but it never got any better. Dr Bailey could do nothing at all. Then along came a gypsy horse dealer. He scraped some mould off a harness strap, put that on a dressing, placed it against the wound and healed it. Magic you might say. Witchcraft, even. But it worked.'

'Do you believe some people – I call them witches for want of a better word – can put a curse on people?'

'Only if the person on whom they put such a curse believes they have that power. I have a cousin working in the mission fields in Africa. When he was home on leave he told me about witch doctors out there. One may tell a man he will die that very night. The man may be healthy, young, fit, vigorous, nothing whatever wrong with him. But as soon as he hears this he will take to his hut and by dusk he is dead. He has simply lost the will to live, and without that, the only alternative is death. The witch doctor's will was stronger than his. The witch doctor killed him, murdered him if you like. But without the use of poison or a weapon. Nothing but words.'

'That could be what happened to my boy.'

'But your son had no contact with Mrs Moore. I doubt they ever even saw each other. The woman told *you* what would happen, not your son.'

'Even so, you will never convince me she did not engineer it all. I'm sorry about the Ballaters, but not for that girl. I feel certain she was involved in some way. I'll never know how exactly. But I'll never forgive her as long as I live.' The laird picked up his whisky, swallowed the spirit at a gulp, then banged the glass down on the table with such force that it shattered. For a moment, the two men sat in silence, looking at the glittering splinters.

Then MacTavish cleared his throat. He glanced at the bottle as though he would pour himself another drink, thought better of it.

'I mustn't keep you, Mr Mansfield,' he said thickly. 'No doubt you have other calls on your time, a lot to do with your flock.'

'I hope I may have something more to do with you, sir.'

'What do you mean by that, exactly? You've carried out your duties admirably. And you have listened to me now and made your case for the woman Moore, although I cannot agree with it.'

'There is something else, sir. You said your lady wife could not bear another child.'

'That is true.'

'I have a proposition to make, which I do with extreme diffidence. But, knowing you as a man of mercy and wide experience of the human condition, as you come into contact with all manner of people through your work as a magistrate, I ask that you will hear me out.'

'Come to the point, man.'

'This woman Moore, who you claim was a witch but who I can assure you most earnestly, to the best of my knowledge and belief and those of others who knew her, was simply a gypsy, leaves a little boy. An orphan.'

'When she came to the back door she said some damn rubbish about a mantrap nearly severing his leg.'

'That was not rubbish, sir. That was true.'

'Well? What of it? What is your proposition?'

'You lack an heir, sir. I believe that this boy is not the son of a gypsy, a tinker mending pots and pans, a person of no consequence. I am sure he is the son of a man of high degree.'

'That's common enough, surely?'

The minister nodded. 'I have seen the bairn several times and he has breeding in his face. He is the son of a gentleman.'

'But his mother was still a witch – or, as you would prefer, a gypsy.'

The minister paused, not quite certain how he should continue. Then he made up his mind. 'What would you say is the more important when you plant your garden, the seed or the soil in which it is planted?' he asked.

'Both are important. The seed must be strong to germinate and survive, for without it the soil is nothing. But without soil the seed will never grow. Why do you ask?'

'Because I believe the same ratio of importance exists between a man and a woman. He impregnates her, and although she carries the baby for nine months, the child is referred to as the father's. This boy lacks a known parent, but he is not without talent. Indeed, I would say he is one of the brightest lads of his age I've come across, bearing in mind he's never been to a proper school. That, to me, shows his breeding, and his potential.'

'So?'

'What I would suggest, with respect, is that you might care to meet the boy. I think that you and your wife would take to him. In God's good time, you both might care to adopt him.'

'Adopt the son of a woman who bewitched my own son? Are you mad?'

The minister stood up. 'I had hoped you would not greet my proposition in that way, sir, but I sympathise with your point of view. Perhaps I was foolish to mention the matter now. But I believe the Lord spoke to me, and this was what I had to do. I feel I am the bearer of the message, not the originator. The boy has been with relations, who have now moved on. They live in a caravan and are people of the road. He will be staying with me until I can either get him adopted or put into an orphanage. I would be pleased if you and your wife would call and take tea with my wife and me, and then you could both meet him casually. I propose this having full regard to your attitude, of course. After that meeting, I will not raise this matter again, unless you wish.'

The laird sat for a long moment, considering the minister's invitation. Then he nodded. 'I'll ask my wife,' he said. The proposition was absurd, of course, but meeting the lad might somehow draw his wife out of the gloom that had surrounded her since the death of their son. 'I shouldn't think she would countenance the idea of adoption,' he added. 'Not for one moment. But a meeting might take her mind off our loss.'

'We spoke earlier, sir, about God working in a mysterious way,' said the minister. 'I feel that the hand of the Almighty is in this.'

'Maybe it is, maybe it isn't,' replied MacTavish. 'Now, Mr Mansfield, I'll bid you good day.'

When the minister had gone, MacTavish sat on, sipping more whisky until shadows darkened, and the only light in the room came from the glow of the dying fire.

Three

The trooper was a heavy, sluggish vessel, sitting low in the sea, and due to be paid off on her return to Liverpool. The first part of the voyage along the west coast of France was pleasant enough, but through the Bay of Biscay the ship began to roll and heave disturbingly. Waves broke over her bows and stern and flooded the decks amidships as she slowly came up, like a weary boxer in an unequal contest.

The soldiers, down on their mess decks beneath the surface of the sea, with hammocks slung at night and only bare boards to sit on during the day, lay comatose or seasick. Those not sick were detailed to swab their decks to remove the foul stench of vomit and faeces.

Anna lay on her bunk and braced her feet against each roll the old ship made. She had never been in a ship of any type, and she felt queasy and wished she could spend the whole voyage lying down. She had to force herself to get up and tend to the needs of her charges.

Eileen Johnson had brought several bottles of specific from her brother to make the boy Johnny sleep. He spent all his waking hours in her cabin. His sister proved a very good sailor, and was nearly always up on deck, playing with other children.

Going into the cabin where Johnny slept, Anna found him lying on the bottom bunk, his mouth open, eyes closed. He had been sick and bubbles of sputum and vomit still formed and broke over his thick lips. Anna felt his forehead. The skin was very cold and his pulse feeble. The Johnsons' cabin was next door. She knocked on the door. There was no answer, so she opened the door and looked inside. Mrs Johnson lay sprawled on her bunk, mouth open, snoring loudly. Anna shook her awake.

'Excuse me, ma'am,' she said. 'But Johnny is not at all well.'

Mrs Johnson sat up and looked at Anna with bleary eyes. 'That's your job,' she said thickly. 'Why wake me up to tell me? You look after him.'

'I think there's something seriously wrong with him, ma'am. We should call the ship's surgeon.'

Now Mrs Johnson swung herself down from the bunk, put up a hand to her head and groaned. 'I feel so ill,' she said miserably. 'This confounded ship. Will it never stop rolling?'

Still grumbling, she followed Anna to her children's cabin, looked down at her son. There was no love, no feeling whatever in Mrs Johnson's eyes. Anna could see she felt ashamed of the boy. His idiocy and total inadequacy were constant reproaches to her and to her husband. They had brought this being into the world. Now he was the cross they would have to bear patiently and stoically until death released them.

'He's all right,' Mrs Johnson said confidently. 'Just been a bit sick. Wipe that vomit off him and he'll be fine. You're not looking after him very well, leaving him like that, I must say.'

Anna sponged Johnny's face, put a new suit of pyjamas on his frail body, took the old ones away to be washed. Then she came back and sat on a fold-down chair in a corner of the cabin near his bunk in case he awoke and needed her. The wooden panelling on the walls groaned like a living thing with every wave that buffeted the hull. A tooth glass slid from one side of a side table to another, hitting the safety rim round the table's edge with each roll. The child lay very still, groaning from time to time, clearly very ill, and possibly growing worse. Anna went to tell Mrs Johnson.

'Go back to your own cabin,' Mrs Johnson said sharply. 'He'll be all right.'

'I still think I should call the surgeon, ma'am.'

'Look, I'm his mother. You're only the nursemaid. I say who's called and who isn't. Let him sleep. He'll be all right directly. Now get out of here.'

Mrs Johnson's voice sounded slurred. Her lips were wet. She pushed something back out of sight beneath her pillow; a half bottle of gin. This would account for her erratic behaviour, thought Anna, the impression she gave of worrying about everything one moment and being full of life the next. Mrs Johnson was a secret drinker.

Anna walked back to her cabin along the creaking, heaving corridor, her arms outstretched to the wall on either side to balance herself. Lucy was combing her hair.

'Where've you been?' she asked Anna.

'With the little boy. He's poorly. His mother doesn't seem to realise it.'

'He's an idiot, isn't he? Probably best for the family if he just turned his face to the wall.'

'You really think so?'

'Well, wouldn't you, if he were yours?'

'I think I'd feel more responsibility for him.'

'You can't be too soft, not in our business. Anyhow, she's a toff, she's the employer. Do what she says. No skin off your nose. Have you had a skim through her belongings?'

'Of course not.'

'Well, you should. I have.'

'You? Why?'

'Because it pays to know who's who and what's what when you're like us.'

'And what was what?'

'She's got some nice jewels in a case lined with red velvet and with compartments for each jewel. I didn't touch them. She'd miss them at once and would probably blame you, and I didn't want that.'

'Thanks,' said Anna sarcastically. 'You do this whenever you can?'

'Of course. But I tell you what I did find. A huge bottle of some white medicine with the name of a Dr Bailey on it.'

'That's her brother.'

'Yes? Well I took out the stopper and had a sniff. It was laudanum. To make you drowsy, send you to sleep. And she must have been ladling the stuff out like treacle. The bottle was half empty. She's probably giving it to the kid. That's why he lies all day like a dead 'un already.'

'But why? To keep him quiet?'

'Most likely to keep him quiet for ever.'

'You mean kill him?'

'Ooh, don't talk so bluntly. Never know who's listening. But, yes, that's the general idea.'

'I can't believe it. His own mother.'

'And who better placed to do it? Only you. Now, enough of that. Feel like a game of cards?'

'Not really. The sea makes me feel dizzy, that's all.'

'Best thing then if you're doing nothing is to lie down. We'll be through the bay before you know it, so one of the sailors tells me. Then it's sunshine all the way.'

Lucy was quite right. Next day, Anna found that her overcoat, gloves and hat were quite unnecessary. On the following day, she took off her jacket. Within a week, she had discarded the vest under her blouse, for now the sun blazed with a heat she had never imagined. She thought that her parents back in Scotland would simply not believe its strength if she tried to describe it in a letter. She wrote a page every day, describing her life; the trooper was due to call at Cape Town and she would post the letter there. But she did not mention what Lucy had told her, or her own thoughts that Lucy could be right.

The warm weather had a bad effect on her charge. Johnny became more listless, so that he appeared almost moribund, lying on his back for hours on end, his mouth open, seemingly oblivious of people around him. Finally, Mrs Johnson did call the ship's surgeon. He looked grave, and prescribed a specific which instantly made the boy sick. Later, Anna went to see the surgeon in his cabin.

'It's about Johnny Johnson,' she explained.

'Well, what about him?' the surgeon asked her shortly. He was a poorly qualified fellow, owing his job to a relative in the War Office.

'He's been very ill for days, sir. Do you think he's dying?'

'We're all dying, my girl, from the moment we're born. What makes you feel he's nearer that moment than the rest of us? I've given him something to settle himself. Opium based. He'll have a good night's sleep and be better in the morning.'

'Is opium – laudanum – a poison, sir?'

'Of course it is if you take too much. So are strawberries and cream, egg custard, anything if taken to excess. Do you think I've given him too strong a dose, then?'

'Oh no, sir. It's just that I was worried. But please don't tell Mrs Johnson I've been to see you. Johnny is her son and she is certain he's doing well. I'm only the nursemaid.'

For some time after Anna had left the cabin, the surgeon sat on at his desk, sipping neat whisky from a glass jar marked 'Specimens'. The girl was worried all right, and he was giving the boy the biggest dose he dared. Mrs Johnson had begged him to do so, to make sure he slept. He seemed pretty sleepy in any case, almost as if someone else was giving him a nip of laudanum as well. That would account for his lethargy, but of course such an idea was ridiculous.

He poured himself another draught of whisky and waited impatiently for the dinner gong to sound.

Each day Johnny's condition grew worse, and after a week Anna realised he was going to die. She had never thought much about death; it was something that happened to other people. Now it was happening to the boy in her charge.

He was wasting away, and lay sweating, yellow-faced, mouth and nose clogged with mucus. His mother spent most of the time on deck with her husband. As a result, Anna was on her own with Johnny when he died. There was nothing dramatic about his passing from one world to another. He simply stopped breathing and lay, eyes staring up at the upper bunk a foot above his head. Anna shook him, but his head just lolled like a doll with a broken neck. She ran out of the cabin, up on deck. An officer stopped her.

'You have a first-class ticket, miss?' he asked her.

'No,' she told him. 'But I'm with a first-class passenger.'

'You need a ticket to be here, you know.'

'Please don't stop me. There's been a death. My employer's son has died.'

'A death? Are you sure?' The man looked at her disbelievingly.

She ran on past him, up the companionway, found Mrs

Johnson asleep in a deck chair, a sun hat over her face. Anna shook her awake gently.

'You'd better come down, ma'am,' she said. 'It's Johnny.'

'What's wrong with him? He was all right when I left him.'

'I don't think he's all right now, ma'am.'

'Have you called the ship's surgeon?'

'No, ma'am.'

'Well, for goodness sake, girl, get him at once. Must I tell you to do the simplest, most obvious things?' Mrs Johnson sat up, giving every appearance of anxiety. Her eyes were bloodshot. Even with the hat to shade her face her cheeks were flushed and perspiration glistened on her forehead. She spent time smoothing back her hair, brushing down her dress, gathering her belongings together – a novel, a shapeless piece of knitting – before she followed Anna down the companionway to the cabin.

The surgeon examined the dead child cursorily. He nipped Johnny's cheeks between thumb and forefinger, nodded and turned to the mother.

'He was, of course, very seriously ill, Mrs Johnson.'

'What with?' she asked him.

'One of these difficult maladies that affect the very young,' replied the surgeon diplomatically. 'It's a blessing he has been taken so peacefully, without pain.'

Looking at the man, sizing up his soft face, his drinker's mouth, his narrow shoulders, Anna could not bring herself to mention Lucy's theory. She had no proof, nothing at all but the word of another girl.

'He didn't sleep well,' she said, surprising herself for speaking at all. Of course, he had slept too well, but she wanted to sting Mrs Johnson into a reply.

'You know nothing about it,' said Mrs Johnson sharply.

'I prescribed a draught to be taken every night,' said the surgeon, surprised. 'That should have helped him.'

Anna looked at Mrs Johnson. She looked back at her, her eyes accusing, as though guessing her thoughts and daring her to speak them.

'You're bearing your loss very bravely, ma'am,' said the surgeon. 'I take off my hat to you. But then such courage is what we expect from an officer's lady.' He took a pen from his pocket, signed a death certificate, pulled up the sheet over the small cadaver. 'I think we can safely say he was always of a weakly disposition. To save any fuss, I have simply written that complications set in, and the patient died. The truth, of course.'

'Thank you,' said Mrs Johnson. 'What about the committal?'

'There could be a burial at sea. But that's rather traumatic. They stop the ship. A service is held on deck, and the body is consigned to the deep and the care of the Almighty. It's a very moving ceremony indeed. I would not wish it upon a lady of your delicate temperament, ma'am.'

'What would you advise, then?'

'That he is buried in Cape Town. You can make arrangements for the grave to be looked after in perpetuity, if you so wish.'

'Yes, that would be best,' Mrs Johnson said quickly. 'What about the – the body, till we dock?'

'I'll take care of everything,' the surgeon assured her. 'If you would care to leave me for a moment?'

Mrs Johnson nodded, went out of the cabin. The surgeon rang the bell for the steward, told him to have two seamen at the door with a small bag. They arrived within minutes. Anna watched them put the body, still wrapped in the sheet from his bunk, into the bag. One of the men carried it away under his arm. He winked at her cheerfully as he passed; he had no idea she had been the dead boy's nurse.

'Where will you keep him?' Anna asked the surgeon.

'In the cold store. Plenty of room there. Damn sight cooler in there than it is out here. Sometimes wish I was there myself. But not in his condition. Why did you say the child couldn't sleep? From what you told me, I thought he slept only too well?'

'I don't know, sir. It just sort of came out.'

'Humm. Truth will out, eh?' He smoothed back his hair, left the cabin.

Anna did not sleep well that night. The cabin felt stuffy; both her companions snored. Shortly before midnight, she went up on deck and stood, leaning against a part of the superstructure, out of the wind, out of sight. The moon was full and threw a wide silver path across the calm sea. Now and then the ship's bell sounded to mark the passage of time. Her bows dipped gently and rose again on the long, slow swell.

Anna felt beguiled, refreshed by the silent emptiness of the ocean. Then a movement to one side brought her back to alertness. A door had opened and a woman came out on deck. She was carrying something close to her body where it would not easily be seen. She turned to make sure no one had followed her, and in that second Anna recognised Mrs Johnson. She took what she was carrying and flung it as far as she was able over the rail. It turned as it fell: a large bottle half filled with a white liquid. Then it was gone.

Mrs Johnson leaned over the rail as though to reassure herself it had landed in the sea and not on one of the lower decks. Then she turned, and holding out both hands to steady herself, she moved towards the door as though in a stupor. Anna was left on her own. Lucy had not lied, but

65

the only evidence of murder was now sinking beneath the silver sea.

When the trooper docked, Johnny's body was carried ashore in a small coffin that the ship's carpenter had made. His funeral took place the next day.

Afterwards, Mrs Johnson called Anna to her cabin.

'This must have been a bad experience for you, Anna,' she said insincerely. 'My husband thinks I may have been a little hard on you, but I have been under great stress. You may take the afternoon off; you have less to do now anyway, with only my daughter to look after. See the city. But remember, we sail at seven. Next stop will be Mamora, up the east coast of Africa. A detachment of troops is going ashore, and then we sail on to Bombay.'

'Thank you very much, Mrs Johnson.'

'I'd like you to know that I don't hold you responsible in any way for what happened to my son.'

'I am glad,' Anna replied, hoping she did not sound ironic. 'I did my best for him.'

'So did I, girl. But I often thought you could have looked after him more closely. However, you're young. One cannot expect an old head on young shoulders, so I have said nothing about my opinion to my husband. That is between you and me. I would advise you to say nothing about it either.'

'About what exactly, Mrs Johnson?'

'About anything to do with Johnny's unfortunate passing. In a way, of course, it was a blessing. His sister will now be able to grow up on her own without this feeling that there's someone not quite himself, not quite up to the mark, at home. She didn't like bringing other children home to play with him, you know. They'd remark on it. Children have a way of speaking out, saying what they think, that can be very painful sometimes. So it's a blessing in a way. We have to look on the bright side.

'Now, your wages are one pound a week, and you have been in my employ for three weeks. I therefore owe you three pounds. I propose giving you one pound now, so that you can buy anything you may fancy in Cape Town – stamps to send a letter home, some trinket to remind you of the place. But I wouldn't say in your letter that anything's happened to Johnny. Bad news like that can only upset people. Especially when they do not know all the facts. You understand me?'

Anna nodded. Mrs Johnson opened her purse, took out a pound note, held it between her thumb and forefinger, snapped it to make sure there were not two instead of one, and handed the note to Anna.

'Be sure you're back on board by six o'clock. That will give you an hour's leeway before we sail.'

Anna went down to her cabin, pleased at the prospect of free time ashore. She closed the door, locked and bolted it. Then she pulled out her bag and removed the small box Jeannie Moore had given to her. She took out a slice of the root, put it in the ashtray, lit it and chewed the warm ash. She could not say why she did this, but she felt it was important that she did. Once more, she experienced a heady yet soporific feeling of wellbeing. She closed her eyes, breathing deeply.

She could see the cabin and its three empty bunks. She opened her eyes again and looked around her. Yes, it was the same cabin. She had been watching it with her eyes closed, or so it seemed. But the view against her eyelids had shown the cabin with clothes thrown across Lucy's bunk, whereas in fact there were none, and the sheets were as neatly turned down as if in a hospital ward.

Anna shut her eyes again and could see herself, as though she was watching an actress playing herself. She was sitting on the end of her bunk, and across from her she now saw Dorothy, although she knew that really she wasn't there. She was seeing an illusion; she was in a waking dream. Lucy's bunk was empty. Then she saw Lucy in another setting. She had come out of a room that seemed to open on to a gallery of the sort Anna had seen on a visit to a music hall in Perth. Lucy was screaming and her clothes appeared torn. All around, people were staring at her in horror or fascination. Then the picture faded and died. Anna was on her own in an empty cabin.

She felt uneasy. Jeannie Moore had bequeathed a strange power to her. She could see a picture – she supposed of future events – but this was not the whole picture. How would she know what these images meant – if, indeed, they had any significance at all? She remembered Jeannie Moore's warning that she had enough slices for four or five sessions and she had already used them twice. This left only sufficient for two or three more. And then? And then?

She must keep them for a genuine emergency when it was vital for her to foresee the future. Having reached this decision, she went up on deck.

Anna had never travelled further from home than Perth, about ten miles away, until she accepted Mrs Johnson's job. Now she leaned on the wooden railing, looking at the docks, wondering what manner of country she had come to. She was amazed at the size of everything under a blazing sun: buildings, godowns, warehouses, cranes, all much larger than anything she had seen at home. Huge carts trundled past pulled by oxen, loaded with goods from the ship's hold.

First-class passengers, officers and their ladies were already going down gangways shaded by scrubbed canvas awnings. Second-class, third and steerage passengers left by simpler gangways. The troops had changed into lighter khaki uniforms and marched off in small groups, awed by unfamiliar surroundings, the strangeness of everything, yet determined not to appear impressed.

Lucy came up behind Anna. 'I'm going ashore,' she told her.

'So am I.'

'But you were ashore yesterday.'

'Only to the funeral of the little boy.'

'Oh, yes. I forgot. I met a fine fellow ashore last night. Name of Piet. Not spelled like Pete, as in Peter. He's Dutch – well, Boer, really. And he's got a friend. Come with me and meet them. We can have some fun.'

'All right,' said Anna, without much enthusiasm. She was not very keen on Lucy, but surely any companion from home must be better than none in a foreign land. Then, remembering her vision, she asked Lucy, 'Are you sure you want to go ashore?'

'Want to go? Of course,' said Lucy, surprised. 'Why ever shouldn't I? I want to see Piet again. He's different from the boys back home, I can tell you. All hobbledehoys, rough red fingers, big boots there. This man's smart, I tell you. Made me buckle to, just to keep up with him. Why shouldn't I want to go? You're jealous, that's what it is!'

Anna shook her head. 'No, I'm not. I've never been abroad before and I suppose I'm a bit nervous. It all looks so – well, so different.'

Anna could not bring herself to explain that in some kind of trance she had seen the ship sail, and only she and

Dorothy were in their cabin, and then there was the strange picture of Lucy screaming.

They walked down the gangway together. Away from the ship, the sun seemed almost unbearably bright and hot. In Liverpool, before they set sail, Anna had seen a few Indian and Chinese seamen working on the docks. But here, dark-skinned men wore what appeared to be white robes. Women walked a few steps behind them. Some wore black gowns that completely shrouded their figures, and their mouths and noses were also covered by a black garment with only their eyes visible.

'It's their religion,' Lucy explained. 'Piet told me. Purdah, they call it. They're Muslims and the men don't like their women to be seen by any other men. They might get ideas, I suppose. Wouldn't do for me, that.'

They walked through the docks.

'Everything's so clean,' said Anna in admiration.

'Oh, well, it's not like England – all that soot and smoke from chimneys.'

Most buildings were white. Behind and beyond them stretched fields or open farmland with scrubby grass and then the great flat top of Table Mountain, with the Devil's Peak to one side.

'My friend Piet said that when there's cloud round the top, they call it a tablecloth. Pretty smart, eh?'

The roads were paved. Shops varied from those with big, double-fronted glass windows to open stalls. Indians sat cross-legged on pavements, chewing nuts and spitting red juice into the dust. On either side they displayed bags of nuts and grain, barley or rice, all open at the top so that potential customers could see and handle the quality of the goods on offer.

One, sitting with a rug on one side, piled with cheap

rings, necklaces, combs, bracelets, held up a handful of trinkets as they passed.

'Look!' he said. 'All good value. Proper gold.'

'They're not gold,' said Lucy dismissively. 'Piet says they're just plated with gold or simply highly polished brass. Rubbish.'

'Not rubbish, ladies. Not at all rubbish. Look at these combs. Made of tortoiseshell. Last for ever. Look, ladies, I give you best price. What do you offer?'

Anna stopped, picked out a comb from the pile. It was studded with little chips of coloured glass that looked like jewels.

'They match your eyes,' said the Indian. 'Very pretty, I am telling you. Only one English pound.'

'That's too much,' said Anna instantly.

'Ten shillings, then. Ten English shillings, that is all.'

'Offer him two, if you must have it,' said Lucy impatiently. 'Then let's get on. We don't want to keep our friends waiting.'

'Make me an offer, lady. I won't refuse any offer, I am telling you.'

'A shilling,' she said.

The Indian put his head on one side, as though acknowledging defeat. He shrugged his shoulders. 'It is as the memsahib wishes. One shilling. Here. It is yours.'

Anna paid him, stuck the comb in her hair. They walked on.

'See the things you can buy here,' said Lucy. 'Wonderful place. *Wonderful*. And you wait till you meet Piet. You'll like him. You'll like his friend, too, I'm sure.'

It was hot walking in clothes never meant for a warm climate, and after weeks cooped up aboard ship the two girls were soon breathless.

'I could do with a drink,' said Lucy. 'Of course, they don't like women drinking here. The bars are for men. No ladies allowed. It's a man's country, so Piet says. And he wouldn't have it any other way, so he says.'

'Where are we meeting your friends?'

'Couple of hundred yards further on. There's a sort of shop – saloon, really. Behind it there's a private room. We can get a snifter there.'

'You've got to know your way around pretty well then?'

'Well, I wouldn't say that, but there's still time.'

'Not a lot, for we sail at seven this evening. Tell me, what do they do, these two friends?'

Lucy shrugged dismissively. 'You'd better ask them yourself. Get it first hand. I don't care what they do so long as they're generous with their money. Here we are.' Lucy paused outside a building with a frosted glass door. 'That's the bar part,' she explained importantly. 'We can't go in there. We go round the side.'

They walked down an alley between two wooden houses of painted clapboard. The air was sharp with the smell of cats' urine and stale beer. Lucy knocked at a side door. It opened immediately. A tall, bearded man, wearing a black hat with a wide brim, stained with sweat round its band, a rough khaki shirt, thick trousers and scuffed boots looked out at them. He had a hard, unfriendly face.

'Hullo!' he said, recognising her and grinning. 'Come in. You've brought a friend, too, have you?'

'Yes. This is Anna. My friend Piet.'

They were in the room now; very small with wooden chairs, rush mats on the floor, a clock with a loud tick on the mantelpiece. It seemed incongruous to Anna in a hot climate that there should be a fireplace. A second man came into the room from the saloon. He was carrying two glasses of thick brown liquid.

'Hullo, Lucy,' he said. 'You've got a girl friend for me, then, have you, like you said?'

'Yes.'

'I'm Jan.'

'Anna.' She shook his hand. It felt rough and hard. He had a red face and a black beard. His eyes were set very close together, flecked with yellow matter in the corners. Anna did not like him. Instinctively, she did not trust him.

'Aren't you going to offer us a drink, then?' Lucy asked Jan, pouting. 'It was hot work walking here, I can tell you.'

'Who d'you think I've got two for?'

'I thought they were for you and Piet.'

'Plenty more for us in the bar. Just come off the boat, have you, Anna? First time out of old England?'

'Yes,' said Anna.

'Then let's drink to the future. To the four of us. To fun. Together.'

He handed her one glass. The drink had slopped over the sides and the glass felt sticky to her touch.

'What is it?' she asked him.

'What they call Cape Smoke here. Cape brandy. Better than you'd get in France. Real good stuff, I'll tell you that.'

He handed the second glass to Lucy, went into the saloon and returned with two more. They clinked glasses.

'Down the hatch,' said Jan, and drank half the glass at a gulp. His face was sweating. Anna guessed that this was not the first or even the second glass he'd had that day. She sipped hers. The brandy tasted very strong. She had never drunk brandy before. Once or twice, out of curiosity when someone at Christmas or after a grouse shoot had given her father a bottle of the locally distilled whisky, she had sipped it surreptitiously but had not liked the taste. But this was far

73

stronger; it burned her throat, her stomach, made her gasp for breath.

As Anna sipped delicately but steadily, not realising how potent the brandy was, she felt a glow of self-confidence come over her. How lucky she was to be in this foreign country, even if she didn't like this man! She had money in her purse, a job to go back to, an exciting future ahead of her. And what would she have been if she had stayed back home in Scotland? At best a tweenie, at everyone's beck and call.

The brandy was moving now in her veins like liquid fire, but she had nothing against which to measure its potency. She only knew she felt good, better than she'd probably ever felt. Even this fellow Jan wasn't too bad looking. She became aware he was watching her closely, looking at the swell of her breasts under her blouse.

'Come on, drink up!' he said and licked his lips. They seemed perpetually wet. Distant warning drums beat in Anna's mind. She tried to dismiss them. Jan wasn't English – or Scottish. He was a foreigner and they behaved differently from people back home. Just for a moment she wished she was in Scotland again, among familiar folk, whose ways she understood, people she could trust. There was that word again. Trust. But why ever shouldn't she trust this man? Was it just because he looked different to other men she had met? If so, was she simply being narrow-minded and foolish?

'Well, what are we going to do?' Lucy asked everyone, looking from one to the other. 'We don't want to drink all day in here.'

'Why not? What's wrong with that? Then we go to bed and sleep it off.'

'So that's what you've got in mind, is it?' said Lucy.

'We'll have to find out, won't we, love?' Piet replied. 'Unless you've any better ideas.'

'What do you do for a living?' Anna asked Jan ingenuously.

'Right now, nothing.'

'Oh? You're very lucky.'

'No. I'm not. Don't call me lucky. I've worked hard, damned hard to get into this situation.'

'What at?'

'Kimberley. Up north.'

She looked at him, puzzled. 'What's up there?'

'You don't know much, do you? They're digging for diamonds up there. Diamonds big as your thumbnail, some big as pigeons' eggs. Lots of them are only just a few inches under the surface. Others are in river beds. More diamonds in some of them than bloody pebbles, I was told.'

'Did you find any?'

''Course I did. That's why I don't need to work. Look at these. Judge for yourself.' He put his hand into his waistcoat pocket, took out a soft wash-leather pouch with a thong round the top, opened it, spilled some rough stones into his hand. 'All right, aren't they? These few stones, just like bits of glass, are valuable. I've lots more back in my lodgings, so I need never work again. *Ever*. I'm going to go to Holland, build a big house, overlooking a canal, tulip fields, everything. I'm going to be rich.'

'You're not going to be,' interrupted Piet, 'you *are*. So am I.'

'You also struck it lucky, then?' asked Lucy, envy edging her voice.

'We worked for it, I tell you. No luck there. Just hard grind. We were up to our knees in icy water, day after day, week after week. We worked for it. About fifty thousand people were up there, doing the same, scratching for diamonds. Not many got even one. We got a couple of dozen. Anyhow, that's in the past. Now, first thing, another drink.'

'What's the second thing?' asked Lucy, holding out her empty glass.

'I'll soon show you, love,' Piet promised her. 'You don't seem so keen to sit here, so let's get a cab somewhere, out in the country.'

'We'll show you South Africa, Anna,' promised Jan. 'Bit different from England.'

Anna drank only half of the next glass. She was reluctant to drink any more for already she felt as though she might be seasick. The walls, the floor, the ceiling of the room had begun to move in a way she had never experienced before, as though they had a life of their own. She felt dizzy.

'Come on, drink up!'

Jan's voice seemed to be directed at her from a distance, and yet he was standing by her side.

'I've had enough,' she told him, and her voice sounded stilted. She spoke slowly, but still the words ran together.

'All right then. Leave it and let's get on our way.'

He led them up the alley to the main street. A horse-drawn cab was passing. Jan hailed it. They climbed inside. The dark-skinned driver on the box looked at them without interest.

'Where to?' he asked.

'Where we tell you,' retorted Jan. 'And get your old nag going if you want to get paid. I could bloody go on my hands and knees faster than this old horse.'

The drink was running in him, too. Anna sat back, closed her eyes. This was not how she had intended to spend her afternoon off, but what could she do now? She didn't know where she was. She opened her eyes as they passed a church with a clock on its tower. Two o'clock. Four hours before she had to be back. Where were they going?

'I've got to be back aboard ship by six,' she said to no one in particular.

'Rubbish!' said Lucy. 'My friend the sailor says we aren't sailing till after nine.'

'Mrs Johnson says it's seven.'

'Who the hell's Mrs Johnson?' asked Jan gruffly.

'I work for her.'

'Ah, working for other people's no good. You've got to work for yourself in this world. Look at me.'

They were outside the town now, and the road deteriorated from tarmac into dry dust. Foothills stretched up to mountains blue in the distance, beyond acres of scrubby vegetation and trees. Anna suddenly longed to reach their shelter, to lie down, to sleep, and to wake up not feeling woozy, sick, bewildered.

After a time, the cab slowed and stopped. The driver had obviously made this journey before. Jan climbed down.

'You look as though you're half asleep,' he told Anna.

'I am,' Anna admitted. 'I'm not used to strong drink.'

'You come with me. Have a sleep, and you'll feel better.'

'Thank you. That's very kind of you.'

Jan laughed. Anna could see Piet going off with Lucy to the shelter of the trees. The cab driver turned his cab so that the horse was out of the sun. The animal stood, head down, asleep on its feet. Anna and Jan reached the trees. The branches were by no means as thick as they had appeared from the road. In fact they gave little shade, and the ground underneath them was rough with clumps of spiky grass, and what appeared to be fir cones.

'Here, this'll do,' Jan told her. He took off his jacket,

rolled it up to form a pillow. 'Put your head on that. You'll be off in a minute and right as rain inside ten.'

'What about you?'

'I'm used to the heat. You're not.'

He sat down in his shirtsleeves, loosened his waistcoat, lit a cheroot. He took out his pouch of diamonds, examined them closely, put them back in his pocket.

Anna lay down thankfully. The cones were softer than she imagined, or she was drunker than she thought. She put her head on his coat. It smelled strongly of brandy and tobacco. She kicked off her shoes and within seconds was fast asleep.

She dreamed that a wild animal had come out of the forest and was looking at her, touching her, nuzzling her. She could feel strange hot breath on her face. She shook her head to wave it away, and it left. Then it returned. She opened her eyes. Jan was lying beside her. His shirt and waistcoat were open. He had slipped off his trousers, his underpants. One hand was under her skirt, feeling her thigh roughly. Anna wriggled.

'No!' she cried. 'No! It's wrong!'

'It's wrong! It's wrong!' he repeated sarcastically, imitating her voice. 'What's wrong about it, you stupid little English girl? What do you think you're out here for?'

'I thought to see the countryside.'

'Don't be absurd! You know damn well why you're here. You and your friend Lucy. You're a teaser. Well, I won't be teased by you, you bitch.'

Jan ripped her blouse open. He seized one of her breasts roughly, squeezed it, then tore off her skirt. He was naked now except for his shirt, and reared above her like a beast. She saw his phallus, huge and engorged with blood. Anna brought up her knee, kicked out into his groin. He screamed

with sudden, unexpected pain, clutched himself as he fell
to one side. His head hit the bole of the tree as he fell. He
gave a grunt and lay, both hands still pressed down on his
groin.

Anna staggered to her feet, shook sand and fir cones
from her skirt, which she pulled on hastily. Her blouse
hung in tatters. She still felt slightly dizzy from the alcohol.
In a daze of shock and bewilderment she put up one hand
to smooth her hair, and found that her new comb was
missing. She had bought it only an hour ago; she must find
it. She went down on her hands and knees, running her
hands through the scrubby grass. The comb lay about a
yard away, but some of the little pieces of coloured glass
had fallen out. She must find them, too; she could not bear
to lose them because of Jan's behaviour.

She put the comb in her purse and then began to search
for the glass segments. She found several pieces, and
picked up each one carefully, put it in the handkerchief in
her purse. Then she stood up.

Jan still lay where he had fallen, groaning and moving his
legs and arms slightly; he was coming round. Anna knew
she dare not be here when he stood up. He could kill her.
She called to her friend, 'Lucy! Lucy! I'm going!'

There was no answer. Lucy had gone much further into
the trees. It was possible she could not hear her. Well, she
could take care of herself – or let Piet take care of her. Anna
was secretly surprised at her own feelings. She would
usually have worried about a companion and waited for
her. But now a new hardness possessed her. She had not
been very successful so far in looking after herself. Now she
would be.

She put on her shoes, walked back through the trees to
the cart. The driver was sitting with his back against a tree,

dozing. She called to him, and when he did not respond quickly, shook him awake roughly.

'The docks,' she told him briefly. 'Now.'

'What about your friends?'

'They're coming later.'

'It will cost you two shillings,' he said.

'The docks,' she repeated. 'I'll pay you then.'

She climbed up under the hood, and sat down thankfully on the warm wooden bench. The cart moved forward. She put out both hands to steady herself against the swaying of the old vehicle. In half an hour they were back at the docks. She paid off the man, walked up the gangway. Dorothy was sitting on the deck reading a novelette.

'You're back early,' she said, almost accusingly.

'What's the time?'

'Just gone five.'

'Well, six o'clock was the time I was told to be here.'

'Where's Lucy?'

'With her friend.'

'Oh. She told me she'd met one. She had one for you?'

'Yes. But I didn't take to him much.'

'Your blouse is all torn. And your hair is messed up. Been in a fight, have you? Had an argument?'

'Sort of.'

'Oh, well, it's all experience. That's what my old mother used to say.'

'I suppose it is. Of a kind.'

Anna went down to her cabin, took off her blouse. It was ruined, only useful now to make rags for cleaning. She undressed, pulled on an overcoat – she had no dressing-gown – and, carrying a towel and a big bar of red carbolic soap, went along the corridor to the communal bath. The sea water ran hot, but the soap did not lather. Even so, afterwards she felt better, cleaner, but she still had a slight headache and a pain behind her eyes.

Back in the cabin she emptied the contents of her bag onto the little table by her bunk. She carefully unfolded the handkerchief, washed the little stones in the basin, dried them, tried to fit them back into the holes on the comb. Each hole had a tiny metal tongue that could be bent to keep the stones in place, but to her surprise the stones would not fit. It took her a moment in her fuddled state to realise why. They weren't the original stones; these were different.

She looked at them more closely. These were the diamonds Jan had taken from the pouch in his waistcoat pocket. When he fell, he must have dropped it, and the diamonds scattered. She must return them to him – but how could she find him? She had no idea of the name of the place to which the cab had taken them. Perhaps he would escort Lucy back to the trooper and she could give them to him then. If he didn't come back, she would keep them. He had others, so he said. She must conceal them somewhere, at least until the ship sailed.

Anna thought of boring a hole in the heel of her shoe and hiding them inside it. But she had nothing to bore a hole with. She couldn't swallow them, nor could she risk keeping them in the little box Jeannie Moore had given her.

Then she saw the bar of carbolic soap she had carried into the bathroom. This was one of two she had brought aboard with her from home. She took the other one out of its paper wrapping, picked up her knife, pushed it into the soap, and began turning it round as though coring an apple.

She pulled out the round whorl of red soap, squeezed the diamonds into the hole and then with her thumbs pushed back the whorl. She smoothed the side of the bar so that no sign remained of the hole. Then she put it back in its wrapper and into her bag.

She lay back on her bunk, closed her eyes. She had gone ashore with a pound note from Mrs Johnson. She was about to leave with a fortune from a Dutchman she had known briefly and unhappily as Jan.

Was this Jeannie Moore's prophecy coming true? Or was it only a foretaste of far greater riches to come?

Four

Davey Moore sat at one end of the scrubbed table in the kitchen of the minister's house. Mrs Mansfield sat protectively at his right hand, watching him eat a slice of toast smeared with dripping. He was a tall, grave boy with widely spaced eyes and a sensitive mouth. He looked, she imagined, as a young poet might look, or maybe an actor playing the part of a young poet. There was something almost ethereal about him, she thought.

The Mansfields did not have any children, and she had been grateful to welcome someone young into their home, although she knew that Davey's stay would only be temporary. She also knew he felt lonely after the death of his mother, and her own solitary spirit went out to him. She wanted to feed him up, as she put it, and put more flesh on his bones. She had suggested to her husband several times that they should adopt him, or at least let him live with them indefinitely – permanently, if possible – and treat him as their own until he could decide what he wanted to do.

'That would not be fitting,' Mr Mansfield told her firmly.

'But why not? You preach every Sunday in the kirk about helping the poor and needy, and maybe entertaining an angel unawares. Here's the only chance we've ever had to do what you so strongly advise others to do.'

'I don't want the boy in the house,' her husband replied.

He could not explain the real reason to his wife. Just

looking at Davey, who was obviously much better bred than he was, and good-looking, while he was plain, the minister felt seeds of jealousy and resentment grow within him. Life was so unfair. Why should this son of a wandering gypsy be so handsome while he would always be stocky with dull features?

It would be altogether different if Mrs Moore's child had been a girl; there would have been no jealousy then. But there was now, and he could not bring himself to tell his wife how strong this was. Two's company, he thought. Three's none, and never would be.

Mr Mansfield knew that his wife regretted they had no children, and sometimes he regretted this himself. But that was surely God's will, something which they could not change. The best means of helping Davey was to persuade the laird and his wife to adopt him. He explained to his wife that this was what he wished to do.

'But yon MacTavish is a cruel man,' she cried in genuine horror. 'He's no friend to anyone, not even his own folk. So why should he suddenly be kind to the lad? The leopard never changes its spots. And he'll never wish to bring up the boy of the woman he claims killed his own son. Don't you see that? Why are you so insensitive sometimes?'

'I'm not insensitive, wife. I think Davey is the son of some high-born person. You have only to look at him and see how proudly he holds himself to know that.'

'Who was his father?'

'I cannot tell you because I do not know. But just look at his features. You can see at once he is of gentle birth, not like other lads of his age round here, all stumpy and thick-fingered, with rough faces like hogs. He'll get a proper chance in a gentleman's home.'

'We could give him as good a chance here. Better. For it

84

would be with love, which is more than he'll ever get up at the castle if he's there a hundred years. You're a well-read man, Douglas. You could easily coach him. Then there's no saying how far he could go. He could be a lawyer, a doctor.' She paused. 'Even a minister,' she added, hoping that this proposal might produce a more positive approach.

'I said no. And don't argue with me. Please don't mention the matter to me again. A man must be head in his own house.'

'That may be, but the man's wife is the neck that turns the head. At least, that's what I was told.'

'Not in this case, wife. Not in this case. And that's an end of it.'

So now Mrs Mansfield sat watching the boy, storing up in her mind his features, the way he ate, how he moved his hands, so that she could recall these memories when he had left them, for she knew that Davey's time with them would be very limited. That morning her husband had told her that the laird and Mrs MacTavish were coming to tea. She had washed Davey's clothes, pressed his only suit of trousers and jacket in preparation for their visit. Then she had filled the tin bath that hung on the scullery wall, given him a bar of soap, a scrubbing brush and a towel and told him how important it was to make a good impression.

'I hope they're going to bring you up,' she explained, trying to keep sorrow and disappointment out of her voice. 'Give you a real chance in life.'

'I'd rather stay here,' said Davey simply. 'It's what I've always thought a home would be like. What my mother used to tell me things were like when she was a girl.'

'Dear Davey, I wish this could be your home. But the minister wants the best for you, and he thinks this is it.'

'And you don't, Mrs Mansfield?'

She did not answer; to tell the truth would be disloyal to her husband, and she could never be that.

'Were you happy with your mother in Soldier's Wood?' she asked him as brightly as she could, changing the subject.

'I never thought about it, Mrs Mansfield,' he replied. 'We never had much food, not like here, and often it was cold in the wood. But, yes, I was happy. My mother did her best for me. We were very close. I miss her a lot. I always will.'

'Of course you will. But you'll be happy in the laird's house. It's a fine place. A castle. They've got steam heating and lots of servants. You'll have everything you want.'

'I'd still rather be here.'

'I'm sorry, Davey. Just as sorry as you are, perhaps even more. But all of us have disappointments. Life is never exactly how we'd want it or how we imagined it. But if the laird does take you, you'll have chances you'd never get elsewhere to do things and go places and be someone. So when they come to tea this afternoon, you wait here, and then, if he and Mrs MacTavish want to meet you, I'll bring you in. Be quiet, be yourself, don't talk till they talk to you. If they ask you questions, do your best to answer them politely but firmly. Don't say anything just because you think that's what they want to hear. Be yourself, Davey, now and always.'

'I'll do my best, if that's what you want, Mrs Mansfield,' Davey promised her. 'But I tell you again, it's not what I want.'

The laird and Mrs MacTavish arrived at four thirty. The chauffeur opened the door of their Daimler, bowed obsequiously as they stepped out. Mrs MacTavish wore a fur coat and the fixed smile of someone who was resigned to being bored but determined not to show it. She was a dumpy, pleasant, rather vapid woman. Her father's estate had marched side by side with the laird's, and it had been assumed from childhood that in due time they would marry. There was little passion or love in their marriage; it was more a matter of a union of acres of land, a whisky distillery and properties in Perth and Dumfries. They were two people sharing the same house, sometimes even the same bed, but not their lives.

'What a very nice manse this is,' she said as Mrs Mansfield came out to greet them. 'I've passed it so often, but, do you know, I've never set foot over the doorway.'

'Well, that must be my fault,' Mrs Mansfield replied nervously, anxious to make a good impression but not wishing to fawn over their visitors. 'We don't entertain very much, you know. We live quietly. My husband's either out seeing his parishioners most days or he's writing his sermons in his study. It's not the fancy, smart life I suppose you have.'

'I don't think ours is very fancy or very smart,' Mrs MacTavish assured her, trying to put her hostess at ease.

How could this very decent, homely body possibly understand what it was like to live with a man whose temper was as unpredictable as the weather? Had she ever lived under the same roof with someone she sometimes actively hated, whose appearance she loathed, whose voice grated on her like a rusty rasp? When their son was alive, she had been able to focus her pent-up affection on the boy, but since they had been on their own, her misery seemed almost unbearable. Now there was this extraordinary proposition that they might adopt the son of some gypsy woman whom only days previously he had been loudly blaming for Hamish's death. The idea was ridiculous; yet she must humour him or for weeks he would be absolutely impossible to live with.

Mrs MacTavish followed her husband into the little drawing room. White antimacassars covered the backs of the upright armchairs; an aspidistra flowered in a polished Benares brass bowl, a barometer hung on the far wall. The laird glanced at it to see what the day would be like for shooting tomorrow. It was set for Windy. He tapped the glass. The needle swung slowly towards Fair.

'Funny weather we're having, Mrs Mansfield,' he said.

'Yes. For this time of year it is. But I expect we'll get better days soon.'

'I very much hope so.'

Mr Mansfield came into the room, shook hands with his guests. 'Most kind of you to come,' he said unctuously.

'Kind of you to ask us,' Mrs MacTavish replied dutifully.

'Please do sit down.'

They perched uneasily on the edges of uncomfortable chairs. The room had a slight feeling of dampness about it because it was almost never used, not even on Sundays. The visitors looked at lithographs on the walls, bound volumes of Sir Walter Scott, *Blackie's Modern Encyclopaedia* on shelves, a Bible with decorated bookmarks on a side table. They dredged for something to talk about, but soon lapsed into remarks about the view from the window, the size of church congregations.

'Would you take tea?' Mrs Mansfield asked at last, eager to escape from the room.

'When you're ready, that would be very nice,' Mrs MacTavish agreed.

'Before we have tea,' said the laird abruptly, 'I think we should all discuss the matter that has brought us here. My wife and I would like to meet this boy, Davey.'

'I'll bring him in,' said Mrs Mansfield.

She went out into the kitchen. Davey was sitting at the table, turning over the pages of one of the few lighter novels in the house.

'They'd like to see you,' Mrs Mansfield told him. 'Now remember what I've said.'

He stood up, nodded, followed her into the drawing room.

'Ah, a fine, upstanding lad,' said the laird approvingly, as though surprised. 'Tell me about yourself.'

'What do you want to know, sir?'

'Well, your interests, your views on things.'

'My interests so far, sir, have been confined to woodcraft. Setting snares for rabbits, lighting cooking fires and seeing they didn't cause fires in the woods, running errands for my mother.'

'You've been to school?'

'Off and on, sir. My mother had some books, though. She taught me to read and to write – joined up writing . . .'

The laird took down the copy of *Blackie's Encyclopaedia* from the shelf, opened it.

'Read that,' he commanded, handing the book to Davey.

'"Ironmongery,"' Davey read slowly. '"Such articles of iron as are generally used for domestic purposes and are sold in retail shops. Irons. Shackles, fetters, or bilboes for the feet, especially such as are used on board ship."'

'That's well done. So you *can* read. Good.' The laird replaced the book. 'Can you swim?'

'Yes, sir.'

'Can you shoot?'

'No, sir. I've never had a gun. But I have a good eye, so my mother said. I could easily learn.'

'What would you like to do when you are older?'

'I don't know, sir. That depends . . .' He paused.

'On what?' asked Mrs MacTavish, looking at him intently. The lad was better looking than she had anticipated, and he was polite. She tried to imagine her dead son Hamish at this fellow's age.

'On what chances and opportunities there are, ma'am. If I had stayed with my mother, I might have been a woodman. But I think I would have emigrated.'

'Emigrated? Where to?' The laird sounded surprised.

'To Canada, perhaps, the United States. Or Australia.'

'Why?'

'My mother thought there was more chance for a young man in those countries than here.'

'I wouldn't say that,' said the laird stiffly.

'Well, it was rather different for you at his age,' his wife told him sharply. 'You're educated. There's a lot in what he says. If this boy was educated, I think he could go anywhere.'

'"If" is a big word.'

The minister cleared his throat. 'He's a good lad, is Davey,' he said earnestly. 'I can vouch for that. He's a hard worker, and honest. Your wife's quite right, sir. He could go anywhere. He could do anything if he had the chance.'

'If I took you into my family, I could give you a chance of education,' said the laird, addressing Davey, ignoring the minister. 'But you'd have to work hard. Any back-sliding and you'd be out. Do you understand that?'

Davey's puzzlement showed on his face. He looked from the laird to his wife. 'What is back-sliding, sir?'

'Laziness. Mutinous behaviour. Resentment.'

'It's unlikely he'd resent you helping him,' said Mr Mansfield gently.

'On the contrary. Young fellows now are quite different from in our day. You do someone a good turn now and they're liable to hate you for it. Help a lame dog over a stile and you must expect to be bitten.' MacTavish turned to his wife. 'Well, what do you think?'

'He's a nice lad,' Mrs MacTavish agreed dubiously.

'Would you like him under our roof?'

'It's difficult to talk in front of the boy. Send him out for a moment while we discuss it. He has feelings like the rest of us.'

Mrs Mansfield nodded to Davey. 'I'll come with you and make the tea,' she told him.

'Well, now, what do you think?' the laird asked his wife when they had gone.

'I don't want him,' said Mrs MacTavish. 'Every time I looked at him, I'd think of my own boy who died.'

'You mean that, like me, you think Davey's mother killed our son?'

'There's no cause for saying that, sir,' said Mr Mansfield quickly. 'I assure you, there is none.'

'That's your opinion,' retorted the laird briefly. 'We've been over that before.' He turned to his wife. 'I think you could get used to him,' he told her. 'Let's give it a trial – say a year.'

'If you say so,' said his wife meekly, but her eyes showed resentment. She didn't want the boy in the house, but if he was there his presence would reduce the time she had to spend alone with her husband. That could be an unexpected bonus.

'Have his bags packed,' the laird told the minister brusquely. 'Then send him up to the castle.'

'You won't take him back in your motor?'

'No, that might give him the wrong idea.'

'What entrance shall I tell him to come to, sir?'

'I suppose the front,' said MacTavish reluctantly. 'It's

what he will be using from now on.'

As the laird stood up, Mrs Mansfield came in carrying a tray.

'I think, having seen the boy and reached our decision, we won't be bothering you for tea, Mrs Mansfield,' said the laird.

'Oh, I am sorry. And I've made some scones especially for you.'

'How kind. But my wife is a little overwrought. It's a difficult decision to make. Very difficult for her, especially.'

He led the way out to the car. The chauffeur held open the door. The minister and his wife watched the Daimler bowl away. A faint frond of blue smoke from the exhaust hung briefly above the unmade road as it disappeared. The minister turned to his wife. She was crying.

'He'll not be happy there,' she said. 'I know it.'

'He'll have a good chance there,' her husband answered her. 'I'd be failing in my duty if I didn't let him take it. I think this is God's work.'

Or the Devil's, thought Mrs Mansfield wretchedly.

Inside the car, Mrs MacTavish turned to her husband. 'Why are you doing this? You *know* I don't want it. And I don't think you want it, either. Not really, deep down inside you.'

'I'm doing it because I want to get even. His mother took our boy's life. I want to make this lad's life something to remember.'

'You mean be cruel to him? Or give him a chance in life?'

'We shall see what we shall see,' her husband replied enigmatically, and lit a cigar.

Davey Moore had his own room in the laird's castle, high up in one of the granite towers. Through its narrow window he could see the river and the wood where he had lived with his mother. The room was cold, its walls whitewashed, but there was an iron grate in the fireplace. A fire was laid and lit every day by a maid. He had a bowl for washing on a marble table and a ewer of warm water was placed by the bowl every morning.

His bed was narrow, and in the confines of this granite room he felt caged, like a prisoner in a cell. He would stand by the thin window, opening the glass panes to breathe cold fresh air flowing in from the distant hills. He realised he had a chance that would never have come if his mother had lived. But although he might have wider opportunities, the loss of freedom was a high price to pay for anything.

The laird had nothing to do with him for the first few days, then called him down to his study. Davey stood uneasily in the big room, watching the older man as he sat in his favourite armchair, sipping a glass of The MacAllan whisky.

'How are you settling in, boy?' MacTavish asked at last.

'Pretty well, sir. When do I start work?'

'This week. You're going to school. There's a good day school in Perth. You'll go there for a term or so, and if you do well, we'll send you away.'

'How do you mean, sir, send me away? I thought you'd only put me out if I didn't do well.'

'When I say send you away, I mean to a school where you'll board. Live in all the term, with other boys. In that way you develop your character, you learn to stand on your own feet. You can also work harder. And then your chances of getting on in the world are greater. Maybe you'll go on to a university. That depends on you, how hard you work, how clever you are. I understand you told one of the maids that until the minister and his lady wife took pity on you

you'd never slept in a room, in a house, or indeed in a building of any kind?'

'That is true, sir. We lived rough, my mother and I.'

'What about your father?'

'I never knew my father, sir.'

'Did your mother ever see him after you were born?'

'I don't know. She may have done. But when I asked her about him, she told me that it was her affair and no business of mine. He'd been a gentleman, she did say once. One day she thought I might be a gentleman, too, sir.'

'I hope her prophecy comes true. Tell me about her.'

'You never knew her, sir?'

'Well, I'd seen her about, and she came to the back door once, and I swear she put the evil eye on my own son who died.'

'I had heard talk of that, sir. But I believe from her own account she only told you what would happen. She did not make it happen.'

'Well, that's your opinion. You're loyal to your mother's memory and I understand that. Shows you've got guts. But tell me about her.'

'What do you want to know, sir?'

'Well, anything. Must have been a remarkable woman, bringing you up.'

'She did very well by me, the best she could. She taught me how to fish, how to snare. I had no gun but I had a sling like the boy in the Bible story – David. I have his name, sir. She liked those old stories.'

'Ah, yes, I remember that story, too. Of course, you were poaching, stealing fish and game.'

'It did not strike us that way, sir. There was so much. Surely a hare, a rabbit, a fish would not be missed.'

'It depends who owns them. And I own them, so in a

sense I missed them. I like to think I know how much I possess.'

'Not in wild things, sir. They travel for miles. They could have come from some other estate.'

'That's a point, I grant you. But, your mother. She was kind?'

'Very kind. Very proud. She said we owed no one anything, not a living, not a penny.'

'Very few people can say that, Davey. How did she spend her days?'

'She went out selling sprigs of white heather. She kept it in some chemical. Peroxide of hydrogen, she called it. It turned ordinary purple heather white, which is supposed to bring good luck.'

'And did it?'

'It brought us a few pennies a time. That was good luck for us, sir. Sometimes I helped her.'

'Did you go out with her every day?'

'No, sir. Not every day.'

MacTavish was silent, not quite certain how he should proceed. He did not want to offend the boy, but he wished an answer to a question that disturbed him and no one else could supply it.

'Tell me,' he said at last, trying to sound casual. 'How did she get those injuries to her face?'

'A man she was living with slashed her with a knife, sir.'

'Not your father?'

'No. Someone else. She told me he had found out about my father and he was jealous. He said he'd make sure she'd never go with another man.'

'I see. And what happened to him?'

'He went off with a tinker woman, sir. But it was a long time ago, before we came to Soldier's Wood.'

MacTavish nodded. It sounded an extraordinary story, but then some of these gypsy people led extraordinary lives; they were like animals.

'Well, that's all for today,' he went on. 'My wife will take you into Perth tomorrow to get you fitted out with some proper clothes. You don't want to stand out like a sore thumb among other boys at school. I will keep a close eye on your progress.'

'Thank you, sir.'

Davey was relieved to be out of the room. He did not like the laird. Something about MacTavish grated on him. But he was doing his best to be kind. And Davey knew he must take full advantage of the opportunity the laird was offering him. If he failed, he would never have another chance like this.

The trooper ploughed slowly north through the shimmering cobalt sea. Like polished dagger blades, flying fish leapt out of the waves and dived in again beneath the ship's wash. To the left the long, green coast of East Africa sank into the horizon, hazy as a mezzotint.

Anna leaned on the rail, wondering what the next port of call would be like. She and Dorothy were alone in their cabin for this part of the voyage; Lucy had not returned in time to join the vessel before they left Cape Town.

'I feel guilty about her,' Anna had told Dorothy as the ship sailed out and Table Mountain sank behind them in the evening mist.

'Why should you?' Dorothy replied sharply. 'She knows what she's about.'

'But does she? She's left all her clothes here. She must have intended to come back in time.'

'Clothes? Only a trunk full of dirty things she was too

lazy to wash. I bet she's found a man to keep her. She's that type. Lucky. Men go for her. You and I may have to keep ourselves – and maybe a man as well.'

'Never,' said Anna. 'If a man cannot keep me better than I can keep myself, give me one reason why I should become involved.'

Dorothy looked at her quizzically. 'They call it love,' she said. 'That's the reason. So I'm told.'

Now, leaning on the rail alone, Anna remembered this, and wondered where Lucy was, how she was faring. The only address they had was her home in England. She had been going out to work for a family of tea planters in Assam, looking after their children. But if she did not arrive, she would lose her job. And Anna did not think that Piet or Jan were men who would keep a strange girl longer than a night or two. So how would Lucy live?

One of the crew came past, saw Anna on her own, turned back to talk to her.

'We reach Mamora in the early hours,' he told her. 'We only stay long enough to take on water and drop a company of British soldiers. They'll be glad to get out of mess decks after so long. Next stop, Bombay.'

'What's Mamora like?' Anna asked him.

'Great place if you're white. Even if you're black it's quite good, as long as you have money. Better than India anyhow. It's a rich island, one of a group around Zanzibar. Both have been centres of slavery for centuries. There's still a lot of that goes on.'

'I thought slavery was made illegal long ago.'

'So was counterfeiting, forgery, thieving and murder. But they all still flourish, and always will, I expect. The Muslim penalty for a thief is to cut off one of his hands. That stops some, but the rest still think the profits are worth the risk. Same with slavery. It's been illegal since early last century, but in my view they'll never stop it, even if they wanted to, which most people don't round here. There's too much profit in it. In every country I've ever visited there's crime and bribery, right up to the top. And the bigger the profit, the bigger the rake-off.'

'I thought most people were honest?'

'Then you are more stupid than I believed it possible a pretty girl could be. This is the twentieth century. We've just had a war that lasted for four years. That should have shown you how things work. It's everyone for himself in this world and, I'd say, in the next, whatever the parsons may tell us.'

As he walked on, Dorothy came up the companionway.

'I've been looking for you everywhere,' she began accusingly. 'Mrs Johnson has sent a steward to the cabin to see where you were.'

'I have the hour off,' Anna replied.

'That's as may be, but she wants you in her cabin now. Says it's important.'

Anna went down the companionway into her cabin, washed her face and hands, brushed her hair, smoothed down her dress. Then she walked through the door into the first-class section of the ship.

Mrs Johnson was in her cabin, sitting at her dressing table, dabbing a glass stopper from her scent bottle behind her ears. The room smelled strongly of spilled whisky.

She turned round in her seat, moving very slowly as though she feared that if she moved quickly she might overbalance.

'Where have you been?' she asked angrily. Her voice sounded thick, clouded with alcohol.

'You gave me the hour off, ma'am. I was up on deck.'

'A nursemaid who is conscientious never takes time off. Not an hour, not even a minute. You are on duty all the time – or you should be. Perhaps if you had been more conscientious, little Johnny would have been with us still, may God rest his poor, dear, innocent soul.'

Mrs Johnson tried to replace the stopper in the scent bottle, but her hand was trembling. She kept banging the stopper down on the dressing table. Finally, she threw it across the cabin. It splintered against the far wall.

'I was told you wanted to see me,' said Anna.

'Of course I want to see you. I have something very important to say. Very important indeed. I've been discussing you with my husband. As you know, my brother recommended you as someone we could trust to look after our children and especially poor darling Johnny. But I have to say you have disappointed us. It seems to me you have been looking after yourself more than them, up on deck when you are needed here. And little Johnny is dead.'

'I am very sorry he died, ma'am. But I did suggest you should call the surgeon.'

'Never mind what you suggested. Your job is to do what *I* say. I am very disappointed in you, Anna. I hear that when I very kindly gave you a pound to spend and allowed you to have the whole afternoon off in Cape Town, you went off gallivanting with that other girl Lucy. No one knows what happened to her. She never returned. She missed the boat – literally. If you had any common sense you would have thought what might happen to her now in a foreign country with just the clothes she stood up in. Why didn't you bring her back? *You* came back.'

'She was with a man friend.'

'What sort of friend could that be? Not a friend in any sense of the word, only someone who picked her up on the docks, I suppose. That shows your lack of care for others. Just another example of your attitude. I relied on you. You let me down. My dear son died. No doubt poor Lucy also relied on you. But you let her go and came back yourself. Not a very good augury for the future is it, eh?'

'That your son died, which I greatly regret, cannot be blamed on me, ma'am. As for Lucy, I told her the time I was coming back to the ship to make certain we would be here before we were due to sail.'

'Words, words, Anna, but never deeds. Some people think they can talk themselves out of any hole, but my husband and I have decided that in view of,' she waved her hands expansively, 'in view of *everything*, it would be better for all concerned if you did not come on with us to Bombay. We cannot take any more risks, not with only one of our children remaining. It would be folly to do so in all . . .' she paused, dredging for words, 'in all the circumstances. The ship docks at Mamora tomorrow. I will pay you twenty pounds – more than is owing to you. If you wish to pay for a passage on to Bombay from your own resources, you can do so, but our association terminates now. At this very moment.'

'You mean you are getting rid of me, ma'am?'

'I mean exactly that.'

'Will you give me a reference? I have done my best for your children on this voyage.'

'I will most certainly *not* give you a character. How could I, in all the circumstances? I will give you nothing except your money. In my opinion – and in my experience, I should add – you are a sly, deceitful girl. You deceived my brother into thinking you were honest and trustworthy. You assured me my children would always come first. And now my dear son, my only son, is dead, and you stand there arguing, brazen as you like, not a word of sorrow or regret.'

Mrs Johnson bowed her head and began to cry, her plump shoulders heaving with the intensity of her sobs. She looked up, her face streaked with tears and mascara.

'Don't stare at me!' she shouted. 'Have you never seen honest grief in a mother before?' She pulled open a drawer of the dressing table, packed with cosmetics. Pink face powder spilled from a lidless box, dusting a pair of scissors, a silver hip flask, lip salve, rouge. She rummaged in the drawer, found a bundle of five-pound notes, counted out four, crumpled them into a ball and gave them to Anna.

'I don't ever want to see you again, nor does my husband, or my daughter. Just get out of our lives. Now. This moment.'

Anna smoothed the notes and put them in her pocket. 'May I say something, ma'am, before I go?'

'I cannot stop you.'

'Now that I am no longer in your employ, I feel I can speak my mind. You are not getting rid of me because you think I am incompetent. I believe you are getting rid of me because you suspect I know you had a supply of laudanum which you fed to your son in addition to the very large doses the ship's surgeon prescribed for him. You are getting rid of me because you think I saw too much, because I know too much.'

'What a disgusting and horrible thing to say! You ungrateful, lying little bitch! Get out of my cabin before I throw you out!'

Mrs Johnson stood up, bumped into a chair, lost her balance and fell. She drew herself up, seized the scent bottle from the dressing table, threw it at Anna. The bottle crashed harmlessly against the bulkhead and shattered.

'Get out! Get out!' Mrs Johnson shrieked.

Anna opened the door, went out, closed it carefully behind her, and leaned for a moment against the warm, creaking wood, hearing Mrs Johnson's loud sobbing inside the cabin.

Anna knew she was now totally on her own, approaching a strange and alien land, with only twenty pounds in her pocket, and a few shillings remaining from the pound Mrs Johnson had given her in Cape Town.

But she also had half a dozen diamonds and an overwhelming feeling of release. Instead of feeling helpless and downcast, she felt free. Now, from a position of apparent destitution, out of work, without even a reference, surely the only way she could go was upwards?

Abdul Mohammed, the old Sultan of Mamora, lay on his bed in the centre of his tent, wounded, in pain, and alone.

The knotted ropes of the primitive mattress bored like sharpened needles into his tired, bruised body. He moved weakly and uneasily to find a more comfortable position. From boyhood he had lived rough and slept rough, often on hard, cold sand, covered only by a sheepskin or a woven rug, but always he had slept well and soundly. He had been fit, alert in those days, but now he could barely sleep at all. Each time he moved or turned, the wound in his groin searched him out like a sharpened dagger point.

He was wounded badly, he knew that; maybe even fatally, although that was for Allah to decide in his infinite mercy, his infinite wisdom. The sultan had been wounded before, and he thought just as grievously. The difference was that then he had been young and now he was old.

Even more serious than being wounded in the body, he had been grievously injured in his spirit. Abdul Mohammed, whose power until only days before had been infinite, whose request was an order to be instantly obeyed, whose laws were never queried, had faced the cruellest wounds of all: insurrection, revolution, attempted assassination. And even worse to contemplate, these misfortunes had not come at the hands of enemies but from the envy of his own younger brother and his brother's son.

The sultan's loyal soldiers had beaten off the fierce and totally unexpected attempt to seize power, but the clash had been harsher than he had anticipated, for this was not a sudden uprising, born of a whim, the recollection of an isolated injustice, but a revolution long and carefully planned. However, he had prevailed, and as victor had personally decapitated his brother in front of his brother's defeated troops in the muddy square of the capital. His nephew he had spared. But while the sultan could kill one of his own blood, who had sucked the same teat in childhood, he could not destroy ideas that this man had sown like poisoned seeds in the minds of the community.

Officers who had betrayed Abdul Mohammed had also been put to the sword, including some he had known from boyhood and counted as his friends. A few he had regarded almost as brothers, and he smiled wryly at the thought that his own blood brother had led them against him. No matter, the punishment for treason was death. They were fortunate that he had ensured that they died quickly.

A number of the common soldiers had been castrated, but allowed to live. Peasants he could forgive; they could not all know right from wrong. But the fact that they had risen against him greatly concerned the sultan. His personal physician had prescribed a draught to ease his pain, mental and physical, but this had not soothed him. He had vomited out the bitter liquid onto the carpets that were piled with prodigal generosity on the sandy floor.

Years previously Abdul Mohammed had fought on his father's side to take over the kingdom from an uncle. Now his brother had tried to take it from him; his only brother and uncle to his fifty-two sons and thirteen daughters. History, like a turning prayer wheel, was repeating itself. Violence begat violence; peace of mind and honour and confidence were always the first casualties.

A slave saw his master move, his face etched with pain, skin tight around his eyes, and offered him a silver beaker of water, but the sultan waved it away impatiently. He did not want water or opium for the pain. He wanted to turn back the clock and have his brother as a friend. But this was a dream that could never come true. What was done was done.

Around his bed, the high canvas walls of his tent billowed gently like the sails of a great ship. Beneath these walls, and through double canvas doors at the front of the tent, sand filtered in on the restless gritty wind. The desert was a shifting sea of sand, never still, never the same. It had ebb tides, flood tides, always moving with that strange almost metallic rasping of millions of grains of sand, one against the other under the ever-changing winds of heaven.

In the past Abdul Mohammed had found the sound soothing, almost comforting – but why should a man as powerful as he had always been need comforting? The sound of the sands had been a lullaby to him in childhood. It would be there long after he was dead. But now its restless and constant rustling disturbed him. He lay back, closed his eyes. The day after tomorrow was the start of the fast of Ramadan which lasted for a month in which, according to his teaching, Allah revealed to Mohammed the first verses of the Koran. During the month of Ramadan the armies of Mohammed also won their first victories in the battle of Badr.

It was the holiest month in the calendar. Every Muslim had to fast from dawn, when there was just light enough to tell the difference between a white thread and a black thread, until evening when it was too dark to tell one from the other. During that time, the faithful must not eat or drink; they must turn away from women during these hours. During this fast, which could last up to sixteen hours in the burning, baking heat, the very devout would not even swallow their own saliva.

And now, with revolution and anarchy only just avoided, the sultan must not risk offending any of his subjects, and certainly not the mullahs. He must drink plenty of water before the first day of Ramadan, because he did not know how he could survive for so many hours in such pain and heat without even a sip to wet his lips.

What troubles were caused to mankind by the zealots, he thought. The Christians had their problems too. They had often gone to war, not simply against the Muslims, whom they considered infidels, but against each other. So many wars, and both sides believing that they were fighting for their god. Yet perhaps there was only one god, but with different names? Abdul Mohammed's thoughts pursued this idea for a moment. Then he heard footsteps on the soft carpet and opened his eyes. Razadin Shah, the captain of his guard, was standing by the bed.

'You have a message for me?' the sultan asked him. It was the rigid rule that he always spoke first. Any breach of this would cause him deep displeasure.

'A private message, Highness.'

The sultan dismissed his slave, who crept away through a side flap in the tent. These fellows had ears, and whoever heard what might not be fitting for him to hear could pass that knowledge to others who might put it to terrible use.

'Well?' the sultan asked Shah when they were alone.

'May your Highness live for ever. May his shadow never grow less,' began the captain nervously.

'I appreciate your hope. But I doubt that my life has been lengthened by my wound. What private message have you to tell me?'

'I hesitate to pass on news of such gravity, Highness, but I feel I would be lacking in loyalty and eschewing my duty if I did not speak, much as my words dislike me.'

'To the point, Captain. What have you to say that a slave should not hear?'

'There are evil rumours in the town, and messengers have come in from outlying villages and districts to report that the same rumours have also reached them. They believe you have been more grievously injured than has been officially admitted.'

'That is truth, not rumour,' the sultan said drily.

'It is feared, Highness, that your brother's son, who has been spared by your merciful hand, may attempt to seize the kingdom, unless . . .'

'Unless what?'

'Unless you can prove to a whole concourse of people, hundreds, thousands, that you are still the leader you have been from youth.'

'And how do you suggest I do that?'

'Again, I hesitate to make the suggestion, Highness. Others, more versed in matters of state, have made it for me.'

'But they lacked the courage to come and tell me face to face? That does not surprise me. In old men, courage runs as thin as their blood. What is this suggestion? Come, you are like a camel going round a thorn bush. Speak out or hold your peace.'

'A cargo of slaves is due to be landed tomorrow from further down the coast. I am told there are a few women among them, young women. I hesitate to suggest this, Highness, but I only carry the commission of the elders. They ask that you go down to the market place tomorrow, at noon, and take one of these girls, a virgin, and deflower her, and so prove that, whatever foul lying rumours may say, you are still a man. *The* man.'

'Is that what they wish me to do? What the elders lack the courage to tell me themselves?'

'It is, Highness.'

'And afterwards I can rest until my wounds are healed?'

'Indeed, Highness. This public act of manhood will slay all rumours. Word will travel faster than the fastest bird, to the north, the south, the east and west of your kingdom. The sultan's manhood is unimpaired. His virility is as it always was. His seed is the seed of kings.'

The sultan looked up at the captain of his guard. How easy it was to talk like this, to make such a proposal when you were young and fit. And how difficult to carry out what to a young man was a brief and easy pleasure, when not only your body was ailing, but your mind was also weary. Even so, he recognised the truth in what the elders proposed on the eve of Ramadan.

'I will do as you ask,' he said gravely, 'as the elders wish. I agree that it is imperative for this to have the widest circulation. I will deflower a slave girl in front of thousands. That is my command. Fill the main square and every street round about. Put people in the upper rooms of all the buildings so that all see that Abdul Mohammed is a man.'

'It will be done, Highness,' Shah assured him. He bowed in farewell and went out of the tent, leaving the sultan alone with his thoughts and his pain.

Five

Razadin Shah was young, ambitious – and now nervous. The revolution had disturbed him greatly. He did not care for the man who had tried and failed to overthrow the sultan, nor for the son who now plotted another uprising. But he knew that they commanded a great following among people who did not appreciate the old sultan's worth and how well he had led and served them.

Any person with a grievance, serious or trivial, could ask for an audience with Abdul Mohammed and be granted one, face to face, to state their case. This had not always been the custom. But young men wished for changes that could bring them power and riches. Exactly how they could achieve these desirable aims was never made clear, but promises had been given. To many of his subjects, simple, illiterate, unskilled even as labourers, this was evidence enough of their future prosperity.

Razadin Shah did not share these comfortable beliefs. He had prospered under the rule of the sultan, serving him first as a member of the guard and then as its commander, chosen simply because the old man trusted him and, more, liked him. Shah was the son of a distant relation, a merchant who came of a line of merchants. He knew that the sultan had lain with his mother before he was born; indeed he had been born prematurely after his mother's marriage. But he did not know that the sultan considered him to be his own, unadmitted, naturally, in these circumstances, but a favourite son for all that.

Shah considered he now had two overriding priorities: to guard his master against any danger, physical or political, and then to preserve his own life.

To achieve both aims in a volatile clash of families, clans and tribes was not going to be easy. If someone was content to remain a peasant, ready to obey without question the orders of others, and to keep his eyes on the dust, to observe every tenet of the faith and never harbour the hope that he could raise himself to greater things, then his life might be free of dangers. But Shah was not content with existence at this low level and never had been. He accepted risks. He believed he knew his enemies and his friends, but nowadays this was not enough to ensure survival. Enemies could prosper, friends could die – or conveniently forget the claims of friendship.

Shah had consulted his late mother's father on the problem. His grandfather wore the dyed red beard of a man who had visited the holy places of Mecca and Medina. He was a rich man, but he had entered these sacred cities as a pilgrim, dressed in the special garment, *ihram*, that consisted of two strips of plain white material, chosen so that all pilgrims, whether rich potentates or poor peasants, looked the same when they came before their Lord.

The old man spent his days now reading the ancient books of law. Razadin Shah was his favourite grandson; he admired his ambition and his promotion in a military world about which he and his family knew so little.

'You should be careful, my boy,' he said – he always talked to Shah as though he was still a child. 'Life is like a turning wheel. One moment, people who are down at the bottom suddenly rise to the top. Then they descend to the depths again. You may not always keep the high position you have reached. To be ambitious is to be a mountaineer, climbing a glass mountain. The slopes grow steeper as you approach the peak. You grow weary, so you rest. You close your eyes, you sleep, and as you slide back, the spears of the envious are there to await you. A successful man is like a mirror. His success reflects the failure of others and they hate him, and would kill for it. Gladly, quickly, without a thought.'

'But I am the sultan's guard commander, Grandfather. I have always served my master loyally.'

'Of course. Which makes you all the more vulnerable. You may know too much about too many people – or they may think you do. And such knowledge can be dangerous. It is because you are who you are, and what you are, and where you are, that I speak thus, my boy. The sultan is only human, like the rest of us. He is also a climber on the glass mountain, and maybe even he will fall. If so, you could fall with him.'

'And then?'

'And then, for a day or two, perhaps a week, a month, whoever takes over will not know quite what to do with you. You have been loyal to one ruler. But will you be loyal to another? He cannot afford to make a mistake, because he is also climbing the same slippery slope.'

'So what will he do, Grandfather?'

'He will jail you, for a day or a week, until he decides whether to torture you, banish you, kill you, or keep you.'

'And how can I possibly help myself? That is why I seek your advice, Grandfather.'

'You must take steps so that when you are in the jail you can also get out. You must assume the worst. You cannot guard against it but you can make sure you suffer as little harm as possible.'

111

'But it is impossible to escape from the jail. I know that well enough. I have escorted many malefactors to it. There are seven doors and seven locks.'

'Do not tell me what I already know,' said the old man. 'But each cell has its own grating to let in light and air. The gratings are just large enough for a man to squeeze through if he is not too fat. You must therefore instruct a locksmith, giving him any excuse, to fit concealed locks to one of the gratings. Keep the key hidden in the cell behind a brick where no one will think of finding it. You have every opportunity of visiting these cells now, voluntarily. No one will question your diligence – now. But if you delay, you may not have the chance to come and go as you please.'

'This will be difficult to arrange.'

'Success, my boy, is always difficult. So is survival. It is only ever easy to fail. But the knowledge you hold a secret key to freedom will give you confidence. You will know that, even if you are cast into the dungeon, you can escape.'

'Did you ever need to make such plans for yourself, Grandfather?'

'No. But then I never was ambitious, my boy. I had enough money for my needs. And now I am old, ambition is like a withered gourd – useless. But I live again through my pride in your achievements.'

Shah had heard growing rumours of discontent in the bazaar, in the souks, and he followed his grandfather's advice. He walked along the Street of the Silversmiths to the shop where a locksmith carried out his trade. This locksmith had a son, a wild young fellow. It was widely claimed that he drank the cursed alcohol bought from sailors off the ships. The sentence for this was death. Shah explained the situation to the lad's father, not accurately, of course, nor quite truthfully, because truth is a strong drug, sometimes too strong for others to savour.

'I have come to see you,' he began gravely, 'because your son may shortly appear again before the magistrates. And this time the sentence could be heavy. Indeed, the ultimate punishment is death. He may escape this but at the very least will receive a public flogging. One hundred lashes.'

'On what charge, Captain?' asked the locksmith in horror. Not many men survived such a terrible punishment.

'The charge of drinking Western liquors. He has been suspected many times. Now it is urged he is made an example. As you are a man of influence and importance in the city, others will take notice if your son is flogged or executed. But I think I can save him.'

'How? I beg of you, how? He is a good boy, wayward maybe, but he is still young. He will settle down as he grows older, I can assure you.'

'*If* he grows older, perhaps. Now this is what I want you to do for me. I am about to incarcerate someone who is guilty of an even more grievous crime. He has foolishly been arrested before a proper investigation of all the background and his associates was made. Thus we have caught one man, but others more dangerous, infinitely more venal go free.

'This man will be placed in a dungeon until he is taken out to die. I want you to refit the window grating in this cell so that it can be removed. I would like you to attach special tongues to it, such as fit in a lock, in all four corners. Slots can be cut into the stone so that the tongues hold the grating securely in place. The key will be hidden in the cell. This man will be told about it by another prisoner. When he escapes through the grating we will follow him to the homes of his chief associates and arrest them all. Can you do that for me?'

'Yes. If I can have access to the cell, and the services of a skilled stonemason.'

'I cannot give you a stonemason. You will have to cut the stone yourself. It should not be difficult with a hard chisel and a hammer. Your fee will be your son's freedom – this time. But I tell you, he must watch himself and his behaviour.'

'You're a good friend, Shah. I do not know why you do this for me.'

'Friends should help each other,' Shah replied gravely. 'As it is written, "The bird has a nest, the spider a web, a man has friendship".'

The locksmith did his job quickly; Shah hid the key in a hole in the wall of the cell. His grandfather was right; it was wise to take such a precaution. In fighting an enemy in front, one must always make sure that another does not tread closely behind. And as his grandfather had said, the knowledge that he possessed a secret key to freedom if all went against him provided him with a warm glow of self-confidence.

The Scotsman Drummond was in his small house by the docks in Mamora when Shah came to see him. Drummond was red-haired, bearded, wild looking. No one knew his first name and he never referred to it. He had been a sick-bay attendant in a British cruiser and jumped ship during a state visit to the island some years before. He had been drunk at the time – he was often drunk, before and since, and had he thought about the matter he would never have stayed in Mamora.

But, as with many young men who make decisions that can change their entire lives, Drummond hadn't really thought much about it at all. He had given far more thought to the colour of a new neckerchief or the cut of a jacket made by an Indian tailor in the bazaar than to a sudden decision that had cut him off for ever from his own kind, his own country.

He told himself often enough that he had made the best of things. He found a native woman, who satisfied him in a way none of the cautious, nervous, raw-boned Scots lassies had ever done. Or maybe the heat of the place, and the fiery food – spiced chicken and mutton cooked in rice, and sometimes a sheep's eye to eat as a delicacy – compensated for his lonely exile. But lust was no lasting substitute for love, and sometimes the heat and stink of a tropical harbour made him miss the mists and cool landscape of the Sidlaw Hills where he had grown up. But when these melancholy thoughts took hold, he would have another drink or maybe pleasure the woman roughly, as though he could purge his homesickness and regret by harshly handling someone weaker than himself.

Drummond wasn't a Muslim, so when slavers brought in cargoes of rum in exchange for slaves, he would take his share. He always kept twenty bottles standing like soldiers in a row, side by side, on a shelf in the back of the house.

He had been drinking now, although it was noon, and everyone knew that for white men in Mamora to drink in the middle of the day was madness. But then he was just recovering from days of depression, comparing his present position, worse than that of a remittance man, with what he told himself he might now be if he had not jumped ship.

He was eating his midday meal, sitting on the floor cross-legged like a native, scooping up the greasy rice with his right hand from the polished copper plate, when Razadin

Shah's tall body darkened the doorway. They were on easy terms, but the captain was an officer, and Drummond would always be someone who took orders, never gave them, except to servants or his woman.

Drummond called himself a physician. He knew a little about some basic medicines, and he could lance a boil or pull a tooth. Local Arab doctors could not all be trusted to keep silent about the nature of every ailment they cured or attempted to cure. Drummond could. He had learned to keep his counsel, for he was a stranger in a strange and not altogether friendly land. As such, he could be useful at times. This was one of those times.

'Is this a social call, sir, or professional?' he asked Shah, standing up deferentially.

'Professional,' said Shah. 'Not for me, but for the sultan.'

'I hear he's been badly wounded.'

'Yes.'

'Rumour has it his cods have been cut off,' said Drummond bluntly.

'I would advise you not to mention such a rumour outside these walls.'

'But is it true?' persisted Drummond. The rum and the spice and the heat of the day were working in him.

'I cannot answer that.'

'But you have your suspicions, Captain?'

Shah shrugged as though he could not commit himself.

'A Scotsman will turn his hand to almost anything – for a fee,' said Drummond pontifically. 'But even I can't sew a man's balls on again.'

'I'm not asking you to. I don't know that they're even damaged. He has been struck a cowardly blow in the groin by a sword. That I do know.'

'He's been treated by your people though, hasn't he?'

'Yes. But now I seek a rather special sort of treatment for him that possibly only you can provide. Others could talk. If they were initially disinclined to speak, they might be captured by revolutionaries and tortured until they did.'

'I thought that the revolution was put down?'

'You can lance one boil, Dr Drummond. But, as you know, poison can remain within and erupt elsewhere.'

'And that could happen now?'

'That's what I fear, unless you can help me.'

'If I can, I will. You've always been fair to me, treated me like one of yourselves. What is it you wish?'

'It is a great indignity for any man, and worst of all for any leader, to lose his virility. He should be able to pleasure any woman at will. Women regard that as an honour. They laugh at men who cannot act like men. Low people who make up scurrilous ditties write songs about such things for eunuchs to sing.'

'But how does this affect the sultan? Has he suffered in this way?'

'He has been grievously wounded in his private parts. That I admit. In time, he will no doubt be restored to his full manhood, but now he is downcast, and rumours abound as to the extent of his injuries. He has to prove he is still a man – in the basic, most important sense of the word. And not just to himself or to his physicians, but publicly to his people. And not at some future date, but now – and here.'

'And how will he prove that?'

'A slaver is about to anchor offshore. I hear that a number of young women slaves are aboard. I have assured the elders that the sultan will pleasure one of these slave women in the city square tomorrow. They will pass the word. Thousands will come, not just to see him as a person, but to see for themselves whether he can do what any real man can do.'

'And you think that this may be doubtful?'

The captain nodded. 'As I say, he has been grievously wounded. And not only in his body, but in his mind. His own brother rose against him. The sultan struck off his brother's head himself. Now his nephew is rallying the disaffected.'

'I have nothing to help him do what you say he must do, Captain. Herb roots and rhino horns are sold to make old men feel young, but I'll tell you frankly, they are mostly rubbish. The will lies in a man's mind. Young or old, he sees a woman who attracts him – and that's the only aphrodisiac he requires. No amount of ground rhino horn will do anything for him if he has not the will and the wish, and if the chemistry of attraction is missing.'

'I am well aware of that, Doctor, so I have another proposal. I want you to take the intestine of a sheep or a goat. Cut this to the length of a man's member. Dry it, strengthen it in whatever way you can with alum, anything. Then the sultan can slip this on his flaccid part like a glove.'

Drummond looked at Shah in amazement. 'And what of all the people round about? Will they not see this deception? If they do, his situation will be worse than ever. He will be likened to a eunuch who pleasures idle women in the harem with the likeness of a member carved in wood.'

'Agreed. But they will not see. I will make sure that people do not press too closely. When he raises his robes, he stands triumphant, a man erect. Then he does what he has to do – and he saves the kingdom, and himself.'

Drummond regarded his visitor doubtfully. 'When is this to take place?' he asked.

'Tomorrow morning, at about nine o'clock, before the day becomes too hot.'

'It's Ramadan next day.'

'That is why it has to be tomorrow.'

'I've never heard of this with an intestine,' said Drummond dubiously. 'What is the fee being offered?'

'Ten pieces of gold. In your hand. Five now, five when the act has been performed.'

'I don't like it,' said Drummond. 'If his member is soft and shrunk with illness, this intestine may drop off.'

'You must cut two holes in it. Fix a thread that goes round his body so that it cannot drop off. Dye it the same colour as his flesh. You can easily do this, Doctor. In fact, you must do it.'

The two men looked at each other. Drummond sensed the unspoken threat. If he refused, and the captain put a word against him, perhaps that he had insulted someone in authority or interfered with the women in the harem or the boys of the court, he could be a dead man by nightfall. Many believers would welcome this. He was not in any position to bargain or decline Shah's proposal.

'I'll do my best,' he said unwillingly.

'The best is not always good enough, Dr Drummond. This *has* to succeed. Everything depends on it. Maybe even my life – and yours.'

'I said, I'll do my best. No one can do more. Now, Captain, let's see the colour of your money.'

Shah delved into the recesses of his robe, took out a purse, counted out five pieces of gold. Drummond bit each one, not because he could tell a true gold coin from a false one, but because he liked to give that impression. He wanted time to think. He had to find the gut of a sheep, cut it to size, dry it, prepare it he was not sure how – and all against the clock.

He put the coins in his back pocket, clapped his hands for his slave to take away his half-finished rice. He had lost his stomach for food. There would be time to eat, time to drink, when he had done what he had been told to do.

As the trooper came into harbour, Anna went below decks to her cabin to pack her belongings. Dorothy was already there, sitting on the bunk.

'You look odd,' said Dorothy. 'As though you've had a bad shock, and yet you're quite cheerful.'

'That about describes my feelings,' Anna admitted. She explained Mrs Johnson had dismissed her, and how, even so, she did not feel in any way depressed or concerned about her future.

'So you're going ashore here on your own?'

'I have no option. I can't afford to pay for my passage on to Bombay. And even if I had the money and went on, I'd be even further away from home in Bombay than I am here. I might as well try my luck here.'

'But how will you live? What will you do?'

'I'll find something. Don't worry. I'm not like Lucy. I won't get picked up and end in a whorehouse as you think she may have done. I shouldn't think they have whorehouses here, for one thing.'

'They've got much worse, I can tell you. Slaves. They still deal in them. Bring them up from the south, sell them – blacks and whites alike.'

'One of the sailors told me about the slaves. I can't believe it. We're in the twentieth century, you know, not the eighteenth or even the nineteenth.'

120

'That has nothing to do with it. They still sell blacks to the West Indies, and those they can't get rid of there to rich families here. The whites, mostly very young kids, they sell as indentured servants. That's what they like to call them anyhow, black and white. The buyers, again in the West Indies, or the States or here, give them nothing much above their food for seven, or even ten years. Then they're free to go – but to do what?'

'You may be right, but I doubt it. In any case, none of that affects me. I feel confident I'll survive.'

'I wish I had your confidence,' Dorothy admitted enviously.

'You could have, if you believed in yourself.'

'It's different when you've got money and background, or if you've got a trade of some kind. Best of all if you can marry a rich man.'

'I can do a bit better than that and I mean to,' said Anna firmly, and began putting her things into her bag.

As she did so, both girls heard the faint and distant rattle of anchor chains running out. The ship's engines stopped, and the vessel was suddenly silent. They had become so used to a constant trembling of the metal hull and a muted hum of distant machinery that these had become part of their lives. But now the voyage was over – for Anna at least.

'Will I ever see you again?' Dorothy asked her, almost tearfully.

'I'm sure we'll meet somewhere if we're meant to. *Kismet*. Fate.'

'That sounds like the Muslims.'

'Then it's apt here because Mamora is a strictly Muslim place. Here's my home address in Scotland. I'll tell my parents where I'll be when I know myself.' Anna scribbled the address on a piece of paper, handed it to Dorothy.

Anna would have liked to say goodbye to the little Johnson girl and to her father. She had scarcely seen Major Johnson on the voyage. He seemed a quiet, decent man, and she was fond of his daughter. But when she knocked on their cabin door, no one answered. She turned the knob. The door was locked. She had to leave without saying farewell.

She walked down the gangway to the shore. It took a few moments for her to become used to being on dry land, just as it had done in Cape Town. She walked slowly along the docks, stopping every few paces because her bag was heavier than she expected. She suddenly realised that the optimism she had expressed to Dorothy was misplaced. She had nowhere to go, and she knew no one.

She stood, irresolute, watching a squad of British soldiers march past. They wore tropical uniforms with pith helmets, rifles slung over their shoulders. Behind, on trolleys pulled by other soldiers, came piles of kitbags. One soldier had obviously been here before. He saw a woman he recognised standing in the shade of a dock building and shouted cheerfully to her. She waved back to him. The woman was in her forties, sallow skinned, probably a half-caste. When the soldiers had passed, she strolled over slowly towards Anna.

'On your own, dearie?' she asked her. 'Or waiting for someone?'

'On my own. I'm looking for somewhere to stay.'

'Much money?'

For a moment Anna paused before replying. What was the point of pretending? But she did not think it wise to admit she wanted to find a bank to cash her diamonds.

'Very little,' she admitted. 'I want to get a job here if I can.'

122

'As what?'

'I came out on the trooper as a children's nurse.'

'Jobs like that are difficult to find here. Got rid of you, did they?'

'Yes.'

'Why? Husband touching you up, wife found out?'

'Nothing like that. She was a drunk.'

'Oh. The tropics sometimes take women that way. They either get randy in the heat or they fall back on the bottle.'

'But who are you?' asked Anna.

'I was married to a soldier. My mother was Indian, my father a sergeant in the Buffs. He came here and died of a fever. There's a lot of that about, I can tell you. The water's poisoned in my view. Or it's the mosquitoes or the drains – or lack of them.'

'What do you do now?'

'Try to make a living any way I can. Like telling you where you can get a good lodging while you look around for something.'

'I've no money to pay you.'

'Don't bother about that, dearie. I'll be paid by the landlord. Now let me give you a hand with your bag.'

'Thank you very much.' Anna felt a surge of gratitude. Here was a stranger offering to help her.

They walked along the docks, out through the gate into a street, thronged with Arabs and Indians. Men rode ponies bareback and dug sharp goads into their flanks. Strings of donkeys were so heavily burdened they could scarcely keep upright.

'It's just down here,' said the woman. 'Only a few more yards, and you'll be all right.'

A strong smell of spice and wood smoke hung in the air, not unpleasant, simply strange and mysterious. They came to an entrance between two open-fronted shops.

'How do you know they'll have a room?'

'I know. That's why I'm here. Now, follow me through this doorway.'

They went into a small room with a bead curtain over another entrance. A scented joss-stick burned on a carved wooden table. The woman put Anna's bag down on the carpet.

At that moment, hands gripped Anna from behind. A thick bandage came down round her eyes, her head, her mouth. She could breathe, but only just. She tried to cry and shout and scream, but the only noise she could make was a low moan. Then she felt a sudden sharpness like a thorn in her right arm, just above the elbow, followed by sudden silence and then oblivion.

The two men who had seized Anna carried her beyond the bead curtain into another room, and laid her down on the rope mattress of a bed.

'Get her bag,' the woman ordered them. She would receive a fee for bringing in the girl, but the kid might have all kinds of trinkets in her bag, and she would have no use for them where she was going. The two men went out, came back with the bag. They fumbled with its padlock.

'Get a hammer and break it off,' the woman said sharply. She had no time to look for keys in Anna's pockets, and if she didn't take whatever the bag contained, someone else would. One of the men produced a hammer and a chisel. With two hard blows the cheap lock shattered.

The bag contained clothes – nothing of value there, nothing at all. At the bottom, the woman saw a small wooden box. She opened it carefully, thinking that it might contain jewels. She did her best to shield what might be inside it from the covetous eyes of the men. But all that it contained were bits of dried root or plant stems.

'Nothing in there,' she said bitterly. 'Look for yourselves.'

They looked and nodded. She dropped the box back into the bottom of the bag, rooted around until she found a flannel cloth wrapped around a bar of red carbolic soap, then a towel, a toothbrush, a tube of toothpaste, a comb, a hairbrush. Nothing worth a damn here. How could anyone travel so light? She must have had some money on her, surely? If not, how could she pay for even one night's lodging?

She searched in Anna's pockets with expert fingers, opened her purse, found a handkerchief and four five-pound notes. She'd have those, at least.

'Here.' She gave one note to each of the men. 'Take that.'

She kept two for herself, snapped the purse shut, replaced it in Anna's handbag.

'Right,' she said briskly. 'Wait with her here. I'll be back as soon as it's dark. But don't let anyone in and don't interfere with her. You understand?'

They nodded. They had worked with this woman many times before, and sometimes there were more pickings for them – in cash or kind. But this girl was only a European servant of some kind, pretty enough in a Western way. In such circumstances five pounds sterling each was not unreasonable.

Sean O'Grady, the American captain of the slave ship, raised his telescope and scanned the shoreline, grimacing with distaste. He had sailed into this port several times, but never with any pleasure. He felt there was something sinister about it, something dead, evil. He always warned his crew not to go ashore singly if they could avoid it, or even in couples, but in threes. He had repeated this warning early that day, when land first came in sight.

'You're afraid we're going to get kidnapped, are you, Captain?' asked the first mate, amused. He had never landed on the East African coast; he could not believe rumours he had heard about the ferocity and greed of the locals.

'That's how most slaves get taken,' O'Grady pointed out. 'Then sold for money or traded for beads, cowrie shells, iron bars. And once you're caught, you'll never escape.'

'And I thought we were the villains, carting them off in a slave ship! Seems like their own people are even worse.'

'Much worse, but because they've got black skins, white folk back home, psalm singers and missionaries all over the place, will not hear a word against them. But remember, there's a market for white slaves, just as there is for black. Whites fetch more money from different buyers. Think about it.'

The captain lowered his telescope, put it on one side. He took a cheroot from his top pocket, bit off the end, lit the weed and drew on it heavily. The smell from the bowels of the ship was like a vast open latrine; the sharp smoke from his cheroot could only disguise it briefly. His whole ship was a floating sewer. Cigarettes, cheroots, clay pipes which the crew smoked almost continuously, barely kept the stench of dung and suppuration out of their nostrils. Some believed that tobacco had a medicinal value, and prevented fever, but its main advantage was that the smoke cloaked the smell.

O'Grady had run slaves for many years, but now the trade was not what it had been when he began. His father had been a slaver before him, and then, in his words, had 'got religion'; O'Grady's younger brother was a priest. And from them both O'Grady, believing in nothing except his own strength, his own ability to survive and one day soon to retire, had often heard the origins of what was known then as the 'three-cornered trade' or the 'triangular run'.

Many years earlier, ships would set off regularly from Lisbon and Marseilles, from Bristol and Liverpool, packed with cotton clothes, iron bars, cheap cutlasses and muskets, for the Guinea coast of West Africa.

Here, in stockades and pens, a human cargo for the next stage of the voyage had already been assembled to await their arrival. Sometimes, the local chief sold dozens of his tribe against iron bars or cowrie shells. The iron bars could be sawn up and smelted to make hoes or knives or spearheads. Cowrie shells were a generally accepted currency up and down the coast.

One tribe might have been at war with another, and then prisoners of war would be sold. It could be too dangerous to repatriate them, or maybe their tribe had been decimated and they had no homes to which they could return. The best way to be rid of such people was to sell them at whatever price slavers would give. Other unfortunates were kidnapped; individuals or groups of young men and women who strayed away from their villages would be seized and brought in irons to the coast.

As the area became devoid of fit people who could be transported, catcher gangs went inland as far as two or three hundred miles. When they caught the victims they put head collars on the men and marched them back by the dozen. The metal bands round their necks were attached by chains or ropes to long logs of wood resting on the slaves' shoulders, one behind another. The women, often with young children, were given the loads to carry. If they collapsed under the weight, their children might be left to die in the bush. Sometimes, the kidnappers brained the babies with stones. This, they claimed, was merciful because it prevented them dying slowly, preyed upon by wild beasts.

It had always been a cruel, heartless trade, and its profits fluctuated enormously. Only a small proportion of the slaves could withstand what was called the 'middle passage' from the west coast of Africa to the Bahamas or to the southern parts of the United States to work in the cotton fields, or cutting sugar cane.

Most people in the West thought all this had been stamped out years ago in the nineteenth century. But the profits were too large for the trade to be allowed to end. So now, in 1919, it still continued. Not overtly as before, of course, but still largely centred on Africa's western coast.

O'Grady turned to the mate. 'We'll need to be rid of as many as we can here, and then the rest in Zanzibar. So we'll take on food and water as quickly as we can. I don't want to hang about. I don't trust these bastards.'

'You don't trust anybody, Captain.'

'This business is not conducive to trust,' O'Grady retorted briefly. He lit another cheroot. Now that the vessel was moving so slowly, the stench from the slave decks had increased. The cargo had been caught, as usual, on the west coast, and then, half way across the Atlantic, a British cruiser had seen the slaver. There was never any real need to board a suspect vessel; usually the smell gave away the nature of her cargo from a distance of several miles downwind.

On this occasion O'Grady had run up the stars and stripes, and the cruiser had signalled he could proceed. Americans would buy slaves but not run them; it was rarely considered worth the effort to board a vessel flying an American flag.

Even so, O'Grady felt it wisest to turn back and go round the Cape of Good Hope and up the east coast to be rid of the slaves there. They were worth rather less than they would fetch in the New World, but then their voyage had been shorter and they had eaten less food.

The stench came from their faeces, for slaves in transit were denied room even to sit up. They lay on their backs on racks of wood with a space of eighteen inches at most above their heads to the underside of the upper deck. The slaves were chained or fettered, ankle to ankle, wrist to wrist, and defecated and urinated as they lay. The filth dropped through holes in the racks into the bilge. Sometimes the slaves suffered from what past generations of physicians called the 'bloody flux' – dysentery. They passed yellow stools flecked with blood, which dripped and stank with the fearful odour of death and decay. Soon six feet of filth, bubbling and suppurating, swirled to and fro in the bilge with each roll of the vessel.

How odd to recall that this terrible commerce had ever stemmed from the best of good intentions!

Standing on the bridge, watching the misty shoreline approach and from a faint green haze develop into palm trees, a white sandy beach and little local fishing boats bobbing at anchor, O'Grady thought of what his father had often told him about its beginnings centuries ago.

In the year of Our Lord 1495, the old man would begin, in the island of Hispaniola, now Haiti, indigenous Indians had suddenly risen against Spanish settlers who had only recently arrived, and marched on the tiny settlement of Isabella (named after the Spanish Queen).

Christopher Columbus had landed on the island shortly

before this, bearing strict orders from King Ferdinand and Queen Isabella to honour the local Indians – 'to treat them well and lovingly' as the king's writ declared. But the Spaniards needed gold, and the only people to produce gold were these Indians. They were set to the task for between ten to fourteen hours a day, working in mountain streams.

At first, they accepted this drudgery, but they had never worked such hours before, and the novelty soon palled. They were accustomed to run naked, to picking fruit from trees, catching fish and whatever small animals they could snare. They were so innocent indeed that when Columbus first saw them he thought he had somehow rediscovered the Garden of Eden, and tried to identify rivers he found with the four rivers of Paradise – Gihon, Pison, Hiddekel, Euphrates.

Gradually, the Indians realised that their peaceful way of life would end for ever unless they killed these pale-faced newcomers, and so a hundred thousand of them marched on the new settlement.

Columbus's men numbered only two hundred and fifty foot soldiers and twenty cavalry, with as many big dogs, bred in Spain to pull down boars and wild bears. In theory, the Indians could not fail to massacre them, but the Indians had no idea of warfare. They did not realise the fearful injuries that bolts from arquebus and crossbow could inflict on naked bodies.

Some of the Indians threw stones at the soldiers to try and drive them away as they might attempt to be rid of a pestering dog. Others hit the soldiers with reeds. A volley of arrows and shot from the Spaniards soon scattered them. Then Columbus went in with his cavalry. They rode until their horses were so weary they could no longer trot.

Indians who managed to flee were hunted down by the hounds. All were then sent to work in the mines, rather than in the river beds.

They had never been captured before, and they had no spirit for servitude. They died by the thousand, unable to comprehend what was happening, or that they would never again go free.

One observer was Bartolomé de las Casas, who held the religious title of Apostle to the Indies. He was shocked to see how casually his compatriots would seize an Indian – any Indian – and burn him alive at the stake simply as an example to his fellows to work harder.

When Bartolomé returned to Spain, he sought an audience with the king, Charles V, who had succeeded Ferdinand, and begged him to spare these gentle people.

'I know we must have men in the plantations and the mines,' he said. 'But the Indians have never had to labour and are quite unsuited to this work. On the other hand, Your Majesty, I have noticed that Negro slaves, who have been brought here, are happy. Could we not import more? Say twelve slaves for each Spanish colonist, as an act of Your Majesty's mercy towards the Indians?'

Since the Indians were almost unemployable, while Negroes were used to physical labour, the King of Spain gave to a favourite courtier a letter entitling him to move four thousand Negroes to Spain's colonies in the West Indies.

'This was the first *asiento*,' said O'Grady's father. 'A licence to ship as many slaves as could be found to Spanish colonies in the New World. For hundreds of years this licence was something that Dutch, French and English would fight and die for so that their nation in turn could possess it. That was how the slave traffic started from

Africa to the West. I have had my share of it, and I want no more. What started as a well-meant intention has become a terrible crime.'

While O'Grady would agree that it was indeed terrible, it nevertheless provided a profit. Times were hard for seafarers, and where else could he make so much money so easily? He found it easy to put all thought of regret from his mind.

'Anchor the ship fifty yards offshore,' he told the mate now. 'According to the charts, the water's deep. We'll let them come out to us. It's safer that way.'

He feared becoming entangled with these harsh Arabs who might easily seize his ship, steal the slaves and put the crew to the sword. This was a risk slavers ran, but he could minimise it if he did not moor alongside.

'You trust no one,' grunted the mate again.

'You told me that before,' O'Grady retorted. 'And because I trust no one, you and all our crew are still free. Now, to your duties and less moralising talk.'

Six

Usually, on a state occasion, the sultan rode a white horse, or sometimes a camel, but his wound made this impossible.

A few years ago, a visiting Portuguese dignitary had presented him with a carriage. It was rarely used and its varnish had to be polished, axles greased, and leather straps oiled to make it presentable for even a short journey. But the carriage was sprung, and so infinitely more comfortable than any saddle. Even so, as Abdul Mohammed sat on the cracking leather seat, he could feel the hardened edge of the sheep gut digging into the lower part of his body, sharp as a knife. What a ridiculous charade this was, he thought. And what a humiliation if the captain's assurances proved false!

He looked at the crowds of people who lined the square, ten deep. Above them, rows of other dark faces peered intently down at him from open windows. Every balcony and flat roof was packed with spectators. How could he possibly conceal his weakness and his wound from so many thousand inquisitive eyes?

Perhaps he had been unwise to allow Shah to convince him that he could, and yet he knew he had no alternative. His manhood had been challenged. If he did not respond, the rumours would be believed. And, of course, they were not simply rumours; they were true.

Shah had told him exactly where the girl he had to assault would be placed. She was fair-skinned and therefore easy to recognise. The sultan looked at the ranks of slaves, some naked, others with tattered rags about their loins. Flies buzzed around their faces, but they were too weary and dejected to brush them away. They stood with shoulders hunched, wispy beards uncombed, eyes dull and lifeless. Then he saw the young woman. Third from the left, Shah had told him. If he were young, if he were fit, he might enjoy taking her. But now, he had nothing but loathing for the thought, and for himself.

He was more grievously wounded than he admitted even to himself. Pain pulsed through him at every beat of his heart. The square shimmered with waves of heat, even though the hour was early. He could see nothing but brown faces, white teeth grinning at him, wide eyes watching lasciviously.

The sultan shut his eyes, and against his tired eyelids he saw more faces, heard shouts, huzzas, cheers, wails. This was a nightmare performance, and he was to be the main player.

Captain Shah rode a white horse by the side of the carriage, his curved sword drawn, its blade glittering in the sun. He dismounted, bowed in ritual obeisance to the sultan. A slave opened the carriage door and the sultan stepped down slowly. He could not move quickly because of the pain. He turned to the crowd, his back to the slaves, and raised his right hand in greeting. The morning sun caught a glitter of diamonds and rubies in rings he wore.

The crowd responded with a great roar – of what? Approval? Loyalty? Challenge? He started to walk towards the male slaves, and wrinkled his nose at the stench of faeces that clotted their legs. Some, he knew, were ill with the flux. In such cases, the custom was for unscrupulous traders to ram a ball of alum into a slave's back passage to prevent them discharging until they were sold. Once money changed hands, the slaves' new owners had to deal with whatever afflictions possessed them. They stood wretchedly, some dying on their feet.

He passed the men and paused opposite the girl. She stood, eyes downcast, looking at the ground. He could see that her body had been rubbed with coconut oil, possibly to make her appear more attractive, or to make his entry easier. Did the girl know what was about to happen? Or was she totally unaware of his intention? The sultan felt a small and totally uncharacteristic feeling of shame and remorse at what he was about to do.

He put out his hand, took the girl's chin, raised her head. She kept her eyelids lowered.

'Open your eyes, child,' he said. His voice sounded hoarse and tired, the voice of an ill man. She opened her eyes wide and looked at him. He saw dread in her eyes, and something else; a cloudiness. She had been drugged in case she resisted him and refused to play her part in this grotesque performance. He took her hand and led her out to the square. Here, slaves had brought a great mattress of furs and goatskins, and laid it on the stone paving.

He nodded towards the goatskin. She looked at him, puzzled.

'Lie down,' he told her.

She did not understand. Shah ordered two servants to seize her and place her on the ground. She lay on her back, arms by her sides, fists clenched, legs close together, terror now in her eyes. The sultan turned to face the crowd.

'I have heard it rumoured by unfriendly and evil tongues that I am not the man I was,' he said in as strong a voice as he could muster. 'Rumour is like a poisonous and deadly serpent. It crawls about its loathsome business and strikes in the dark, never making accusations face to face, man to man.

'I have therefore invited you to see for yourselves whether I am fit or ill. I will take this girl now in front of you all. I will mount her, pleasure her.'

At this, Captain Shah gave a quick signal. Trumpeters blew a fanfare. The sultan began to raise the hem of his white robe slowly, deliberately turning away from the crowd. He knelt down in front of the girl. She looked up at him with horror, at last realising what was about to happen, silently beseeching him to show mercy. He raised his robe again, parted her legs and pressed himself down on her body. He smelled the fragrance of the oil on her skin, saw her eyes wide in terror, and the whiteness of her teeth as she screamed in fear. The harsh edge of the hardened intestine cut into her. Instinctively she raised both her legs in pain, and he was through the narrow passage, his body in hers.

The sultan lay on her for a moment, grateful for the slightest rest before he had to begin the motions of the act of procreation. When he moved, the girl screamed and writhed beneath him like a live animal impaled on a sword point. The crowd cheered wildly. Truly the sultan was still a man, Allah the ever merciful be praised.

Dimly, the sultan heard the cheers and shouting behind him. Waves of sound broke like distant surf on a stony beach. He could feel blood gathering in his body, engorging his weakened organ, and then a sudden release. Heart racing, mouth dry as an empty desert gourd, he sank forward across the girl's body.

She put up her hands to force him off. In that split second, her face grew misty, as though seen through a fog. The sun shrank in the sky, and the heavens grew dark. The sultan fell to one side, and lay, face down. Shah bent over him, making certain that his robe still concealed the subterfuge. Then he knelt down by the sultan's side, felt his pulse. There was no beat. Abdul Mohammed was dead.

Shah stood up, raised both his hands above his head. His sword blade caught the sun like a semaphore.

'You have seen that the sultan is our leader,' he shouted. 'And you have seen something no other person in this land has ever seen before – the death of our king. He proved his manhood. His wounds he bore for your sakes. Now his death is on your conscience. May he walk tonight in Paradise! May we always live as he would have wished, who gave his life for all of us!'

The crowd cheered, not knowing what else to do. What an extraordinary way to die, pleasuring a slave in front of thousands of people! Truly, only a great man could die like this.

Guards lifted the sultan's body, carried it reverently to his carriage. Then the captain saw Drummond in the crowd, called to him.

'Take her away,' he commanded.

Drummond nodded. It was imperative that they kept the girl out of sight, out of communication with anyone, in case any discovered how deeply she was cut. If this secret were ever revealed, the sultan would have died in vain, and instant revolution would result.

Drummond took the girl's hand, pulled her through the crowd into his house. She sat on the floor, sobbing miserably. He brought a bowl of water and a sponge, handed these to her and a towel. She wiped herself clean. Then he gave her a mug of milk to drink. She crouched on the carpet like a captive animal, drinking greedily, thankfully, still fearful, still fuddled by drugs.

She was pretty. Pity the old sultan had to humiliate her

like that. But of course he had no option. His throne depended on such a public display. And now he was dead, and only Shah and the girl knew of the deception involved. He did too, of course, but he would never reveal it. Shah would sell the girl somewhere, he felt sure – if she wasn't killed because she knew too much.

He became aware that his native woman stood, watching him sulkily from the back of the room, her eyes sullen. He couldn't trust her; he couldn't trust any of these locals. She might reveal that he was sheltering the woman Captain Shah had brought in. That could be as good as a death warrant for him, as well as the girl.

He took a bottle of rum from a shelf and three mugs, poured four fingers of spirit into each, handed one to his woman. She usually accepted a drink, she liked the sweet taste of rum, but not this time. She shook her head. Of course, it was the eve of Ramadan. Muslims weren't supposed to drink alcohol in any case. He handed one to the girl, took the third himself, raised it in a toast.

'Good luck,' he said, not expecting her to understand, but wishing himself as much good luck as he wished her. She nodded.

'Thank you,' she replied.

He stared at her in amazement. 'You speak English?'

'I am English. Or rather, like you, Scottish.'

'Than what the hell are you doing here? You're coloured?'

'No. That's dye. I only realised this when I saw myself in your mirror on the wall.'

'Who brought you to Mamora? Who are you?'

Anna sipped the drink gratefully, holding the mug in both her hands. The spirit ran through her blood, reviving her. She glanced at the native woman.

'Does she understand English?'

Drummond shook his head.

'Even so, I don't trust her. She's jealous.'

'She's all right,' said Drummond doggedly, trying to convince himself.

Anna shrugged. 'If you say so. I was in a troopship, a nursemaid to an officer's family. The mother didn't like me, put me off here. Some woman I met on the docks said she'd find me a place to sleep – I had nowhere and didn't know anyone. I wanted a job, desperately. She took me into a back alley somewhere, and I felt something sharp being stuck into my arm. I must have passed out, for the next thing I remember was standing in line with all those slaves. Then that awful man . . .' She shuddered at the memory.

'You'll forget it in time,' Drummond assured her.

Anna looked at him dubiously. 'What if I'm pregnant?'

'You won't be. I know. I'm a doctor – well, sort of. Did you have any belongings?'

'One bag. It had my money in it. Twenty pounds. All I had.'

'Whereabouts on the quay did this take place?'

'I could show you.'

'Do that,' said Drummond. He heard a faint noise behind him and turned. His native woman had gone. She'll be back, he told himself. She's only gone on some errand, to buy some food before Ramadan. But he felt uneasy. She believed he was going to be unfaithful with a woman who spoke his own language. It wasn't safe for him to stay here, either with this girl or alone.

'There's a back way out of here,' he said. 'Come with me.'

Anna gulped down the rest of the rum, followed Drummond out through a labyrinth of narrow passages. They came out on the docks.

'Cover your face,' he told her.

Anna pulled a cloth low over her face, tried to keep up with him, her feet slithering in the locally made leather sandals someone had given her instead of her European shoes. She recognised a shop, and a blind beggar holding his hands out for alms, eyes opaque as marbles turned beseechingly to the sky.

'It's the next alley from here,' she said.

'That's Mrs Murphy. It's her beat.'

'Who is she?'

'A procuress. Whores for the sailors or for anyone else. Follow me and let me do the talking.'

Anna followed him up the alley she recalled so clearly. Drummond knocked heavily on a door. It opened, the woman Anna had seen looked out and, recognising her, attempted to shut it. But Drummond had his foot in the door, pushed it open against her.

'Where's this girl's kit?' he asked Mrs Murphy bluntly.

'I don't know what you're talking about.'

'Don't waste my time, woman, or you'll get a clip round the ear.'

Under a bed he saw a cheap bag of imitation leather. He lifted the coverlet.

'Is that it?' he asked Anna.

She nodded. He pulled it out. Anna bent over the bag. The five-pound notes had gone, but the bar of soap was still there, and Jeannie Moore's box with the slivers of stem inside; Mrs Murphy must have thought them valueless, not worth stealing. Anna pulled out some clothes, keeping the bathing costume her mother had given her.

'Is that all you want?' Drummond asked in surprise.

Anna nodded. 'I can't carry a heavy bag with me everywhere.'

He turned to Mrs Murphy. 'Who did you take her to?' he asked.

She shrugged, looked away.

'Don't waste my time, woman,' he told her sharply. 'You may want my help one day when one of your girls has pox. I'll not help you then unless you help me now.'

'Captain Shah,' Mrs Murphy said at once, not looking at either of them, keeping her eyes downcast.

'You know what he wanted her for?'

She nodded.

'You should be bloody well ashamed of yourself, doing that to another woman. But why did he choose her? How did he even hear about her?'

'He wanted a woman slave from the slaver in the harbour, Captain O'Grady's ship. But that cargo didn't have any suitable women. He was very concerned, for he had to find a girl quickly. He came to me, hoping one of my girls would oblige. But they wouldn't. They guessed what would happen afterwards. That they'd be killed.' Mrs Murphy nodded towards Anna. 'She'll be dead, too.'

'Not if I have anything to say about it,' Drummond retorted. 'She's Scottish, like me. Now you keep your mouth shut, woman. If anyone asks, we've not been here. Remember, I'll know if you talk, and you may want a good turn from me one day.'

He led Anna out into the alley.

'Where are we going now?' she asked.

He looked at her blankly for a moment. Where the hell were they going now? He did not believe it was safe to return to his house in case his woman had told the police about Anna. He would have to lie low for a time until tempers cooled. There was always trouble in these tropic ports; it must be due to all the spices these people ate, and the heat. Ramadan added to the hysteria and the confusion. When your religion forbade you to drink one drop of water through all the hours of the hottest period of the year, what could you expect but sudden, irrational rages?

He'd holed up during previous troubles, and he had survived. But this kid, he couldn't keep her. That was too dangerous. Yet he could not stand by and see a fellow Scot murdered for no reason whatever. He had to get Anna off the island somehow before she was discovered, because then it would be too late. He glanced across the quay. The troopship had gone, but in a far berth he saw the slaver.

'Yon's Captain O'Grady's ship,' he told Anna. 'The slaver. I'll get you aboard that somehow.'

'Where's she sailing to?'

'God knows. But anywhere out of here will be safer for you. You must go while you can. It's your only chance, believe me.'

'You know O'Grady?'

'I've met him. I'll get you aboard somehow.'

'Will he want favours from me?' Anna asked nervously.

'No. He's not interested in women. Only money and boys. Maybe not even in that order. He's not a bad fellow at heart, though. If he takes you, he'll take care of you.'

Could she trust him? Could she trust anyone in this terrible place?

'There's just one snag I can see, and it's a big one,' Drummond continued. 'No point in denying that. It's going to cost money. Maybe a lot of money. And you've lost all you had.'

'Yes. But I might be able to raise some more,' said Anna. 'How?'

'Give me five minutes on my own and I'll show you.'

'You're not trying to do anything silly?' said Drummond

dubiously. 'You're not going to run away or kill yourself?'

'Kill myself? No. I'd never do that. And where could I run to? If I had any chance, we wouldn't be talking now, would we?'

'All right. Five minutes. At the outside.'

Anna walked up the alley for a few paces and then, making certain Drummond could not see her, she removed the bar of soap from the piece of flannel.

Drummond stood on the quay, wondering what his future would be like under the new sultan, if indeed he had any future. Was now the time to pull out from this dangerous island? Should he also try for a passage aboard the slaver and start a new life somewhere else with another local woman? He felt a sudden spasm of unease, remembering how his woman had disappeared when this Scots girl arrived. Was she loyal to him or to someone else? After all, she had her own future to consider, just as he had his.

Before he reached any conclusion, Anna returned. She held out her right hand. In her palm he saw the glitter and twinkle of a tiny diamond.

'It's real,' she assured him.

Drummond picked it up carefully.

'I can see that,' he said. 'I've handled a few in my time.'

The stone glowed wickedly, like a tiny fallen star, its sharp edges blue and amber.

'That should pay for my passage,' said Anna.

'If we can exchange it for money, yes, easily. It must be worth a hundred pounds at the very least, probably much more. But this stone on its own, no. O'Grady mightn't believe it's genuine, and he won't have the contacts to exchange it. I have. Come with me, and don't say a word, even if you're spoken to, and keep that cloth over your face. On no account let anyone know you are not local.'

Anna followed Drummond along the quayside, a few paces behind him, like a dutiful Muslim wife. They turned into a narrow street. Its central open drain ran purple with putrescence, thick with flies. Drummond knocked at a door, green paint faded by unnumbered summer suns. A piece of wood slid to one side behind an eyehole. Drummond whispered a name. The door opened. Anna followed him into a courtyard. A servant sat grilling a large fish over a charcoal fire. He did not look at them as they passed on into the house.

A dark-skinned man, plump and wearing a light linen suit, frayed at the cuffs and too tight for his bulk, stood up to greet them.

'Dr Drummond,' he said unctuously. 'What a pleasure to see you. What brings you to my humble home?'

'A matter of great urgency, Mr Khan. So urgent that I fear I must come to the point at once. I think you will agree, sir, that I have helped you and your family in a medical way when suffering from complaints you did not wish your own doctor to treat.'

The man bowed his head in acquiescence. His eyes, dark as olives, and just as expressive of his real thoughts, flickered between Anna and Drummond, trying to gauge their relationship. The girl was not local; she had blue eyes.

'I now seek a favour from you,' said Drummond nervously.

'Speak,' Khan commanded him.

'I want this girl smuggled aboard the slaver.'

'Who is she?'

'Names do not matter, but I can tell you that the sultan died on her in the main square this morning.'

'Ah, yes. I have heard that the new sultan wishes her to

144

be silenced. It is very dangerous to have anything to do with this woman.'

'I cannot abandon her.'

'Then what you ask will cost a lot of money, if it can be done, which I doubt. I have my own position to consider. With a new ruler, old loyalties are suspect.'

'That is why I came to you, sir. I can trust you, as you, in the past, have trusted me. How much money do you need?'

'I fear more than either of you possess.'

Drummond put his hand in his pocket, showed him the stone. Khan took a jeweller's glass from a side pocket, held the diamond between thumb and forefinger, examined it under a reading light.

'This should be sufficient,' he admitted, impressed by the purity of the stone.

'So will you help me and her?' asked Drummond.

The man nodded, but without enthusiasm. 'If I can, I will. But you keep the stone until all has been arranged. It is better that way.' He did not add that as far as he was concerned it was also safer. If the diamond was found in his possession, questions might be asked to which he could not give answers.

'As a merchant,' he continued in his sugary voice, 'I have always found it prudent never to pay until the goods are delivered satisfactorily. I have insisted on that code of conduct all my life. I will not alter it for myself. Give me the stone when she is away from Mamora.'

'You trust me?' asked Drummond, surprised.

'You are not likely to sail on the slaver,' said the man with a smile. 'And there is no other ship about to leave the island. So I trust you. Now, has this woman any luggage?'

'Just the one bag.'

'Good.'

Khan nodded. 'We'll get you aboard in this.' He pointed to a large wicker crate that was standing on the floor. 'Stay inside it until you are in your cabin, and don't try to leave the cabin until O'Grady opens the door and tells you. He will know when it's safe.'

'Thank you,' said Anna.

'Don't thank me, thank the doctor. This is a business transaction, nothing more. The box may be roughly handled, even tipped up. You must not make a sound whatever happens, or you will be discovered.' Khan handed Anna a plate with a small white tablet on it and a glass of milk. 'Swallow this,' he told her. 'It will send you to sleep for an hour or so. After that you will be safe.'

Anna looked at Drummond. 'Do you trust him?' she asked bluntly.

'I trust him,' Drummond replied. 'So must you.'

Anna swallowed the tablet and climbed into the crate. The lid was fastened. She heard Khan talk in his own dialect, giving orders sharply. She felt the crate being lifted, smelled the sweat of coolies, and then through a sense of increasing drowsiness she felt the crate sway as they carried it along the quay.

Khan and Drummond followed at a slight distance, walking slowly and in step. Behind the roofs of the nearest buildings the sky glowed red, lit up by sudden flashes of orange. Fragments of burning wood and cloth floated past them.

'Signs of revolution,' said Drummond nervously.

'Yes,' Khan agreed. 'Uprisings are so easy to start, but who can say when or how they will end?' His face, visible in the glare of the distant fires, was set. Drummond saw deep furrows of worry on either side of his mouth, his forehead, and felt concern once more for himself and his future. The memory of his native woman returned.

Both men kept in the shadows as they approached the slaver. Despite Captain O'Grady's misgivings, he had finally brought her up to the quay to discharge the slaves. Now he wanted to be away as soon as possible. It was doubly dangerous to linger here with more revolution a possibility.

O'Grady saw Khan, whom he knew slightly, and came down the gangway.

'I'll speak to him here,' said Khan. 'It's safer than going aboard. People might get the wrong idea, think that I was leaving.'

He crossed the quay. Drummond could see the two of them shake hands. They began to talk, Khan gesticulating, O'Grady shaking his head at first and then nodding reluctantly as he glanced towards the crate. Khan's two servants picked it up and carried it up the gangway into the ship.

There was something in this for all of them, thought Drummond. O'Grady would have a fee, Khan the diamond, and Anna her freedom. He was the only person getting nothing out of this, and he was the prime mover. But then, he was helping a Scots girl in a deadly situation. Surely that should be sufficient reward? But he did not feel too sure about it.

Khan approached him. He was smiling. 'It is agreed,' he said. 'All is well.'

They began to walk back along the quay.

'Come to my house,' said Khan, more relaxed now. 'Have a coffee with me, and I will take the stone.'

'I will give it to you now,' said Drummond, putting his hand in his pocket.

'No, no. There is no need to conduct business in the street. Someone might see us and wonder.'

'As you say,' Drummond agreed, but uneasily. He scented danger and betrayal in the air, and wanted to put as much distance as possible between himself and this quayside.

Khan had played his part. Why wouldn't he accept the diamond now so that Drummond could be away? He did not want to go back with Khan, yet he could not risk offending him by not accepting his invitation.

As they walked, both men gradually became aware of a faint roaring noise, growing nearer, louder. At first, this seemed too distant to be of any concern to them, but as it intensified they suddenly realised what it was: the sound of thousands of people on the march, shouting hysterically, madly, and coming towards them.

They heard the crash of doors being smashed open, a splintering of glass, and then the mob came round a corner on to the quay, and Drummond saw to his amazement that Shah was apparently leading them. Or was he being chased by them?

Suddenly, Shah stopped. The crowd surged around him. He had seen Drummond, who at once realised his own deadly danger. He was the only other person who knew what actually had happened in the square. Like Anna, he knew too much. His knowledge could incriminate Shah, if ever he chose to reveal it. And the sultan's torturers would leave him little chance to keep silent. In that same split second, Shah also realised his own danger, and instantly reacted.

'There he is, the man who killed the old sultan!' he shouted furiously, pointing at Drummond. 'There is the traitor.'

Drummond turned to Khan, to appeal to him, to beg

him to address these ruffians in their own tongue and assure them of his loyalty. But Khan had prudently disappeared up a side alley, through one door, out of another, into a second street, down a staircase and away. He wanted no part of what he knew would follow. It was better to lose a diamond than his life.

'You're wrong, Captain Shah!' shouted Drummond desperately. 'Quite wrong! Let me explain!'

But by then the mob was on him, and the time for words was gone. Drummond had a sudden nightmarish view of dark and furious faces surrounding him, faces grotesquely distorted by hate, by hemp, by misery at their own wretched lives, all eager to purge their fuming resentment by killing a non-believer. They fell upon him exultantly, punching, kicking, tearing first at his clothes, then at his flesh. Drummond sank beneath the ferocious attack, and died as he fell. Then the mob raced away over the stones of the quay, seeking another victim, a new target. Death to all unbelievers.

Shah stayed behind. When the mob had gone, he knelt by Drummond's side. He felt no shame, no remorse at having betrayed the man who had helped him. It was a simple matter of survival, and he had survived. Until he saw Drummond, he had feared that the mob might lynch him. It only needed someone to denounce him for serving the old sultan, and they would have turned on him as swiftly and ferociously as they had killed the Scotsman. Some, he knew, had already recognised him as a loyal retainer of the former ruler.

Drummond's native woman had been in the crowd; she had also stayed behind and now came and knelt on the other side of her dead master.

'When I told you he was helping the white girl I did not

imagine this would happen,' she said miserably.

'I assume not,' replied Shah coldly. He did not wish to have to endure any hysterics now. 'But it has. We have both lost a friend.'

The woman began to weep noisily, beating the paving stones first with her fists, then with her forehead.

As she did so, Shah went through Drummond's pockets methodically in case there was anything in them that might incriminate him in the farce of proving a dead sultan's manhood.

He found nothing except a small stone the size of a single pebble, hard as steel, bright as a cat's eye. He put it carefully into his pocket. Then he stood up and walked along the quay, sweating with relief. He had been on the point of death, and his own quick reactions had saved him, Allah the ever merciful be praised.

But before Shah had gone ten paces, he was suddenly seized from behind, his arms pinioned.

Captain Shah stood with a soldier on either side of him, facing the new sultan, Abdul Karim, the dead sultan's nephew.

Abdul Karim was a thin man in his early twenties. He suffered from chronic indigestion, and chewed on a piece of root which court physicians had assured him would ease his discomfort. His face was pale and unhappy, lined with furrows of pain. The root was not food but medicine and therefore allowable in Ramadan.

He sat uneasily on the throne his uncle had occupied until recently, and regarded the man before him with neither pity nor interest. In Ramadan it was not fitting that even an enemy should be put to death, but Ramadan only lasted for a month and Shah knew that his days were very few.

'What have you to say for yourself, Captain?' Karim asked him, pushing the root from one side of his dry mouth to the other. 'My guards found you on the quay near the body of the Scotsman, Drummond. Not a very loyal subject, I may say. And, I believe, a friend of yours. Speak.'

'Highness, I have always done my duty,' Shah replied. 'I am innocent of any disloyalty to you. I have honoured the sultan who gave me authority. I carried out his orders and commissions to the best of my ability. I have kept the faith.'

'Had you any hand in the killing of my father?'

'I did not kill your father, Highness.'

'But you were involved. What part did you play?'

'I was commander of Abdul Mohammed's guard.'

'And no doubt privy to his thoughts and his intentions. A new rule, a new regime mean new loyalties. There is no place for you in this new kingdom. You have enjoyed the good days. You have felt the warmth of royal approval on your face. Have you anything to say, Captain?'

'I would serve you with loyalty, Highness,' said Shah, his voice dry. He had not drunk even a sip of water since dawn, and it was already late in the afternoon. He felt dizzy with thirst and misery at his situation.

'It is written, "A man cannot serve two masters. He will honour one, and hate the other and hold him in contempt. No one can serve two masters equally." I do not doubt that you served my uncle well, but his interests were not mine, nor those of my father. Until we decide on a suitable punishment, you will stay in a dungeon, where in the past you put so many who supported me.' He nodded to the guards. 'Take him away.'

They seized Shah roughly and retreated from the presence of the sultan, moving backwards. All three bowed, then turned about. The guards marched Shah out of the tent and across the square.

The sun felt very hot. It hung almost vertically above the palm trees. The captain kept his eyes on the pavement. Some people recognised him and shouted, 'Look at you now! You who commanded so many others! You who gave orders to hundreds! You will wish you had died at birth, that your mother's milk had poisoned you.'

Shah did not look up. He pretended he had not heard them, but he knew what they said was true. There was no escape now, no escape at all unless . . . unless . . .

He turned to the guard on his left. 'What dungeon are we going to?'

'Number three.'

'No,' said Shah, shaking his head. 'That is too light a punishment. In that dungeon a big grating lets in sunshine, the daylight, fresh air. I know. I have sent many people to that cell. Why not dungeon five?'

'Why not?' said the other guard. 'That's half the size and stinks like a sewer. We'll put the bastard in there. Then he can see what it's really like to be a prisoner. The sultan was too merciful.'

They reached the prison house; the first guard hammered on the gate. A jailer opened it, let them in. Shah kept his eyes downcast. He did not want to meet the gaze of a man who had been his subordinate only days previously. The revolution had taken place so quickly and so successfully, it was almost as if the new sultan was actually the old ruler's legitimate heir.

The door opened, shut, and clanged behind them. They went down the corridor to the next gate. At each of the seven gates they stopped and waited until a jailer unlocked it. The entrance stank slightly of urine and faeces. By the time they reached the end the smell was almost overpowering.

'Cell five,' said the guard. 'That is what you wished. It is the law that a man about to die can be granted one wish. This is yours. Get in there.'

They undid two bolts on a wooden door, studded inside with sharpened nails. It opened on to a filthy cell twelve foot square. There was a gutter in one corner, which stank of sewage. The place was dank, semi-dark, crawling with flies. Rats scuttled away along the gutter at the sound of the intruders and stood, backs hunched, ready for further flight. Their eyes glowed green in the gloom.

'Where do I lie?'

'On the floor, where you have condemned so many others to lie, in their own dung. See what it was like for them. Taste the bitter wine of punishment.'

They went out. Shah heard the door slam; the bolts were hammered home. Then he heard the other doors open and close, voices growing fainter as the guards walked away.

Shah walked round the cell, accustoming his eyes to the gloom, deliberately postponing the moment of searching for the hidden key, in case it had already been found and removed. Did the guards know about it? Or had they so readily agreed to his request for cell five because this would be a further humiliation for him?

He peered up at the grating. It opened to another floor, and, although narrow, was just large enough for a man to squeeze through. He began to feel along the slimy walls, slipping on dung on the floor, trying to find the loose brick. In his anxiety he could not remember exactly where it was. Was it on the left of the door or on the right?

At last he found it, and stood for a moment, his heart beating like a huge drum. Then he pulled out the brick, felt desperately inside the hole. The thunder of his heart eased slightly as his fingers touched the key.

He reached up, holding the key firmly, feeling with the fingers of his other hand through the filth and rust and slime for the small keyhole in the grating. He came to a slight indentation, gouged out the dung with which it was plugged and pushed in the key. It moved easily. He turned the key twice, three times. The tongues of the bolt slid out and the grating almost fell down on his head. He pushed it out of the hole on to the floor of the room above the cell.

He took out the key, put it in his pocket. Then he stood on tiptoe, braced his elbows at the edges of the hole and heaved himself up. Soon he was in the upper room. He carefully replaced the grating upside down, so that he could lock it in place again. They would assume that an accomplice must have come from outside to help him. Let them assume what they liked. Their thoughts did not matter now. What mattered was that he was free. He would survive. May Allah the all-seeing, the ever merciful, be praised!

The new sultan sat uneasily on his uncle's throne. He was beginning to realise how precarious his position and his power was. Many who had helped him to seize power expected immediate rewards far beyond his ability to provide. He moved the piece of root from one side of his mouth to the other, trying to extract some comfort from its faintly minty taste. The pain in his stomach throbbed with every beat of his heart.

The newly appointed captain of his guard came into his tent, bowed deeply and stood in silence awaiting his orders.

'Step forward,' Abdul Karim commanded him brusquely. 'Speak.'

'I have here one of the two men who accompanied Captain Shah to the jail.'

A second man now came into the tent, bowed low, stood nervously, head lowered.

'Come closer,' ordered the sultan. He did not want to raise his voice. Unless he spoke in a whisper, the pain became excruciating. He wondered whether the root was helping him. It was a pity that the Scottish physician Drummond had died. He might have been able to ease his agony. With a conscious effort, he brought his mind back to the present.

'Who are you?' he asked.

'The jailer, Highness.'

'What happened?'

'As you commanded, Highness, we marched the captain to the cells.'

'And?'

'On the way, Captain Shah asked to be placed in cell number five. He gave as his reason that this was less commodious than any of the other cells. He felt it would be a fitting penance for him to be incarcerated there. He did not know we had discovered that this cell had a hidden key.'

'How did you discover it?'

'The locksmith told us Shah had threatened that his son would go to jail if he did not help him. The locksmith believed him. When he found out that Shah had lied, he took his revenge.'

'And when Shah asked to be put in this cell?'

'We agreed, Highness, and took up position, as our captain had instructed us, outside the window of the room directly above the cell. Within a matter of minutes, Captain Shah appeared at the window, then came out and went into the bazaar. I followed him.'

'Where did Shah go?'

'To see his grandfather. He stayed for an hour. He cleansed his body of the filth from the cell, and, wearing a European suit, he came out and went down to the docks.'

'Did he lead you to any of his accomplices as had been hoped?'

'No, Highness.'

'So where is he now?'

'My colleague is watching him. Captain Shah is taking coffee in a coffee house.'

'And the old man?'

'He is in his house, Highness.'

'You have found out Shah's intentions from him?'

'He said he had no idea what his grandson intended. But as far as he knew, he had no money with him.'

The sultan turned to the officer. 'Make the old man talk, or you will force me to the unhappy conclusion that you cannot remain my guard commander.' He turned back to the jailer. 'From what you tell me, if the locksmith had not informed you of the whereabouts of the hidden key, you would not have found it.'

'That is so, Highness.'

'In fact, you had no idea it was there at all.'

'No, Highness.'

'So you admit gross negligence and slackness in not searching every cell every day in case prisoners have hidden some item to help them escape.'

The jailer did not reply, but stood trembling, his head bowed.

The sultan turned to the guard commander. 'Give him a hundred lashes,' he told him brusquely. 'Now, go!'

The men bowed, backed away nervously from the sultan's presence.

Abdul Karim sat for long after the men had gone, rolling the root on his tongue. Surely this agony could not simply be indigestion? Was it possible that no one in his kingdom could cure him? Was there a cure? Or was he waiting for the cure for all diseases that Shah's grandfather and this incompetent jailer would doubtless experience within the hour?

Seven

Captain Shah sat at the back of the coffee shop where he could watch whoever came or went.

He drank a cup of thick, gritty coffee slowly and gratefully. Then, feeling in his pocket for a coin before he ordered another, he discovered he had no money. The jailers had taken everything from his pockets: coins, banknotes, his fountain pen. Such items they kept as their perk; prisoners were rarely in a position to ask for their return. And when he changed his clothes in his grandfather's house he had neglected to ask the old man for any money.

Shah dared not reveal who he was, or that he could not pay, so he kept ordering more cups of coffee, sipping each one very slowly to spin out time, hoping that somehow he could think of a way out of his predicament. He sat until heat began to drain from the day and, after the short tropical twilight, dusk fell like a swift and gentle curtain. Now he would have to leave. He stood up, walked towards the entrance. A waiter hurried up to him with a scribbled bill on a plate.

'I'm sorry,' Shah explained shamefacedly. 'I have no money with me.'

'No money?' repeated the waiter, as if he had never heard the words before and could not understand them.

The proprietor came out of the shadows. He was a big man. He carried a stick.

'What have you been doing, drinking in the back if you

have no money? You've been in here two hours. Who are you? A tramp?'

Shah turned to him. The proprietor recognised him at once.

'I know you,' he said slowly. 'You're captain of the old guard. I've seen you on parade with the former sultan.'

'Yes. You do know me. I will pay you. It is just that I have foolishly left my money behind.'

'You never came here when the old sultan was alive. I wasn't good enough for you then, eh?'

'Not at all. But I am here now. Let me go. I will pay.'

'You're in trouble, Captain. You're on the run.'

'I *will* pay!' Shah shouted desperately. He pushed them both out of his way, ran into the darkened souk. It would be ludicrous to be ignominiously handed back to the authorities over the price of a few cups of coffee.

He walked quickly, stepping now and then into a doorway to look back over his shoulder in case he was being followed, but the streets were dark and empty. He could not see anyone who appeared to be following him. He wanted to run, but a running man always attracts attention, so he fought the wish to do so and walked as quickly as he dared.

He came to a junction with two narrow alleys. He knew this area well. The main street ahead was where his grandfather lived. He could not go back there, so he continued on through winding narrow passages until he reached the quay. It seemed deserted. That in itself was unusual. At this hour it should be crowded with sailors and touts. This could mean that the docks were being watched. If so, the watchers must be looking for him. If he was caught now, he would die, for he would have no defence: he had been caught trying to escape. Somehow, he did not know how, he had fallen into a trap.

He saw a ship, larger than the rest, preparing to sail on the dark tide. A few stevedores on the dock were already coiling up ropes that had held her to the quay. He recognised the slaver.

At that moment, a whistle blew, scattering his thoughts. Instantly, men ran out towards Shah from dark alleyways, the doorways of shops. They carried sticks and clubs. For a second Shah stood, mesmerised by the sight. There must be ten, twenty of them. There was no escape now.

Yes, *there was*. The ship. This was his only hope, his last thin chance. He raced across the docks like a gazelle, fighting aside men who thrust at him and tried to bring him down. He reached the edge of the quay, paused for an instant by the stone bollards. Far beneath them the water glittered with oily filth, pieces of wood, orange peel, all the debris of a dock. He took a deep breath and jumped. As he fell he prayed there would not be a boat moored underneath that could break his fall and smash his legs.

He landed between two narrow, high-prowed country boats, and struck out wildly away from them. Fifty yards away, the slaver was turning sluggishly to meet the tide. Her propeller churned up the water. He must avoid the blades. He swam on with the terrible strength of despair, knowing that to fail now was to die horribly. Gasping for breath, he reached the slaver, saw a tarred rope trailing in the water. He reached out and gripped it.

The vessel's hull was now between him and the quay. Her movement forced his body against the scummy metal plates. Boltheads and barnacles ripped his jacket and scored his flesh. He held on grimly. At least, he could not be seen from the shore.

Slowly, painfully, Shah hauled himself up on the rope.

Sobbing for breath, he threw himself thankfully on the deck as the slaver headed out towards the open sea.

Captain O'Grady had the prudent custom, born of many years commanding ships which Lloyd's might consider unseaworthy, of always staying on the bridge when he left a port, until all sight of land had disappeared and his vessel was safely out at sea. Only then would he feel free to hand over to the first mate and retire to his cabin for his usual evening drink of half a pint of rum and fresh lime juice. When he was carrying a cargo of slaves he would remain on the bridge until an hour after dusk, no matter when he set sail. As day turned to darkness he knew that the restlessness of his captives would decrease. If there was going to be any trouble, any attempt at insurrection, it would usually come just before sunset on that first day out of port. All creatures, with two legs or four, became more docile after dark.

Always at that hour, when the day began to die, a strange and eerie sound would echo round the ship. It never failed to move him, sometimes even made him regret the trade in which he had worked for so long, but such thoughts were easy to put to one side when he considered the profit each voyage represented. The sound always began in a small way, as though one person was moaning in almost unbearable pain. Then it spread, becoming louder and more pronounced, so that the whole ship seemed to groan with a melancholy wailing.

On O'Grady's first voyage, as a young man, he could not work out what it was. An old hand soon told him.

'It's the slaves,' he explained. 'They're mourning the loss of their freedom and their families and friends. Suddenly they realise they'll never see Africa again, never be free again. It's a cry of anguish that comes from the depths of their hearts. It's animal, and it's frightening, I can tell you. And it happens every time. You get used to it. If you don't, you'll have to quit the trade.'

All manner of people were run as slaves. Criminals evading the police could be seized and sent out west. Children would be tempted by offers of sweets or the excitement of seeing a strange animal, and then kidnapped. They would be passed on to willing buyers, usually in the States, under the description of indentured servants. But their indentures could last as long as they lived.

This girl who had been carried aboard earlier in the day was one who might face a similar future. He'd place her easily enough. That was the word he liked – place, not sell. She'd probably end up in a whorehouse, and many people would take a share of the profit as she passed through their hands. That was not his concern; he had received fifty sovereigns already from Mr Khan and his fee would be probably twice as much again when he found a place for her.

O'Grady had two cabins aboard the ship, one which he used, and the other given over to what was delicately called 'private trade'. He did a brisk business in such items as hubble-bubble pipes for curio shops, elephant tusks, camphor, gold dust and powdered rhino horn which, when mixed with harmless, peppermint-flavoured syrup, was regarded as a potent aphrodisiac. He was also carrying large tins full of a fish scale mixture, for which he had discovered a new and lucrative market among artists and sign-writers in the United States. The thick glutinous liquid stank of rotting vegetation and foul fish, but when mixed with spirit it produced a luminous paint. An inn sign painted with it would show up clearly in the dark.

There was no obvious communicating door from

O'Grady's cabin. O'Grady had insisted on this when he took command in case any over-inquisitive Customs investigator claimed that he was responsible for whatever dutiable or forbidden goods might be discovered in this second cabin. A pedal concealed behind a fixed chest of drawers in his cabin caused a section of panelling to slide to one side. Under the floor of this second cabin he kept a secret cache of six revolvers, in case he had any trouble with the crew. A bullet could answer arguments when soothing words failed.

The girl Khan had delivered was safely in this cabin, its porthole secured and the main door bolted on the outside. He must go down and see her some time, but not yet. Girls were not his taste. He knew many captains who would have been down there throughout the voyage – on her, in her, under her. But he had no interest in women; boys and young men were O'Grady's preference. As far as he was concerned she was simply merchandise, human cargo to be sold, as with all the slaves. But to get the best price for her, she had to be well cared for on the voyage.

She would be quite safe, as long as she kept to her cabin, away from the crew. He was running the vessel with very few men. For the ship's final voyage he did not want to pay off more than he had to, some perhaps even demanding a share of the profits and threatening him if he disagreed. He would make sure she fully understood the need to stay out of sight.

As the sun fell behind the far horizon, the sea turned to ink. Within seconds, the tropical twilight vanished. Gradually, the wailing stopped. The first mate came up on the bridge.

'You take over now,' O'Grady told him. 'I'll go below. Anything to report?'

'Nothing, sir. The girl seems very quiet. I looked into the cabin, but she was unconscious – or asleep.'

'You don't think someone gave her a bit too much to knock her out and killed her?' asked O'Grady anxiously. He did not trust traders who supplied white boys or girls. They were much rougher than those who dealt only in Negro slaves, perhaps because they were dark-skinned themselves and resented white folk. To drop a dead black slave of unknown origins over the side was one thing; to do the same with a white British subject was quite another.

'I felt her pulse, sir. It's slow, but it's steady. She'll come round.'

'Good. Anything else?'

'Yes. There's a bloody Arab lying on the main deck.'

'Dead?'

'No, alive.'

'Where's he from? Who is he?'

'He swam out from the quay. Quite an educated fellow. Speaks English. Says he is Captain Shah. He commanded the old sultan's guard. From what he says, his mistake was serving the wrong master.'

'So what's he doing here?'

'He says he was being chased for his life. His only hope of survival was to jump in the harbour and swim. So he did. Then he caught hold of one of our ropes and climbed up on deck.'

'You believe him?'

'I think so. But you have a word with him, sir.'

'I will. Is he free? You haven't tied his wrists or ankles?'

'No, he's free. Looks knackered. He'll not give you any trouble.'

'I hope not.'

O'Grady found Shah leaning against the stern rail.

Behind him, the vessel's white wash stretched like a luminous pathway to infinity against an indigo ocean. O'Grady approached, one hand in his pocket gripping a knife. You could never trust these Arab fellows. You never really knew where you were with them. This bugger might have come aboard intent on making trouble with the slaves. That had happened once before aboard a sister vessel when someone smuggled in a copy of the master key each captain carried to unlock the shackles of the slaves. They overpowered the crew and literally tore them to pieces.

O'Grady kept his distance now, pausing ten paces from Shah. One suspicious move, one step too close and the man was dead and over the side. O'Grady had been a tough street fighter; he had not lost his skills.

'You are the captain, sir?' Shah asked him nervously.

'I am. And you're a stowaway.'

'That may be so, sir, but I throw myself on your mercy. I served the old sultan loyally for years, but under the new regime I was flung into jail. I managed to escape but I was cornered in the docks. I could not go back, so I jumped into the sea. Your ship was leaving. I swam out to it. I beg your indulgence, and I ask your mercy as a human being.'

O'Grady took a pace closer to him. Under the lights on the outer deck he could see Shah's face. It was drawn and haggard, and O'Grady recognised him; he had seen him before on ceremonial parades. How swiftly could the wheel of fortune turn!

'You know this is a slaver, Shah?' O'Grady asked him more gently.

'I am aware of that, sir.'

'You must have sent many men to be transported as slaves. You gave them no mercy. Why should I show you any now?'

'What you say I cannot argue against. I can only throw myself on your goodness and charity as a Christian.'

'You're a Muslim. Would you give me charity and mercy in this position?'

'Sir, it is written, "In my father's house are many mansions." We worship the same God, if under different names.'

'That may be.'

'I have some knowledge of navigation, sir. I also know the dialects these men speak. I could be useful as an interpreter. And when you dock, I will disappear. I give you my word.'

'And then maybe you'll tell people on shore a slaver's just come in, and I'll be arrested. I don't like the sound of that, Shah. I believe you're telling me the truth, that you're running for your life. But in a sense I'm running for my life, too, and my liberty. So are my crew. You're on passage aboard my ship, uninvited. In days gone by, many captains would have thrown you into the sea. However, if I transport you, I cannot put you down with the slaves. They'd tear you to pieces if they had the slightest chance, or club you to death, shackled as they are. I saw once how they killed a man they thought was an informer. They ripped out his heart and his liver with their bare hands and ate them raw while the bugger was still alive.'

O'Grady paused. He did not explain that he had a girl in his second cabin.

'I'll have to put you to work with the crew. You will wear a pair of trunks, or a loin cloth, but no shirt, nothing where you can conceal any weapon. You understand me?'

'I understand, sir, and I thank you.'

'Good. Then wait here while I get the second mate.'

He went below decks, turned the mate out from his bunk.

'We've got an Arab called Shah aboard as a stowaway,' he explained briefly. 'He was the captain in charge of the old sultan's bodyguard. Now the new sultan wants his head. He has sought safety aboard with us.'

'In a slaver?' asked the mate incredulously. 'He must be bloody mad, sir.'

'I agree. But it was either that or certain death. I can't throw him over the side, and I can't put him below with the slaves for obvious reasons. So I'm going to let him work with the crew. But without a shirt, and in a loin cloth or his underpants only. No shoes. He'll have nothing about him where he could conceal a weapon. You understand?'

'Where will he mess?'

'In the fo'castle. We have a Portuguese crew. He can muck in with them, sling his hammock there.'

'You're being very merciful all of a sudden, Captain.'

'It's my last voyage. But if there's any trouble, Shah goes over the side. For the time being, though, I don't want a dead man on my conscience.'

'You'll have several before long. One of the slaves has dysentery. It's pouring out of him like out of a tap.'

'I can't help him. Shah is someone I can help, and as far as I can I will because he can help us, and without being paid a penny piece.'

The wooden floor moved slowly, like a living creature. Then the roof sagged, and the walls bulged and grew together again as though they were breathing.

Anna shook her head to try to rid her mind of these terrible images. She was lying on a bunk in a tiny square room. It had a circular window with a brass rim and two metal levers holding the glass tight against the wall. She remembered the porthole in the cabin aboard the trooper. Of course, she was in a ship, but of what kind? And where was she bound – Bombay, or back to England?

The floor dipped and heaved and rose again, and all the walls quaked. She remembered now. She had been ashore minutes ago. Or was it hours ago? She glanced at her watch. She sat up, terrified, confused, forcing herself to think back. Gradually she remembered the Scotsman, Drummond, taking her to see Mr Khan; and the pill Khan had given her with a glass of milk. Of course, she had been drugged, that was why she still felt so strange. But for how long had she been unconscious? And where was this ship going?

Then she saw her familiar bag, with the lock blown away. She opened it, went through all her clothes hurriedly; nothing seemed to be missing.

She shouted: 'Help! Help! Is anyone there?'

The only answer was the creak and dip of the floor. She stood up and crossed the room. A metal washbasin was hinged up against one wall. She opened it, pressed a tap against a spring. Tepid water dribbled out. She rinsed her mouth, washed her face, her hands, and dried them, felt slightly better.

The cabin door was locked. She beat on it furiously, until she heard the scrape of a key in the lock. The door opened, a man came in. He locked it behind him and pocketed the key. He was of medium height, in his forties, with sandy hair and pale blue eyes.

'Who are you?' Anna asked him with more bravado than she felt.

'The captain of this ship. Sean O'Grady. And you?'

'Anna Ballater. Where are we sailing?'

'The West Indies.'

'I don't want to go to the West Indies. I was going to India.'

'Often we make plans to go somewhere, to do something, but events change them. You're going west with us now.'

'To do what?' she asked.

'To take up a position there. Have no fear, I'll see you get a good one.'

'A position? With whom? Doing what?'

'With a family perhaps, or maybe working in a hotel. Who knows?'

Anna fought to stay calm, or at the least to appear calm. Drummond had told her the ship was a slaver, but did this mean she was a slave now, a person to be sold? She had given Drummond a diamond. Surely that was sufficient to ensure her safety?

'You mean, you're going to sell me?' she asked hesitantly. She had to find out.

'Place you is how I'd describe it.'

'However you describe it, that's what you're going to do. But what about the diamond I gave to the doctor? He said that would pay for my fare.'

'Diamond? I know nothing about any diamond. A man I've dealt with in the past, Mr Khan, asked me to take you aboard as a favour. I did so for a small fee. You'll cost me for food on the voyage, and there's the use of this cabin. I can't afford to do this for nothing.'

'A slaver,' said Anna dully. So what Dorothy and the sailor had told her was true – and she had not believed them.

'You've slaves aboard?'

O'Grady nodded. 'Yes.'

Anna sat down. She had never imagined this; it was

beyond all imagination, to be a slave, a white slave.

'You'll be all right,' O'Grady assured her. 'You're our only white passenger. But there's a poor devil who was run out of Mamora. A Captain Shah. He's not a slave, though in the past he's dealt in them, like so many on that island. I'm letting him work his passage as a member of the crew.'

'I could work, too, if that would buy me freedom.'

'Doing what? Pulling on ropes? Swabbing decks? Don't be bloody silly. You stay here. You'll be safer here than out on deck. Know what I mean?'

'I can guess.'

'Remember, Miss Ballater, your name is not on any manifest, and we have no passenger list. Officially, you don't exist – anywhere.'

'I do exist,' Anna retorted.

O'Grady shrugged. 'I'll send you in some soup and bread. The water in that tap is drinkable, by the way. And I'll see you in the morning. In the meantime, keep your door locked – for your own safety.'

He went out, leaving Anna sitting on the bunk. She found she was trembling. She put her face in her hands and wept like a lonely child.

By the fourth day at sea, Anna had grown used to the sway and roll of the ship. The second mate opened the porthole for her now there was no risk of her climbing out and attempting to swim to the shore, and she breathed fresh salty air thankfully. Food was brought to her three times a day, and she was allowed a brief daily walk on the aft deck, with the second mate as her escort.

On the fifth day she realised that she must escape this virtual incarceration. Somehow she had to come to terms with the captain, otherwise she would be sold when the ship landed, perhaps as a potential whore under the convenient guise of being a housekeeper or a cook. The only way she could think of dealing with O'Grady was to offer him one or more of the diamonds concealed in her bar of soap. But could she trust this man to honour any arrangement they might make? If she gave him one diamond, or even all of them, what was to prevent him still selling her to any bidder? Nothing at all.

Anna sat considering the problem. Finally, she took the little box that Jeannie Moore had given her, tipped out a slice of dried stem into her hand and chewed it thoroughly. She drank a glass of water to wash out her mouth and sat, hoping for some reaction.

For a few moments, nothing happened. Then she began to feel drowsy. She lay down on the bunk and closed her eyes. Halfway between sleep and wakefulness, she saw a single bottle of Long Glen whisky, the drink produced by the laird's distillery. She had first noticed its distinctive label of a heather-covered hillside and a stag poised on the peak when the estate bailiff brought a bottle for her father as a Christmas present.

As she attempted to find a reason for this unexpected sight, the single bottle became two, then three, a score, a hundred. Then all faded and in their place she saw two ships on a sunlit sea, one large, the other small, with a bright blaze of flame. And as before, when she had seen this same vision aboard the troopship, she saw herself swimming in a sea of deepest blue.

What could it mean? Disappointed, she tried vainly to answer the question. Then she fell asleep, and slept more soundly than at any time since she had left home.

Pierre Montagne was feeling unusually pleased with himself;

this was the morning of his twenty-seventh birthday and it was starting very well indeed.

He sat in the stern cockpit of the former French navy torpedo boat *Josephine*, which he had commanded for the last six months of the Great War. The sun felt warm on his face; in one hand he held a glass of Napoleon brandy, in the other, a half-smoked Gitane. The future looked as agreeable and promising as the glittering expanse of sunlit sea. By this time next year, on his twenty-eighth birthday, Montagne calculated he could be a rich man.

Half a dozen former junior officers of the French navy, all his contemporaries, had chipped in together to buy this vessel which would otherwise have been scrapped. Montagne held the majority shareholding and was determined that his investment should pay speedy returns. During the previous few months they had run regular trips loaded with cartons of cigarettes from Marseilles across the Mediterranean to the Bay of Naples. Here, at dusk, they would drop anchor and, after an exchange of signals, a flotilla of local Italian fishing boats would come out on the evening tide. The cigarettes would be exchanged for wads of thousand-lira notes. Then Montagne and his crew would be away, heading westward, before dawn lit up the sky.

The market for foreign duty-free cigarettes in Italy seemed insatiable and the profits were high. Their illicit trade was also relatively safe because the Italian Customs authorities did not possess cutters fast enough to catch a torpedo boat powered by two twelve-cylinder Hispano-Suiza engines. And although the Italian government threatened all manner of retribution, sometimes using navy vessels in attempts to stop large-scale cigarette smuggling, many senior Customs officials had their price. They would warn the Frenchmen when a corvette or even a light destroyer was heading their way, and advise them when the ship changed course. The price Montagne paid for such information was always added to the cost of the cigarettes, so the smugglers did not suffer any loss of profits.

These were regular runs, but repetition to young men can soon become boring. During the war, Montagne had escaped from the drudgery of clerking in a Lyons lawyer's office and was determined never to return to any life of dreary and predictable routine. The prospect of making easy money indefinitely from smuggling cigarettes was agreeable, but perhaps other prospects could offer even greater and quicker profits?

With this hope in mind, they sailed *Josephine* out of the Mediterranean and headed south. They called at the ports of Freetown and Lagos in West Africa, but prospects of profitable trade of any kind seemed remote. Now the plan was to aim for Lüderitz, where the Namib desert met the sea in southern Africa.

This was at the suggestion of one of the crew who had spent the last few months of the war interrogating German prisoners of war, two of whom had been born and grew up in Kolmanskop, near Lüderitz, an outpost in what until the war had been German South-West Africa. They had told him stories of diamonds in such numbers that they could be picked up in the sands. They described how dealers would put rows of natives on their hands and knees and order them to move forward slowly, picking up any stones that glittered. Some were only pieces of quartz, of course, but many more were diamonds. Here, fortunes could be made, literally, overnight.

Understandably, the South African authorities had now instigated very tight security over the whole area. Smuggling diamonds out was said to be virtually impossible, but Montagne calculated there must be loopholes somewhere. And only a very few diamonds could set them all up for years, even for life. Anyway, this was a challenge he could not resist.

As he sat savouring the prospect of future riches, a member of the crew came through the main cabin to him.

'There's a ship, travelling west, about ten knots, possibly two miles away,' he reported.

'Have they seen us?'

'Probably not, for we're pretty low in the water. But I can't be sure.'

'Go hard to port. Keep out of sight. But get ahead of her, and then maybe we can say hello.'

After his experiences off the Italian coast, Montagne felt wary of other vessels whose identity he did not know. This could be an innocent merchantman, or a South African patrol boat.

'How far are we from Lüderitz?' he asked.

'Difficult to say. We're only about five miles from the Namibian coast, though.'

'Right.'

'Meanwhile, *mon capitaine*, I will have a glass of that brandy before you finish it all,' said his colleague, and poured himself a beaker from the flagon.

The second mate approached O'Grady as he came down from the bridge.

'That slave I told you about, sir, the one with dysentery. He's dead.'

'Any others ill with the flux?'

'Several, sir. But not to the death, I would say.'

'We've no treatment for them,' said O'Grady regretfully.

'Open all the hatches. Let the air get in on the deck, and maybe their natural strength will pull them through.'

'You're optimistic, sir. I think the flux will take a few more yet. I'm glad this is the last trip I'm making with these poor bastards.'

'I don't want any moralising from you,' retorted O'Grady. 'This trade pays your wage. If you don't like it, you should have quit long ago.' He took the mate's arm. 'I'll come below decks with you,' he said. 'Help you get the dead man overboard. Order the Portuguese to play hoses on the rest for half an hour. That will clean up the muck and cool the air. May even wash some germs away.'

He led the way down a ladder onto the second deck. Before they reached it, the smell of faeces, sweat and urine became almost overpowering. The mate choked and spat over the side. The captain lit a cheroot against what he believed could be a potentially deadly stench.

The slaves lay in a circle on their backs on the deck, their heads towards the portholes, their feet pointing inwards. Every man was shackled to his neighbour by a handcuff at each wrist, and a leg iron round each ankle. They lay on strips of oak, nailed three inches apart. In the centre of these naked bodies, glistening blue flies swarmed around cooking pots.

The slaves were not allowed knives or forks or spoons lest, in a sudden ferocious rage at their situation, they might somehow manage to attack each other despite their irons. Worse still, they might fashion a key to open the locks on their legs and ankles and then attempt to seize the ship. Food was put down on metal plates between them and they had to eat as best they could, rolling on their sides, feeding themselves with their fingers. For drink, a crew member would spray their faces with water from a hose.

They looked up now as the captain stood surveying them. He saw a hundred pairs of eyes, reddened with sickness and salt and hatred.

'Where's the dead man?'

'On the end, sir.'

'You have the key?'

'Yes.'

The corpse lay in a puddle of yellow pus, streaked with blood. Flies covered his mouth, his nostrils, his open eyes.

'Get him out, then,' said O'Grady, 'and move the rest up.'

The mate unlocked the handcuffs and leg irons, pulled out the body, dragged the next man across the space, reshackled him.

'Don't try to carry him yourself,' said the captain. 'Get the Portuguese here. I'll have a look at the rest meanwhile.'

He walked up the row of sweating Negroes. The stench made him choke, even though he pulled vigorously at his cheroot. Most looked healthy enough, but a few lay damp with fever, flesh shining with sweat, crawling with greedy flies.

On some runs it was not unknown for captains to lose half their slaves, but O'Grady reckoned he would lose only a few on this one. He would hose the slaves down twice a day as he approached port. This had the effect of freshening them, so that when they appeared for sale they did not look so wretched and woebegone.

He went up on deck. Two Portuguese sailors came behind him carrying the dead slave. They laid him down on the deck.

'He can't stay there,' said O'Grady irritably. 'Get him into the sea.'

'Do we wrap him in a blanket, Captain?'

'Of course not. He's dead. Blanket's no use to him now, poor devil. Heave him over the rail as he is.'

One of the Portuguese crossed himself. 'Do we say a prayer for him, sir, to save his soul?'

'If you want to, you can. But how do you know he's got a soul? He's a heathen.'

The Portuguese mumbled a few words in his own language, bowed his head, and again made the sign of the cross.

They picked up the dead slave by his shoulders and ankles. He sagged. They were small men, and panted with the exertion; the slave was at least half a foot taller, and of very heavy build. They levered the body up onto the rail, balanced it for a moment, then pushed it over. The corpse landed in the sea with a great splash. They all stood staring as it floated away.

As muscles twitched and tightened, the corpse raised its right arm as though in ironic farewell. Then came the telltale flutter of fins and tails as ravenous killer fish attacked the flesh. The blue sea darkened with a dead man's blood.

The body had left streaks of grease, sweat and dung on the varnished wooden rail.

'Get this clean,' said the mate irritably. He did not care to appear slack in front of the captain. O'Grady was not a bad fellow by some standards, but in the mate's view the captains of slavers always had a tendency to bad temper, even madness. He remembered one ship in which he had served, when the captain was taken ill by some painful stomach disease and sought relief from his own agony by hurting others. He had ordered two sailors to carry him round the ship while he struck the faces of any members of the crew he disliked, gouging their flesh with a penknife blade. One man had ducked away to avoid the blow. The captain ordered him to be taken down to his own cabin, tied naked to his bunk and flogged while he enjoyed the spectacle at close quarters.

O'Grady turned away from the rail. This was the first time he had been below decks to inspect the cargo on this voyage. He would not go again.

There were all kinds of jobs, he told himself, where profit entailed necessary suffering, even death – to others. He would not care to work in a slaughterhouse, for example, and every day see the floor run red with blood from cows and hogs and oxen. Nor could he bear to be a surgeon's assistant, carving up the living, tossing away their limbs, sinews and bowels; nor in a mortuary, breathing dead men's putrefaction and decay. And this was his last trip, after all. He had savings, he was single, and he would find another job; but not slaving, not ever again.

He went down to his cabin, poured himself four fingers of rum, swallowed the raw spirit in a gulp, poured himself another measure. The smell of the slave deck hung in his nostrils, his clothes, his hair, surrounding him like an unclean fog. He would have a bath and be rid of it with disinfectant in the water.

As he went into the bathroom, there was a knock on the cabin door.

'Who is it?' he asked irritably. 'Not someone to announce another death, surely?'

'Second mate, sir. Message from the crow's nest.'

'Well?'

'Vessel in distress, sir. Dead ahead.'

'What flag is she flying?'

'British flag, sir. White ensign.'

'A navy vessel, eh? Then we'll have to see what we can do to help.'

He turned on the bath, stood watching the frothing salt water pour out of the tap. There could be money in this, he told himself. Salvage fees. He might make as much helping a distressed naval ship as on a cargo of slaves, maybe more. But he could not have one without the other. If he wasn't shipping slaves, he would not be in any position to help a naval vessel in distress.

Soothed by this thought, and the rum and the steam, he climbed thoughtfully into the hot water.

Captain O'Grady focused his binoculars on the small boat that lay five hundred yards ahead, bobbing up and down on the South Atlantic swell. She was flying the white ensign upside down, sign of a Royal Navy vessel in distress. She sat low in the water, held steady by sea anchors out aft and from her bows. A sailor was standing on the afterdeck waving to him. O'Grady raked the ship with his glasses. He could just make out her name on the side – *Clarissa*. He turned to the mate.

'Check her in the book.'

The mate quickly thumbed through the pages of Lloyd's List of Shipping which contained details of nearly every ship afloat.

'Here she is, sir. *Clarissa*. Was a wartime patrol vessel, powered by two Thorneycroft diesels. Launched Portsmouth, 1913, still in restricted use for Admiralty research purposes, whatever that may mean.'

'What the hell can she be researching out in the Atlantic?' O'Grady removed the plug from the speaking tube. 'Half speed, port engine,' he told the engineer.

The slaver slowed, began to turn. About a hundred yards from *Clarissa*, O'Grady ordered the engineer to go down to a quarter speed. He picked up a megaphone.

'Who are you?' he shouted.

'*Clarissa*. Research vessel undergoing Admiralty tests,' came the reply. 'We've run out of fuel.'

'A Royal Navy ship out of fuel?' shouted O'Grady sarcastically. This was extraordinary, something he had never heard of before. For a moment he stood, savouring the situation. Here he was, a renegade captain, commanding an illegal slaver, and being asked to help a Royal Navy vessel by some incredible folly out of fuel on the high seas.

The irony amused him; he'd play the bugger along for a bit. Then he remembered his own situation. He could not afford to let the Royal Navy discover the cargo he was carrying. They had only to radio the information back to the Admiralty and he would be in dire trouble. His best plan was to give them some fuel and be on his way as quickly as possible, trusting they would not report the matter, since to do so would only expose their own negligence.

'Can we come aboard for it?' shouted the sailor. 'We can pay you in English pounds or American dollars, however you wish.'

'How much fuel do you need?'

'Minimum, two hundred gallons. Anything above that we'd be very grateful for. But two hundred would get us back to port.'

'Where's that?'

'Simonstown naval base, South Africa.'

'Right,' said O'Grady. 'Two hundred gallons it is.'

'We have a fuel hose here with a metering gauge. Can we tap it into one of your tanks?'

'Yes,' agreed O'Grady. 'But don't be long.'

'We've been here for some hours already,' the man replied sharply. 'We want to get away as much as you do, before Simonstown starts getting concerned. We won't drag our feet, I assure you. Can you come alongside us? We have no power to reach you.'

O'Grady put down his megaphone, gave new orders to the engineer. He had brought his ship safely into many strange harbours, without pilots, without tugs, and on moonless nights. Within ten minutes, she was alongside *Clarissa*. A crewman lowered a cluster of thick fibre ropes and old motor tyres over the side to stop the two hulls rasping against each other.

Two sailors now appeared on *Clarissa*'s deck. They wore white shorts and shirts and thick rubber gloves. Between them they carried a heavy hose. O'Grady dropped a rope ladder, for there was a difference of more than twenty feet in the deck heights of the two ships. They climbed up the ladder, pulling the hose after them. O'Grady came down from the bridge to meet them. They saluted him smartly.

'Where do we connect, sir?' asked the first one.

'He'll show you,' O'Grady replied, pointing to a Portuguese crewman. The man led them towards the stern of the vessel, bent down to turn a spoked wheel that controlled access to the fuel tanks.

As O'Grady watched them clip the end of the hose into the nozzle, he heard a faint crack, like the sound of a distant whip, or a dry twig breaking. To his astonishment, the Portuguese sailor crumpled and fell forward across the hose, and lay spread-eagled on the deck. The first and second mates came up to O'Grady.

'What's the matter?' the first mate asked him anxiously. 'What's happened?'

Had the sailor had a fit, a seizure?

Then the two sailors from *Clarissa* turned. Each man

held a revolver. The slaver's two mates raised their hands nervously.

'Stay right where you are,' the first sailor shouted to them. 'Don't move an inch or you die.'

O'Grady stood, staring at the scene in disbelief. Was he going mad, imagining all this? Why should two British Royal Navy sailors shoot a crewman and now threaten them?

'You've killed him,' he said flatly, in disbelief.

'So what? Six million people died in the war. What is one more?'

'Who are you?' O'Grady asked. Surely these could not be British sailors.

'We're French.'

'French?'

'Yes. I thought my English accent was quite good, eh? I had an English mother, you see.'

As he spoke, other sailors swarmed up the rope ladder in rubber-soled canvas shoes. They surrounded O'Grady and the mates. Back aboard the small boat someone was unhooking the name *Clarissa*. O'Grady saw now that it had only been painted on a board and suspended by two wires from the gunwale. Beneath it he read the ship's real name – *Josephine*. The sailor pulled down the white ensign.

'What do you want?' O'Grady asked weakly, unable to accept what was happening, let alone comprehend it.

'The contents of your safe, Captain,' Montagne told him. 'That's all.'

'Who the hell are you?'

'You can call us what you like. Pirates. Buccaneers. Corsairs. But we're not here to toss words to and fro. This isn't a social call. It's business.'

As the man spoke, the first mate jumped at him. The

sailor fired. The mate fell. As his companion bent over him, the man fired a second time. The second mate collapsed.

'You've murdered them! You'll never get away with this,' shouted O'Grady furiously. Then he remembered the transmitter in the radio room. Unconsciously, he glanced up at the long aerial wire that stretched between the tops of the two masts.

'Your radio isn't working, Captain, so don't get ideas about that,' replied Montagne, guessing O'Grady's thoughts. 'We've already put a man in to smash the valves. Sorry to say he had to treat your operator in the same way. He became belligerent. Now, your safe.'

'There's nothing in it,' said O'Grady stubbornly.

'We'll see for ourselves, Captain.' Montagne nodded to two of his colleagues. 'Go below and open the main water cocks. You will then have under ten minutes before we sink.'

'You're bloody mad,' cried O'Grady desperately. He had the vague feeling that if he kept talking they might somehow be persuaded to go away.

No one answered him. The two sailors still stood silently, revolvers trained on O'Grady. The slaver wallowed uneasily in the troughs between waves. Then they heard a deep boom of metal striking metal far beneath their feet. The seawater cocks were being hammered open.

The fellow was right, O'Grady thought, he had done his homework; they had ten minutes at the most before the ship sank. O'Grady decided he must tell them where the safe was while he still could. Then it was just possible they would not scuttle the ship, *his* ship.

'The safe only contains enough money to pay off the crew. It's absurd to scuttle a ship for a few hundred pounds,' he said desperately.

'I'll decide that, Captain. Where is it?'

'On the bridge.'

'Give me the keys, but don't try anything when you put your hand in your pocket. It's as easy to take keys off a dead man as a living one. Probably easier.'

O'Grady put his right hand in his jacket pocket, took out a bunch of keys attached by a leather thong to his belt. He undid two of them, threw them on the deck.

'Take 'em,' he said bitterly.

'If they're not the right ones, you're dead,' said Montagne grimly.

'They are the right ones.'

'Maybe, but I still don't trust this bastard,' said Montagne to one of the sailors. 'Lock him in his cabin and keep the key. And check he hasn't a pistol hidden away somewhere. Most English captains travel with one.'

Two men frog-marched O'Grady across the deck, down the companionway and into his cabin. Then they ripped open all the drawers, turned out the cupboards. They found his pistol and a clip of cartridges under a pile of shirts. They pocketed the weapon, tore the sheets off his bunk in case he had another concealed under the mattress. Then they left, locking the door.

O'Grady heard them remove the key, and the sound of their feet die away. He sat for a moment on his bunk, head in his hands. There must be some way out of his predicament, there must be. He had to escape before the ship went down or he would go down with her.

Eight

Shah had dropped flat on the deck when he saw the two Frenchmen follow the Portuguese sailor towards the bows. Long experience of living on the edge of danger, of sensing the faintest nuances of approaching disaster, made him scent death in the air. When he saw one man fall, and the glint of sun on the blue metal of revolvers, he knew that, once again, his basic animal instinct for survival had not failed him.

Shah had heard of many instances of piracy in the Arabian Sea. Like slavery, such incidents were everyday events, but he had never been personally involved. He believed that pirates were creatures of habit. They would board a ship on some plausible pretext, such as a request for help, then kill the captain, or lock him up with the crew below decks. They would then loot the ship and scuttle her. Dead men could never give evidence, and pirates were always, by nature, careful. They had to be if they were to survive. Usually, the risks they took were slight, or they would not attempt to seize the ship in the first place. Most ships of the size and type they attacked did not carry wireless sets, and if they did, they would speedily put them out of action.

Having escaped the vengeance of the new sultan, Shah had no intention of dying at the hands of unknown French sailors of fortune. So far, the boarders had not seen him; he was certain of that. But he guessed he had only minutes at most before someone would see him if he stayed where he was, so he crawled across the deck to the nearest companionway. He climbed down it slowly, holding the rail tightly so as not to slip on the smooth, diamond-shaped treads of each step. Any unexplained noise could be fatal.

Below decks, breathing the familiar oily smell from the engines, he paused for a moment. He did not want to go right down to the engine room. That could be one of the first places the Frenchmen would visit to smash the engines, in case someone attempted to start them and escape. Most probably they would simply cut the fuel feeds and then set fire to the ship as the oil poured out.

Shah moved along the corridor, tried the first door. It was locked. So was the door next to it. Then he heard breathing behind the panels. Someone was hiding inside.

'Let me in,' he begged in an urgent whisper. 'Quick! It's a matter of life and death!'

His life, he thought, his death. A pause, then a key turned in the lock. He heard a bolt being withdrawn. The door was opened cautiously half an inch. Shah forced his way in, locked and bolted the door behind him and leaned against it, thankful to have found sanctuary of a sort until he could decide on his next move.

Facing him was the girl he had brought, drugged, to Mamora's main square for the old sultan to rape.

Anna did not recognise Shah at first. Then she did and her eyes narrowed.

'*You!*' she exclaimed in horror. 'You were in the square at Mamora!'

Shah nodded. This was no time to lie.

'Bastard!' said Anna thickly. She looked around desperately for anything to use as a weapon to strike him.

'Listen,' said Shah, seizing her arms. 'I can explain everything.'

'Let me go, you swine. You can explain nothing.'

'I can. *Everything*. But not now. We've been boarded by pirates. Within minutes they will sink us – if they don't kill us all before.'

'You're making that up.'

'I wish to God I were. It's true, I tell you. That's why we've stopped.' He released his grip on her gradually, cautiously, in case she struck him.

'So why come and tell me?' Anna asked him.

'I didn't know you were here. I just wanted somewhere to hide, to give myself a moment to think what I could do.'

'And what can you do?'

'I don't know. But if we're quiet, they may not discover we're here.'

'They'll find out. They're bound to.'

They could hear noises, banging, shouting, through the wall. Men were in the corridor, beating on the door of the next cabin, trying to force it open.

'That's the captain's cabin,' Anna continued, thinking aloud.

'There isn't a connecting door to this one,' said Shah. 'I know. I had a look round it one day when the captain wasn't there.'

'There is,' Anna corrected him. 'It's hidden in that cabin. But not in this. You can see for yourself.'

Shah took a step nearer to her. Anna backed away nervously.

'Keep away from me,' she warned him.

'I mean you no harm,' he assured her earnestly. 'I am very sorry for what happened then, but my life was at risk. So was the old sultan's. I had to find a woman somehow.'

'So you found me.'

'I can only say again, I didn't mean any harm to you. It was simply a matter of my own survival.'

'So you deliberately had me publicly raped and humiliated.'

'But I got Drummond to take you out of the square afterwards,' Shah replied defensively. 'If I hadn't, you would almost certainly have been raped again, by goodness knows how many men, or even lynched. That crowd was in a very dangerous mood.'

'What happened to Drummond?' Anna asked.

'He's dead. I was arrested, but managed to escape and swam out to this ship. Captain O'Grady said he would give me passage wherever they were going.'

As he spoke, the door into O'Grady's cabin opened on oiled hinges. Captain O'Grady stood framed in the doorway. He was wild-eyed, his hair tousled.

'How the hell did you get here?' he asked Shah in amazement.

'Through the outer door.'

'The pirates will be in my cabin within seconds. They've already opened the water cocks. The ship will go down like a stone.'

As the two men looked at each other in horror, and the cabin floor dipped slightly as the ship began to list, Anna remembered her two visions: two ships, one large, one small, and she was swimming in a cobalt sea. There must be a way of escape, she thought, and suddenly it came to her. At last she could read some of the images she had seen in the eye of her mind.

'I have a plan,' said Anna quietly. 'If either of you has a gun of any sort.'

O'Grady did not reply. Instead he opened a drawer. It

appeared empty except for a folded newspaper. He lifted this, took out a screwdriver hidden underneath it. Then he kicked a loose rug across the floor and unscrewed four brass screws that held down a floorboard. Between the wooden joists lay six revolvers wrapped in oily rags against corrosion. He checked they were loaded, handed one to Shah, another to Anna, put two in his own pockets. He replaced the floorboard and the rug.

'Now, what is your plan?' he asked her quietly.

'I didn't see anyone come aboard. So they must have arrived on the other side, away from us. Right?'

'Obviously.'

'We open this porthole, which is on their blind side. I'll jump out and swim round to their boat, still on their blind side.'

'They're bound to have look-outs. They'll see you.'

'I'll swim underwater, so they won't.'

'You couldn't make that distance, round our stern and halfway along the port side.'

'I have to, unless you have any better suggestion.'

'Go on,' said Shah. 'We haven't heard yours yet.'

'You follow me, and take out any pirates you can. I'll deal with those on their boat – my father taught me to shoot. But before you start, wait till you hear my shots, which will distract them. Then go in.'

'Sounds risky,' said O'Grady doubtfully. 'But it's better than staying here, waiting to be shot.'

Anna pulled off her clothes, put on her swimming costume, tucked the revolver into its belt. Then she picked up her bar of carbolic soap from the washbasin, put this into her spongebag which she also tied to her belt. O'Grady was about to ask her what she could possibly want soap for at such a moment, but thought better of it.

Anna looked round the cabin as though searching for something. She saw a hubble-bubble pipe, snapped off its bowl and the crimped mouthpiece, blew through the tube to check it was not clogged.

'Ready?' O'Grady asked her impatiently.

'Ready.'

O'Grady opened the porthole a few inches and peered out cautiously. They could hear footsteps drumming on the upper deck, shouts, and faint cries for help from the shackled slaves down below.

Anna squeezed through, swung round and dropped, holding her nose against the sudden rush of warm salt water. She surfaced briefly, glanced around her. The sea lay empty, blue as in her vision, dappled with sunlight. She took a deep breath, put one end of the hubble-bubble's tube in her mouth, and dived. She swam on her back, a foot beneath the surface of the sea. She went round the stern of the slaver, then came up briefly to check her position.

Ahead of her a much smaller boat was bobbing up and down; the small ship she had seen in her dream.

Two men were still aboard, looking up at the slaver, watching their comrades. *Josephine*'s engine was running, ticking over with a lazy thump-thump.

Anna dived and swam underwater until she saw the boat's dark hull almost above her head. She surfaced again, hauled herself carefully up the far side. Then she pulled her revolver from her belt, shook seawater out of its barrel and gave a great shout: 'Ahoy!'

The two sailors turned towards her in astonishment. Their hands went down to pistols strapped to their waists. Anna fired twice before they could draw. They fell sideways over the rim of the hull into the sea.

At that moment a crackle of revolver shots came from

the deck of the slaver. Anna climbed aboard the smaller vessel and untied the rope that held her close to the slaver. Then she ran back to the controls, accelerated the engine. The little boat backed off in a flurry of foam from her propellers, until a couple of yards separated the two vessels.

The slaver was already settling in the water, several feet lower than when Anna had left her. Montagne appeared on her deck. He aimed his revolver at Anna. She fired first, but the hammer fell with a useless click against the cartridge. Salt water had ruined the charge. She saw Shah race along the slaver's deck and bring down Montagne in a rough tackle as the Frenchman fired. Montagne's bullet ripped into woodwork above Anna's head. Then she heard the crack of another shot. Shah leaned over the rail.

'All clear!' he shouted triumphantly.

Now there arose a great clanking of irons and manacles as the slaves tried desperately to break free in their confined space between decks. Their terrified shouts sounded like the braying of shackled animals in a slaughterhouse. Slowly, the slaver began to list to one side as water poured into her hull.

O'Grady called from the bridge. 'I'm going below. If I can turn off the sea cocks, we may still save her.'

He reappeared within a few moments, dragging the ship's safe at the end of a rope. He heaved this over the side onto the torpedo boat's deck.

'The water's reached the engines,' he reported. 'The sea cocks are already under feet of water, and the level's rising fast. We have no power, and so the pumps won't work. That's it.'

'Have you a master key to unlock the slaves' shackles?' Anna asked O'Grady.

'Of course.'

'Give it to me.'

O'Grady removed a large key from the bunch at his belt.

'I'm going back aboard,' said Anna. She turned to Shah. 'You saved my life,' she said gratefully.

'Maybe I owed you that,' he replied awkwardly.

'Maybe,' she agreed. 'Come on, then.'

Together, they raced along the deck and down the companionway to the slaves' deck.

'Tell them in their own language we're going to set them free.'

'They may not believe us. If they think it's a trick, they'll kill us.'

'Tell them if they attempt anything, we'll all die. This old tub will sink any moment. But if we can take her in tow we may just make the shoreline before she does.'

'Land's several miles off.'

'But it's shallow water. Look, the sea's so clear you can see the bottom even out here. We'll put them all ashore in their own country, Africa. Then they'll be free.'

Anna took O'Grady's master key and unlocked the main padlocks that held the manacles, while Shah addressed them.

O'Grady came down to their deck. 'The ship's sinking quicker than I thought,' he reported. 'And the more water she takes in, the quicker she'll go. You can't waste time down here.'

'We're not wasting time, we're saving these poor devils,' Anna retorted. 'Then we can tow the ship within sight of land before she goes under and let them loose.'

'The waves break so high on that beach you can only land there on one or two days a year. The wind blows constantly – locals say for eight days every week. And it's so strong it covers houses, whole villages with sand. Next day, the wind blows the other way, and they're all free again. It's the wildest, emptiest part of the whole continent. The Namib desert. What Hottentots call the "Place of No People".'

'Even so, it's the best we can do. If we can tow the ship far enough in, she'll simply ground on the sand. Then they can wade ashore.'

Anna ran down to the cabin, tore off her bathing costume, dried herself hastily and put on her clothes. Then she crammed all her belongings into her bag and was about to leave the cabin when she paused, ripped up the carpet, lifted out the two revolvers O'Grady had left behind. From now on she would be on her own with Shah and O'Grady, and she had strong reservations about both men. She would feel safer if these weapons were in her keeping rather than theirs, but where and how to conceal them? She could not very well tie them to her belt or keep them in her bag where they could easily be discovered.

She looked around the cabin, then saw the tins of fish scales. She prised open the lid of the nearest one, pushed the guns beneath the stinking, luminous mass. Then she carried the tin and her bag up on deck.

Shah threw a line from the bows of the slaver. O'Grady climbed into the torpedo boat to make it fast. *Josephine* moved forward slowly, taking the strain. The thick rope twanged like a gigantic violin string. Hairs burst off its rough hessian surface. Gradually, the waterlogged slaver began to move, slowly and sluggishly at first, then more easily.

As they came within sight of land, they could see a water tower, and the tin roofs of houses behind a high white rim of breaking surf. The slaver grounded gently on the sand, trembled with the strain, and stuck fast. Shah released the rope. O'Grady coiled it up in the stern of the torpedo boat.

The main deck of the slaver was now crowded with slaves, almost naked, many with wrists and ankles raw where their fetters had eaten through flesh. They stared in horror at the thundering waves, then back at Shah.

'That's the south-west shore of Africa,' he told them in their own dialect. 'You can either swim to it and take your chance or you can stay here. I expect the South Africans will send people out to see what's going on and bring you in. Or you can lower the lifeboats and make a dash for it. What ever you decide to do, you will be free.'

One of the slaves addressed him. Shah turned to O'Grady. 'He's asking what we intend to do.'

'We're going off in this boat,' O'Grady told him.

'What if the South African authorities follow us?'

'What if they do? They don't know who we are or where we're going. We'll have a head start on any pursuers. The Portuguese crewmen can go ashore too. I'll open the safe and pay them off before we leave. They can make their way up to one of the Portuguese colonies, Angola or Mozambique. They'll have no problems.'

'The South Africans will find the bodies of the Frenchmen,' Shah pointed out.

'Of course. Maybe they can work out who they were but they'll never know who killed them,' Anna said.

'What about my ship's owners?' asked O'Grady.

'What about them?' replied Anna. 'They'll collect insurance on the vessel. They're most unlikely to come searching for us. And if they did, where would they start looking?'

Shah climbed down the rope ladder while O'Grady manoeuvred *Josephine* against the rusting hull of the slaver. In the last hour the relationship between all three of them had changed subtly but irrevocably. Captain O'Grady was no longer clearly in charge. But who was, Shah or Anna?

'What's your plan?' O'Grady asked now, looking from one to the other, subconsciously accepting his new position. While he captained his ship he was in charge, his word was law. But now he had lost his ship, and with it his automatic right to command.

'We go west,' replied Anna at once. 'First to the Azores. We can refuel there, and then on to the Bahamas, where you were heading with the slaves. Any questions?'

The two men shook their heads. The Bahamas were about as far away from South Africa as they could go, which was prudent – at least until they could decide their next move. The two men glanced at each other, sharing the same thought. This girl was in charge now. She had said what they were going to do, and they had agreed. But how had the transformation occurred, from being virtually a slave to taking command? Had she the stronger character naturally, or had recent experiences weakened theirs?

'One last thing,' said Anna. 'These slaves may stay marooned here for days if no one on shore sees over that surf that the ship is aground. We had better signal their arrival.'

'How do you propose to do that?'

Anna picked up a Very pistol from a wooden cupboard packed with distress flares.

'Set fire to the ship. That's how. That will concentrate the minds of the slaves; and coastguards on shore will see a ship has gone aground, and come to the rescue.'

So it came about that the last view Anna had of the slaver was of a grey ship erupting in a sheet of flame with white breakers behind her and a smaller ship alongside – the enactment of her vision. She thought then that she really must possess the gift of foreseeing events – or at least part of them. But could she ever use this ability to any real advantage and decipher what appeared to be isolated and unconnected scenes?

She could scarcely believe that she had deliberately aimed to wound, perhaps to kill, another human being. But somehow out here, surrounded by open sea, with two men she had no reason to trust, and others clearly determined to kill, values that obtained in a remote and peaceful Scottish village seemed suddenly out of place. Paradoxically, although she felt she should also be out of place, she knew that she wasn't, that somehow she was in charge and would stay that way.

Anna watched Shah cut the torpedo boat adrift. His action had a symbolism that brought her back to reality. It was as though Shah's knife had also cut her links with the past. Now, all that concerned her lay ahead. If life was going to be harsh and tough, then she would learn to cope. Later, there might be time for reappraisal, maybe even for regret. But that time was not yet.

With O'Grady at the wheel, they turned out towards the open sea. Gradually, the outline of the slaver, grey against breaking waves, with a pall of black smoke spiralling upwards, diminished and disappeared.

Anna turned to O'Grady.

'Switch off the engines,' she told him. 'There's something I want to make clear before we sail any further.'

Shah came out of the cabin, and the two men stood staring at her, puzzled and uneasy.

'How much money have you in your safe?' Anna asked O'Grady bluntly.

'About five hundred pounds sterling,' he replied. 'Why?'

'We will probably need all that to buy fuel and stores in

the Azores and Bermuda. Do you have sufficient charts in the locker to cross the Atlantic?'

'I have checked them out,' O'Grady told her. 'Those Frenchmen had enough to sail round the world. The only trouble is, everything is written in French, but I think I can cope with that. What do we do when we reach the Bahamas?'

'We'll decide when we do,' Anna replied enigmatically, for she had no idea herself. Her basic instinct was to put as much distance between them and what had happened. The Bahamas seemed the most logical destination.

'Fewer questions are going to be asked about us over there than in South Africa. Now, our first priority is to change the name of this boat. We can't continue as *Josephine*. A search party might fly out and see us. And *Clarissa* is equally impossible – if that is a real Admiralty name.'

'What do you suggest?' Shah asked her.

'What one of the Portuguese sailors said when he saw land just now, and he knew he was safe. *Boa Vista* – a good view.'

'Strange name for a ship,' commented O'Grady.

'Strange ship,' Anna retorted.

'I'll paint it on the bows,' said Shah quickly. He did not want any argument. 'I've found some tools and paints and brushes in the engine room.'

'Start now,' Anna told him. 'We have no time to lose.'

'What flag do you suggest we fly?'

'American,' replied Anna. 'Anything European, and the Royal Navy might decide to have a look at us.'

'I'll go along with that,' said O'Grady approvingly. 'But how come you are so full of ideas?'

'I don't know,' Anna admitted. 'But I do think they're right – unless either of you have any other proposals?'

The two men shook their heads. What Anna said made

total sense, and neither felt in a strong enough position to argue. One had a price on his head and the other had abandoned a slave ship of which he was captain. One day, both could face questions they might not care to answer.

'Now, as to quarters,' said Anna. 'I will take the forward cabin. You two have the aft cabin. I propose we split our watches, three hours on, six off.'

'Can you steer a ship?' O'Grady asked her doubtfully.

'If you set the compass and tell me the error of drift, yes.'

While Shah hastily painted over the torpedo boat's name and stencilled in *Boa Vista*, Anna went into the cabin. She emptied all the drawers, sifted through clothes the French leader had worn. Each had his name tag, Pierre Montagne, or his initials sewn on it. She took them out, handed them to Shah and O'Grady.

Within half an hour, they were on their way. Anna checked the provisions and brewed a huge pot of coffee. She took a mug to O'Grady. Afterwards Shah followed her into the cabin.

'I would like to see you alone,' he said nervously.

'About what?' She still felt hostility and distrust towards him, but it would be unwise to show this. They could not afford to fall out until they reached the Bahamas, if then. Also, he had saved her life when her revolver refused to fire.

'I want to say I'm truly sorry for what happened in Mamora,' Shah explained awkwardly. 'Words aren't much use, I know, so I have something I would like to give you just to show how bitterly I regret it.'

'What's that?' asked Anna.

He unclenched his right hand. In the palm a diamond glittered.

'Drummond had this,' he explained. 'I know it's real, and it's the only thing of value I've got. It's what you in the

West might call a kind of peace offering. Please accept it.'

Anna put out her hand. She recognised the stone as the one she had given to Drummond. She wondered how it had come into Shah's possession, but this did not seem the moment to ask.

'Thank you,' she said. More of her dislike receded. It was always easy to blame other people for events that harmed you, and probably Shah had only acted in self-preservation, as he claimed. She might have done the same in his situation.

'Let's call it quits, then,' she said.

They shook hands.

'Thank you.'

Anna still did not like him, but the hatred had gone, leaving a void. She really felt nothing towards him. Hatred, even distrust, was a luxury none of them could afford on a trip across the Atlantic in a small boat in midwinter.

In the Azores, and again in Bermuda, they refuelled, took on more provisions and water. Thereafter, the weather steadily grew warmer and the sea calmer. They were sailing into Caribbean sunshine, but hundreds of miles to the north-west, in New York, winter was still at its height.

That night, 16 January 1920, and every night during the previous week, the temperature there stayed relentlessly below twenty degrees. A driving wind lifted clouds of powdered snow from sidewalks and blew them away like frozen fog. But now, despite the cold and the lateness of the hour, every street was crowded with cars and trucks. Horses pulled heavy carts; men pushed wheelbarrows; women hurried with prams. All seemed oblivious of the Arctic conditions. The streets of nearly every other city in the United States were equally crowded. It was as though a bitter January night had suddenly been turned into the busiest day anyone could remember.

Most of the cars and trucks contained only a driver; all were so heavily laden that their springs had flattened under the weight they carried. Wooden crates and cardboard boxes were piled in car luggage boots, on the seats, in prams and push chairs. They contained bottles, packed by the dozen, the score, the hundred. Millions of dollars worth of whisky, gin, brandy, wine and beer were on the move in the United States that midnight.

All through the previous day and evening, more loads, equally heavy, had been hurried from bars, liquor stores, and warehouses to people's homes, garages, lock-ups. People were not taking them to celebrate the three hundredth anniversary of the landing of the Pilgrim Fathers, but to mark an historic happening of quite a different kind. Unbelievably, this was the last night when it would be legal for anyone in the United States to buy a beer at a bar, to order wine with a meal in a restaurant, or even to sip a sherry in front of their own fireside, and no one could say when, if ever, this law would be rescinded.

After midnight, the Eighteenth Amendment to the American Constitution was due to come into force. From then on, any person found possessing alcoholic drink anywhere in the United States would be liable, as a first offender, to a fine of one thousand dollars and six months' imprisonment. Subsequent offences would bring higher punishments. The Eighteenth Amendment specifically prohibited the manufacture, transportation, import or export, sale or consumption of what the law described as 'intoxicating liquors'.

Congressman Andrew Volstead, a prosecuting lawyer in Minnesota – a 'dry' state before Prohibition – had proposed this law which thereafter bore his name. 'Intoxicating liquors' were defined as any beverage that contained more than one half of one per cent alcohol.

Those who regretted the onset of Prohibition were largely in towns and cities and of Irish, Italian or Jewish descent. They came from countries where drinking beer or wine was as commonplace as a glass of water or milk. They were known as 'wets'. That night they conducted macabre ceremonies of their own to mark the moment.

In New York, the Park Avenue Hotel staged a mock funeral for John Barleycorn. Waitresses wore black dresses, and guests sat at tables covered with black crepe cloths. In a restaurant in Upper Manhattan, the Irish proprietors held a solemn wake, and gave each customer a miniature casket to keep as a memento of this night. Estimates as to how long Prohibition would last – could last – ranged from a matter of days to years.

The 'drys', mostly from small towns and villages, gathered in churches all through the evening to give thanks for the defeat of what they called the Demon Rum. They and their forebears had fought for nearly two centuries to ban all alcoholic drink. They could not let this moment of victory pass without celebration. The Anti-Saloon League issued a special statement: 'At one minute past twelve tomorrow morning a new nation will be born . . . Now for an era of clear thinking and clean living. The Anti-Saloon League wishes every man and woman and child a Happy Dry Year.'

Early American colonists, in the seventeenth and eighteenth centuries, would not have subscribed widely to these sentiments. They frequently drank excessively, choosing beer, rum, wine and cider. They claimed that alcohol helped to purify bad water or contaminated milk, and indeed such drinks were often cheaper than imported tea or coffee. By the nineteenth century, some physicians and ministers of religion began to voice concern at increasing instances of drunkenness and heavy drinking. They believed that this habit would lead to poverty, immorality and disease, and urged people to be more temperate. Employers added their views. Workers who drank heavily were poor time-keepers, and with increasingly complicated machinery being used in factories, they were more likely to injure themselves than employees who did not drink alcohol.

The temperance movement grew steadily, and gradually came to mean not simply less drinking but no drinking at all. Finally, its leaders demanded total prohibition of all alcoholic drinks.

By the second half of the nineteenth century a dozen states passed prohibition laws. In the early twentieth century, saloons became a focus of criticism. Many abolitionists felt that if alcoholic drinks could be banned completely, large numbers of new immigrants pouring into the country – Irish, Italians, Middle European Jews – might then become what they called more 'American' in their outlook. Under this pressure, more states passed what were known as 'local option laws'. These gave them the right to ban the sale of alcoholic drinks within their borders. A law was also passed forbidding the shipment of alcohol from a wet state into a dry one.

When the United States entered the Great War in 1917, many felt that Prohibition should be adopted as a patriotic gesture. Sober soldiers and workers were obviously preferable to drunken soldiers and workers. Also, it was claimed that grain could be put to better use making bread rather than whisky. Lastly, anything identified with Germany instantly became unpopular, and many of the country's most famous breweries and distilleries had been founded by German immigrants and still traded under German names. There was also a vague but widespread feeling that after the war the world would somehow be a cleaner, happier, friendlier place. In such a dream, drunkenness clearly had no part.

The Senate passed the Eighteenth Amendment after only thirteen hours of debate. The House of Representatives ratified it after one day's consideration, and so the law came into force.

That January midnight, while no one knew how long Prohibition would remain, very few could foresee the totally unexpected consequences it would bring, not only in the United States, but worldwide. And as Anna, Shah and O'Grady headed into the welcome sunshine of a new Caribbean morning, none of them imagined how this American law would totally change their own lives.

'We should make land by nine o'clock local time,' O'Grady told Anna. 'I'm heading straight for Nassau, which has a good harbour.'

Anna nodded, picked up a set of earphones, handed a second set to O'Grady. She turned on the radio and began to turn the heavy Bakelite controls, hoping to pick up a news broadcast. Throughout their voyage from South-West Africa up to the Azores, then on to Bermuda, voices and music, at first from Europe, and then from powerful transmitters along the eastern coast of the United States had helped to diminish their sense of loneliness and insecurity. They felt they were not simply two men and a woman in a tiny boat tossed by huge Atlantic waves. The radio was their link with both worlds, old and new. It gave them confidence that in any emergency they could call other ships in the area to come to their aid. Also, they hoped that news of the slaver grounded off the Namibian coast might be broadcast and give perhaps a hint of what investigations the South African authorities might be making. But so far they had heard nothing about it.

Static squealed and hissed, and then Anna heard the American accents of a newscaster. His voice rose and fell, distorted by distance. Sometimes it was a hoarse shout, then it diminished to a strained whisper.

'New York. One o'clock in the morning,' he announced. 'Prohibition is exactly one hour old and how's God's own country reacting to a ban on all beers, wines and spirits? Two items may hold an early clue. First, Chicago. Here, just after midnight, six masked and armed men drove a heavy truck into a railway freight yard. They tied up the yardmaster and the night watchman. One bandit then held six men at pistol point, while his colleagues piled crates of whisky, valued at a total of one hundred thousand dollars, from two box cars into their truck.

'The whole incident only took twenty-five minutes. By the time the night watchman struggled free and raised the alarm, the truck and its cargo were – who knows where? For where, in a country suddenly gone dry, can hoodlums ever hope to sell so much whisky?

'Late last evening three ships sailed out of Baltimore harbour, bound for Nassau in the Bahamas, their holds packed with whisky which the owners knew they could not sell here. Their cargo is worth at least five and a half million dollars. If the ships had not sailed, all this whisky would have been impounded.

'So, while we in the States say goodbye to the chance of a whisky on the rocks, down south in the sunny Bahamas will they be saying hello to the greatest party ever?'

Anna switched off the set, removed her earphones.

O'Grady opened a cupboard beneath the set, took out a bottle of whisky, poured two fingers into a tin mug.

As he did so, she noticed the label, Long Glen, and at once she remembered her vision of one bottle of that whisky, then two, a score, hundreds. In that instant, Anna knew what the future held.

'Makes me thirsty just thinking you can't get a drink anywhere right across the States, coast to coast,' O'Grady remarked thoughtfully as he drank. 'It's hard to believe that's really the case. They must be mad. They'll never stop people drinking – even in their own homes.'

'Agreed,' said Anna. 'So how will that affect us?'

'Not at all, as far as I can see. Why should it? We're heading for the Bahamas. They're not dry there. Nor are they ever likely to be.'

'Exactly. Those three ships are also bound for Nassau. What goes up must come down. That's a basic law of nature. I say, now, what goes out must also come back.'

'I don't get you,' said O'Grady, frowning. What the hell did she mean? He poured himself more whisky.

'Give me a dram and I'll explain,' Anna told him patiently.

Anna stood by the porthole in her cabin, peering through salt-encrusted glass as the shore of New Providence Island came slowly into focus. Half a dozen small sailing boats, sails furled, bobbed in the lapis-lazuli water of Nassau harbour. Beyond them, she could see three cargo ships flying the American flag. These must be the steamers the American broadcaster had mentioned.

Behind the harbour stood a rash of white buildings with red tiled roofs, then a hill. This was crowned by a pink-washed colonial house, surrounded by palm trees. The

Union flag drooped from a white mast. This was Government House. To its right were more long buildings, more palms, then a long white beach with breakers pounding it – Cable Beach, according to the charts.

She turned away from the porthole, relieved to be near shore at last.

'The quay is dead ahead,' O'Grady reported. 'I'm going to bring her alongside.'

'As soon as we dock, we'll need to get some money,' Anna told him. 'We've used all we had in the safe to buy fuel in the Azores and Bermuda.'

'How do you propose to raise more?' O'Grady asked her.

'From a bank. That's their business, money.'

'Why should they give you any money without security? You going to pledge the *Boa Vista* for a loan?'

Anna shook her head. 'I've a better idea,' she replied enigmatically.

She went into the cabin, opened the bar of soap with a knife, removed the diamonds, wrapped them in a twist of tissue paper. Then she came up on deck and stood, feet braced against the slight roll of the vessel, as O'Grady brought her expertly alongside huge wads of coiled and knotted rope that hung from the stone quay to prevent paint being scratched.

From a small office, not much bigger than a telephone booth, the harbour master watched them arrive. The office contained a desk, a chair, a telephone and a Lloyd's List of Shipping. He focused his binoculars on the name, *Boa Vista*. Portuguese. A good view. Of what? he wondered.

Joe Garcia was a half-caste Bahamian with yellowish skin and black, bristly hair. He skimmed through the List but could not find any vessel registered under this name.

Was she simply one of the boats that since Prohibition were coming in every day from Florida? Most were not registered anywhere. Many were just fun craft, with drums of petrol lashed on their decks in case they ran short of fuel on the journey. All had the same aim: to collect crates of whisky and rum and carry them back to sell illegally in the States.

Garcia closed the book. Carefully locking the door behind him, he walked down the quay. Captain O'Grady, recognising authority, gave him a vaguely nautical salute.

'Sean O'Grady,' he said. 'We've just arrived from Bermuda.'

'Harbour master. Joe Garcia. On vacation?'

'Sort of. Also looking for part-time work – fishing, any kind of thing.'

'Doesn't look like a fishing boat to me,' said Garcia doubtfully. 'You've no swivel seats. You need those. Sportsmen want to be strapped in, you know. They're all rich men – too rich to be pulled into the sea by a big grouper.'

'I guess you're right. But we're strangers here. It's our first time in the Bahamas.'

Anna came and stood beside O'Grady, nodded a greeting to the harbour master.

Garcia looked her up and down appreciatively, and then turned back to O'Grady.

'How are you going to pay the dues?'

'When do you want them?'

'Like now. In advance. You have an arrangement with a bank here?'

'Not yet. But my colleague here, Miss Anna Ballater, is going to tie that up.'

'What bank you dealing with?'

O'Grady shrugged, unwilling to admit he had no idea. Anna stayed silent.

'Any one you particularly recommend?' O'Grady asked.

'I've always found the Bank of World Indemnity gives you a square deal. Mention my name. Say I sent you. Meantime, we'd like cash up front.'

'You can have it soon as we get it. What does a week's mooring cost?'

'Hundred dollars. US. Twenty pounds sterling.'

'That's pretty high for a little boat like this.'

'That's the going rate. Take it or leave it.'

'We'll take it, then, since we have to.'

'Come up to my office and we'll do the paperwork. Got your ship's papers handy?'

'As a matter of fact, no.'

'Where are they?'

'We ran into bad weather, got swamped. They went over the side.'

Garcia nodded understandingly. He did not believe the excuse; it was one he heard almost every day from new arrivals like this. Either that, or they'd left the papers at home, or maybe they'd somehow burned them by mistake. What did it matter, really, as long as he got the money? Half went to him and half to the Nassau Port Authority. Fifty dollars a time each way. It was better than working, but peanuts compared to what these little boats could make running liquor up to Florida. You had to look after yourself. No one else ever stepped forward to help you. But maybe he'd also lever himself into the big time one day.

Anna watched O'Grady follow the harbour master to his office. Shah joined her.

'I'll stay aboard,' he told Anna. 'It isn't wise to leave the vessel unmanned.'

'I'll be back as soon as I can,' Anna promised.

She walked along the edge of the harbour, past sailing boats and motor cruisers, and a pyramid of conch shells, stinking in the sun. A string of donkey carts headed for the quay where the cargo vessels were anchored. This instantly reminded her of her first view of the docks in Mamora, and she shuddered at the memory of what had happened afterwards. Each cart was heavily loaded with bulky packages encased in covers of plaited straw.

From the harbour she walked along Bay Street, the widest and richest street in Nassau. It stretched from the Yacht Club and the harbour to the British Colonial Hotel. The pavement was uneven, and every few yards pillars supported tiled roofs built to shield pedestrians from tropical sun and rainstorms. Some pillars bore hooks where, in earlier days, horses had been tied.

Cars moved slowly, as though to show off their beautifully polished paintwork. Black Bahamian chauffeurs wore smart white starched uniforms with peaked caps. Behind them sat the owner or a lady out to do her morning shopping.

Above the shops were offices, and through open windows Anna heard a busy click-clack of typewriters. Black-painted doors blocked off staircases leading between shop fronts to the upper rooms. The doors carried the names of companies, each neatly painted in gold script – merchants of various kinds, lawyers, accountants, agents.

She came upon a row of banks at the far end of Bay Street, where a statue of Queen Victoria in white stone looked across a dried stretch of grass, and ancient cannon pointed empty metal mouths to the sea. The smell of sewage was strong. Black land crabs scuttled up an alley-way on scaly, rasping claws. She shuddered. Like the conch shells by the harbour, they pointed to another more unsavoury side of Nassau.

Gilded signs hung over the pavement, like signs outside old-fashioned English taverns. The Bank of World Indemnity had one of the largest. She passed it, walked to the end of the street and then back again, suddenly and unexpectedly nervous. She had never met a bank manager. Now she was arriving without any introduction, without knowing anyone, to make a business proposition to a total stranger. What if he refused to help her?

As Anna paused irresolute, a woman of about her own age, wearing a wide-brimmed straw hat to shield her fair skin from the sun and carrying a huge and expensive alligator-skin handbag, came out of the bank. She raised a hand and snapped her fingers imperiously. An open Buick that had been parked a few yards down the road now moved towards her. The uniformed driver jumped out, opened the rear door, bowed deeply as the woman climbed in.

I must teach myself to look like that, poised, confident, Anna told herself. If she can do it, so can I – and much better. She pushed open the swing door and went into the entrance hall.

It had a polished wooden floor, a long wooden counter. Brass rails edged frosted glass partitions to provide each client with some measure of privacy. Three Americans were drawing out wads of dollar bills at the far end. They were chewing gum. One ran a thumbnail expertly through the bills as though they were cards. He put them in his back pocket, looked up and winked at Anna.

'Hiya, kid,' he said easily. He had very dark hair, a sallow face. But what struck her most forcibly about him were his eyes. They seemed cold, without feeling, like the eyes of a dead fish.

'Hello,' she replied, surprised at the greeting. This must be the way they did things here and in the States, she thought; all free and easy, everyone friendly. The thought cheered her. She approached the nearest teller.

'I would like to see the manager,' she told him.

The clerk was a young man in a white jacket with a nervous face, greasy, spiky hair. 'You have an appointment, madam?' he asked her.

'No. I would like to see him about opening an account.'

'I could do that for you here.'

'I'm sure,' she said. 'But I would still like to see him. I have an introduction from Mr Garcia, the harbour master.'

'Would you please wait a moment?'

The clerk walked along behind the counter, through a side door. Anna waited, drumming her fingers on the counter, hoping she looked as confident as the woman who had driven away in the car. What if the manager wouldn't see her? The clerk returned, beckoned to her.

'If you will just come to the end of the counter, madam,' he said, 'Mr Rettini will see you now.'

Anna walked to the end of the counter. A door opened in the facing wall. A plump, balding man stood in the doorway, regarding her.

'I am the manager,' he said. 'Mr Rettini.'

'Anna Ballater. Miss. Could I see you privately for a moment?'

'Please come in.'

Rettini led the way into a small office. The ceiling fan was not working, and the air felt flat and dusty. The window had a horizontal slatted blind against the sun, which even at this hour of the morning was strong. Rettini indicated a seat. Anna sat down.

'Mr Garcia advised me to come to this bank,' she

explained. 'I want to open an account.'

'That will be my pleasure. You have money or securities you wish to put into it?'

'Neither, I am sorry to say.'

'No? Then how would you wish the account to operate?' Rettini asked her gently, eyebrows slightly raised as he looked at her. She was pretty, sure enough, but she seemed a little nervous, a little unsure of herself. Was she a new front woman for rum runners he did not know?

Anna took the twist of paper from her pocket, unfolded it on the manager's desk. The diamonds glittered.

'I have these,' she said. 'I will put these in as security, until money starts to arrive.'

'They are real diamonds?'

'They are.'

'Do you know how much they are worth?'

'I have no idea. You would have to value them here.'

'Where did they come from, if I may ask?'

'From a friend,' Anna replied. 'A man friend.'

'I see. I'm not a valuer myself, as you will appreciate. But I can have them valued for you very quickly. A jeweller here in town would do it. He would charge you a fee, naturally.'

'Based on what? The time he takes, the value he gives, or their real worth, which would probably be much more?'

The manager's eyes narrowed. This girl might be young but she was no fool.

'Usually he bases his fee on his valuation.'

'As a buyer or a seller?'

'That I really don't know, Miss Ballater. You'd have to ask him yourself.'

'When can I do that?'

'Almost immediately – if he's in his shop.'

The manager picked up the telephone, jiggled the rest impatiently until the operator answered. He asked for a number, and sat, the way people do when waiting for a line, with nothing to say, yet feeling they should say something. Anna heard a man's voice. The manager's face brightened.

'I've someone in here with some diamonds to value,' he explained. 'Do you think you could come round? It shouldn't take very long . . . Thank you.' He turned to Anna as he replaced the receiver. 'He'll be here directly,' he explained.

The jeweller was a fat, lugubrious man with a Dutch accent. He looked at Anna closely, his small eyes hanging critical price tags on her clothes. He did not ask her name, and the bank manager did not introduce them. The jeweller took out a magnifying glass from an inner pocket, breathed on both lenses, wiped them carefully with a silk handkerchief, put the glass in his eye and examined the diamonds.

'They're quite good,' he admitted grudgingly.

'I know,' Anna replied. 'But what are they worth?'

'It's difficult to sell uncut diamonds right now, though things may improve, for we expect more American tourists. With Prohibition, they'll come south for sunshine and a drink – we hope.'

'How much would you give for them?'

'The lot? Fifteen hundred pounds sterling. Now. In your hand.'

'That means they must be worth rather more.'

'Only if I can find a buyer. It's one thing buying, and another thing selling, as you know. I may have them on my hands for months. Anything is only worth what someone will pay for it. All that money tied up, losing interest.'

Anna paused for a moment, as though giving the matter

thought, although she had already decided what to do. She turned to Rettini.

'If I let you keep these diamonds as security, Mr Rettini, would you allow me credit for fifteen hundred pounds?'

The two men exchanged quick glances. The jeweller gave an almost imperceptible nod.

'Yes, I would,' said the bank manager. 'Of course, any money you borrow will attract interest at two per cent over base rate. That's five per cent total now. Non-reducing. For a three-month period, in the first instance.'

'Then I'll open an account here and now.'

The manager turned to the jeweller. 'What is your fee, so the lady can settle up now?'

'Two and a half per cent of my valuation. Thirty-seven pounds ten shillings.'

'Please pay the money out of my overdraft of fifteen hundred pounds,' she told the manager.

'Right,' said Rettini. 'Now, if you'd care to sign these forms, madam, which I think you'll find in order – really only a formality – I'll issue you with a cheque book.'

'How long will that take?'

'You can collect it this time tomorrow. Or we can deliver it to your hotel.'

'I've just arrived by boat and I need money. I have two companions with me. We are not staying in a hotel.'

'There are no tourist ships in,' said the jeweller pointedly.

'We came in our own vessel, the *Boa Vista*.'

'Where from?'

'Bermuda. We need money for fuel and other expenses, harbour dues, and so on. Could I withdraw money to the extent of this security now?'

'I'd like you to retain, say, two hundred or so in the account just to keep it alive, and service the loan meantime.'

'Thank you.'

'Don't thank me, Miss Ballater. I must thank Mr Garcia for suggesting you called. I wish all my transactions were as simple.'

Nine

O'Grady sat on a bollard on the edge of the harbour, thankful to be back on dry land and feeling the sun warm through his thin shirt. He hoped that some likely cabin boy or messenger would stroll by, and they could make contact. But he had to be very careful how he did it, what he said. If the lad wasn't amenable and his approach was crude and unmistakably sexual, he could be in deep trouble. He had made mistakes before in London and New York; he had managed to escape charges of importuning but only by bribing policemen. He could not expect to be so lucky every time.

As he sat, he watched two men in shorts working on the engine of a big cruiser moored about twenty feet away. Every now and then they started the motor. It would run lumpily for a moment, then backfire and stop. Each time, a cloud of blue smoke blew out of the exhaust. They did not seem to be making much progress, but were clearly in a hurry to repair whatever the fault might be.

O'Grady heard footsteps, turned round. The harbour master was standing behind him, rolling a cigarette, watching him, gauging his man.

'Those boys have sure got trouble,' Garcia said conversationally.

O'Grady nodded.

'So it seems. Who are they?'

'Americans. They've blown a gasket. They're trying to

cobble it up without taking off the cylinder head. They'll never do it. I've told 'em that, but they know it all. They've poured all kinds of rubbish into the cooling system to try and stop the leak, but water's still getting into the cylinder. It's *kaput*, my friend.'

'They seem in a hurry.'

'Know why?'

'Tell me.'

Garcia lit his cigarette, puffed on it vigorously until he was certain the tobacco was burning strongly. He was enjoying his moment of importance.

'See those three steamers out there? They've come down with millions of dollars worth of booze from Baltimore. If they hadn't shifted it, the whole damn lot would have been seized, like as not poured down the drain. Criminal. And do you know where it's going now?'

'No idea. Where?'

'Right back there.'

O'Grady remembered Anna's words after she had heard the radio broadcast from New York, but he gave no indication he knew anything about Prohibition.

'Why, if it's just been thrown out?' he asked innocently.

'Because it's going to be smuggled in. That's why those guys are working their butts off to get that engine going. If they can't, everyone here with an available motor boat will be called in to help shift that cargo. There's a fortune in each trip for everyone who makes it. So most of our boats are involved.'

'What do you mean by a fortune?'

'Depends how much booze your boat can carry, that's the only limiting factor. Looking at yours, I reckon you could shift fifteen hundred cases easily.'

'A lot of cases.'

'Sure. And you've quite a journey to New York – about eight hundred miles. You'd need barrels of fuel strapped to the deck so you don't have to stop to fill up on the way. Too goddamn risky to do that with Revenue cutters prowling around.'

'Where else are the boats going?'

'Florida. That's under two hundred miles. But if you want to make the real money, you head for New York.'

'What are the snags?'

'That they catch you red-handed with the booze. The Yanks can board you, impound your boat, and then jail you. And they will, for you've no defence whatever if you're caught with that cargo.'

'I'm not an American subject.'

'That doesn't matter a damn. You're violating American law. On the other hand, the cutter that intercepted you might have an amenable crew. They could be Irish, or at least have Irish names, like yours, Captain. Then you could cross their captain's hand with silver – a lot of silver, like the gypsy said – and you might be free. Or you might not. That's the gamble. Of course, you might then face a far bigger sentence for trying to bribe a Revenue officer. Or they might pocket your bribe and still turn you in.'

'I don't fancy ending up in a United States penitentiary on a smuggling rap. What's the other side of the medal – if we're not caught?'

'On each case you make ten dollars profit. Clear. Fifteen hundred cases, fifteen thousand bucks, with a small commission to me for putting things your way.'

'Like how small?'

'Two dollars a case.'

'And who pays me?'

'The fellow who organises it here. When you deliver

there. He's of Italian background, or Sicilian. We call him Bill Castle.'

'What did his mother call him?'

'Maybe Giuseppe Castiglione. I don't know and I don't want to know. That's nothing to do with us here, so let's keep it that way. Mr Castle likes to quote an old proverb, "The man who sees nothing, hears nothing, says nothing, lives for a hundred years in peace".'

'He talks sense, this Mr Castle. You trust him?'

'Captain, my old mother told me, trust no one. An honest man has hair growing in the palm of his hand, she said. And that's a two-sided question you ask, for can Castle trust you? You might take off with the booze, flog it yourself. But I wouldn't advise that.'

'I wouldn't do that,' said O'Grady.

'Of course not. I just told you because one or two have done just that. Thought they'd be smart.'

'And were they?'

Garcia shrugged. 'They don't come round here any more, that's for sure, so I can't ask them. They just sort of disappeared.'

'How would Castle know if anyone did that?'

'There are only so many people buying at the other end. Many of those had Italian mothers, too. It's a small parish. You follow me?'

'I'm beginning to. I'll think about it.'

'Don't think too long. Those guys will never get that motor going. But if others hear that and offer to help out with the cargo, there's your first deal gone. You get your foot in now. If Mr Castle likes you and you deliver on time, you could end up a rich man.'

'Or in jail.'

'Sure. And those Revenue guys aren't idiots. They'll

have bigger boats soon. Some already carry one-pounder guns that could blow you out of the water.'

'You make it sound an attractive job.'

'The job's crap,' retorted Garcia, throwing away the stub of his cigarette. 'It's the profit that's attractive.' He turned. 'I see your lady friend approaching. How did you get on at the bank?' he asked Anna. 'You went to the one I suggested?'

'Of course. And they let me have some money. Mr Rettini was pleased you'd remembered him.'

'You must have great powers of persuasion if he lends you money so quickly,' said Garcia, clearly impressed.

Anna smiled. 'Now, we want to fill our fuel tanks right up to the top. How do we go about that?'

'I'll arrange it,' said the harbour master, and left them together.

O'Grady told Anna about Garcia's proposition.

'That fits in with what I said when I heard about Prohibition on the wireless,' she replied. 'You trust him?'

'No,' O'Grady admitted. 'But there's money in it for him. Two dollars a case. Three thousand dollars for doing nothing except have a chat, make a suggestion. He runs no risk. We do.'

'Let's speak to this Mr Castle before we decide. He's the prime mover. Can you arrange a meeting through the talkative harbour master?'

That evening, O'Grady, Anna, Mr Castle and Joe Garcia met in the bar of the British Colonial Hotel. Shah stayed on board the *Boa Vista*. They sat on a terrace hung with coloured lights, overlooking the ocean. Anna recognised Mr Castle at once; he was the man she had seen counting dollar bills in the bank. Close to, he looked older than he had seemed across the entrance hall. His chin was blue, as though he had shaved only an hour ago, and would need another shave very soon. His eyes still fascinated her. No, that was the wrong word. They frightened her.

'I've had a look at your boat,' he said. 'She should make the distance all right.'

'I should hope so,' said O'Grady. 'We crossed the Atlantic in her.'

'Thought you came from Bermuda?'

'We did.'

'And before that?'

'South Africa,' Anna said vaguely.

'I see. Well, Joe here has told you the terms. Are you on or not? One boat we had hoped would take some of the stuff is a non-starter – like that big cruiser with the crappy motor. All the rest of the cargo has been shared out. There's just one load left.'

'How do we get rid of it at the other end?'

'Easy. I'm not putting all this into New York after all. We've had a bit of trouble there. The Revenue guys have to pick on a few vessels, just to show they're not entirely in our pocket, though in fact most of them are. We're going to land the cargo at the mouth of St Catherine's Sound in Georgia. I'll have a lighter there, ready for you to transfer everything.'

'How will you get up there before us? The *Boa Vista* doesn't hang around. She's got two big engines. She was a torpedo boat in the war.'

'Is that right? Even so, I'll beat her this trip. I'll fly up by seaplane.'

'When do we get paid?' Anna asked him.

'When we meet. In dollar bills, or as you want it. Any currency you like.'

'What happens if things go wrong?'

'That's your affair.'

'But say your seaplane couldn't take off or something. Or you had bad weather or engine trouble, and you couldn't meet us.'

'Then someone else will. I'll deal with all that. No problem. Now, are you on or not? Yes or no?'

'On one condition, yes,' said Anna.

'What's that?'

'I understand Mr Garcia here takes two dollars a case.'

'Sure. Agent's fee. Without him you wouldn't have a deal.'

'Agreed, but without us nor would he – or you, Mr Castle. So put his cut on top of our ten. Then we get ten clear as he said. Fifteen thousand dollars in our hand. He gets his share on top of that, not out of that.'

'You drive a hard deal, ma'am. There are plenty of skippers down here would take it for ten dollars a case, not twelve.'

'Then why don't you get one?'

'You know why. We're stuck at the moment. I'll offer you eleven.'

'Twelve.'

Mr Castle picked up a bread roll, tore it viciously in half. He looked out at the sea, bright red and green and yellow under the fairy lights.

'All right,' he said at last. 'This time, as we're pushed, twelve it is. But remember, we can also drive a hard deal. So make sure you're there on time. No excuses. No engine failure, storms, illness or crap of that kind. OK?'

Anna nodded. 'OK,' she agreed.

The night was cold and stormy. Mountains of water mushroomed off the tossing deck and streamed back into the sea. Against the *Boa Vista*'s windscreen, with its wiper busy as a metronome, the wind threw rattling spears of rain. O'Grady looked up at Anna from his charts, while Shah busied himself at the ship's controls.

'According to my calculations, we're just outside the twenty-mile limit,' he said. 'And we're keeping there. If we go in any closer we run the risk of a Revenue cutter catching us.'

'In this weather?'

'Especially in this weather. Castle should be looking out for us, so I'll give him a signal and see how he reacts – if he can see it.'

O'Grady picked up a long wooden pole to which were bolted four chromium spot lamps, which Castle had told him he had bought from a car accessory shop in New York. O'Grady clipped a coloured lens over each one, red, then green, then two more red. He went up on deck, and steadying himself against the side of the cabin, held up the pole. Anna connected wires from the lamps to a plug on the boat's dashboard. Green and red beams shone out eerily across the heaving sea.

If a Revenue cutter approached and hailed them to find out what they were doing, they could hastily unclip the coloured lenses and throw them overboard. They would then be left with four harmless bright lights on a pole. Their explanation was that they were holding this over the side of the vessel to dazzle fish and so make larger catches more certain, a ploy popular among local fishermen.

But in this storm, with wind whipping the sea into long, curling waves, no Revenue cutter could be seen. At O'Grady's signal, Anna switched off the lights. Above the roar of the wind he had heard an outboard motor approaching. A small speedboat with Castle and two men aboard came alongside, bobbing up and then diving deep down in the troughs between waves as her pilot strove to keep her close to the *Boa Vista* without dashing against the much larger vessel.

'We can't unload out here!' Castle shouted through a megaphone. 'Too rough.'

'But if we go inshore we can be picked up,' O'Grady shouted back.

'I've fixed that,' Castle assured him. 'Follow me.'

O'Grady climbed down into the *Boa Vista*'s cockpit. 'You heard what he said. At the worst, I suppose we can dump the whisky over the side before anyone tries to board us. I'm not going to be caught and jailed on my first run.'

'It won't come to that,' Anna replied. 'Castle's in this for a living. He won't take any risks himself. He's not the heroic type.'

They crossed the harbour bar, where breakers, yellow with sand, spumed and thundered and then, through a shallower sea, they came into St Catherine's Sound. Here, the sea was much calmer. Two barges without lights appeared out of the gloom, led by Castle's motorboat. Hooks held the *Boa Vista* closely to the nearest barge as shadowy figures transferred the cargo. No one spoke. The men from the barges worked silently and swiftly. As Anna watched them, she saw red and green lights coming closer. A coastguard cutter was approaching. She could make out a glimmer of light from the vessel's cabin, and her mouth went dry with dismay. They were trapped, caught, with no way out and crates of whisky already piled in the hold of the barge.

The cutter came within feet of them. She heard the beat of her engine grow louder and louder, and then suddenly the noise diminished until their only memory of the vessel was the smell of exhaust fumes blown by the wind.

'She *must* have seen us,' she said to Castle in amazement.

'Of course she did. But I told you, I fixed it. The crew saw nothing.'

'You do this every time?'

'Most times,' he admitted. 'Those crews can have very bad eyesight – except when it comes to counting dollar bills. I must be away now, but first I'll settle up what I owe you.' He took a waterproof pouch from an inner pocket of his jacket. 'Fifteen thousand dollars,' he said, 'in one thousand dollar bills. Fifteen big ones. Count them.'

O'Grady did so. 'Thank you,' he said.

'Where are you folk heading now?' Castle asked him.

'Back to Nassau.'

'You hope to pick up another consignment there?'

'If there is one, yes. This seemed pretty straightforward, and where else, how else, can we make so much so easily?'

'There's a risk, of course,' Castle replied. 'See the harbour master. He's not doing you any favours. He's helping himself, remember, so he'll look out something for you. I may be back there before you. Or again, I may not. It all depends. I have some other business commitments here and in New York. So now, if not goodbye, until we meet again.'

He climbed down into the speedboat. The engine crackled and the boat disappeared into the mist, the sound of her engine fading into the rumble of distant surf and the rain's steady drumming.

'We'd better get back ourselves,' said Anna.

It seemed an anticlimax, almost impossible to accept that the three of them could be returning with a profit of fifteen thousand dollars – three thousand pounds sterling. And to think that she had worked for a whole year in

Scotland for fifty pounds, had been dismissed by Mrs Johnson with twenty – and had been content with those terms.

She smiled at O'Grady to hide some latent Presbyterian concern that the money had been earned too easily, too quickly. Surely there must be a snag somewhere. The risk Castle mentioned had receded, almost to vanishing point. She began to work out the sums involved if they had a larger boat, perhaps several, all making regular runs to the States. Within a few months, they could be rich – provided they weren't caught. She felt no qualms about the legality of this trade. They were not going against any law of God, only what seemed to be a stupid and totally unenforceable law of man. They were simply traders supplying a need.

'We've got the current with us this time,' she said, bringing her thoughts back from such academic considerations. 'The trip back should be quicker.'

It was. By the end of the week, Anna was once more in the bank manager's office.

'I want to open another account,' she said. 'I will call it the *Boa Vista* account. With permission for my colleagues Sean O'Grady and Razadin Shah to withdraw up to a third of whatever it contains on demand, but no more. The same terms for me. Is that absolutely clear?'

'Perfectly. I assume you had a successful trip.'

'I think so.'

'The first of many?'

'I hope so.'

After Anna left the bank, Rettini stood looking out through the slats in the blind of his window. In the back yard, a goat stood staked to a tree; a few scraggy hens pecked optimistically in the dust. He felt a rising tide of irritation, as frequently occurred when people years younger than himself opened accounts with money involving sums always tantalisingly beyond his reach.

Of course he was pleased when anyone opened a new account with his branch rather than with some rival bank, but there was never any profit in it for him personally, no matter how many new accounts he accumulated. He seemed doomed to watch others he considered far less worthy grow rich within months or even weeks, while he stayed in this office simply observing the phenomenon, worse, even subsidising it, and never with any personal profit, always on the outside, always looking in.

This girl and her companions, whom he had never even met, were newcomers, total strangers, not, like him, born in the Bahamas. Yet they were clearly on their way to wealth, while he must consider himself fortunate simply because they banked with his branch. The irony ate into his mind like etching acid.

He was like that goat, he thought; tethered, when others were free. He waited for ten minutes, brooding on the problem, wondering how he could change this totally unsatisfactory situation, whether he dared to do so in the only way he knew. Then, his mind made up, Mr Rettini lifted the telephone.

Prince Coleridge had been given his name by his Bahamian mother for two reasons. First, she liked the word Prince. She felt that it exuded class and breeding. Secondly, she had read *The Ancient Mariner* at school and became intrigued by the poet's name. She did not know who Prince's father was. He could be one of four sailors, or even a sergeant in the British battalion stationed in Kingston at the time. Now Prince had no idea where his mother was either, and he did not care.

He was a large, plump, coffee-coloured man in his late twenties, who had tried various jobs, all unsuccessfully. He had dived for sponges, and when the market for these collapsed, he served in a bar. Then, as the possibilities grew for running whisky or rum into the United States, he had worked as a mechanic on some of the launches. This job he found hard to hold because his time as a barman had given him a liking for the drink he should be selling. Prince was known locally as a good one-punch fighter, a bully with a soft gut and a hard streak.

When the telephone rang in his wooden shack he was mixing himself a zombie, a potent local drink made of different types of rum. He poured a generous measure of dark rum into a tall glass, added a little olive oil. Then he poured another rum of a different colour, added more olive oil, then a third, a fourth. The result was a long thin glass of neat rums, dark, brown, light, each separated by a thin layer of oil.

The drink took its name from the local word for a walking corpse revived by witchcraft. It was so strong that bartenders would not sell more than one in an evening to any customer. A repeat could be paralysing. But Prince liked zombies and drank so many he would tell himself that nowadays rum wasn't as strong as it used to be; the makers were adulterating it, weakening it. He believed that zombies had no effect on him. Others took a different view. When drunk, Prince was a useful man to carry out a disagreeable or dangerous task which nobody would ever attempt when sober.

He let the telephone ring while he sipped the drink, relishing its punch as the alcohol ran in his blood. Let the bastard wait, whoever it was, he thought. The bell kept ringing, so finally he picked it up.

'Prince here,' he said gruffly, his voice slurred by drink.

'Mr Rettini speaking.'

'Oh, yes, Mr Rettini.' Prince's tone immediately became respectful.

'I've a job for you. Could be a good payer.'

'On my own?'

'You may need a couple of local lads to help you, maybe three. It's quite simple, but we'll have to meet. I can't discuss business on the telephone.'

'We could meet in a bar.'

'I think that might be unwise,' said Rettini cautiously.

'Why?' asked Prince belligerently. The rum was working strongly in his body now, surging round his arteries to his brain. When this happened, he instantly became conscious of his background, his lack of qualifications. Was this banker fellow trying to upstage him? Didn't he wish to be seen with him in a bar?

'A bar's too public,' Rettini explained patiently. 'Come and see me here in the office. Also, I have someone I'd like you to meet. It's really his idea, but it was mine to bring you in. When can you get here?'

Prince curbed his belligerence. He was desperate for money.

'Half an hour, sir?'

'OK. Half an hour. But, remember, the bank shuts early today. Don't be late.'

Castle jumped down from the quay onto the deck of the *Boa Vista* in Nassau harbour. The little ship dipped and rose and dipped again under the sudden weight. Anna came out of the cabin to meet him.

'Another run,' Castle announced briefly, without even wishing her good morning or asking how the return voyage

232

had been. 'Two thousand cases this time. Same profit. OK?'

'OK. When?'

'We load tonight, after dark. Set off as soon as everything's aboard. This time I won't pick you up off Savannah, but off New York. If I'm not there myself – and I may not be because, as I said, I've other business concerns – a colleague will be.'

'How will we recognise him?' asked O'Grady, who had come up from the engine room.

Castle tore a visiting card in two pieces and gave half to Anna.

'He will have the other half. Don't bother about his name. He doesn't know who you are either. It's safer that way.'

Anna nodded agreement.

That evening, a string of donkey carts appeared on the quayside. They were carrying burlap bags packed with bottles of whisky, tied in batches of four. The bags took up less space than wooden boxes and gave the bottles some protection against breakage. When all available space in the *Boa Vista* was filled, the donkeys pulled the empty carts away into the darkness.

The *Boa Vista* sailed just before midnight, lying very low in the water. Shah stood on the quayside and watched her go. He was staying behind to check on the availability of a second launch that might be bought or hired. With so many people involved in running rum and whisky into the States, nearly every locally owned boat was already in use. Old launches, yachts and speedboats abandoned long since because of rotten planks or unreliable engines were now being hastily renovated. Nor was the involvement in bootlegging restricted to the owners of such vessels. Even old Bahamian women who ran stalls in the market selling straw hats and carrier bags to tourists contributed. They wove the bags that protected the bottles on the voyage.

Because of the extra weight the *Boa Vista* was carrying, her engines were using more fuel, and the boat's speed had dropped considerably. O'Grady stopped at noon on the following day to replenish their tanks from drums of petrol they carried lashed on the afterdeck. To cut down on consumption, he now reduced speed. All through that day and most of the night they chugged north.

'We're carrying far too much cargo,' said Anna. 'I didn't realise how this would slow us down. If we run into bad weather like last time, we'll be in real trouble.'

'More cargo, more profit,' replied O'Grady shortly.

'And much more risk. You think the fuel will last out?'

'No reason why not. We've three more drums on deck, so we should be all right.'

To their left as they sailed they could see the headlights of cars on shore roads, and sometimes the glitter of garish red and green signs outside a gas station near the beach.

'We're very close to land,' Anna warned. 'Why are we so far inside the twenty-mile limit?'

'The nearer we can keep to the shore, the calmer the sea, so the less fuel we use.'

'And the greater the risk of a cutter stopping us. Let's keep our distance.'

'We're travelling blind, without lights,' O'Grady reminded her sharply. 'That's illegal, but it's safer. No one will see us.'

At two o'clock in the morning Anna, on watch, saw a faint glimmer of red and green lights far behind. She woke up O'Grady.

'We're being followed,' she told him.

'We can't keep the whole ocean to ourselves,' O'Grady replied easily. 'It's probably only another boat out from Nassau, like us.'

Even so, he increased speed. For a time, the following lights fell away, and then they steadily grew stronger. The unknown ship had powerful engines. Soon, she was only fifty feet astern. Against the hum of engines, Anna heard a voice shout through a loud-hailer.

'Ship ahead, heave to! Prepare to be boarded! United States Revenue cutter! Do you hear me?'

'We hear you,' O'Grady shouted back.

'I told you we should have kept outside the limit,' Anna said furiously. 'Now we're caught on our second run loaded with booze, and without any possible defence.'

'We're not caught yet,' O'Grady replied, trying to convince himself. 'We may negotiate something with them. They're nearly all willing to deal.'

'With what? All our money is in the bank.'

'We have plenty of booze. That's as good as money.'

The loud-hailer boomed again. 'I repeat. Heave to, or we open fire!'

O'Grady shrugged, turned on his riding lights reluctantly, moved back the throttle in its quadrant. The roar of his engines died. The *Boa Vista* slowed, and lay wallowing sluggishly in the Atlantic swell. A spotlight from the cutter played on their deck.

'We're going to board your port side,' shouted someone from her bridge. The cutter now came up close, and nudged the *Boa Vista*. She was a much larger ship than they had realised. A crewman threw across two ropes with sharp metal hooks that bit into the *Boa Vista*'s wooden deck. Two men climbed over the side onto the deck. Both wore dark shirts and trousers, with peaked naval caps, and carried pistols in opened leather holsters on their belts, with two clips of ammunition.

'Why are you sailing without lights? You're breaking the rules of navigation. You got contraband aboard?'

O'Grady did not reply. The speaker kept out of the spotlight's glare so that his face was in shadow. Even so, O'Grady thought there was something familiar about him; his build, the way he stood, his voice. But where could he have possibly seen him before?

The man nodded to his companion. It took him only moments to discover the sacks of whisky.

'Stacked with booze, sir,' he reported triumphantly.

'I'm taking you in tow,' the officer told O'Grady.

'Where to?'

'The nearest land.'

'What authority have you to do this?'

'Authority of the United States Government. You are the captain?'

'Yes,' O'Grady admitted. 'Let's see your papers,' he added, trying to postpone the inevitable.

'Time enough when we reach Florida. Now, no more talk and no trouble or we'll sink your vessel, with all the booze aboard. That way you'll get a helluva lot longer term inside. My ship's keeping her gun trained on you, just in case you try anything. The choice is yours. Understood?'

'Clearly,' Anna replied bitterly.

The cutter moved ahead of the *Boa Vista*. Her crew made fast a tow rope, and then she began to pull them ignominiously through the dark sea. As they moved, Anna heard the exhaust note of the cutter's engine change suddenly and drastically. From being a controlled hum it now began to backfire erratically.

'We're pulling in to the nearest land,' the officer told

them through the loud-hailer. 'We have a small problem with our engine. Nothing serious, so it doesn't affect anything. Don't get any ideas. We'll be on our way again in half an hour. Understood?'

'Understood.'

The cutter towed them into a small cove. Ahead, Anna could see a dark ridge of rock, one of many small uninhabited islands in the Caribbean chain. If only O'Grady had followed her advice and kept outside the twenty-mile limit, they would be safe, still on their way to another profit. Now, they faced confiscation of their ship, a huge fine, and almost certain jail sentences. She had been an idiot to allow herself to be lured by the prospect of fool's gold.

Anna watched as the cutter, engine now thumping asthmatically, brought them alongside a primitive wooden pier. Why would such a pier be built on an uninhabited island? she wondered. Before she could reach any conclusion, the cutter swung out sharply so that the *Boa Vista* bumped against the jetty. A crewman leapt ashore and made her fast and then cast off the tow rope from her bows. The cutter berthed ahead of her. Floodlights came on above her deck, engine covers were raised. Two men with dark skins – Bahamians? Americans? Anna was not sure – went below to work on the engine.

'You two get out,' the officer ordered Anna and O'Grady. 'You the only ones aboard?'

'Yes. But why must we go ashore? We're not staying long, surely.'

'No. Only until we sort out the engine. But it's safer to keep you on shore – just in case you get any crazy ideas about trying to sail away. Last folk who tried that didn't make it. We don't want a repeat performance.'

'I've some things I'd like to take with me, personal

things, just in case we do stay longer than you think,' said Anna.

'Sure,' the officer agreed. 'Take what you like. I'll frisk you before you land, so don't try and smuggle any guns ashore.'

Anna went down to her cabin, lifted the mattress from her bunk, removed one of the two revolvers from the tin of fish scales she had taken from the slave ship, checked it was loaded. She cleaned it, closed the lid, washed her hands carefully. Then she went up on deck.

'I have this revolver,' she told the officer meekly. 'You'd probably have found it under my bunk, so you might as well have it now. Maybe it will count in my favour that I surrendered it willingly.'

'I'll make a special note of that.' He nodded towards the tin. 'What's in that?'

'Concentrated food – fish base. Want to check?'

He nodded again.

Anna prised open the lid, pushed the tin under his nose. He jumped back, coughing in disgust at the foul smell.

'Shut it up,' he told her, wrinkling his face in distaste. 'I wouldn't eat that if I were starving.'

'What about the whisky?' O'Grady asked him hopefully. 'Can't we do a deal?'

The officer shook his head firmly. 'No way. My deals are all with Uncle Sam. And remember, trying to bribe a Revenue officer carries a statutory two years in jail. But in view of your companion's open approach, I'll forget you ever made that offer.'

As he spoke he moved into the light. Anna and O'Grady recognised him at once.

'You're no more a Revenue officer than I am,' she exclaimed. 'Last time we met you boarded Captain

238

O'Grady's ship and tried to scuttle it.'

'So you remember, eh?' Montagne asked her sneeringly. 'You had a man – an Indian, I think – who shot me, but not as seriously as I pretended. The South Africans rescued me. Someone had seen this boat, my boat, the French *Josephine*, sail west. So I came after it. Now you can both sweat things out on this island till you starve to death, while I take back my property. I'm sorry I won't be here to see you die. It won't be a quick end, but I haven't any more time to waste. Now get off my ship, both of you, before I lose my temper.'

Anna turned to O'Grady. 'Let's go,' she said dispiritedly.

They walked away slowly, up the spine of land into the darkness. Montagne watched them, hands on his hips.

Out of range of the cutter's spotlight, Anna sat down on a large stone.

'I suppose it was too good to last,' said O'Grady sadly. 'I never thought that bastard would come back from the dead.'

'And he thinks the same about us, I'm sure,' Anna retorted sharply.

'But do you think their engine is genuinely playing up?'

'No. I reckon that was just a bit of play-acting in case any of his crew wondered why he was dumping us. It gave him a convincing reason. Not that it matters now.'

'You're right,' O'Grady agreed. 'Nothing matters now.'

'Speak for yourself,' Anna told him.

'What do you mean?'

'Exactly what I say. Now, listen . . .'

Montagne lit a cheroot, called down to the men in the engine room to join him on deck.

'They fell for it, like I said they would,' he told Prince

Coleridge gleefully. 'Now, let's get the hell out of here.'

'Hold on, boss,' Prince replied from below deck. 'There's no mad rush. They aren't going anywhere and they've no wireless. It's damn hot down here, faking a breakdown, I can tell you. Let's split a bottle of that whisky before we leave.'

Montagne shrugged. There was truth in what the man said; a few snifters would be very much in order.

'Right,' he agreed. 'Ready when you are.'

Sweating from the heat of the engine room, eyes white in dark, perspiring faces, Prince and another Bahamian climbed up on deck. With a pocket knife, he cut a bottle of whisky from a sack, poured out four fingers into metal mugs.

'How much you reckon they've got aboard this boat?' he asked.

'I counted two thousand bottles,' Montagne replied. 'Good stuff, too. Long Glen Scotch.'

'What are you going to do with the boat?'

'It's mine. I'll take her in tow to New York. Sell off her cargo, then sell her, too, if we can. We don't want her back in Nassau. People could ask questions.'

'Like Mr Castle, eh?' Prince's teeth glowed white as he asked his question.

'Maybe,' Montagne agreed. He did not want any trouble from Rettini or Castle; all he wanted now was to be rich. 'Best sell her off. She's worth a few thousand bucks, for she's in good shape. Got a couple of powerful engines. French. Like me.'

All three men sipped their whisky appreciatively, looked towards the shore.

'Hey,' said Prince suddenly, his eyes narrowing in surprise and alarm. 'I thought you said that island's uninhabited. There's people over there, walking about.'

'Of course. The woman and the man. We dumped them off. That whisky too strong for you, Prince?'

'I don't mean them, Captain. *Look!*'

As Montagne turned, his hand moved instinctively to the pistol in its holster. On the shore, some way up from the beach, he could see the faint outline of something moving. It seemed thin, like a tall cross, or a ghostly scarecrow. No living human being could conceivably be that shape and size. As they watched, they all heard a faint, shrill sound as if someone, or something, was crying out in mortal pain.

'Aaaah – aaah!'

'Bloody place is haunted,' said Prince hoarsely, emptying the bottle into his mug. He gulped the fiery liquid greedily. 'Could be the ghosts of shipwrecked sailors or marooned pirates from the old days. They could put a spell on us. Let's get the shit out while we can.'

'Rubbish!' retorted Montagne. 'There's no one else on the island. You know that. Rettini told me no one's lived on it for years.'

'Maybe these aren't living people, boss. They sure as hell don't look like they're alive,' said the other man nervously. 'You can see that for yourself. No bloody argument.'

'If there isn't anyone living, then it *must* be a duppy,' said Prince, his voice thin with horror. A duppy was the local name for the spirit of a corpse that hovered around the home he or she had occupied in their lifetime. Denied a place in heaven or hell, they were doomed to stay, without substance, in a nightmare death in life, silent wraiths, refused rest or remission until the end of the world.

'Crap,' said Montagne derisively.

As the three men stared, a second figure appeared further along the coast. Long, thin, stick-like arms moved in strange repetitive gestures. Again, they heard the ghostly cry, nearer this time and louder, more threatening in its strength. The men in the cutter felt a chill stab of terror; their flesh crawled with fear of the unexplainable.

'The bloody place is haunted. They *are* duppies,' said Prince. 'Let's go now, while we can.'

'We're going,' Montagne agreed, 'But they aren't ghosts. They're only some sort of hallucination.'

'What sort? I never seen no hallucination like that.'

'Nor me,' the other Bahamian insisted.

'Then I'll bloody show you,' said Montagne angrily. 'It's either that or those bums we put ashore are playing around. This'll answer the matter once and for all.'

He took out his pistol, gripped it with both hands to steady his aim, fired at the first figure once, twice, three times. It kept moving slowly along the beach, and shook its arms as though in ridicule or anger at the shots.

'You see,' said Prince. 'They *are* ghosts. I knew it, soon as I saw them.'

'I don't understand it,' Montagne admitted. 'I couldn't miss at this range.'

He fired at the second moving figure. It also kept moving, and for the third time they all heard the shrill, unearthly cry.

'How can you kill the dead? You're firing at a spirit, a ghost, Captain. Let's go. *Now*, before they come at us.'

At that moment they heard a faint and distant sound, like a dry twig breaking; a small, isolated noise in the empty silence of the night.

Prince gave a gasp of surprise and pain. He stood up unsteadily, as though stung by a wasp or a bee. Then his knees sagged. He lost his balance and fell backwards over the side of the boat into the sea. Montagne and the other man peered down at him. Prince was floating face down, quite dead.

'What the hell?' asked Montagne incredulously. Again both men heard that same faint dry sound. This time, the second Bahamian fell, striking his head on the deck. The air was suddenly heavy with the smell of spilled whisky.

Montagne raced to the controls. Something was happening on the island that he couldn't understand. It might just be some native voodoo ceremony they had interrupted. Whatever it was, this was not the moment to discover.

As Montagne ran, a third bullet hit the side of the main cabin, splintering woodwork only inches from his head. He dropped on his hands and knees. Shielded by the gunwale, he began to crawl towards the rear cockpit. Once inside, within minutes he would be out of range. At least he knew now that he wasn't dealing with spirits but with a good marksman.

The shooting stopped as suddenly as it had started. Montagne raised his head cautiously in case whoever was firing had come nearer and he could pick them off. The two phantasmagorical crosses, glowing green as though with the decay of the grave, were moving along the beach, approaching the jetty.

Montagne was a good shot; he knew he couldn't miss at this range. He raised himself clear of the gunwale to fire again. As he did so, another shot came from the shore. It went wide. Montagne squeezed his trigger, fired twice, and then the gun jammed. He had used all his ammunition. Then a second bullet from the shore hit his wrist.

The pistol dropped from his hand. He went down on hands and knees, scrabbling for it in the dark, and for a new clip of cartridges. But the pain in his wrist was so great that it clouded his vision. He gasped at the stabs of agony when he put the slightest weight on his arm. Then, as though through a mist, he heard a woman's voice he recognised.

'Stand up,' Anna ordered him. 'Don't reach for your gun. Raise both your hands above your head and face the shore. One false move and you're dead, like the others.'

For a moment Montagne stayed where he was. Could he be imagining all this? Was it all a nightmare? Anna spoke a second time, and he realised it was no dream; this was reality.

'On your feet. I will not tell you again.'

Montagne stood up slowly, raised his hands. 'Who are you?' he asked, unable to see anyone beyond the rim of floodlight, only a single pale green outline, now stationary.

'You know damn well who I am.'

'You can get the electric chair for this. You've killed two men.'

'I am sorry about that. I only meant to wing them. I would much rather have brought them back to Nassau in chains with you.'

Anna and O'Grady walked along the jetty, jumped aboard.

Anna held her revolver inches from Montagne's head. 'Now. The truth. Are you working on your own?'

'Yes.'

'Who lent you the boat?'

'Rettini organised it through Prince Coleridge, who owed him money. Rettini said he would take a cut from the profits and let Prince off the hook.'

'And then?'

'I'd sell off the boat.'

'Who to?'

'Mr Castle. He doesn't like competition in this game.

And that's what he's got with you.' He looked from Anna to O'Grady. 'What are you going to do?' he asked nervously.

'Put you ashore.'

'But there's no food on this island. Nothing. I've got to live.'

'Why?' O'Grady asked him shortly. 'You didn't give us much chance when you scuttled my ship. Or when you marooned us. Start walking.'

Montagne climbed over the edge of the boat, walked slowly along the jetty and up the beach, shoulders hunched in defeat, holding his wounded wrist with his other hand.

O'Grady hauled the body of the dead Bahamian across the deck, opened a hinged section of the gunwale, manhandled it into the sea. Anna handed him a whisky. He drank thankfully.

'Never thought your idea of tying bamboo canes together and daubing them with that filthy luminous paint would do any good,' he told her. 'But I was wrong.'

'It wouldn't have impressed a more sophisticated lot,' Anna agreed. 'But these fellows are brought up with fears of voodoo and ghosts that go back to their forebears in Africa. So it worked. Just.'

'When that fellow Montagne started shooting, I thought he'd get us. He was a good shot. Actually split in two the pole I was holding.'

'I know, but I told you to hold it out at arm's length so you were OK. We should have worried if he'd been a worse shot and hit us by mistake.'

'It may be a while before another ship comes calling,' said O'Grady.

'That's his bad luck. He wasn't just dumping us for an hour or so, remember. He was marooning us.'

O'Grady poured out two more whiskies. 'What's the plan now?' he asked Anna.

'We take both boats up north, do our deal with Castle's people, and see if we can sell this cutter. If not, I suggest we sail them both back to Nassau and wait for the next offer. And in future we keep a very close eye on Castle.'

'Agreed. Tell me, where did you learn to be such a good shot?'

'In Scotland, shooting rats.'

'But that's different to shooting men.'

'True,' Anna agreed. 'Men make bigger, easier targets. And rats have four legs, while men have only two. Now, no more questions. You keep us on course, and this time *please* stay beyond the twenty-mile limit.'

As the two boats began to move, Anna looked back towards the shore. Somewhere out in the warm darkness was a man who had once tried to shoot her. Now she had shot him and left him on his own to live or to die. The strangest thing to her mind was that she felt no reaction whatever and no pity for Montagne. He had gambled and failed. She had gambled and won. But why, oh why, had she not seen any inkling of this in the visions she had experienced of her future? Could she trust them? And how could it be that she had changed so quickly from being a girl in a Scottish village, with all the strict disciplines of that life and upbringing, to a woman who could shoot two men and maroon a third without a second thought? What was happening to her?

Sometimes, years later, a whiff of fuel oil from a diesel truck would make Anna relive that trip up the coast of the United States. Because they had to tow the cutter they were late reaching the rendezvous, so they anchored the cutter and then spent two hours cruising up and down the coast after dark in the *Boa Vista*, hoping to locate their contact.

Finally, a small vessel without lights approached them out of the gloom, and drew alongside. Anna recognised one of the men who had unloaded their first cargo. She produced the part of a visiting card that Castle had given to her. The man took out its matching half from his pocket. She handed him a list of their cargo.

'Same price?' he asked her brusquely.

'Same price,' Anna agreed.

He nodded to several younger men wearing sweaters and serge trousers and rubber-soled shoes. They went aboard and unloaded the bottles in their burlap bags with the speed and silence that had impressed her on her first trip.

'I make it two thousand bottles; one empty. Let's say twenty thousand dollars to you,' said the man when the final bags had been moved. 'You agree with that?'

'I agree,' said Anna.

He peeled off the money in hundred-dollar bills. 'What's in the boat you're towing?'

'Nothing – this trip, at least.'

'OK. See you around.'

His ship sailed off into the darkness towards the shore, still without lights and with little sound from a heavily muffled exhaust.

Anna and O'Grady set off on the homeward journey to Nassau. The profit was so great that they could barely assimilate the fact that in a matter of days they had made much more than many people earned in a lifetime.

As they approached New Providence Island, Anna told O'Grady to keep both ships out of sight of the harbour, and to go on round the coast.

'Why?' he asked.

'I want to see Rettini before he sees us or anyone tells him we're back.'

She rowed herself ashore in the dinghy, walked up the beach, past native huts with roofs of plaited reeds and walls made from enamelled metal advertisements for petrol and tea and rum. She reached the main road, hailed a passing car. The driver gave her a lift to the British Colonial Hotel. She waited until he was out of sight, and then walked along Bay Street to the Bank of World Indemnity.

'Mr Rettini is engaged,' a clerk explained.

'I'll wait.'

She sat for ten minutes, thumbing through out-of-date banking magazines until Rettini appeared.

'Miss Ballater,' he said effusively. 'I am sorry to keep you waiting.'

'The clerk told me you were engaged.'

'A bank manager's job is full of engagements,' he explained almost regretfully. 'Please come into my office. As a matter of fact, I didn't expect to see you back so soon.'

He closed the door, stood watching her as she sat down. Anna could sense he was uneasy, nervous.

'Mr Rettini,' she began quietly, 'let us not misunderstand each other. You did not expect to see me back at all. My boat was intercepted by ruffians led by a Frenchman, a pirate who had previously scuttled a ship in which I was a passenger. Now he attempted to maroon Captain O'Grady and me. That failed, but I am sorry to say there was shooting. Two men died.'

'What an extraordinary story,' said Rettini, shaking his head in perplexity. But Anna noticed that his face was damp with perspiration.

'I agree. What I find even more surprising is that I

understand you advised him of our plans.'

'Me? Why would I do a thing like that? That is a ridiculous suggestion, Miss Ballater. I'm a banker, not a pirate.'

'This man contradicted what you tell me. It is my intention to make that public. Here and in the United States.'

'That would be highly defamatory.'

'Which is precisely why I will do it. Your employers will not welcome the publicity.'

'I deny your grotesque charge entirely.'

'We have nothing further to discuss. I will, of course, close my account with you and inform the manager of the bank to which I take it of my reason for leaving you.' Anna stood up and walked towards the door.

'Wait a moment, please, Miss Ballater,' Rettini entreated her. 'You are quite wrong in what you claim. But I understand how a newcomer to the Bahamas can sometimes make wrong assessments. To bring this to court would not help either of us.'

'So?'

He looked at her, trying to gauge her determination.'What do you want?' he asked at last.

'Enough money from your bank to buy a third boat, then maybe a fourth, possibly a fifth. The security for your bank on the initial advance would be the cutter we took from the Frenchman.'

'You are asking a lot.'

'I am *asking* nothing. You wish to do a deal with me. And that is the only deal I will accept. Now. Not tomorrow or next week, but now.'

'Have you any other craft in mind that would be suitable?' Rettini asked, playing for time, hoping desperately he could somehow find a way out of a potentially disastrous situation. How could everything have gone so desperately wrong?

'Mr Shah is looking at several possible purchases,' Anna explained.

Rettini sat down. This woman might be bluffing, but somehow she didn't sound as though she was, and he could not risk finding out. Castle would not take this setback kindly. It could have very serious consequences for him, perhaps even fatal consequences. The thought made Rettini perspire even more.

He would get his own back on this bitch one day. Her proposition might make her rich, but it would also buy him time. And, looking at the proposition from the bank's point of view, the loan would be secured; it would read correctly in his books. In any case, all the banks in Nassau were involved at one or two removes from bootlegging. He would not be out on his own.

'All right,' he said at last. 'I will back you, on condition you drop these ridiculous charges.'

'No conditions,' said Anna. 'But I can tell you that if all goes according to my plan, I will not press charges. After all, if we hadn't been attacked, we would still only have one boat. Now we have two, and your promise of more.'

'Is that all?' Rettini asked her.

'No,' said Anna. 'Two more things. One, I gave you some diamonds as security against a loan. I would like them back.'

'Then we have no security.'

'You have the boats.'

For a moment, Rettini watched her. Anna met his gaze. Finally, he nodded reluctantly. 'All right,' he said. 'I'll give them back. What's the second thing?'

'I told you what the Frenchman said about you putting

him up to his attempt against us.'

'I had nothing to do with it,' said Rettini quickly, too quickly.

'I don't think you have the character, or the guts, to propose a deliberate act of piracy that has ended in two deaths. You were simply the go-between, the messenger. You passed on someone else's ideas. Whose?'

'I don't know what you mean, Miss Ballater.'

'You know exactly what I mean. You also know I intend to have an answer. Not in the future. Now.'

'I cannot help you,' said Rettini. 'It is quite impossible.'

Anna picked up a pencil from his desk, wrote one word on a piece of paper, pushed it across. Rettini read 'Castle'. He nodded.

'I thought as much,' said Anna. She tore the paper into little pieces, put them in the waste basket.

'I understand the *Boa Vista* isn't sailing under her real name,' said Rettini, his voice stronger now. Admission, Anna thought wryly, can have its own therapeutic effect.

She stood up. 'You understand a lot of things, Mr Rettini,' she said, smiling. 'I'll take those diamonds with me now.'

Ten

Dr Bailey heard the sound of firing before he was fully awake.

He sat up, for a moment imagining he was down in the trenches again. Then he remembered where he was and sank back thankfully in his bed. The war had been over for years. This was Monday, 12 August, the Glorious Twelfth, when the grouse season opened. Landowners across Scotland were already out on the moors with their friends and keepers, all eager to bring down the first grouse of the year. Odd how he could have forgotten such an important date, but then it meant far more to them than it did to him. He had encountered too much shooting in Flanders. His sympathies now lay with the shot at rather than the shooters.

Usually, the laird, Mr MacTavish, invited him to join his party, but not this year. Ah, well, he had probably many more important guests to ask, and the doctor felt he had no right to expect to be invited every year. But it was a custom, and the older you grew the more store you set by custom and routine. There was something curiously comforting about both – just as there was about suddenly receiving a totally unexpected legacy.

He washed, shaved, dressed. On his way downstairs he met his housekeeper coming up.

'I was coming to fetch you, Doctor,' she said importantly. 'Mr MacTavish is in the sitting room.'

Bailey nodded. The laird and his wife and some of the

other richer people in the area usually visited him privately at his house to discuss their ailments. Villagers, of course, had to keep to surgery hours – nine o'clock to ten every morning, five to six in the evening. But it was odd for MacTavish to visit him without an appointment. He was a punctilious man. And a visit from him was even more unexpected on the Twelfth. Bailey went into the sitting room.

'Is this a social or a professional visit, sir?' he asked.

'Professional,' said the laird briefly.

Bailey had not seen MacTavish for some time and was surprised to note how his face seemed to have shrunk; his skin stretched tightly across his cheekbones and had turned a peculiarly yellow colour.

'How can I help you?' the doctor asked with professional brightness.

'I hope with one of your pills or potions. I've been suffering the last few weeks from a devilish bout of indigestion. I have tried bicarbonate of soda, been to the chemist and bought patent medicines guaranteed to cure all manner of stomach troubles, but nothing can ease it.'

'Let's have a look and see what we can do. Please take off your jacket and shirt.'

As Bailey placed his stethoscope on the laird's chest, he heard the distant rattle of gunfire. 'You're not shooting this morning,' he remarked casually.

'No. I didn't feel up to it. First time since my teens I've missed it, though. Except for the war, of course.'

He must be feeling very poorly indeed, thought Dr Bailey. The laird set as much importance on custom as he himself did.

MacTavish's heartbeat was heavy and irregular. Bailey checked his blood pressure, and tried to keep his concern from his face. Not since student days had he examined a patient with such high blood pressure. He checked it a second time to make sure he had not made a mistake. Then he motioned to MacTavish to put on his shirt and jacket, and sat down opposite him on an easy chair.

'You've a bit of blood pressure,' he said easily, as though this was no more important than a cold. 'A little high, to my mind. You smoke?'

'About sixty a day. Have done for years.'

'Well, I would cut that down. You don't drink much, do you?'

'Not to my mind, Doctor, though some might disagree. Four whiskies before lunch – usually singles. And the same in the evening before dinner. A port or two afterwards, of course.'

'Again, I would cut down on that, at least for the time being. That amount of alcohol isn't doing you any good at present. Combined with the cigarettes, you are putting an unnecessary strain on your heart and arteries.'

'I would die if I had to give them up,' the laird replied flatly. He looked closely at the doctor. 'Be honest with me, Doctor,' he said. 'I think I'm dying now. What do you think?'

'Rubbish,' Bailey replied decisively. 'Whatever gives you that idea, Mr MacTavish?'

'A feeling I have in my bones, in my water. I've lived all my life in these hills. I know what happens when animals get this same feeling. I've seen old stags, masters of the herd for years, suddenly realise their time has come. Then they go away to some quiet part of the forest to die quietly.'

'Maybe. But you're not going to do that.'

'I know what I feel, Doctor. I do not think you are being quite fair with me.'

'I assure you, I am. Your blood pressure is too high for a man of your age, that's all. You can bring it down quite easily if you reduce your smoking and drinking and cut out sugar and red meat. You are not going to some lonely part of the forest to die. You are going to be Laird of Long Glen for many a year.'

'But only if I live the life of a sheep, a herbivore. I may be all kinds of things, but I have never been a sheep.'

'You are dramatising a very simple reduction of tobacco and alcohol.'

'For how long?'

'Until you feel better. Do you have any pain now?'

'At this moment, no. But if I walk up a hill I have to stop halfway, with a pain in my chest as though I've swallowed a great stone. Indigestion?'

'No. It's caused by blood going through your arteries at greater pressure. As we grow older our pipes fur up, almost literally.'

'Have you any medicine for that?'

'I can give you something to ease the pain, but you have to play your part. Then we'll soon have you right again.'

'I would like to believe you.'

MacTavish left, and as Dr Bailey watched his Daimler drive away, he wondered whether the laird's high blood pressure was worth a letter to *The Lancet*. It would be interesting to know whether any other practitioners had found such high blood pressure in a patient and whether the patient had lived. Then he shook his head. No, he would wait until the laird died before he contacted *The Lancet*.

As he went into breakfast, he heard another burst of shooting, the crackle of a fusillade from a dozen guns, and glanced at his watch. He was late this morning. He would have to hurry his breakfast to be in his surgery by nine, but somehow he did not think too many patients would be waiting for him, not on the Twelfth.

The Writer to the Signet in Perth, Douglas Macleod, was a small man with a black beard carefully combed to a point. He sat behind a huge desk that emphasised his gnome-like proportions. The laird sat in a wing armchair opposite him. The Writer spoke in the precise, neatly clipped way of the provincial lawyer.

'When I received your recent valued instructions, Mr MacTavish, I immediately took your previous will and testament from the deed box and altered it according to your wishes.'

He handed MacTavish a vellum document, creased and folded and bound in pink tape. The laird skimmed through it and nodded.

'I will sign it now. Can you bring in someone to witness my signature?'

'Of course.'

Macleod rang a bell. A clerk came into the office, signed without even looking at MacTavish. The Writer blotted the signature with a semi-circular blotting pad, moving it to and fro importantly as though the man had not simply written his name, but a whole paragraph.

'I will keep this and have copies made, sir,' he said when he felt convinced the ink was dry.

'No,' said MacTavish. 'I would like to read it through again at home more carefully, on my own. I'll take it with me.'

'There is no copy, sir. This is the only one.'

'That's immaterial. Come out and see me tomorrow for

a drink before lunch. I'll give it back to you then. I want to check everything is exactly as I wish it. I am sure it is, but I just want to be certain.'

'We endeavour to give every satisfaction, sir,' said the Writer stiffly.

'Of course. And you always have done as far as I am concerned.' MacTavish put the will into his briefcase, shook the Writer's hand and left.

Macleod stood at the window behind his desk, concealed by the curtain. He stroked his beard slowly as he watched his richest client being driven away.

The Daimler drew up outside the castle. The laird stepped down from his car, went into the house. A servant reached out to take the case from his hand.

'Mrs MacTavish is in the small drawing room, sir. Will you take tea with her?' he asked.

'Yes, I will, and I'll take my briefcase with me,' he told the servant. The pills Dr Bailey had given him were in it. MacTavish walked through the hall, past suits of polished armour, beneath crossed dirks on the walls and old battle standards now too threadbare ever to be washed again. He had grown up here, lived all his life among these reminders of a warlike past. What a tragedy his heir had died and would never feel the pride he felt in the deeds of his ancestors! He walked slowly; the pain had returned and was growing worse. He would take two pills with his tea, in the belief that if the doctor prescribed one, then surely two must do twice the amount of good.

His wife sat reading a newspaper by the fireplace. The grate was filled with dried flowers. Even in Scotland it was unusual to have a fire in August. Within a few weeks, though, when days grew shorter and evenings longer and colder, a fire would be welcome.

He sat down in a chair opposite his wife, opened the briefcase.

'Is it very hot out?' she asked him.

'No. Why?'

'You're perspiring. And you look quite tired. Have you had a busy day in Perth?'

'Not really, but it's full of English tourists at this time of year, which I find an irritation. Pour me a cup of tea, please. I'll take a couple of pills. The doctor's given me some for my indigestion.'

He watched the well-remembered routine of silver tea strainer being held just above the bone china cup as his wife poured with the left hand and kept her right hand on the top of the teapot in case the lid fell off. He found the small wooden phial of pills in his bag, took out two, swallowed them.

His wife was pouring milk.

'Sugar?' she asked him.

He shook his head. Suddenly, he did not want to speak. He just wanted to be quiet, not focusing his mind on such a trivial matter. Oddly, he felt hot and yet cold at the same time. A cup of tea and these pills would set him to rights.

At that moment, the world exploded with a brilliant, orange blast, like peering into the heart of a roaring furnace. Then darkness wrapped MacTavish with the softness of a velvet shroud. He fell forwards on to the floor. Pills scattered like confetti. The cup and saucer shattered. Steaming tea spread in a brown stain across the carpet.

Mrs MacTavish jumped up, crossed to her husband, thinking he had fainted. The suit he was wearing was far too thick for this weather.

She loosened his collar, and in doing so touched the flesh of his face. It felt cold and damp. Then she screamed and pressed the bell urgently for the butler. For the laird had not fainted, he had died.

Dr Bailey arrived within minutes. He had been driving past the castle gates on his way home from seeing another patient, and the lodge keeper ran out and stopped his car.

Servants had already carried MacTavish's body up to his bed and he lay on the silk coverlet, in his suit, still wearing his handmade brogues. Although the doctor dealt frequently with the dying, he never failed to feel surprise at the speed with which life could so often leave the human frame. Only hours earlier, that very morning, he had advised the laird what course he should take to avoid heart trouble. The advice had come too late.

He closed the laird's staring, empty eyes, pulled the curtains across the windows in a gesture of deference to the dead and walked down the stairs. Mrs MacTavish was waiting for him in the library.

'A very sad case of heart failure,' Bailey explained. 'He came to see me this very morning, complaining of pain in his chest.'

'He's had that pain for weeks. He thought it was indigestion.'

The doctor nodded. That was a very common delusion in such cases, but this was not the moment to say so. 'At least he did not suffer. It was just like falling asleep, quietly, peacefully.' He watched Mrs MacTavish as he spoke. He guessed that she and her husband had never been close, but he sensed a nervousness about her now that might not be entirely due to grief. She patted her cheek, smoothed back her hair, kept nodding her head in agreement with what he had said.

'Would you like a glass of something, Doctor?' she asked him.

'No, thank you,' he said. 'It is very kind of you, but in these sad circumstances, I will forgo that pleasure.' He picked up his bag, his hat. 'If there is anything I can do to help, please let me know. I have left the death certificate in an envelope in the hall. You may need it for the funeral arrangements.'

She followed him into the hall. 'You have been very good, Doctor.'

'I have done nothing,' replied Bailey. 'Even if he had consulted me earlier, there was little I could have done, unless he was willing to change his style of life.'

'I know,' she said. 'He smoked too much. He drank too much. And he smoked and drank a lot more after that boy Davey Moore came into this house.'

'Ah, yes, I expect that changed his routine a bit, having a young person here.'

Mrs MacTavish watched him go to his car, then went back to the study. She locked the door, poured herself a whisky, drank it neat, then shook out the contents of her husband's briefcase on the table.

She had glanced at them before the doctor arrived, but now she felt she must check she had not made any mistake in reading the will, had not imagined what she had read, for this will was quite different from the one he had made some years earlier, a copy of which she kept in her bureau drawer. This will bore today's date, so he must have signed it only hours before he died. Would that be before or after he went to see Dr Bailey? Not that this was particularly important.

Attached to the vellum by a paperclip was a handwritten note on a piece of paper: 'N.B. Only copy. This is to be returned by client for copying.' That was something, she thought. If there really was no other copy, it would be difficult for anyone to prove this will had ever existed. The lawyer would know that it had, of course, but knowing was not sufficient; knowledge was not proof. She sat down and reread the passage that had so disturbed her before the doctor arrived:

'To my natural son, who goes by the name of Davey Moore, I give and bequeath all my possessions, with the exception of such properties and shares hereunder enumerated, which I give and bequeath to my wife, Elizabeth.

My son knows that his mother was latterly known as Jeannie Moore. She had another name when I knew her very briefly, long ago. I did not see her for years until she came to my back door, begging bread. Her face was so disfigured that at first I did not recognise her. When I did I drove her away. I thought she might have come intent on blackmailing me, but in this I am sure now I was mistaken.

She never asked anything from me except a piece of bread, and even that I denied her, may I be forgiven.

Mrs MacTavish read on, amazed at the duplicity of her husband. Their son – *her* son – was dead, drowned in an extraordinary accident. And this young fellow Davey was the son of a gypsy woman her husband claimed was responsible for her son's death. Now, he admitted that he was Davey's father – and he planned to leave him very nearly everything.

He must have been unfaithful shortly after their marriage.

Did he realise he was Davey's father when he agreed to bring him up? Or did he discover this later? If so, how and when? No wonder she had not wished to take the boy into her home. That had been an instinctive reluctance. She had sensed his presence could be destructive, without knowing the reason why.

Well, her husband was dead now, and even if he had discussed his intentions with Davey, promised him anything, that would not carry any weight in law. The only thing that mattered to the law was this will.

Mrs MacTavish folded it up carefully, then tore it across three times, put the pieces into the empty fire grate behind the sprays of flowers. She set a match to it and watched each page burn. Then she broke up all the charred fragments, in case any writing still remained, replaced the flowers, poured herself another whisky, and sat down to write an appreciation of her late husband for the local paper. Better to say what she knew was safe rather than risk some reporter nosing around. Who knew what he might uncover?

The appointment Mrs MacTavish had made with the Writer to the Signet to read her husband's will was for three o'clock on the afternoon of the day following the funeral. Macleod had not visited the castle before, and consequently thought it prudent to arrive at the gates a quarter of an hour early.

He was not sure how long the drive was from the gates and there might be some delay in being taken to the study, and he did not wish to risk being late. He was meeting the young man who was due to inherit the whole estate for the first time; it would be foolish to create a bad initial impression.

Macleod drove his Morris Oxford to one side of the front door. It was already open. The butler had been told to expect him.

'Mrs MacTavish is in the study, sir,' he explained.

'And Mr Moore?'

'He's in the end garage, sir. Across the courtyard. Shall I tell Mrs MacTavish you are here?'

'No. I will have a word with Mr Moore first and come back directly.'

'I will wait here for you, sir.'

Davey Moore was cleaning his motorcycle. The laird had given him a second-hand Douglas as a reward for being accepted by MacTavish's old college at Oxford. He looked up in surprise as the door opened and a stranger came in.

'You don't know me,' the Writer explained. 'Macleod is the name. I am Mr MacTavish's lawyer.'

'I won't shake hands,' Davey replied. 'Mine are so dirty.'

'Honest toil,' said Macleod approvingly. 'I wanted to see you to say how sorry I was to hear of the laird's death. My colleagues and I have worked for him for many years, and before that we took instructions from his father.'

'He has mentioned you. I am very sorry he died, too. At first, I was not very close to him – I can admit that to you as his lawyer – but over the past year or so we grew much closer. He gave me this motorcycle, and would come out and sit on an upturned box while I worked on it.

'There was a kind of affinity between us, a sort of bond, that was growing stronger. I kept thinking he wanted to tell me something, I don't know what. He would begin and then suddenly change the subject or say he had an appointment elsewhere or something.'

'I have come here to read his will. You will be in the study at three to hear me read it, I expect.'

264

'I don't think so. It really doesn't concern me,' Davey replied. 'To be frank, I don't know what is going to happen to me now. Mrs MacTavish was never very welcoming to me, not like her husband. And she has hardly spoken to me since he died. I expect she is too upset.'

'I expect she is,' Macleod agreed. 'But I would like you to hear what I have to say, all the same.'

'What about Mrs MacTavish? Will she mind?'

'I would be very surprised if she did.'

'If you say so. Then I had better clean myself up a bit.'

Macleod crossed the courtyard, listening to the cooing of doves above the garage block. He felt the afternoon sunshine warm on his face, and wished he had been the one fortunate enough to inherit this huge property with the thousands of acres of land that surrounded it, and to feel part of a long line of succession that stretched back across the centuries to the reigns of the early Scottish kings.

The butler was waiting for him near the open front door.

'Will you be coming in now, sir?' he asked.

'Not for a moment. I'll wait for Mr Moore.'

'There's no need to,' said a voice from the end of the hall. Both men turned. Mrs MacTavish was standing outside the study door.

'The will does not concern him, Mr Macleod. It is purely a matter between you and me, and of course the wishes of my dear, dead husband.'

'I still think he should be present, Mrs MacTavish.'

'Why?'

'I would not wish to discuss a client's instructions here, ma'am, as I am sure you will appreciate.'

'Very well then, let him come,' she said. 'It is really immaterial to me, although why you feel it involves him is quite beyond me.'

At that moment, Davey Moore arrived. He and Macleod followed Mrs MacTavish into the study. She sat down in an armchair, indicated to Macleod that he should sit behind her husband's desk where he could spread out any papers he might need to consult. Davey Moore stood rather nervously at one side.

Macleod looked expectantly at Mrs MacTavish.

'Well, what are you waiting for?' she asked him sharply. 'Read the will. That's what you're here for.'

'I think you have the document, Mrs MacTavish. That's why I'm waiting. Your late husband took the only amended copy from my office the morning he died. I expect it is with his papers here.'

'Really?' Mrs MacTavish's voice sounded shrill with surprise, almost disbelief. 'He made his will years ago. I have a copy here.'

'He did, Mrs MacTavish,' the Writer agreed. 'But he made some important changes just before his death. He wanted to go through them again when he came home.' The lawyer looked round the room, saw the briefcase. 'He had that case with him. Perhaps the will is still in it.'

'Perhaps. Open it and see for yourself. Only do let us hurry. This is a very traumatic time for me, as I am sure you will appreciate.'

Macleod picked up the briefcase, shook out its contents on the desk. The will was not among them.

'It is not here, Mrs MacTavish. He said he wanted to read it again himself. Is there any place you think he could have put it?'

'He didn't have time to put it anywhere, poor man. He came in and dropped dead, literally, at my feet as I handed him a cup of tea. If it is not in the briefcase, it is not anywhere.'

266

'What exactly do you mean by that, Mrs MacTavish?'

'Exactly what I say. But why all the concern? You must have a copy, surely?'

'We have not. That is the point. He wanted to bring the document back so that he could peruse it in the privacy of his own home, as I have explained. He was going to give it back to me the following day, so that my clerk could copy it.'

'Well, I have here the will he made some time ago, which I am sure is the same.' Mrs MacTavish picked up a document lying on a side table, handed it to Macleod. He skimmed through it rapidly, then glanced at the date.

'I remember him making this out years ago. But I can tell you, it is substantially different from his later will,' he said slowly.

'But there *is* no later will,' replied Mrs MacTavish patiently. 'You as good as say so yourself. You have no copy. Neither have I. Am I not therefore right in believing that the will you hold in your hand is the only one containing my dear husband's instructions?'

Macleod inclined his head. 'In the absence of any other will, that is so.'

'Then please read it and let us be done with arguing.'

'I have to tell you, my clerk witnessed the second will. He knows what it contains. As I do.'

'But since there *is* no will, that point is surely academic. Please read the only will we have.' Mrs MacTavish turned to Davey Moore. 'There's really no need for you to be here. You are not mentioned in the will.'

'Not in this one, agreed,' Macleod said. 'But this was made before your husband took Mr Moore into his care.'

'Of course it was. Now, for the last time, are you going to read this will or are you not?'

There was something odd here; something Macleod did not like. He looked up sharply at Mrs MacTavish. Their eyes locked like swords. He saw hostility, contempt, triumph in her gaze and guessed she had destroyed the altered will. He looked across at Davey Moore.

'As Mrs MacTavish says, there is no need for you to stay,' he said gently. 'I am sorry to have brought you here.'

'Presumably you thought there was need for me to stay – if that second will could be found?'

'I cannot comment on that, as I am sure you will understand,' said Macleod quietly.

Davey stood up, bowed to Mrs MacTavish and left the room.

'Now, *at last*, can we read my husband's will?' Mrs MacTavish asked him petulantly.

Mrs MacTavish poured herself two fingers of whisky from the bottle her late husband kept in his desk. She noticed that the level was going down very quickly. She was drinking more than she should; but the spirit cheered her and provided confidence she lacked. For days she had kept postponing the meeting she must have with Davey Moore to tell him what she had decided about his future.

It would be best to be rid of him as soon as possible, just in case another copy of her husband's will was discovered. It was not impossible that the lawyer could find one; she didn't trust lawyers. Indeed, she didn't trust anyone. She put down the empty glass on the desk, wiped her lips on a silk handkerchief, and rang for a maid to ask Master Davey to come to the study at once.

While she waited she wondered how much she should offer him. A hundred pounds? Five hundred? A thousand? She decided on the middle figure. It seemed reasonable. A thousand was altogether too much to spend. But what if the boy refused to carry out her instructions? Could she force him to do so?

Davey knocked at the door, came into the room.

'Do sit down,' Mrs MacTavish told him, as kindly as she felt able. Then she paused, not quite certain how to begin. All her life she had been sheltered and cosseted, first by a rich father and then by her husband. She had never been required to make any serious decision on her own. The most she was ever asked to do was to agree with their judgements, their conclusions. She had no idea about money, no conception how the estate ran. Her husband employed accountants and a factor and a bailiff to deal with such matters. She had never even dismissed a servant, with all the unpleasantness this could sometimes involve. Such matters were her housekeeper's concern.

She took a deep breath. 'I have asked you here, Davey, because now that my husband is dead, I feel we have to discuss your future. How old are you now?'

'Eighteen next birthday, Mrs MacTavish.'

'I thought so. You are not a boy now, Davey, but a man. My husband, bless his dear heart, had planned for you to go to the university to follow some career or profession, as I expect he told you. But as you are a man, I know you can accept disappointments and changes of plan that might be crushing to a boy's hopes and expectations.'

She paused.

'I have to tell you frankly, my finances are not as I expected. The estate is burdened with debt. Farming does not pay, and as a result some of our largest tenant farmers are quite unable to meet their rents, modest as these are. And all the time the cost of everything continues to increase alarmingly.

'For years our distillery has produced Long Glen whisky for sale all round the world. Our largest overseas market has been the United States of America. Now their government has passed a ridiculous law prohibiting the sale of all alcoholic drinks, which has lost us the sale of thousands of bottles of Long Glen destined for New York. I tell you this to show that the future looks extremely bleak.'

Davey said nothing, waiting for her to continue. Mrs MacTavish eyed the whisky bottle longingly, but decided against another drink. That might be construed as weakness.

'I wanted to tell you these unpleasant facts face to face. I think it is better to do this than for you to hear them at second-hand. To be blunt, there is simply no money for your university fees. You are not mentioned in my husband's will, but I know how he regarded you, and I intend to give you a cheque out of my own pocket.'

Mrs MacTavish paused again.

She would never have peace of mind as long as Davey stayed here; he was a constant reminder of her husband's treachery. And if he ever discovered he was her husband's son, he might make all manner of difficulties. The Writer to the Signet knew the facts, and so, presumably, did the clerk or whoever in his office had drawn up the second will. Either of them might tell Davey, so the sooner he was moved as far away as possible, the safer she would feel.

'I imagine that, in these bleak circumstances, you will want to go out into the world and make your own way,' she went on. 'I therefore propose to give you five hundred pounds, and suggest that you leave within the next week. When one is young and starting out in life, there is no point in delaying departure. Have you any plans in mind?

'I haven't,' Davey admitted. 'Until this moment I had

assumed I was going to train for some career, as your husband suggested.'

'You are very keen on mechanical things,' said Mrs MacTavish. 'I have seen you with your motorcycle. There must be openings in that field for a young man of your ability. You could become apprenticed to a manufacturer in Coventry or Birmingham and learn that trade. Alternatively, you could emigrate. I remember that when my husband and I first met you in the minister's house, you said that this was already in your mind. There are great opportunities in Australia and Canada. I believe you can get a free passage there, and financial help until you are settled in. The prospects must be far greater in such huge countries than here in these small islands. You will easily find a job if you decide to take that course, and my five hundred pounds will help you until you do so. I am sorry if this seems sudden and harsh, but we must all accept changes now my husband is dead.'

'I quite understand that, Mrs MacTavish, but could I not take a job here, say in the distillery, working with the machinery? Perhaps I could then work my way up to something better.'

'We will be shedding staff from the distillery very soon in view of Prohibition,' Mrs MacTavish replied quickly. 'I'm sorry, but there's nothing there for you at all.'

Davey nodded. It was clear that she wanted him away as soon as possible, and in these circumstances he could see no point in delaying his departure.

'I would not want to impose on your hospitality any longer,' he said. 'I am grateful to your husband for paying my school fees, and keeping me so generously for so long. I will always remember his kindness, and will try to be worthy of his generosity, and I thank you for your gift now.'

Mrs MacTavish nodded approvingly and with relief. He was going quietly; he wasn't going to make any trouble. She opened a drawer in her desk, took out a chequebook and wrote out a cheque for five hundred pounds, payable to Bearer, and handed it to Davey.

Only when he had left the room did she reach for the whisky bottle. This time, she poured herself four fingers.

Davey Moore walked back to his room and started to pack. Then, on an impulse, he walked down to the village to the public telephone box and telephoned the Writer to the Signet. He did not want to use the telephone in the castle because he felt he could not bear to be further indebted to Mrs MacTavish, even to the small extent of paying for a local telephone call, since she had made it clear she wanted to be rid of him as soon as possible. There was also the possibility that others might listen on an extension, and what he had to say was for Mr Macleod's ears only.

A secretary told Davey that the Writer was engaged with a client. Would he please ring later? Davey walked up and down for half an hour and rang again. This time the Writer was in conference. He telephoned a third time. The Writer was just leaving for an appointment with counsel. Could he please tell the secretary what he wished to discuss? Davey explained that it was a private matter.

He suspected that the Writer had no intention of speaking to him, and even if he telephoned tomorrow or on every one of his tomorrows, there would still be some excuse why he could not do so.

Davey walked back to the castle, climbed on his motorcycle and rode into Perth. The Writer's office was in a converted private house. The front garden had been concreted over to make a car park for several cars. Davey recognised the Writer's Morris Oxford and parked his motorcycle nearby. He sat down on a low wall until five o'clock, when Macleod left his office. Clearly, the message that he was leaving earlier had been false.

He frowned when he saw Davey approaching him.

'I could not reach you on the telephone,' Davey explained, 'so I felt the only way to speak to you was to come and see you.'

'I am very busy,' replied Macleod petulantly. 'I cannot discuss anything with you now. I am already late for an appointment.'

'Mrs MacTavish has given me a cheque for five hundred pounds and a week's notice to go. I wanted to ask you, while I am still in the area, if you could tell me something about this other will you mentioned.'

'I cannot divulge any details about a client's instructions. It is most improper of you even to ask me.'

'Some might consider it unfriendly and unhelpful not to answer a question of the utmost importance to me. I am about to leave this country. You will probably never see me again. I accept that I am not mentioned in the will to which Mrs MacTavish referred, but I believe I must have been mentioned in the will that cannot be found, otherwise you would not have asked me to be present when you read it? Am I right? Simply answer me that one question.'

'Let me tell you something, Davey,' said Macleod, more kindly this time. 'All manner of people tell relations or friends that they intend to leave them something when they die – maybe a fortune, a house, perhaps only a book, but something. Often they genuinely mean it at the time, although sometimes they only say it to get good will, or a favour from that person. In any event, for whatever reason, they do nothing about it, and that is the end of the matter.

Others go a step further, and actually make a will mentioning this person or persons. But they may not have it witnessed, or they don't sign it. Or they do both, and then, somehow, the will just disappears.'

'That is what happened here, sir, is it?'

'It would appear so,' the Writer said carefully. It seemed clear that the young fellow had no idea MacTavish was his father. 'You will understand that I cannot tell you what was in the missing will, but there is nothing confidential in the fact that the laird took it away with him on the morning of his death.'

'And there's no copy?'

'That is so. He promised to return it so that it could be copied.'

'The inference then is that someone destroyed it.'

'That is a *possible* inference,' agreed Macleod cautiously. 'But not a conclusion based on any evidence whatever. Mr MacTavish may have put it somewhere for safekeeping – in a file, a drawer, anywhere – and died before he could remove it. He might even have had second thoughts about it and destroyed it himself.'

'Do you believe it will be found, sir?'

Macleod shook his head. 'In a fairly long career, I have on several occasions come across this situation of missing wills. But I have never ever known one to turn up. A lost will stays lost. That is one of life's basic truths, in my experience. You will have to accept that. But all this belongs to the past. Tell me, where are you planning to emigrate?'

'I think to Australia or Canada.'

'Do you know anyone in either country?'

'No, sir.'

'I have a relation in Canada. He works for a chemical

company in Toronto. Quite high up in it, I believe. It makes pills and patent medicines and so forth. I am sure he would give you a job of some sort, at least until you find something else if you don't like it. Come here tomorrow and I will give you a letter of introduction. His name is Tam Douglas.'

'That is very kind of you, sir.'

'Not at all. I would like to help you if I can. Who knows, you may make your fortune and come back to Scotland and require my services.'

Both men smiled. Neither imagined that this could ever come about.

Eleven

The Royal Mail ship *Benares Castle* trembled under blasts from her siren as hawsers were cast off and she moved away from the quay. Against a grey afternoon sky, seagulls swooped, calling shrilly and angrily through the winter chill. Clouds rested on the top of buildings. As the tugs hauled the liner into midstream and let go towing ropes, the ship's engines took up the strain. The siren blasted a farewell to England, and with a tremble like a giant animal shaking herself free, *Benares Castle* headed for the open sea.

Down on E Deck, Davey Moore sat on his bunk, one of six in the cramped cabin. He wore his best suit, because he felt that somehow this was appropriate to starting a new life in the New World. He had the letter to Mr Macleod's relation in an inner pocket with a flap that buttoned down on it, and a letter from a Perth bank authorising any bank to advance him up to the equivalent of £500. Every now and then he touched the edges of these letters with the tips of his fingers to reassure himself they were still safe. The Writer's letter he regarded as more than a card of entry; it was a key to a new life, because in spite of his outward appearance of confidence, Davey felt nervous and alone.

The five other young men who shared the cabin were all on their way to find work in the United States or Canada. One had brought with him carpenters' tools in a carpet bag. Another had a set of spanners, each one fitting into a shaped recess in a blue tin case.

'You won't find those much use,' said the carpenter.

'Why not?'

'Because they're Whitworths and in the States they use different threads altogether.'

'Well, maybe I'll find someone who has British machinery.'

'I doubt it,' retorted the carpenter.

This underlined the fact that they were not going to another part of Britain, but to a totally new country. Still, Davey wasn't alone; thousands had sailed before him. If they could find work, then so could he. Thus cheered, he went up to the very small patch of deck that steerage passengers were allowed to use.

The passengers were divided into decks according to their class – first, second, third and steerage. This last took its name from the fact that accommodation was either on or just below the water line, down in the belly of the ship. Feet away from their tiny cabins great chains controlling the rudder slithered through a mass of thick grease and scummy oil. The propeller shaft revolved slowly, and the thunder of its blades reverberated throughout the stern of the ship as if in an echoing metal canyon.

Steerage passengers were allowed only a small section of the deck up forward. There were no deckchairs, and indeed no seats of any kind. If they wanted to sit down they had to perch on anchor chains or coils of thick oily rope and oil drums lashed to the side of donkey engines that winched in ropes and anchors.

The wind was fresh, and the bows of the *Benares Castle* slowly dipped and rose again in stately motion. This was a bad place to stand for anyone who felt seasick, but Davey found that the movement was exhilarating. He stood, legs apart, bracing himself against the rise and fall of the deck, his arms folded, imagining himself at the prow of a vessel setting out to explore an uncharted and seemingly endless sea.

Up on the top deck, huge windows, six feet tall and nearly as wide, sheltered the first-class passengers as they took their morning promenade. Some walked in groups, deep in earnest conversation; others in pairs, a few on their own. The men cast appraising eyes on any single women. Some men bowed to them and smiled, hoping that in the five days of the Atlantic crossing it might be possible to conduct an affair with the comforting knowledge that both parties would accept that it ended the moment the ship docked.

Along one side of this promenade deck a row of striped canvas chairs had been set out. Wrapped in rugs, several passengers had already taken up their positions. Attentive stewards, having calculated who were the most likely to be liberal tippers, hovered about them solicitously, offering hot drinks or bouillon.

Maria did not want beef tea or bouillon; she wanted excitement. But while she waited for whatever opportunity this trip might bring, she had allowed herself to be tucked up on a canvas chair with a rug round her legs. Glancing to left and right, all her companions seemed very old; grey-haired men, women with sunken faces and dull, discontented eyes. On the impulse, she threw aside the rug, walked across the deck and looked out through the wide windows at the rise and fall of the bows. As she looked, she saw Davey in silhouette.

He did not move for several minutes. Then he turned and, as though feeling her intent gaze on him, looked up at her. He could only make out the faint, foggy outlines of a girl's face through the misted glass. She wiped condensation away and waved to him. He thought she must be waving to someone else. He turned round, but there was no one else. She was pointing at him now and smiling. He waved back uneasily. Then she left, and he was staring at the empty blank glass, wondering whether he had imagined the whole incident.

For the first time, Davey realised how lonely he was. He knew no one aboard ship or in Canada; he had no friends in whom he could confide, with whom he could share this new adventure. Worse, he had no trade. All he had was a letter in his pocket and a bank credit for £500. What would it be like to be travelling first class, like that girl, who no doubt knew all kinds of important people?

Maria flicked her fingers at a passing steward. He hurried across to her.

'Yes, madam?'

'There's a young man down on the lower deck. I'd like you to take a message to him. Have you a piece of paper?'

He handed her a small writing pad and a pencil marked with the name of the ship. She scribbled a note with her cabin number, opened her purse, took out a ten-shilling note.

'You will see him down there. Give it to him.'

'If he is on that deck, madam, he is travelling steerage. He cannot come through to the first class.'

'Not even if he's invited? I'm inviting him.'

'It's very difficult, madam. One of the strict rules of the ship.'

'I never obey other people's rules, strict or otherwise,' said Maria. 'I make my own.' She smiled, and put another ten-shilling note on top of the first. 'I'd like to see him,' she added and turned her back on the steward. He scurried away.

Maria went down to her cabin, lit a cigarette, and sat in one of the easy chairs, waiting impatiently for the knock on the door that would tell her the young man had arrived. She caught sight of herself in one of the long, gilt-edged mirrors that lined the walls and smiled at her reflection. Only a few years ago she would have been travelling steerage, like the young man, if indeed she would have been travelling anywhere. But now she was a first-class passenger, with a state room, able to buy her way through any kind of rules and regulations. That's what money meant; or rather, that's what being married to a very rich man meant. The fact that he was a gangster was irrelevant.

Maria had been brought up a Catholic and knew the difference between right and wrong, but now she rationalised her situation. What did it really matter how money was made, as long as it was made and you could enjoy it. You could argue that however the money had been acquired, its possession allowed you to give work to other people who might otherwise have been unemployed. Anyhow, it was infinitely better than being a waitress, which is what she had been before she met Giuseppe. Yet, on reflection, if she hadn't been a waitress, she would never have met him. And in that case she would still be carrying out other people's instructions, like the steward to whom she had just given the note.

Maria's transformation from one who took orders to someone who gave them had come about in a most unexpected way. From the age of sixteen, she had worked in a modest ice-cream parlour in Chicago, near the corner of Halstead and 14th Streets, not far from the Maxwell Street ghetto. The customers there were predominantly working class, mostly of Italian origin. Some brought their families to the parlour for a treat, fondly watching their children guzzle huge ice-cream sundaes, marshmallow flips, or thick, malt-flavoured milk shakes.

Then, as Prohibition became law, Maria noticed that fewer women and children customers came in, and many more men. They were not workmen wearing overalls and dungarees, with oily hands and dirty fingernails, who sat on the bar stools or at the tables with their wives. These were a different class altogether: shopkeepers, clerks, sometimes lawyers. Without any trace of embarrassment, they ordered sickly sweet concoctions which previously had been the children's favourites. And they would not simply order one but two, or three or even four, and devour them all with remarkable speed and obvious enjoyment. This seemed an extraordinary situation, but Maria was an innocent girl then and could not understand the sudden appetite of well-heeled men for ice-cream sodas and sundaes.

One day, a man who had ordered a cherry sundae was called out by someone who came to the front door. He left in a hurry and did not return. He had not touched the sundae, but it had been paid for, so Maria could see nothing wrong in taking it behind the counter and eating it herself.

To her, the taste seemed disgusting. She had never drunk anything alcoholic, and so she did not recognise the cheap whisky flavour.

'There's something wrong with this,' she told the owner.

'You think so?' he said, grinning. 'You notice we've been doing ten times as much business here since they banned liquor outside.'

'Yes. But this sundae is revolting. I can't eat it.'

'You don't have to. It's not for eating, it's for selling. It's spiked.'

'What do you mean?'

'It's flavoured with liquor. Cherry sundae is the code for whisky, malt sundae for brandy. You can get gin, vodka, anything. In other places people are drinking cups of tea. But there's very little tea in those teapots and a lot of liquor. That's why we've jacked up our prices. Didn't you notice?'

'I thought that was just because more people were coming in.'

'Sure. That's one of the reasons. But the main one is, liquor costs a lot of money. We buy from one source and we have to pay others not to tamper with us. Protection money. You've been walking around with your eyes shut, girl.'

'I must have been,' Maria agreed.

'How else could we afford to redecorate this joint? Long may Prohibition last, that's what I say.'

Shortly after this conversation, she met Giuseppe. Then, she didn't know who he was, or how important. He would come in on his own, usually in the late morning, and sit in a corner drinking a black coffee and smoking a cigar. He never ate ice-creams or sundaes, and he was always polite and well dressed. One day, he was the only man in the ice-cream parlour. They got talking.

'Business is good,' he remarked. 'Yes?'

'Yes,' she agreed. 'Though I tasted one of the sundaes myself and I didn't like it.'

'Then you must be in the minority. Worked here long?'

'Couple of years. And you?'

'I was a waiter. Cicero's Restaurant.'

'I've passed that. It's very flash.'

'That's right. It's even flashier now.'

'Do they serve drinks spiked with liquor?'

'Well, that's not for me to say. It's illegal to serve alcoholic beverages. But I think you might just find one or

283

two whiskies there, if you looked hard enough.' Giuseppe smiled, amused at the girl's obvious innocence and naivety. After that, they had a chat every time he came in. One day, again when they were on their own, he looked her up and down sharply.

'You like nice clothes?'

'Of course. But I can't afford too many on what I'm paid.'

'I thought not.'

He put a hand in an inside pocket, removed a wallet, extracted a hundred-dollar bill. 'Buy yourself something nice – underwear as well as what I can see.'

'That's a lot of money. Why are you giving me it?'

'Because I like you. Because, having been poor myself, I now have a lot of money – relatively speaking. And I'm going to get a lot more.'

'How, if you're a waiter?'

'Oh, I left that job. Now I'm a customer. You're waiting on me. So I'll have another black coffee, with lots of sugar.'

They might have gone on like this indefinitely, Giuseppe buying coffees, Maria serving them, until perhaps they reached the point of going out together and maybe going to bed together.

Maria bought a dress and a coat and black underclothes and silk stockings and shoes with buckles and very high heels. She had little change from the hundred-dollar bill, and found she did not relish having to wear shabby, cheap clothes again.

Then something happened on a hot afternoon that changed her whole life.

One day she was walking near Oakwood cemetery when she saw people standing in groups, obviously waiting for something or someone to pass along the road.

'It's Big Jim's funeral,' someone told her when she asked.

She did not know who Big Jim was – she did not read newspapers then – but she waited as funeral cars, covered by mountains of white wreaths and crosses, came slowly by, followed by an army of mourners, five thousand strong. All the women wore black dresses and the men black suits, walking behind the cortège with heads down. Next morning, wondering who could have been buried in such style, she read a newspaper in the ice-cream parlour. To her astonishment, she learned that Big Jim's pallbearers included two congressmen, a state representative, three judges, an assistant state attorney, eight Chicago aldermen and, behind them, the main singers of the Chicago Opera Company.

One alderman, John Coughlin, knelt by the coffin and recited Hail Marys. It was noted that the Roman Catholic archbishop had refused to allow the use of the church at the cemetery, on the grounds that Big Jim had been divorced.

When Giuseppe came in for his coffee, she told him she had seen the procession. Giuseppe knew so many people; had he ever met him?

'Yes. I knew him slightly,' he admitted. 'It was a fine send-off he had. A great man, Big Jim.'

'What did he do, exactly? Someone in here this morning said he ran a restaurant, Colisimo's.'

'Sure did. And he ran other things too. But never mind that now. What about another coffee, now I'm here?'

Next day, on Maria's way to work for the afternoon shift, she passed a group of children playing hopscotch on the pavement. Suddenly, they stopped playing to stare at a large black car parked against the kerb.

There was nothing particularly unusual about the car; what was unusual was the fact that four men were roughly manhandling a fifth into the back of it. For a moment Maria thought they must be police in plain clothes, arresting a felon. But the fifth man had a look on his face of such horror and terror that she felt this was too easy an explanation. The car accelerated away, the hopscotch game continued, and Maria walked on into the ice-cream parlour.

Giuseppe was a little late that day. He seemed preoccupied, just nodded to her curtly as she brought him his black coffee. He sat until late in the evening, working out figures in a notebook. She missed his conversation. She wondered if she was boring him, if he'd found someone else to talk to, someone more attractive perhaps, prettier. She approached the table.

'I saw something odd here today,' she began.

'What was that?'

'Four men were sort of kidnapping another right outside the parlour.'

'You saw their faces?'

'Of course. I was as near to them as to you.'

'Would you recognise them again?'

'Yes. Specially the man they were putting into the back of the car.'

'Sit down,' said Giuseppe sharply. He glanced round the room. Three middle-aged men were enjoying raspberry sundaes at a corner table; elsewhere, men on their own were reading newspapers and sipping milkshakes. Giuseppe looked at them; they did not appear to have heard what Maria had said, but he did not like to take risks.

'Keep your voice down,' he whispered to her. 'You've seen something which it could be dangerous for you to admit seeing.'

'But why? They were policemen, weren't they?'

'Not exactly. But they were carrying out duties that in the interests of justice sometimes do fall to the police. Forget what you saw. Don't mention it to anyone. Put it right out of your mind. Now.'

'Why?'

'Because it's dangerous.'

'All right. If you say so.'

'I say so. It could be very dangerous for you if you ever mentioned it.'

'But why me? I don't know those men. I was just passing by.'

'You could recognise them. Every face has a name.' He put his notes in his pocket, laid a five-dollar bill on the table. 'That'll cover the coffee,' he said. 'And remember what I say. Remember to forget.'

He went out. Two days later, in a newspaper again left behind by a customer, Maria saw a picture of the fifth man. She instantly recognised him. His name was given as Steve Wisiewski, and his body had been found at the roadside in the small town of Libertyville, twenty-five miles north of Chicago. He had been shot several times in the head.

Maria sat down, numb with horror and fear, still holding the paper. She had seen an abduction – four men taking away a fifth to kill him. Now she realised just what Giuseppe had meant when he said she could be in danger if she spoke about what she had seen.

The telephone rang, making her jump. She was alone in the ice-cream parlour – her employer had gone to the bank – and so she picked up the receiver. Giuseppe was on the line.

'Get out of that cafe,' he told her urgently. 'Now.' He gave her an address. 'Come over here. I'll be waiting for you.'

'But I'm on duty. I can't just walk off. Pedro, the owner, is out. I have to wait until he comes back.'

'Do as I say. Now. This is deadly serious.'

What did he mean? Why such urgency in his voice? It frightened her. Maria stood irresolute, drumming her fingernails on the top of the counter. Through the window she could see children playing hopscotch on the corner where that man with the strange Polish name had been kidnapped.

As she watched them, a car drew up, stopped across the road. It was the same size as the one that had stopped then, but that had been black. This car had black wings and a blue body. Four men climbed out. She recognised them instantly. They were the men she had seen on that previous occasion. They approached the children. One of the men tossed a coin to the oldest boy and asked him some questions. The boy pointed towards the ice-cream parlour. Instantly Maria guessed why they were here. Somehow they had heard she was a witness.

Instead of coming to the ice-cream parlour, the men returned to the car and brought out what appeared to be banjo cases. What an extraordinary thing! Were they going to play? Were they musicians wanting a job? Then she saw that all the children had run away. Suddenly the street was empty and quiet. The men crossed the road, looked in the window. They could see her standing there, just as she could see them, and in that moment she ducked, sensing danger as an animal hears the approach of a hunter.

From the banjo cases the men took submachine guns. She recognised them from newsreel films of gangsters. Their shots crackled all over the front of the shop, splintering the glass, going through door panels. By then, Maria was crawling out from the parlour into the kitchen. She opened a back door, ran into the yard and then on into another street. As she ran she heard more shots spatter the walls of the cafe, then a squeal of tyres as the car accelerated away.

She ran without stopping until she reached the address Giuseppe had given to her. It was a rooming house. She felt surprised he lived here, in a poor area. On the doorpost half a dozen bell pushes had names or initials written on bits of cardboard and stuck with paste or drawing pins.

She did not know Giuseppe's name, so she pressed the bell push marked 'G.C.' It seemed the nearest to Giuseppe. A window opened upstairs, Giuseppe looked out.

'I'll be right down.'

He let her in, took her up the stairs to his room.

'Those men,' she said, trembling. 'They came again. In a blue and black car. They fired machine guns all over the cafe.'

'You're not hurt?'

'No. I was behind the counter. I went down on all fours and crawled out. But why me? Who are they?'

'You've no idea?' he asked her, looking at her quizzically. 'Well, you *are* innocent. It's all tied up with those funny-tasting sundaes. Booze. Prohibition. That funeral you saw. Big Jim Colisimo.'

'What's he got to do with it?'

'Nothing, now. But for the last twenty years he was the prime mover of all the gangsters here in Chicago.'

'But all those famous people, all those politicians, were at his funeral.'

'Of course. He owned them. They were his men. He paid them in cash, and they repaid him with silence. Let me give you a rundown. Like me, like you, Big Jim was the child of Italian immigrants. He was a shoe-shine boy, he sold newspapers. Then he joined the Black Hand gang from the old country, enforcing shopkeepers, cafe owners, all kinds to pay their dues or have their places raided or their kneecaps smashed. He became rich.

'He was a strong-arm man. For a cover he worked as a street sweeper. Then he had the idea to enrol all street sweepers in the city into a kind of club.

'Big Jim dumped his wife and married a woman who ran a brothel. He expanded this single cat-house into a chain, and started his own cafe. Soon he was earning half a million bucks a year in cash in his back pocket.

'To show how rich he was, he wore diamonds sewn on his suit, had diamond rings on his fingers and he carried little leather bags of diamonds in his pockets. As he'd talk, he'd run his fingers through them. Newspapers called him Diamond Jim and he loved the publicity. But he caused a lot of envy among his colleagues in the Black Hand. When you're making money you attract criticism if you throw it about, which he did, so they decided to take him out.

'Big Jim heard of this and hired a hit man from New York, one Johnny Torrio, to look after him. Torrio has a brain like a calculating machine. He doesn't like all this killing that's going on because it makes for bad publicity and cuts into profits. One guy shoots a rival and then the rival's friend shoots him, and so on, multiplied many times over, day after day. He wants peace and quiet, and everyone's energies focused on one object – making money.

'Old Big Jim couldn't understand this at all. He couldn't change. He'd drunk too much, screwed too much, and he wanted an easy life. So one day Torrio got rid of him – and then went to his funeral, which he organised. Now that is style for you.'

'But how does this affect you or me?' asked Maria.

'Because I work for Torrio. What he can do, I can do.'

'So you're a gangster? Like the men who shot that Pole?'

'In a loose sense, yes. Some people have to organise Torrio's deals. I'm one of those. I hear all kinds of things, and I heard you could be in trouble. So I'm taking you out of trouble. I'm going to marry you. Then you'll be quite safe.'

'But we don't know each other, apart from exchanging a few words over your coffee. You don't know my parents. They're very strict.'

'Maybe. But they'd rather have a daughter a bride than one in the graveyard under a marble cross. I'll give them five hundred bucks as a wedding present. That'll show them I'm serious. We'll get married now.'

'But I don't love you, Giuseppe. I like you, but that's not the same thing.'

'This isn't a question of love. That's for women's magazine stories. I don't want to see you rubbed out. I like you. You're so innocent, you're a treat. Anyhow, you haven't much choice. Those guys who killed Wisiewski won't make life hard if you're my wife because they'll know that if they did, they wouldn't live long enough to make another mistake.'

'But this is terrible!' cried Maria in anguish. 'I don't want to get involved with killers.'

'You won't, with me. I'm going to be rich and you'll be rich with me. You won't need to go back behind a bar, ever.

'Now there's one other thing I want to make clear. I'm changing my name. Most of the gangs are Irish, Italians, Jews, all with foreign names, like ours. I want a proper American name. I'm going to be king one day, king of the castle. So I'm changing my name to Castle. William Castle. And you're changing yours to Mrs Castle.'

Now Maria sat, as Mrs William Castle, in her state room

and waited for the young man to arrive. Since her unexpected and unwanted marriage she had often waited for other young men to call, because her husband was not interested in her despite his claim that he liked her, sometimes that he even loved her.

She soon discovered why her husband had wanted to marry her so quickly. The excuse that otherwise she might be killed as a potentially dangerous witness was not the reason. Castle prided himself on being a hard man. The shooting of a waitress in an ice-cream parlour was of little account to him; he was directly or indirectly involved in a shooting every few days, for despite his claim that Torrio wanted peace, others resented Torrio's growing influence and it fell to Castle, among others, to deal with them.

Castle married Maria to provide a cover for his lack of interest in any sexual liaison, with either women or men. He dreaded being classed as a homosexual or, worse, an impotent, and marriage to a young girl would surely put an end to innuendoes and sneering remarks. His colleagues and contemporaries boasted of their affairs with chorus girls, some even with stars. Castle was simply not interested. His sole interest was in making money, as much as possible and as quickly as possible and by whatever means.

He carried a small notebook in his pocket and itemised all profits and expenses every day. He had been doing this when Maria thought he was too busy to talk to her and wondered whether she could have offended him.

But although Castle was so keen on becoming rich, he never thought what he would do when he was rich, how he would spend the money. The aim was simply to acquire it.

For Maria, her discovery why Castle married her was traumatic and humiliating. At first, she sought release in the whisky he sold in such quantities. Then slowly and carefully, she began a number of discreet affairs, vaguely hoping she might find a man who liked her for herself, not simply for her availability and new-found wealth. So far, she had been disappointed. Perhaps she was asking too much and, being married, too late. This particularly depressed her, and again she sought escape in whisky.

Castle knew that she played around on the side, and insisted she must be discreet about her liaisons. It wouldn't do for anyone to know; they might laugh at him. But on this ship there was no risk, for no one knew her. To the other passengers she was simply another rich American woman who had been over to Europe and who was now returning to Chicago and her apartment on Michigan Avenue. This was in the same block as the Torrios, so she had met him several times. He seemed so quiet, it was difficult to believe he was a totally ruthless killer. He had a large collection of classical and operatic records, and on most evenings he would sit listening to them. He looked like a successful businessman and, of course, in his own way he was. He wore dark suits and never raised his voice. She found it almost incredible that he was now one of the most powerful and feared men in the United States, a millionaire without an office, controlling politicians, judges, mayors, lawyers by the score.

A knock on the cabin door scattered Maria's thoughts like the imitation snowflakes in the cheap kaleidoscope her mother had bought her on her tenth birthday – her only present then, she remembered now. What a long time ago that was!

'Come,' she called imperiously. She had heard an actor in a play about the French Revolution give this one word of command to an underling knocking on his door, and it had impressed her. She hoped it also impressed others.

The door opened. Davey came in, and stood looking in admiration at the state room. This was far more luxurious than any room he had ever seen; it made the cabin he shared seem like a cupboard. And what to him was strangest of all was that this room, with its panelled walls, brocaded sofas and armchairs, flowers on a huge table, piles of magazines scattered on a smaller one, shelves full of books, was actually in a ship, at sea. Somehow, he had vaguely imagined that all cabins aboard the *Benares Castle* were as primitive and spartan as his.

'You like it?' Maria asked him, sensing his feelings, which would have been hers only a very short time ago.

'Very much, ma'am.'

'It's sure got a good view of the ocean. And being in the centre of the vessel it doesn't roll. It's just like being on dry land, in the Waldorf or the Crillon. This is the first transatlantic voyage I've made. A lot of people told me I'd be sick, but I haven't been the least queasy at all. You travel much?'

'No, ma'am. This is my first trip, too. But what do you want to see me about? The steward said you had a message.'

'Oh, these stewards, they'll say anything. I just saw you looking lonely up in the bows, so I thought I'd ask you up here for a chat. Have a drink?'

'What of, ma'am?'

'Whatever you like – cocktail, Scotch on the rocks, beer, anything. I've got a cabinet of it here.'

'I don't drink alcohol.'

'You're not keen on Prohibition, are you?'

'I don't know anything about it, ma'am.'

'I'll tell you some time,' said Maria, amused. What a hick this kid was, and yet so good-looking. His naivety added to his charm. 'Meantime, sit down and have a cocktail with me. A really dry martini. You know how to mix one?'

'No, ma'am.'

'Well, I'll show you.'

She picked up bottles of gin and vermouth, poured the spirits into a shaker, added ice, shook it, decanted the cocktail into two glasses.

'Your health. Do you know, I don't even know your name.'

'It's Davey. Davey Moore.'

'I'm Maria Castle.'

Davey sipped the drink. It tasted very strong. He was not quite sure that he liked the taste, but the drink certainly had a kick that was not unattractive. He sat down on the edge of the sofa, looking at the woman. As she crossed her legs, he glanced down involuntarily at her silk stockings. She crossed them again, more carelessly this time, so that he could see a brief flash of white thigh.

'Well, you *are* a quiet young man,' said Maria, watching him, half amused. Her expression concealed far deeper feelings. This young man, hardly more than a boy, was as innocent as she had been when she married. Totally unspoiled. Virgin, without a doubt. The sort of person she could mould to make her ideal man. He was tall, good-looking, well-mannered, with a brand of old-fashioned courtesy about him that was missing in all her husband's friends. They chewed gum and spoke out of the corner of their mouths, often without seeming to move their lips. The shoulders of their suits were too heavily padded, their trousers too wide at the turn-ups. They wore brown and white shoes. Davey Moore wore grey flannel trousers, a blue cotton shirt, a tweed jacket, polished brogues. He was different. Maria searched for the correct word to describe his appearance, found it: *wholesome*. She sipped her drink appreciatively. No doubt about it, a stiff drink sharpened the mind.

'Another?' she asked him.

'I haven't finished this yet, ma'am.'

'You'll soon get in the habit of it.'

She mixed another martini, topped up both their glasses, raised hers to him in a silent toast.

'I'm getting ahead of you,' she said. 'Drink up. You can't let a woman beat a man.'

'Is it a race, then?' Davey asked her.

He was beginning to feel slightly woozy, as though he was not actually here but somehow only observing everything. Through the brass-rimmed portholes, the far horizon rose and fell slowly with the gentle movement of the ship.

'Not really a race,' said Maria. 'But a brisk walk, a trot, if you like.' She glanced at her diamond-encrusted wristwatch. 'It's almost lunchtime. Where are you lunching?'

'There's a mess room downstairs on my deck. I was going to eat there. They have two sittings, there are so many people.'

'A *mess room*? Two sittings? No way. Come and lunch with me.'

'That's very kind of you, ma'am, but I haven't much extra money. I've paid for my fare, which includes meals . . .'

'Ah, you're a real Scot, I see. You don't want to be done out of anything you've paid for.'

'It's not that, exactly. Though I wouldn't argue against what you say. The fact is, that's all I can afford.'

'I'm asking you to be *my* guest. You can afford to do that, surely? Come and lunch with me. But finish that drink first. They've got some very good wine on this ship. My steward tells me that it's something we should treat ourselves to. You drink wine?'

'I've never drunk wine. Never really drunk anything.'

'Tell me, how were you brought up? What do you do for a living?'

'I was brought up in the country, in Scotland, by my mother. My father wasn't there.'

'What happened to him?'

He shrugged. 'I don't know. My mother never talked about it. Then my mother died and the local laird – that's the landowner – he took me into his home.'

'That was kind of him.'

'Yes. It was. He was a nice man. He had a baby son, killed in a drowning accident. Then he died, poor fellow, and his widow – she and I never really got on – she gave me some money so that I could emigrate.'

'How much money?'

Davey paused. A stranger had no business asking this, but somehow he did not resent it. She was obviously so rich that the sort of sum Mrs MacTavish had given him was of no importance to her.

'Five hundred pounds,' he said.

'And what are you going to do in the States?'

'Go on to Canada. I've a letter of introduction from the laird's lawyer to a relation of his in a chemical works in Toronto. I hope to get a job there.'

'Doing what? Are you good at anything special?'

'Well, I like mechanical things – motorcycles. Bit of a self-taught engineer, really. I'm going to learn a trade if I can.'

'Good for you. Perhaps we can learn together.'

'What do you mean, exactly?'

'Oh, all sorts of things. Now, come and have lunch. But

as I say, finish your drink first. There's plenty more where that came from.'

'I think I've had enough,' said Davey.

'Never say that. Like money, you either have none or you don't have enough. You can *never* have too much drink or too much money.'

Davey gulped down the strong drink quickly and followed her out of the state room along the corridor. Although the sea was calm, he was thankful he could reach out and keep one hand firmly on the rail. The scrubbed planks of the deck seemed to be moving in a way he had never experienced before. Or maybe they were stationary and his two feet were moving oddly.

They reached the restaurant before he could make up his mind. Again, this was like no room he had ever seen: white walls edged with gold, tables aglitter with silver knives, forks, spoons of all sizes, three crystal glasses by each place.

'We'll sit by the window,' said Maria. 'I like to watch the sea.'

Davey was glad to sit down. A waiter appeared, holding two menus bound in leather. Davey saw they were written in French.

'You choose,' he said. He did not want to appear ignorant in front of her. After all, she was not much older than he was. And yet she seemed to know everything about this kind of life and he knew absolutely nothing.

'What I would suggest is that we have Mediterranean prawns in their shells, and then perhaps a grilled sole or a steak.'

'A steak,' said Davey firmly. This sounded familiar. He could not make a fool of himself with that.

'A bottle of Chablis to start with,' she told the wine

waiter who now hovered by the table, his gilt chain of office glittering in the weak sunshine. 'Is there any wine you particularly recommend for the steak?'

'We have some very fine clarets, madam.'

'Good. I want the very finest.'

'It will be my pleasure.'

Davey drank very little. He was grateful for the glass of iced water by his plate that the waiter kept refilling. He enjoyed the prawns and the steak, but more than either he enjoyed the extraordinary feeling of confidence that these opulent surroundings inspired.

'Come back and have a coffee and brandy in my room,' said Maria casually.

He followed her along the promenade deck, not needing to hold on to the rail this time; the food had steadied his stomach.

Maria opened the state-room door, locked it behind her casually, as though this was something she always did whenever she was in her suite.

'I think I had better be getting back,' said Davey.

'There's no hurry,' she said gently. 'We're going nowhere faster than the ship. Have a brandy?'

'Are you?'

'Of course. We've real French brandy here, not some bootleg gut rot. Take off your jacket and relax. Make yourself at home.'

'It's a very luxurious home,' he said hesitantly.

'It'll do in lieu of anything better. Yes, it'll do.'

Maria had seduced many young men, but none so deliberately and with such pleasure of anticipation as Davey Moore. It was all so easy that in a way she felt slightly mean. She wondered if the older men who had seduced her since her marriage had felt the same about her. She thought probably not. She poured two Hines, watched Davey sip the drink appreciatively. Then she suggested he took off his shoes and lie down; unaccustomed alcohol had begun to affect him, he was looking a bit dozy, she said.

'Why not undress and go to bed? Have a sleep. There are two beds in the bedroom.'

He felt sleepy and agreed willingly. He kicked off his shoes, waited modestly until she left the room, then undressed to his underpants. He climbed into the second bed and was almost immediately asleep. As he slept, Maria undressed completely and climbed in beside him. From then on it was as though everything had been predestined. She let him sleep for a time, stroking his body gently and expertly. How firm and whole his flesh was! How infinitely more attractive than the hairy, older bodies of some of her other lovers.

She awoke him by kissing his chest first, and then his lips, then moving down his body. They were lying very close together. She could feel his hard phallus pulse with every beat of his heart.

'Have you ever done this before?' she asked him.

He shook his head. 'I've never had a chance,' he admitted.

'Well, I'm giving you the chance.'

'But this is wrong. We'll make a baby like this.'

'No. We won't.'

'Are you sure?'

'Take my word for it.'

She moved on him now, guided him into her.

Afterwards they slept and woke again and then made love a second time, a third, a fourth. He seemed tireless, and always ready to learn. She rang for the steward to bring a bottle of champagne. They sat in pink chairs while they waited for it to arrive. Maria was quite naked. Davey had wrapped a towel round himself.

'What about the man who brings in the drink?' he asked her nervously.

'What about him? Do you want me to seduce him?'

'No, no. I mean, won't you feel embarrassed with nothing on?'

'I'll put on a dressing gown, just for him. Or rather, for you,' she said, and gave him a butterfly kiss on his forehead.

For the rest of the voyage, Davey moved into her state room. He assumed that Maria paid whatever difference was owing on the fares, but he did not enquire. He was learning that sometimes it was unwise to ask questions.

They came on deck as they approached New York, passed the Statue of Liberty. She pointed out the row of windows at the top.

'You can climb up there,' she told him. 'It's a wonderful view.'

'I like the view here with you,' Davey replied.

'You're very sweet. But I must tell you, from now on we'll have to be more careful. I'm married.'

'You never told me,' said Davey, staring at her, horrified. What had he let himself in for here? He felt like the male equivalent of Cinderella; the ball had been great, but now it was all but over. Midnight was about to strike. 'I had no idea. I would never have behaved like this if I'd known.'

'That's why I didn't tell you.'

'But what about your husband? Will he find out?'

'I think it's unlikely. But he doesn't really care for me. He's not interested in me.'

Davey looked at her incredulously. 'You don't mean that.'

'Oh, but I do.'

'And he doesn't mind if you do – what we have done?'

301

'Not if I'm discreet about it. He wouldn't like his friends to know, though.'

'I can well imagine that.'

'That's why we must be careful. For his sake as well as ours.'

'Will I see you again?' Davey asked her.

'Of course. My husband will give you a job.'

'But I'm going up to Toronto.'

'I think not. He'll offer you more. I'll ask him to.'

'Where does he work?'

'All over. We have an apartment in Chicago and one here in Manhattan. He works from both of them.'

'What is his work, exactly?'

'Oh, all kinds of things,' she said vaguely.

'What can I do?'

'Well, me for a start, silly boy. Often. Any way you like, as hard as you like.'

'But I mean, I can't do that if he's there, can I?'

'He's not there. Right now he's mostly down in Nassau in the Bahamas. They're islands, about eight hundred miles south of New York. Paradise islands, always sunny.'

'What does he do there?'

'He's involved with trading, shipping goods up to Miami and New York.'

'What sort of goods?'

'For your ears only – booze. Not the wines we've been drinking, but whisky. It comes over to Nassau from Scotland, sometimes from Ireland. My husband and a number of others, probably hundreds of others, ship it up.'

'But that's against the law, surely, with Prohibition.'

'That's right. It is. But what we've been doing on this voyage is also against the law. It was rather nice, though, wasn't it? Anyhow, Prohibition is a law of man, not a law of

302

God. There's a difference. Though what we've been doing was against both laws, all laws.'

'I suppose so.'

'I'll get you a job in Nassau, working on the boat engines maybe. Something like that. I'll fix it,' she promised him.

'No,' Davey said, suddenly wanting to be independent. 'I'll get one myself. Then we can see.'

'See what?'

'What happens then.'

'You don't trust me to help you?'

'Of course I do. But I think it would be better if I helped myself – at least now.'

'All right, if that's what you want. We can meet when the boats come to the States. Or I sometimes go to Nassau. You'd like that?'

Davey nodded.

'Anyway,' said Maria. 'Here's a present for you.' She opened her purse, took out five one-hundred-dollar bills. 'Keep them,' she told him. 'Money's always useful – even to a proud Scot.'

He would have liked to say, I love you, but he didn't; not to someone else's wife, and he didn't really know whether it was true or not. He only knew that this heady amalgam of unaccustomed, unbelievable wine, delectable meals, and a lovely passionate woman, surrounded by an ambience of wealth, had changed him totally.

He didn't really give a damn now what he did, as long as whatever he did could provide these previously unimagined rewards. Well, he did give a damn. But not a very big damn. He knew he wanted all these things more than he had ever wanted anything. But how could he ever acquire them?

Twelve

The first thing Anna did when she began to make a lot of money and realised that this desirable (and, to her, almost incredible) situation could continue indefinitely, was to buy herself the house she had been renting.

Like many people who started life in a small cottage with a minimum of tiny cramped rooms, she longed for space. The house was large, with a garden stretching to the beach. Bougainvillaea, frangipani and all manner of flowers bloomed by day and filled the air with scent at night. Sometimes, in the evening, when the sun dropped down into the sea, she would sit on the patio, breathing in the honeyed air, watching luminous waves break on a bone-white beach only feet away. This was like fairyland, she thought. But even as she told herself how fortunate she was to enjoy such luxury, she remembered that all the fairy stories of her childhood also had a darker side with ogres, giants, witches.

Witches. Jeannie Moore. *Was* she a witch? Could she ever have been one? Here, in the sun, the idea seemed absurd. But sometimes, when Anna walked away from the beach towards the centre of the island, the idea became less absurd. Many Bahamians, descended from African slaves, still practised voodoo. She would see chickens, their throats cut, feathers clotted with blood, hanging upside down from the branches of trees, and masks and crosses, and bones on the ground set about with rings of stones.

Once, she asked her Bahamian housekeeper what these things meant. The woman only rolled her eyes.

'It's from the old country, ma'am,' she said vaguely. 'Don't interfere with them. They're bad news for everyone, unless you know it.'

'And who knows it?'

'Some of the elders, the old people. It's handed down. Don't touch anything like that. And don't ask questions, please. That's not something God-fearing, chapel-going folk talk about.'

She was so serious about the matter that Anna did not ask any more questions, even when she saw men crouched, seemingly in a coma, or under the influence of some powerful drug, around these hidden and somehow sinister shrines.

When her house was furnished, Anna invited her parents over to stay with her. She told them she would send money for their fares, and they were welcome to stay for as long as they liked. But they did not come.

'I cannot understand how you can afford to make such an offer,' her mother wrote, almost in rebuke. 'Your father has made some enquiries from a travel agent in Perth, and the fares alone would run into two or even three hundred pounds, going first class, as you suggest. How can you spend so much money if you're a nursemaid? I know from your letters that you left the employ of Dr Bailey's sister some time ago, but who are you with now? Please tell me. Your father and I are worried about you. It's not in our knowledge for anyone to make as much money as you seem to be making now.'

Anna explained that since she had ceased to be a nursemaid she and two colleagues had gone into business together, and it proved altogether easier to make money out in these sunshine islands than in Scotland. But her parents still stayed at home. It was far beyond their experience and even imagination to live as their daughter appeared to live, although Anna deliberately never told them just how much money she was making.

Since they would not come and visit her, and for the moment she could not spare the time to return to Scotland, she sent them a regular allowance. But then her father wrote and said that it was far too much; they would only take a pound a week from her. That's nothing, she thought, nothing. But to them it meant a great deal, so she did as they requested.

She could barely believe she really could be so fortunate and still be so young. And yet, despite her new ability to buy anything she wanted, she could not buy what she wanted most: companionship, and something that was not often mentioned in her family, love.

She and O'Grady and Shah were partners, but they were not friends. Try as she might, Anna could not put entirely from her mind the memory of Shah and the dying sultan. Through Shah's involvement, he had actually died on her, in her. The thought still made her flesh crawl, brought back by such unlikely things as listening to the Bahamian police band at some state function, smelling the coconut oil that American tourists rubbed on their faces and bodies to stop sunburn.

Anna's relations with Shah were therefore formal. He was useful when it came to finding suitable boats and men to crew them. Sometimes she would have selected one particular man, but Shah would shake his head and say, 'He's no good, he's soft inside. He only looks tough. You need someone who's hard. If they have a fight with the crew of a Revenue cutter, they must fight to win.'

'Does it often come to that?'

'It has done.'

'I didn't know,' she said.

'They don't tell you everything.'

'But they do tell you?'

'If they don't, they're out of work. I choose them, hire them, pay them.'

'Perhaps you could tell me,' she said. 'We are partners, after all.'

'Of course, if that is what you want. But partners, to my mind, are like different parts of the human body. Like them, we all have different duties. The arms don't do the work of the legs, for instance. The head doesn't bother about the feet, and so on. Each of us has his own task. You're very good with ideas. It was your idea that we went into this business in the first place. If we hadn't, goodness knows how we would have fared. You keep on with that side of things. I'll deal with the crews, and O'Grady can handle the sailing times and so on.'

The three of them rarely met socially, and when they did it was only for a rather formal dinner, either in Anna's house or in the British Colonial Hotel. Shah bought a house near the yacht club. He did not invite O'Grady or Anna to visit him there. She had no idea what style he kept, but she heard that a local native woman had moved in with him.

O'Grady lived his own peculiar life. He liked to drink in bars on the edge of the harbour. Here he found companions and lovers, if not friends, from cooks and stewards and cabin boys off the big yachts or the cruise liners that came in twice a week during the season. Once, Anna had seen him out driving in his open Buick, a young boy at his side, glancing across adoringly at him. Anna could not recall ever seeing O'Grady in conversation with a woman; he did not like women.

'You're the only one I've stayed with all this time,' he told her once when he had drunk too much rum.

'Is that a joke?'

'I never joke about these things. It's fact. I had a rough time with my mother. Nothing I did was ever right. She never wanted me. She'd wanted a girl, someone different. So I became different. Each to his own, they say. I don't corrupt anyone who's not already corrupted. And by now no one can corrupt me.'

'You're not really interested in money either, are you?' she said.

'Only for what it can buy. I like a good gold watch and a nice car. When I have a boy friend I like to buy him clothes, presents he wouldn't be able to afford on his own. Last one, I bought a speedboat. Then I caught him two-timing me with the bosun off a cargo ship. That was the end of things between us.'

'What about the speedboat?'

'He sold it.'

'Are you sorry?'

'About the boat? Hell, no. I could buy a dozen more tomorrow. About him? Of course. At the time, I was devastated. Worst thing, I had to keep my feelings secret. If a girl had jilted me, everyone would understand, and maybe even sympathise with me. But not where a boy is concerned. I have to keep quiet about that, say nothing, do nothing. It's a secret and has to stay that way, always.

'Life's like a wheel, Anna. It goes round and round. You get over these things, in time. You get over everything in the end. I count myself lucky I had a wonderful experience with him. Now, it's all in the past. So I look forward to the next one. But . . .'

'But what?' Anna asked him.

'More than money I'd like to be free to be myself, to admit openly who I am, what I am. You and Shah don't mind, but nearly everyone else seems to. I've got to be so careful. People do time if they're caught. So I'm always cautious in case anyone's watching me. I'd like to be free of all that. But I doubt I ever will be, so I have to make the best of things as they are.'

Anna enjoyed a social life which to someone in a Scottish valley would be almost impossible to comprehend. She was invited regularly to dinner parties and dances. She was asked to help crew a yacht in island races. Young men wanted to partner her at swimming parties, at moonlight parties on the beach, at barbecues. Several of them wanted rather more. Their hands strayed across her breasts or touched a thigh. No matter how attractive they were, whenever this happened Anna always felt herself stiffen in revulsion and her throat tighten. Their fondling reminded her of Mamora and the sultan and sudden, disgusting pain and death.

Sometimes, looking at her escorts, she saw briefly in their faces the old sultan's tortured face. It seemed they were consumed by lust, and this was not what she wanted; lust was not love.

Instead of these escorts who all seemed to wear well-pressed white flannel trousers and smart short-sleeved shirts, she would prefer someone who wasn't so overpowering, someone altogether more sensitive. There must be such men about, she told herself, but she began to realise that, if they were, her wealth probably frightened them away.

Young men were not used to women personally involved in running liquor to the extent of tens of thousands of dollars' profit from every trip. No one really knew quite how many ships she and her partners controlled, for they rented some from Out Islands in the Bahamas chain, others from as far away as Jamaica. All that anyone could say for certain was that they were rich, and such incontrovertible success brought envy. At dinner parties Anna deliberately sought out shyer men, but she soon discovered that most of them were already married.

So, as time passed, Anna's loneliness grew. She began to wonder what things were like back in Scotland. Her parents were not great letter writers. The longer she stayed away, the more remote their village gossip and the mention of local births and deaths seemed to her. She had heard that Davey Moore had left the castle after the laird's death. Apparently, Mrs MacTavish had never got on with him. She had given him a handsome cheque to leave, and he was supposed to have emigrated, some said to Canada.

Davey Moore. He would be nineteen now. She wondered what he was like. She had only seen him twice, both times as a small boy, with his leg caught in a mantrap, then at the back door of the castle with his mother. She remembered Jeannie Moore's face, viewed through the window of the boot room, when the laird had turned her away and Anna had run after her with a loaf of bread. How strange life was! She could afford to give her anything now, but now was too late.

She still had one piece of the dried stem that Jeannie Moore had given to her. Sometimes she wondered if she should throw it away or keep it as a memento. She was making her own decisions now, not relying on what she told herself must only be superstition. But while she still had this slice of stem, she felt that in some way it was an insurance, or at least an icon, a totem. If she could only understand all the pictures she saw in the visions, then she would be much better placed to take advantage of the gift. Perhaps one day she would be able to do so. And maybe Davey Moore could help her. He might even know from what plant his mother had taken the slices and could get some more, if she needed them. In a curious sense, she felt that she did – and yet she didn't.

But if she could read the pictures in her mind, what would she want to see now in her future? She had money, she had authority. What she really wanted to know was something far less tangible, but now, to her, more important. She wanted to be reassured that she would not always be on her own; that she would find someone to share her life as she would share his; someone she could love, and who in return could love her, not for what she had become, but for who she was.

One night, when Anna was on her own, sitting after dinner looking out to sea as the cool wind of evening tossed the lamps that hung in the rafters above the patio, Shah came to see her.

'Join me in a drink,' she said.

'No. I'm still a Muslim, you know, and I don't drink alcohol.'

'A soft drink then?'

'No, nothing, thank you.'

'What brings you here now? Not trouble, I hope.'

'Not trouble. Just an idea. That's rather your province, Anna, but I have them from time to time.'

'And what's this one?'

'First, the bad news. We're not getting enough whisky to ship. I could have sent up five launches full today, but I only had enough crates for three. And that isn't the first time, though it's never been as short as this.'

'Where is it going?'

'Castle's got other friends he's feeding it to. He means to squeeze us out. That's my reading of the runes. We have to buy it all through him. Now he wants ten dollars more on each case. I won't pay.'

'I should think not. So, what's your idea?'

'That we bypass him so we won't need him any more. He's using some young fellows, American students on vacation. He's told them that with the money they'll make they'll never need to go back to their studies. Whisky's going up on their boats at his price. But they don't know the game. The Revenue men will crucify them if they catch them. They have no idea of the sort of man Castle is or who is behind him, one of the worst hoodlums of all, Johnny Torrio.'

'What's the solution?'

'You're Scottish. Whisky comes from Scotland. Why don't you go back home and buy a distillery?'

'What distillery?'

'Any distillery. Only a few have been servicing us here through Castle. The rest must be in pretty low shape, because their biggest market was always the States. And without America, they'll be running at a loss. You could pick one up cheaply.'

'That's a hell of a good idea,' said Anna enthusiastically.

'I thought it was too. I'm glad you agree.'

'There's one in my home village, Long Glen. And if that's not for sale, I can easily find one that is. I'll go right back, first passage I can get.'

'You trust O'Grady and me to run things here?'

'Of course. We're partners, as well as traders.'

'Yes,' said Shah. 'Partners.'

'You don't sound so sure.'

'I am. I know how you must still feel about me for what happened. That will always be a kind of cloud between us. But somehow I feel I'm on the outside, looking in.'

'You shouldn't.'

'You're white. So is O'Grady. I'm not. I'm coloured.'

'So is almost everyone here in these islands. That has nothing to do with it.'

'Well, maybe my religion is some kind of barrier. Anyway, I feel I don't fit in. Maybe I'm just homesick. I left in a hurry, you know.'

'Do you hear much about Mamora?'

'Bits and pieces. People there are having a rough time with the new sultan. He's an ill man. He's thought to have cancer. He was in constant pain when I saw him last, and that's a long time ago. Like so many people in that situation, he tries to make life hard for others. It's as though that can help him get rid of his own agony.'

'I don't know about that,' Anna replied. 'But now you're certainly going to get rid of me. I'm booking a passage tomorrow morning.'

Castle was driving his Packard roadster with the hood down along the coast road when he saw Shah walking towards him. Castle had driven along this road two or three times every day since he had last seen Torrio. He wanted to meet Shah, but was determined that the meeting should appear casual, by chance, not in any way intentional. He knew that Shah often walked on this road, near the sea, but until now he had not seen him.

Castle was concerned at the success of the three partners. They could make life hard for him with Torrio; he meant to

314

break them up. And he guessed the weakest of the three was Shah.

Castle stopped, switched off his engine. White breakers thundered on the beach; the palms waved their fronds like huge upturned feather dusters. On the other side of the road lay the big houses that American millionaires used when winter gripped the East Coast of the United States. As Shah approached, Castle waved cheerfully to him.

'Hot day for a walk,' he said.

'Not where I come from,' Shah replied.

'I suppose not. Hop in. Ride with me.'

'But you're going in the wrong direction.'

'I'll turn round and go in your direction.'

'No, no. Don't let me take you out of your way.'

'You're not. I wanted to see you, anyhow.'

'About what?'

'We've never really had a chance to talk much since you've been in Nassau.'

'I've been busy,' said Shah defensively.

'I've been thinking. Maybe we could do some business together. On an individual, private basis.'

'I wouldn't do anything that cut across the others.'

'I'm not asking you to. Cigar?'

'No, thanks.'

Castle lit one, flicked the match carelessly over the car door. 'I've been doing a bit of research into conditions these days in Mamora. Where you came from.'

'Well?'

'I am told that the people aren't too happy with that new sultan they've got.'

'I know that. But he's been there some years. They should be used to him by now.'

'People often think they want something, or someone,

new. They rarely realise just what a good deal they already have until it's all too late. Maybe you could make it better by going back.'

'What do you mean?'

'I have contacts in Mamora, Shah. They tell me the people look back wistfully to what they call the old days. I asked my friends if they knew you. They told me something interesting.' He paused.

'What's that?' asked Shah.

'You may be surprised, and I do not wish to offend you by telling you what they told me.'

'Tell me what you found out.'

'Right. First, did you ever meet your father?'

'No. Never. I knew my mother's father, my grandfather. I went to his house before I jumped the slaver. He was tortured, poor old man.'

'So I hear. I have found out who your father was. The old sultan. The man you served so loyally, whose guard commander you were.'

'Are you serious?'

'Yes. The sultan had many sons. I don't know how many. Some say forty, others fifty, born within marriage, and outside. You were one of the latter, but he always liked you, had a special feeling for you. You were a favourite. That's why you became guard commander – so I hear.'

'Can you prove that?'

'If I have to.'

'How?'

'Through my contacts.'

'The old sultan, my father? So I was the heir?'

'One of them. As I said, he had many sons. But most of them were feeble. They didn't want to fight. You were different. You were – you are – a fighter.'

'I ran away.'

'You had to. You'd have been tortured and killed if you'd stayed. Remember, he who fights and runs away lives to fight another day. Now that other day is coming.'

'What do you mean?'

'I am one of a pretty powerful consortium of businessmen. We're trading in drink now, as you know. But one day Prohibition will be repealed, and when that happens the market goes bang overnight. So we're being prudent and moving out into other areas.'

'Like what?'

'I won't go into details now, just the basic facts. As you know, we ship a hell of a lot of liquor up from here to the States. But in the States people are making as much, maybe more, in bathtubs, zinc tanks, anything. They sell their hooch in bottles, just like us. But ours reaches us in bottles. Theirs doesn't, so they have to bottle it. They've had to buy thousands and thousands of bottles, millions of bottles. And then they have to paste labels on 'em, to say what's in each bottle – whisky, gin, vodka, and so on.

'So they say, what the hell? Why should we buy these things? It's much cheaper and makes more sense to buy the firms that make 'em. So now they own whole bottling plants. They have printers to make the labels, trucking firms to carry the stuff about, warehouses to store it. And in the former distilleries they've picked up cheaply they're making meat pies, pastries, chocolate bars, anything except booze. And suddenly, from being gangsters in the street, they're hiring lawyers and accountants, men with button-down collars and button-down minds. They've gone legit. They're in the trucking business, in property, real estate, bottling plants, printing. You name it. We're big business now, very, very big. And there's the biggest business of all still waiting to be broken. We've got a share of it, and we want it all.'

'What's that?'

'Drugs.'

'You mean pharmaceuticals, pills, medicines?'

'Hell, no. Don't be naive. I mean dope. Coke. Heroin.'

'But there's not much of a market for that, surely.'

'At the moment it's mainly with show business people, singers, trumpeters who blow their brains out every night in some crappy club. People who need a lift or they'll crash. It's hard as hell to give a concert every night of the week or take the lead in a play each night, two performances every Wednesday and Saturday. But a sniff of the white powder takes away the tiredness – for a while. When the effect wears off, you're down worse than before. So they need more. Which we can supply.'

'So how does this affect me?'

'We get our supplies mostly from South America. But they keep jacking up the price. We want new sources, and the best comes from the East. It's the purest and, more important, the cheapest. Mamora could be a handling post for that trade.

'I'll make you an offer, Shah. We put up money so you can buy mercenaries, pay bribes, spend it how you like, as long as you get back into power as the new sultan. And once you're there, we want a blind eye turned to what goes on.'

'That may be difficult. Mamora's part of the British Empire. They're strict.'

'So are the Bahamas, part of the British Empire. But what people don't see, they don't know about. And what people discover, they can then be paid to forget. I'm willing to pay whatever it takes to put you on top in Mamora. Are you willing to play?'

'Let me think about it. I didn't know about my father. I had no idea. It puts all sorts of things in a totally new light. Give me time to work it out.'

'Keep in touch with me,' said Castle. 'Don't leave it too long.'

'I'll think about it,' Shah replied doggedly.

'I'll ring you tonight, ten o'clock. That gives you long enough to make up your mind. I want your answer then. Yes or no.'

Castle telephoned Shah exactly at ten.

'What is it?' he asked.

'Yes or no?'

'It's yes,' said Shah. 'Yes.'

Davey went up on deck as the *Benares Castle* docked. He watched Maria walk demurely down the first-class gangway, under its scrubbed canvas awning. A chauffeur waiting on the quayside approached her, saluted respectfully and carried her bags to the Customs post. She turned, shading her eyes against the pale sunshine, looking back at the liner. She could be looking for anyone, of course, but Davey told himself that this was her special goodbye to him.

Now that she had gone, he felt bereft, lonely, curiously vulnerable. This was the first time he had been abroad. He booked a room in a small hotel, then took a cab to the shipping office. For fifty-five dollars including taxes they offered him a berth on a boat sailing to Nassau in two days' time. He gave them one of Maria's hundred-dollar bills, put the ticket with the change in his back pocket.

For the next two days he walked through the streets, surprised by the size of everything, the noise, the way that drains steamed in the centre of the roads. The height of the buildings impressed him; so did the striped awnings that led from big apartment blocks and the smartest hotels right across the pavement, so that people alighting from limousines and taxis could walk on a red carpet across the paving stones. This was all very different from home.

So was Nassau. He had not known quite what to expect, but standing on deck as his steamer came into the harbour, the rash of small white buildings, yachts bobbing against the sunshine on a sea that glittered like polished steel, gave the impression of a fairytale world. He had never imagined the sun could be so warm and the water so clear. He carried his bag ashore, feeling ill-dressed, provincial, a hobbledehoy among men who wore lightweight tropical suits and panama hats, with women in smart silk frocks. A procession of big open cars with their Bahamian chauffeurs wearing starched white uniforms drove in line along Bay Street.

He found a rooming house near the Royal Victoria Hotel and took a room for a week, then went out and bought himself a ready-made lightweight suit, with a spare pair of trousers, white shoes, dark blue shirt. After a morning spent walking round the town trying to get his bearings, he approached the harbour.

He was surprised by the activity. A dozen motor launches were moored, bows in, while relays of labourers packed them with square crates or odd-shaped bundles wrapped in basket weave or burlap bags.

He saw a man in uniform smoking a cigarette, watching the activity. Davey approached him.

'Excuse me, sir,' he said politely, 'but I'm a stranger here. Just arrived. What's being loaded on all the boats?'

'You kidding?' asked Garcia, the harbour master.

'No, sir. Just asking.'

'Where are you from, then?'

'Scotland.'

'Ah. Home of the whisky, eh?'

'That's true.'

'Well, this is whisky too. But maybe not all from your home town. It's going on up to the States. Prohibition. Whole damn country's dry. These fellows with the launches are trying to make it a bit wetter.'

'Smuggling, rum running? I read about that in the papers.'

'Well, here it is, boy, in all its native glory.'

Garcia noted Davey's pale face, his obviously ready-made suit. He didn't look rich, so what exactly was he doing here?

'On vacation?' he asked him.

'No. Looking for a job.'

This seemed more in keeping, thought Garcia. 'As what?'

'Anything to do with engines.'

'What kind of engines?'

'Petrol. I started off with motorcycle engines. Car engines and boat engines just mean an addition of more cylinders.'

Garcia nodded. 'If you're any good, I might be able to find you something,' he said. 'For a fee.'

'What sort of fee?'

'Your first week's wages in my hand.'

'That's quite a hefty fee. How am I going to live for the week?'

'That's your affair. You got here. You're still alive. So you must have some money.'

'Isn't there an employment agency here in Nassau?'

'Not that I've heard of, and I was born and bred here. You play ball with me and I'll help you. I'm the harbour master. Joe Garcia. Better to have me as a friend than not.'

'I can see that. What sort of job have you in mind?'

'Come on and I'll introduce you to a few friends. But you have to know your stuff. Don't try and bluff these guys.'

Davey followed Garcia across the quay to a shed where a launch had been lifted out of the water by a crane. The hull was propped up with big beams. One man was repainting the keel, another was inside working on the engine. Davey could hear a hammer tapping on metal.

'I've got a possible helper for you,' Garcia told them.

The man put his head over the rim of the hull. He was sweating, his face smudged with grease.

'Doing what?' he asked shortly.

'Depends what you need doing,' replied Davey.

'Well, put your head over here and you'll see what I'm doing. We've got a water leak, a blown gasket head. These old engines are run at full stretch day after day, and she can't take it. The best of their life's been ripped out of them. Ever cut a gasket?'

'I could learn,' said Davey.

'Ah, hell. I don't want to have to teach you.'

'Just show me.'

'You'll get your clothes all dirty.'

'I need a job.'

'All right. Climb up.'

Davey climbed up a small ladder against the hull, dropped down inside. The bilge was awash with oily water. The whole boat smelled strongly of rotting wood.

'How far do you hope to go with this engine?' he asked.

'Up to Florida and back. Why?'

'The wood's rotten in the hull. I can smell it.'

'Oh, we'll treat it, patch it up. It's the engine that's the heart of the thing. Here's the old gasket.' He held up a long thin sheet of copper. 'Cut holes in this for each cylinder and

322

the valves. Here's a pair of shears.'

'What's wrong with the old one?'

'It blows, that's what.'

'It's solid metal,' said Davey, examining it closely. 'It shouldn't.'

'Well, I'm telling you it does.'

'If we put sealer on each side of it, it couldn't,' said Davey. 'That will save a lot of time, instead of cutting a new one which may also blow.'

'We ain't got no sealer.'

'Well, get some. And I'll have that engine ready in half a day.'

'You're on,' said the man, impressed.

Davey kept his word. The engine was running by late afternoon.

'But don't keep it at full throttle for too long. Old engines are like old people. They can't take too much pressure.'

'We don't have to sail the thing. We're just paid to get it running,' the man retorted. 'Now, what are you doing tomorrow?'

'Looking for a job, like I was today.'

'OK, we'll pay you for a full day today. My name's Rafferty. Jim Rafferty. Come and join us tomorrow. Wage, five English pounds a week.'

'I hear people are making fortunes running this booze,' said Davey. 'A fiver doesn't sound a lot of money to me.' He remembered that Joe Garcia would also claim his first week's wages.

'You're not running booze,' replied the man. 'I can hire plenty of people at a fiver who can tinker with engines.'

'You don't seem to have had much luck in finding them so far.'

'We haven't tried too hard. You want the job or not?'

'I'll take it,' said Davey. 'For the time being.'

Rafferty owned the boatyard which, until Prohibition, was so small that he could do all the work himself. This had been limited to scraping the hulls of racing yachts, varnishing woodwork, checking steering and rigging. Now he hired every freelance labourer he could find who had any knowledge of woodwork or engines. There weren't too many on the island with those skills, and most were already working in other yards.

Within two weeks, Davey's wage was doubled to ten pounds. As he was working on an engine, the other men chatting or whistling alongside him suddenly fell silent. Davey looked up to find out why. A stranger was standing in the doorway in silhouette. He came in slowly, moving like a lithe animal. His rubber-soled shoes made no sound on the yard's concrete floor. Rafferty nodded to him respectfully.

'Morning, Mr Castle,' he said.

'I heard you've got a new hand,' said Castle.

'Yeah. Pretty good, too.'

Castle came on into the shed, paused opposite Davey. 'You know the business?' he asked.

'I do, sir.'

'We could use half a dozen of you, then. Where you from?'

'Scotland, sir.'

'You heard there was good money down here?'

'Yes, I did.'

'Even in Scotland, eh? What part? I've been to Glasgow and Inverness.'

'A village you've probably never heard of, sir. Long Glen. Near Perth.'

Castle's face clouded. 'You know the distillery?'

'Yes.'

'Who owns it?'

'Mrs MacTavish, the widow of the laird.'

'I hear she's trying to sell it.'

'I didn't know that, sir.'

'A guy I know in Scotland sent word. A woman here called Ballater is said to be interested. Know her?'

'No, sir. But I met her, I think, when I was a little boy. She was kind to my mother. Her name rings a bell.'

'Small world, isn't it?'

As Castle turned away, Davey found he was sweating. This must be Maria's husband. Did he know, could he conceivably guess, that he had had an affair with his wife? He turned to Rafferty.

'Who is that man?'

'Don't ask dumb questions like that, boy,' said Rafferty sharply. 'He's the big noise. Bill Castle. A gangster. He organises a lot of the booze, and he's sore as hell at that Scots woman Ballater. He thinks she and two fellows she's in with over here are going solo. He doesn't like that one bit. Castle tried to bump up the price of his booze to them and they wouldn't pay.

'He thought they'd have to because he controlled all the booze coming in here, and going out. He never imagined they'd try to buy a distillery themselves. But buying it is one thing, running the stuff in and out is another. Mr Castle's a hard man, and he's got even harder men behind him. He won't let Anna Ballater get away with it for long, I'm telling you. Don't you ever cross him, boy. He's bad news, a killer.'

Davey nodded.

Rafferty looked at him sharply. 'You all right, boy?' he

asked. 'You've gone pale. Feeling the heat – or too much rum last night, eh?'

'Something like that,' Davey agreed, wiping sweat from his face. But it was nothing like that. The thought that Castle might discover his involvement with Maria, and what he might do if he did, was what had disturbed him, despite Maria's assurance that her husband didn't mind her affairs.

Davey had been working in Rafferty's yard for six weeks when he received another shock. He saw Maria.

He was walking to work round the edge of the harbour when he saw her being driven past in an open car. She looked at him. He did not know whether to acknowledge her, but she didn't wave, so he walked on as though the passage of the pretty woman in a touring car was of no interest to him. But the sudden thumping of his heart belied his calm. That evening, back in his rooming house, he found that a sealed envelope had been pushed under his door. He had not received any mail since his arrival and wondered who this could be from. He took it into his room, opened it. The note inside was from Maria, written in capital letters.

'Tonight. Eight o'clock. Villa Maria, Cable Beach. Burn this. M.'

Villa Maria. Had her husband named the house after her? Davey had passed the house often enough, one of the bigger, flashier homes overlooking the ocean, with a white picket fence, a double garage. Dare he go there? Surely Maria would not ask him unless the coast was clear? Davey had a bath, shaved carefully and burned the letter, holding a match to it, then flushed the ash down the lavatory.

He walked from his lodging along the coast road until he came to the house, and then he walked past it. By the high iron gates a night watchman stood in a small hut, like a sentry box. Davey waited, wondering whether he should go in or forget all about the invitation. He had not expected to find a guard on the gate. He made up his mind, turned and walked in through the open gates. The man looked at him sharply, but did not stop him, so presumably he had been told to expect a guest. Davey knocked at the front door. Maria opened it.

'Hullo,' he said awkwardly, not knowing whether anyone else was in the house. She smiled and shook her head, making her black hair fan out.

'Don't worry,' she said. 'We're on our own.'

'There's a guard at the gate.'

'Oh, my husband insists on that. He doesn't bother anyone.'

'You're sure?'

'I know. Have you had supper?'

'No.'

'Well, I've something cold here for both of us.'

They went into the dining room. It was laid with four places, three glasses by each one.

'We're not eating here,' she explained. 'This was laid for lunch with a couple of friends. But Bill couldn't make it.'

'Where is he now?'

'In the States.'

She led Davey on into the kitchen. This had so many polished white surfaces it looked like a hospital ward. There were three sinks, not one; taps for hot water, cold water, iced water.

Maria opened the refrigerator, took out a split lobster. She set out plates, found a bottle of wine, opened it. They sat on stools at a bar counter, talking awkwardly because Davey still felt ill at ease. He feared it could be serious if

327

Castle found him here with his wife, or even heard he had been a visitor. He would wonder how Davey knew his wife, why he hadn't mentioned this when he met him at the boatyard. He told Maria his fears.

'Relax,' she said easily. 'Don't worry. I told you, he doesn't care. Anyway, he's taken a seaplane up to Florida. Then he's going on to Chicago. Got to report to his boss, Mr Torrio. He's miles away. Now, let's not talk too much. We've only so much time. You will be staying the night?'

'No,' said Davey tensely. 'I can't. I'd like to, but I'm on duty at seven thirty tomorrow. I've got to get back and change my clothes. Someone might see me leave.'

'You worry too much,' Maria said easily, running her fingers through his hair. 'The guard on the gate saw you come, but I've given him five bucks. He's already forgotten all about you.'

'Someone else may give him ten bucks to remember.'

'Not on your life. Come on, cheer up. Let's eat and then to bed.'

Davey left in the early hours. He walked back to his rooming house along empty roads, past shuttered houses. He had to admit that as far as he was concerned the evening had not been a success. They had made love at first with passion, then, later, almost as a kind of duty – at least on his side.

What had been exciting in a state room aboard a liner hundreds of miles out at sea, now in another man's house, actually in his bed, seemed sordid, and very dangerous, because the woman was a gangster's wife. Davey could not see how he could possibly conduct an affair here without someone knowing and telling Castle. He suddenly realised that he wanted out. He was afraid. All his instincts were warning him to keep away from Maria. Concealment of their affair in this tiny colony would be impossible, and discovery would be as dangerous for Maria as for him. Despite Maria's repeated assurances of her husband's indifference to her behaviour, he remembered Rafferty's words about Castle: he's a killer. He must not see Maria again; at least, not in Nassau. In New York, things might well be different, but they weren't in New York.

As he walked, donkeys pulling carts down to the quay from the rum distillery were already clop-clopping along the dusty road. Work started early here, where booze was involved. He walked behind one of the carts, head down, hoping no one would recognise him.

He was six yards down the road before he remembered that the watchman had not been on duty when he left. Was that significant, or was it just Bahamian slackness?

Johnny Torrio, the man newspaper reporters called the 'uncrowned king of Chicago', a description that irritated some of his contemporaries who would have liked the title for themselves, was wearing his usual evening attire of a silk dressing-gown over a starched white shirt.

He lolled back on a brocade sofa in his apartment, one hand along the back, fingers tapping in time to music coming from his gramophone. He was going out to dinner with his wife and he had instructed Castle to see him before he went. Castle sat nervously on the edge of a chair. In the indifferent light, diffused by thick red silk shades, he could see the polish on Torrio's fingernails – he had them manicured every day. Castle thought they looked like claws, and the similarity disturbed him. He was also disturbed by the fact that Torrio had telephoned him to come to his apartment only minutes before he was due to go out. A brief abrupt interview could only mean one thing: the big man's displeasure.

Torrio rarely invited Castle on his own. Usually, Mrs Torrio would telephone Maria to ask whether, if she and her husband had no other engagements, they could come up to their apartment for what she called a 'bite to eat' or a drink. The invitation might seem casual, but it was a command. No one ever turned down an invitation from the Torrios.

Mrs Torrio was not in the room this evening, and there was clearly nothing social in the summons; no whisky on the table between the two men, and Torrio had not offered Castle a cigar. These little things might mean nothing, but more likely they meant he was about to be reprimanded, or that he was seriously out of favour.

The trouble was, no one ever really knew with Torrio, or with any of the gangsters. There was something odd about them all, thought Castle miserably. They could be roaring with laughter one minute, slapping you on the back, and the next they were thrusting their face right into yours, their mean, vicious eyes hot with hatred, all because of some minor happening on which you had not wasted a single thought. They were like wolves, he thought; and of course they were all mad, certifiable, except that they wielded so much power no one would ever dare to say so.

You realised then that you were mad, too, to be with them. But having joined the pack, you could not bow out. The only way out, they liked to remind subordinates, was feet first in a wooden box, or in a concrete block dropped into the river, never to be found. No grave, no epitaph, no religious service, nothing but oblivion because you had ducked out, ratted, gone chicken.

Castle licked lips that had suddenly gone dry as he watched Torrio draw on his cigar. Why the devil didn't the man speak, say what he had in mind? Torrio tapped half an inch of expensive ash into a gold ashtray.

'I got you here,' he said and paused.

He used the word 'got', thought Castle; not 'asked' or 'invited'. Got. Things were bad. But what things? What had he done wrong?

'I got you here,' Torrio repeated because he liked the phrase, 'for I want to talk to you frankly, man to man. No horseshit.' Again, he paused.

Castle looked at him, meeting his eyes, hoping his face was composed, that the thunder of his heart could not be heard across the white Aubusson carpet.

'I been hearing things. Things I don't like.'

'About what?'

'About your wife.'

'Maria? Really? I'm surprised.'

'Maybe you are, maybe you ain't. But I'm telling you this. She was on the *Benares Castle*, the crack British liner that nearly won the Blue Riband for crossing the Atlantic so fast.'

'Maria was in Europe, visiting the old country.'

'Is that a fact? But on the boat she was behaving in what you might call the old way, which I don't like. It cheapens you, it cheapens me. Most important of all, that kind of behaviour cheapens our business.'

'I don't quite follow what you mean. She was travelling on her own.'

'Sure, she was travelling on her own, and you were picking up the tab. I don't know about the trip out, but on the way back she's not on her own. She picks up a young fellow, a stud. He was travelling steerage. Hung like a bloody donkey, according to the steward, who saw him all but ball-naked in your wife's room, or rather in her suite.

Someone of your class don't let your wife travel in a room or a cabin. She has to have a whole goddamn suite now, because you're rich. But being rich brings special responsibilities, Castle. And the first is you don't flaunt your wife around. Her tail is for you, not for anyone else who can make a grab at it.'

'I wasn't flaunting her. I had no idea she was with anybody.'

'No? Then let me put you wise. I got a list in my pocket here. I can give you the names of other people who have been screwing her, here in Chicago and in New York. And there's something else I have to tell you. She's not just content with screwing on an Atlantic liner. She's actually doing it in your house, in your bed, in Nassau.'

'That's impossible,' said Castle quickly.

'Nothing's impossible. You know that. Especially not where hot-tailed women are concerned. And it's happening. I can prove it. I've witnesses to it. Tell you which positions they used, what sort of underwear your wife had on – or took off. Everything. But you don't want to hear that, really, now do you? Just take my word, it's fact.

'OK, you can make a fool of yourself, be a cuckold, do as you like. It's your life. But you don't make a fool of the outfit, because that's more than your life's worth. It's the lives of a lot of important people. Very rich, powerful people. And we don't like it – any of us. So you do what you have to do. Stop it. Now.

'What you get up to on your own with your wife is your business. Right. But what *she* does on her own with other men is also your business, if she does it so that others notice. And your business is my business.'

'I'll certainly speak to her about it.'

'You won't speak. Like I say, you'll stop it.'

'She's always been a good wife to me.'

'Yeah? So maybe now she's being a better wife to other men. *Stop* it. Not tomorrow, not next month, next year. Stop it *now*. Do I make myself clear?'

'Perfectly, Mr Torrio.'

'I'm glad, for if you don't, there's no place for you in our business.'

'What do you mean, exactly?'

'What I goddamn well say. Can't you make sense of that? There's no place. You're out. Finished. *Kaput*.' Torrio drew on his cigar, brushed a silk sleeve over his heavy, diamond-studded watch. 'It's almost time to go. Got a car outside?'

'No, I took a cab.'

'Well, take another cab. I can't give you a lift, tonight. I'm going out with my wife. You go see yours and tell her what I told you. Understand?'

Castle nodded. He felt too weak to speak.

Maria stayed in Nassau for longer than she had anticipated because her husband's return had been delayed by his unexpected trip to Chicago. Every afternoon, a note was delivered by hand to Davey in his rooms: 'See you on the beach. Eight.' or 'The house. Nine.' The venue might change, but the action was the same, and each time he made love to her he felt more and more concerned, but he didn't know how to end their relationship. Discretion was something he sensed that Maria did not possess, and she simply could not understand Davey's fears about her husband.

'He's not here,' she would say with rising exasperation, as though addressing a backward child. 'How can he possibly find out? Anyhow, I've told you, he doesn't care.'

On the night she left for New York, she gave Davey a card on which was printed her address and telephone number.

'I'll try and get you up to New York on some pretext,' she promised. 'There may be parts you need for an engine or something like that.'

'They ship the parts in here.'

'Well, I'll think of something. My husband has so many interests. You should work for him. It would be easier then.'

'No,' he said firmly. 'I couldn't work for him.'

'Why not? Scared?'

'I suppose in a way I am, yes. I feel mean, and I've only seen him once.'

'Anyhow, let's not spoil our last night talking. Here's the address. And here's something to remember me by. Just in case you need money for a postage stamp.' She opened her purse, took out five one-hundred-dollar bills.

'I can't take those,' he said.

'Why not? They're a gift. My husband took them from somewhere. I took them from him. You take them from me. Money's round, it's meant to go round. Here you are. Now, no more words. Deeds!'

Thirteen

Mr Mansfield, the minister in Long Glen, was sitting in his back garden in his shirt sleeves writing next Sunday's sermon. It was a hot Friday afternoon, and his wife was away in Perth visiting her old mother. From time to time, he sat back in the chair, rubbing his eyes, bored with his work but thankful to be out in the open air. He had written and declaimed so many sermons that now the phrases had become routine. Sometimes, he even wondered whether he still believed what he declared so passionately from his pulpit, whether, in fact, he ever had believed. This was one of those times.

A ring at the front door bell on the other side of the house brought a frown to his face. This was probably some parishioner in trouble, or maybe wanting to give notice of a baptism, a wedding, a funeral, the three pivotal points in most family lives. He put down his spectacle case on the papers in case the wind blew them away, slipped on his jacket (he felt it somehow demeaning to appear to a parishioner casually dressed), and walked round the side of the house.

He saw a car parked in the road outside, a hired black Minerva of enormous size. Who the dickens could this be? He took a few more steps and saw Anna standing by the front door.

'*You!*' he cried in amazement. 'You've come home!'

He went forward to greet her, arms outstretched, his

face lit with genuine pleasure.

'But you should have let me know,' he said. 'Then I'd have prepared a proper welcome for you. Did you tell your parents you were coming?'

'No. I told no one. I wanted to keep my visit a secret.'

'What a pity! They will be absolutely delighted to see you back. Your mother was telling me the other day how regularly you wrote to her, and how well you were doing. She and your father are very grateful for the money you send them every month. They have often mentioned it to me. Lots of children, my dear girl, promise to remember their old parents. You are one of the few who has done so, indeed the only one I have ever heard of round here. You have clearly taken to heart and acted on the saying of our Lord, "Honour thy father and thy mother that thy days may be long in the land". Where are you staying?'

'In Perth. The Fair Maid Hotel.'

'Are you here for long?'

'For as long as it takes to do some business. That's why I came to see you first.'

'I'm not a businessman, Anna. I have tried to serve God, not Mammon. You should see the Writer to the Signet, Mr Macleod.'

'I intend to. But first, I wanted your advice. Which, as a businesswoman, I will pay for.'

'Anything I can give you in the way of advice is yours for the asking, Anna. I do not seek payment. I am delighted if I can help you in any way. That is payment enough – and more. Come into the back garden. My wife's away for the day, but I'll make some tea and we can have it out here in the sunshine.'

Anna followed him into the kitchen. He brewed up tea, put two cups and saucers on a tray with milk, sugar and a plate of homemade scones, carried them into the garden. He brought out another chair. They both sat down.

'Now,' he said as he poured out the tea. 'What can I do for you?'

'I'm involved in the Bahamas with the export of various things to the States,' Anna began carefully. There was no need to involve this decent man with details of Prohibition, bootlegging, the rule of the gun. He would not understand that business; it was pointless even to mention it. If she told him she had been aboard a slave ship captured by French pirates and forced to shoot her way out, or that she had marooned a man on a deserted island, he would not believe her. She must stay carefully within the narrow parameters of the minister's own experience. How great a distance from this village she had travelled since she left, a journey not only measured in miles!

'I think there's a great market for Scotch whisky,' she went on. 'I came over to see how the Long Glen distillery is doing.'

'You'll never get a better dram than is distilled here in Long Glen,' Mr Mansfield assured her firmly.

'I know that. Do you think the laird's widow would ever sell the distillery?'

'I can't say. You'd better consult Mr Macleod. He handles all her business matters. She might well consider it. She's a lonely old person now. Lost her only son years ago, as you know, and then her husband. She's not of an age or a type to make new friends easily. But certainly the person you should see is Mr Macleod. You are going to visit your parents, too, I hope?'

'Of course. But first I want to settle the matter of the distillery. If she will sell, I'd like to give my father a decent job there. He's a good craftsman.'

'He is that. And Dr Bailey acted in a true Christian fashion, giving your parents a cottage. But of course he hadn't the opportunities to offer a craftsman like your father. He'd be very glad of a steady job, I know. But who are you acting for? Who wants to buy the distillery?'

'A group of people I have been working with,' Anna explained vaguely.

'I see. You really are a success now, aren't you? I found it difficult to believe your parents when they told me how well you were doing – you know how parents tend to exaggerate their children's successes. Now I feel like the Queen of Sheba when she saw for herself the splendours of King Solomon's court. "The half of it was not told me."'

'I hear you were very kind to Davey Moore,' said Anna, deliberately changing the subject.

'Not really. I only persuaded the laird to give the lad a home. But when he died, Mrs MacTavish decided to terminate that arrangement. He emigrated. I hope he will do well. He is a lad of spirit.'

'Jeannie Moore,' said Anna. 'Are there any other people like her in Soldier's Wood with her gift to tell the future?'

'None,' he said firmly. 'The wood's quite deserted. People still won't walk through it at night, just as in your day. They think there's something harmful there. But I think that the harm is probably in their own minds. They imagine it.'

'Is the lawyer likely to be in his office now?' asked Anna.

'Use my telephone and find out.'

'Thank you,' said Anna. 'I said that our discussion is on a business basis. Is there anything you'd like personally, or your wife?'

'You are very kind, Anna, but there really is nothing. We have no family, and we have enough to live on. I could not

338

possibly take any money from you, but it is extremely generous of you to make the offer. I appreciate your thought.'

'I have a cheque here which I have made out to Bearer,' said Anna. 'Please cash it. Use the money to help anyone you know who may need some. Or you could pay for anything in your kirk that may need repairing. I leave that to you. But please don't refuse it.' Anna opened her handbag, took out a folded cheque and handed it to Mr Mansfield.

He unfolded the cheque. 'But this is for a *thousand* pounds!' he cried in astonishment. 'I couldn't possibly take it.'

'You're not *taking* it,' Anna replied drily. 'I'm *giving* it.'

The Writer to the Signet's clerk showed Anna into the lawyer's office. Mr Macleod stood up behind his desk, came round to shake her hand.

'I don't think we've met before.'

'No, we haven't,' Anna agreed. 'But this, I hope, will be the first of future meetings. I used to be a maid at the castle.'

'So I heard. Your father and mother and you were put out by the laird after that most unfortunate business when his infant son died.'

'Yes. But Dr Bailey took in my parents. I've been in the States and the Bahamas on business. It's on a business matter I'd like to see you now.'

'If I can help you, I will. Please take a seat. Would you like a cup of tea?'

'No, I've just had one with the minister. I'm only over here for a short visit, so I hope you will understand if I come to the point at once.'

The Writer inclined his head.

'Good,' said Anna. 'I believe you handle the business affairs of Mrs MacTavish, the laird's widow.'

'That is true, yes. I am favoured by her instructions.'

'Would she ever sell the Long Glen whisky distillery?'

'I could certainly ask her.'

'If she decided to sell, would it be unethical to ask you to act on my behalf as the buyer, as well as on hers as the seller?'

'It would be unusual, but I could ask another member of my staff to act for you.'

'That's settled then. First, before I make a bid on behalf of a group of interested investors, is it possible to see any of the accounts?'

'That would be irregular.'

'I don't wish to be irregular, Mr Macleod. But I'm only over here for a limited time. I want to buy that distillery on behalf of my colleagues. I will pay cash for it, in pounds sterling, in American or Canadian dollars, however you or Mrs MacTavish may wish it. There is no mortgage needed, no bank loan, nothing of that kind. If there are any searches to be made on the ownership of the property, they would have to be done quickly.'

'This may take some time, Miss Ballater.'

'I repeat, I do not have much time, Mr Macleod. Unless I can get a quick decision, I will be forced most reluctantly to go elsewhere. I have a list of other distilleries in Scotland whose owners wish to discuss business if Mrs MacTavish doesn't. So I do ask you to help me here.'

'Please don't think I am being difficult, Miss Ballater. I quite understand your need for haste. In view of this, I will show you the accounts, but in the strictest confidence, of course.'

'Of course.'

He pressed a bell on his desk. A clerk put his head round the door. Macleod gave him instructions. Within minutes, the man was back holding a buff folder bound in pink tape. The lawyer opened it, skimmed through several pages until he came to the one he wanted, handed this to Anna.

'There you are. Last year's sales. Not very good, you'll see.'

'Why is that? I hear the whisky is excellent.'

'It is. But the market's not. Prohibition in the States has hit their profits a fearful blow. At least ninety per cent of the whisky went over there. Not a lot is sold here, as you can see. People are very fickle. And new-fangled drinks brought in from France, to make cocktails and so on, are the current fashion here.'

Anna nodded. She skimmed through the figures, surprised that the sales were so small. 'I thought it was a bigger enterprise,' she admitted.

'It used to be. But if you look at the following sheet you will see the enormous gallonage of whisky that is stored in vats.'

'Why?'

'The company is hoping for better times to come, as politicians always assure us will be the case.'

'On the basis of a low return, plus a bit for good will, which is probably minimal now, and the freehold of the premises, how would twenty-five thousand pounds, on the table, strike you?'

'As an interesting sum, Miss Ballater.'

'Will Mrs MacTavish take that view?'

'I'll ask her. I can see her this evening. Where can I reach you?'

'Until seven this evening, I'm at the Fair Maid Hotel in

Perth. After seven, my offer is withdrawn. But please do not tell my parents I am here. I would like to surprise them myself.'

'Of course. I will tell no one you are here. Not even Mrs MacTavish.'

'There is one other thing perhaps you can help me with. Soldier's Wood. Does she still own it?'

'Yes, she does.'

'Any idea just how big the wood is?'

'I would think about ten acres.'

'I understand it still has the bad reputation it had when I lived here?'

'I fear so. Locals still claim it is haunted in some way. I doubt that myself, but in these country places old views die hard.'

'Do you think Mrs MacTavish would sell the wood as well?'

'You would like to buy it?'

'Yes.'

'I can easily find out. Would you wish your name to be mentioned in connection with that purchase?'

'Not if you can avoid it.'

'I think she may well be willing to sell. The wood is totally useless land, and she is feeling the pinch, like many landowners now. Farm rents are low and the cost of living is high. I'll do what I can.'

'Thank you. The minister told me that Davey Moore has emigrated.'

'Yes. He's a fine, upstanding lad.'

'Where did he go?'

'Canada. I've a relation in Toronto, Tam Douglas, a partner in a firm making patent medicines. He's done rather well. He was over here during the war in the

Canadian Army, and he has just come back on a visit. I gave Davey a letter to take to him, but I think it must have crossed with Tam on his way over here, for he hasn't heard from him. He will find Davey a job if he can. At least for the time being.'

'And then?'

'Who knows? One step at a time in this life, Miss Ballater.'

'I agree with that. But let me have your relation's address in Toronto, just in case I'm in Canada. I could get in touch with Davey through him.'

'You'll not recognise him now. He's a big fellow, you know, grown up.'

'I suppose he is. We forget how quickly time passes.'

As she spoke, Anna realised she was also forgetting how fast time was passing for her. It seemed now that she had been working at the castle in another life, almost in another world, and in a sense that was true. A curtain had come down on her past life the moment she had set sail for South Africa. She knew that it would never really rise. She now spoke a different language, and found it difficult to understand and accept the small ambitions and petty day-to-day happenings that were so important to people she had left behind.

Was this a good thing or a bad? She wasn't sure. But she realised, and accepted, that in acquiring so much money so quickly she had lost something else. Was this peace of mind, contentment, happiness, or perhaps an amalgam of all three?

Anna had ordered the hired Minerva for five minutes past seven. If the Writer to the Signet had not rung her by then, the deals were off. She found herself feeling curiously calm about this; she did not care greatly either way. Perhaps she had only been glad of an excuse to come home. But at five to seven the telephone rang.

'I have spoken to Mrs MacTavish,' Macleod told her. 'She is agreeable to sell the distillery for the price you name.'

'Did you tell her who was bidding?'

'No. I told her it was a company in the Caribbean.'

'Good. And Soldier's Wood?'

'She'd also be willing to be rid of that. She told me that no good had ever come out of that wood. A thousand pounds more and it's yours.'

'Excellent. Please draw up all the paperwork and I'll sign whatever I have to.'

'I fear that, hurry as I may, this will take some time, Miss Ballater. There are a lot of documents to go through.'

'I'm sure you can deal with everything as quickly as any lawyer, Mr Macleod, and quicker than most. Remember, God made the world in six days and rested on the seventh. This deal is much simpler.'

Anna replaced the receiver, went down to the waiting car. She had calculated that Dr Bailey's surgery would have ended well before seven o'clock, and she was right. As with the minister and Mr Macleod, the doctor appeared pleased to see her.

'This is a most welcome surprise, my dear,' he said. 'I'd no idea you were even in this country.'

'I only arrived a day or so ago. I haven't seen my parents yet.'

'They tell me you've been doing amazingly well. They have shown me some of your letters, so I know just how well. I must congratulate you.'

'Thank you. I have come to see you, Dr Bailey, to

discuss two things. First, I want to thank you personally for what you did for my parents after the death of the laird's son. And if it hadn't been for your kindness in giving me a reference, I would never have had the job with your sister.'

'Have you heard what happened to her?' Bailey asked.

'No, I haven't.'

'A sad story. She drank, you know – but I expect you probably noticed that. Her husband admitted this to me later, but I had no idea at the time, none at all.'

'Where is she now?'

'She died as a result of an accident in India. She went out riding at a friend's house when she was inebriated. If she'd been sober she would never have chosen the horse she did. The groom warned her the animal was headstrong and unsafe for anyone except a most experienced rider, which she wasn't. But Eileen wouldn't believe him. She had a strong will, and she was thrown. She died instantly.'

'I'm very sorry. She dismissed me, you know.'

'Yes. She told her husband you'd not looked after the children, and she also wrote to me about it, saying how surprised she was that I had recommended you. I believed her then, but since her husband has returned here with his regiment, he has given me a rather different account. Apparently, after the death of her sickly little boy, Eileen went completely to pieces. She was drinking a bottle a day by the time the ship reached Bombay.'

Anna nodded. She could understand the reason, but this was not the moment to tell the doctor – if there ever would be one.

'You've been exceptionally kind to my family,' she said. 'You've given them your cottage, and put what work you could in my father's way. But I am now able to give him a job myself, and to buy them a house elsewhere. They don't know this yet. So please let all the details wait till he tells you himself which, from what you say, I am sure he will soon enough.

'When they move out, I'd like to pay to redecorate your cottage completely and maybe add another bedroom or two and a bathroom if you want, and put in electric light. This is my attempt to thank you in a positive way for your kindness to all of us when we had absolutely nothing.'

'There's no need for that, Anna,' said Dr Bailey, clearly moved by the unexpected offer.

'There's no need for many things in this life, Doctor. But kindness is one for which I think there is a need, and it certainly should be rewarded. Believe me, I will get as much pleasure out of this as you will. So let's consider that closed.'

'Well, if you say so. And thank you very much indeed. Now what's the next matter you have come to see me about?'

'Soldier's Wood. Again, for your private ear, at least for the time being, I'm buying it. The whole wood should be mine before I leave.'

'What on earth do you want that for?'

'Because there's something odd in that wood, and I want to know what it is. I'm never likely to find out while Mrs MacTavish owns it, but I might – I won't say I will – once I do. People say it's haunted. When I was a girl, I was afraid to walk through it, yet if I hadn't gone into it when I heard a woman cry out for help my whole life could have been totally different.'

'What do you mean?'

Anna explained.

'I heard something of that,' the doctor admitted. 'Jeannie

Moore once asked me to treat her son who, I hear, has emigrated.'

'So Mr Macleod tells me. My father and the farrier, Donald Coupar, who lived next door, went into that wood one night. Coupar wanted to ask Jeannie Moore, who he thought had psychic powers, to contact his wife who had just died. But before they even met Jeannie, they saw a number of hooded figures and a goat as big as a man standing in a circle, and they panicked. A huge cat jumped at my father, who fired his pistol at it. He hit the animal – at that close range he couldn't miss. Next day I went into the wood and found Jeannie Moore dying, with terrible head injuries – exactly where the cat had been shot.'

Bailey nodded. 'He did mention this to me. He thought that the cat had somehow miraculously changed – metamorphosed is the scientific word – into the woman.'

'It seems absurd, but Donald Coupar thought the same.'

'At the time, maybe, but not later. I can tell you that categorically. One day Donald was shot accidentally when he was out on the moors beating for some shooters up from London. I was called out to attend him and found him mortally injured. Before he died, he wanted to get off his conscience the thought that he had somehow shot Jeannie Moore.

'Apparently, later that night, after he and your father came home, Coupar went back into the wood on his own to try and see her. He was determined to ask her to contact his dead wife. He told me he heard a noise like a great beast moving in the undergrowth. He lost his nerve, for he thought it was going to attack him. So he fired blindly into the bushes and ran.'

'And the next day I found Jeannie Moore dying,' said Anna.

'Yes. Two versions of how she received mortal injuries.'

'Which do you believe?' said Anna.

'As a man of science, I tend to the second one. But, also as a man of science, I agree with you that there is more in Soldier's Wood than has been discovered so far.'

'What do you mean, more?'

'I don't know. I have my own theories, but for the moment I think it best not to mention them. But there is something strange in there.'

'Would you be willing to try and find out what it is?'

'On my own, no. I lack the facilities. I have no laboratory to conduct any tests that may be necessary.'

'Do you know anyone who has those facilities?'

'Well, Macleod has a relation, Tam Douglas, who runs a very successful patent medicine firm in Toronto. He's over here to set up a laboratory in Perth. His idea is to comb the hills and glens and woods for all the herbs he can find and gradually wean people away from chemical drugs to natural ones. Originally, of course, all medicines were herbal. It's always impressed me to see how many of the old remedies really work much better than new ones. He was having dinner with me the other night. A most interesting man. We got on well.'

'So you could work together on this?'

'I'd be happy to. Just let me know as soon as you own the wood, and I'll tell Douglas, and we'll go through it together – keeping our own counsel, of course, about what we are doing. I'll say we're collecting wild flowers for my niece to press, or something like that.'

Anna felt embarrassed to arrive at her parents' cottage in such an impressive car, even if it was only hired from the man who owned station taxis in Perth, so she asked the driver to stop about a hundred yards from the house.

She walked this last distance, smoothed down her dress, adjusted her hat, patted her hair. She felt strangely nervous, wondering whether her parents had changed much in the time she'd been away, and whether they would think she had also changed.

Her father was in the garden, tying a rose to a trellis near the porch. As she reached the gate, he turned at the sound of the latch, and stood, transfixed, a pair of secateurs in one hand.

'Anna!' he cried. 'Is it *really* you? You're back!'

'Yes! It's me,' Anna replied, smiling at his astonishment.

He turned, called to his wife. 'Annie! Come here! She's home!'

Anna's mother came to the door, wiping her hands on a dish towel. As soon as she saw Anna, she threw the towel to one side and ran down the garden path to embrace her daughter.

'Oh, it really *is* you! You're a sight for sore eyes,' she said. 'Are you here for good?'

'Not this time. But, one day . . .'

'Where are you staying?'

'In Perth, the Fair Maid Hotel.'

'What's wrong with your home? Or are you too grand nowadays to stay with us?' her father asked her, only half joking.

'No, I'm not too grand to stay here. You know that. This is my home. The one place in all the world I call home.'

'Then it's a pity you're not here with us.'

'You haven't a spare bedroom,' Anna reminded them both. 'That's the reason I left.'

'Of course,' said her father. 'I'm sorry, I'd forgotten. For the moment I thought we were all back in our old home.

But come in. Tell us about yourself. What brings you over here?'

Anna followed them into the kitchen and sat down. The black dog she remembered so well – greyer now about the muzzle, a little thicker in the body – looked up at her, beat his tail on the floor in welcome before he lay down again in front of the fireplace.

'See, he remembers you. Everyone does round here. We show people your letters. They don't believe how well you're doing, though.'

'People would rather commiserate than congratulate,' said Anna. 'It's human nature.'

'You're quite right. Now, I'll put the kettle on. You're staying for supper, I hope?'

'I'd love to.'

'Well, tell us about yourself. What's happening? How's your business going? *My*, those clothes. That must have cost a pretty packet,' said her mother, fingering Anna's dress.

'You have to look smart when you employ yourself, as I do. You're your own ambassador, and often the only one.'

'Well put. And what's the ambassador got to say for the country she represents?'

'I'll tell you. But first of all, you tell me how things are doing here.'

Her father shrugged. For a moment his face fell. 'Oh, it's not too bad, no matter what some people say. Dr Bailey's very kind. We don't pay him a penny rent, which is remarkable these days. And I make things for people in Perth – a table here, put up a set of bookcases there, or mend sash cords in windows, things like that.'

'He's only half employed,' her mother explained. 'He does his best, but . . .' She held out her hands. Anna could see how careworn they were, how rough.

'I send you a bit each month,' she said.

'We're very grateful for it. But the cost of everything has gone up.'

'So have shares,' said her father. 'I read the doctor's newspapers when he's finished with them, and I see that shares are climbing all the time. It's amazing. There are people here who did not have two bawbees to rub together, and now they've got motorcars, maids, everything.'

'And you're going to join them.'

Her father smiled. 'How?' he asked, puzzled.

'I want you to take charge of all the maintenance, and all the repairs, in the Long Glen Distillery.'

'Aye, I'd like a job like that. But how can you say I'll do it? Mrs MacTavish owns the distillery.'

'She does, yes, at this moment. But within twenty-four hours my company will own it.'

'*Your* company?'

'I'm a partner with two men. One is a retired sea captain and the other an army officer from Mamora, an island in the Indian Ocean. We've been very lucky and have formed a company, Traders Incorporated. Our company has just bought the distillery.'

'Are you joking?' asked her father sharply. 'You've not come to make fun of us, have you?'

'I wouldn't dream of it. We own the distillery. You can name your own salary. You both looked after me when I was young. You gave me a good background, and more than anything you taught me to stand on my own two feet, to look people in the eye, be true to what I believed, and what *you* believed. Now it's my turn to pay you both a dividend on your kindness.'

Her father was crying. Anna could not bear to see him

351

weep, so she said to her mother quickly, 'Come into the kitchen. I'll help you peel some potatoes for supper.'

'Your father can't stand too much good news,' Mrs Ballater explained. 'We've both been through a rather bad time recently.'

'You should have told me.'

Anna's mother shook her head. 'No,' she said. 'You've been so kind and generous to us. We couldn't ask for more.'

'But you're not asking. I'm giving – and delighted to do so.'

'I've got a bottle of Long Glen in the cupboard,' said Mrs Ballater, diplomatically changing the subject. 'Let's all drink to you being back here and all the good things that are going to happen. Never mind your father, he'll soon cheer up. He's only crying because he's so happy.'

After supper, Anna took them in the hired car to her hotel in Perth. She was so used to expensive things now that it seemed quite modest, almost primitive. She saw with surprise how awed her mother and father appeared by the surroundings – the large entrance hall, the chandeliers, waiters padding about noiselessly, carrying trays of drinks. Of course, they'd never been in a place like this; but then, neither had she until she left home.

They sat in the lounge, drinking coffee. Her father had a Long Glen Malt.

'You'll not be staying long, I suppose,' her mother said.

'Unfortunately not this time.'

'We hope you'll come back one day. Now you've got the distillery here to look after, it gives you an excuse. If you've no other excuse.'

'What do you mean?'

Her mother smiled archly. 'Well, your father and I aren't

getting any younger. And we both hope you might want to settle down.'

'I am settled down,' said Anna.

'We hope you may get married. You don't want to be a spinster all your life, doing good works, putting flowers in the kirk, that sort of thing.'

'No,' Anna said. 'I don't think I'll ever do that.'

'Well, marriage is an alternative I would recommend, having been married to your father for nearly thirty years.' She smiled, patted her husband's hand affectionately.

Marriage, thought Anna. What it implied brought back an instant recollection of burning sun on a bare body, the smell of coconut oil rubbed into flesh, the silhouette of the old sultan looming over her, temporarily blocking out the sunlight. Symbolically, he was of the dark. And then came the indignity, the pain, the revulsion against him, against herself, against Shah, against the whole idea of sexual involvement.

Marriage. She hadn't really thought of it. Well, she had, often, but not in any serious sense. She had not met anyone she wanted to marry, and she could not divorce from her mind the memory of rape.

On the liner back to New York, Anna recalled her mother's words. She was still very young. She was also, amazingly, rich. And yet what sort of life was she leading? Basically, she was a smuggler on a big scale; that was the truth of the matter, the reason for her wealth. Traders Incorporated owned or rented a number of fast launches and speedboats. She did not travel in them now from the Bahamas to Florida or further up the American coast. There was no need to; others were pleased to take that risk. Sometimes, they were arrested by Revenue officers in American cutters, and fined or jailed. Sometimes, the launches were impounded. But, no matter. The profits were huge. After a dozen trips, even a crewman could make enough to retire. And where else could anyone make that sort of money? It was worth risking time in jail for the prospect of a fortune.

And yet Anna had an increasing sense that somehow she was only running on the spot, going through the motions of progress, confusing a routine – admittedly an astonishingly profitable routine – with real and lasting achievement. Of course, with all the money she had saved, she need never work again. That was a situation for which most people scrimped all their lives, 'to put a little by' to keep them in their old age. When widows and single women grew old, unless they could live with a family, the future was often bleak indeed. Not for Anna. But her future might well be bleak in emotional terms.

Money was surely not the only currency by which achievement could be counted. Happiness was a better one. And she was not happy. She was lonely.

She had a magnificent house on Cable Beach, an apartment in New York. But, apart from servants, there would be no one to greet her in either place when she returned. In essence, her house and her apartment were hollow shells, waiting to be filled with laughter and with love. In the meantime, they were both as empty as her life, as her heart. What could she do to change things? She had no one in mind.

Each night on the voyage, when she went to bed, she lay awake, with the curtains open. How different from her first trip west in the *Boa Vista*. The liner dipped and rose slowly and the moon cast its silver path across the calm waters. And she wondered, would there ever be a sign to tell her which way to go? She thought of the pieces of root that

Jeannie Moore had given to her. She had only one piece left, and she did not want to risk using it in case she saw only a cloudy picture and could not understand its significance. Was everyone's destiny written in the stars before they were even born? However you might try to avoid it, you could not do so, for it instantly bent back again, like a bow when the arrow has fled.

Finally, as dawn began to paint the sky pink, Anna would go to sleep, and wake up tired, still wondering whether she was doing right, whether she was going wrong, and what she could do about it in either case.

Castle sat at his desk in the study of his house in Nassau, a twenty-dollar cigar in one hand, watching the night watchman who stood opposite him. He was a shambling, gangling figure wearing shabby, frayed cotton trousers and blue shirt, faded by many washings. His eyes rolled nervously as he faced his employer.

'How many visitors have come to the Villa Maria while I've been away?' Castle asked him pleasantly enough. No need to alarm the man – yet.

'Only ones I was told to let in, sir.'

'Who were they?'

'Friends of Mrs Castle, boss.'

'What sort of friends?'

'Women friends. They came for the English custom of taking tea in the afternoon.'

'Any men?'

'No, boss. No men.'

'You're lying,' said Castle shortly.

The man swallowed. Mrs Castle had given him five dollars to forget he had ever seen the Scotsman arrive. Five dollars was a big tip, but if Castle found out (and maybe his wife would tell him, you could never trust women if things were going against them), five dollars would not keep the night watchman and his wife and four children for long. This might even be a test of his honesty: you couldn't trust anyone any way. He made up his mind, swallowed again.

'I forgot. There was one man, boss. He works at Rafferty's yard.'

'Who's he?'

'A Scotsman, boss. Name of Moore.'

'What did he want?'

'He called one evening.'

'Why didn't you tell me before?'

'I forgot, boss.'

'Now you've remembered, was that the only time he called?'

What did the boss know? He dare not risk lying now. He was in too deeply already. 'No, boss. He called on several evenings.'

'And Mrs Castle told you each time to let him in?'

'Yes, boss.'

'What did she give you?'

'Give me, boss?'

'You know what I goddamn well mean. What did she slip you to keep quiet?'

'Oh, nothing, boss.'

'Nothing?'

'Well, she's a generous lady, boss. She gave me five dollars.'

'Right. Now get out. If you say anything to her or to anyone else about this, you're fired. At once. Out. Understand?'

'Yes, boss.' He bowed, shambled out of the door.

Castle sat for a moment, drawing on his cigar. Then he

picked up the telephone, spoke to a colleague in Nassau.

'I want you to find out all you can about a man called Moore, working at Rafferty's. Check where he lodges. Then go through his belongings. Don't break in. Do it quietly. Don't let him suspect anything. Bribe your way in. It'll be some kind of dosshouse, so it won't take much.'

'What are you looking for, exactly?' asked the man at the end of the line.

'Anything you might think is surprising for a Scotsman in a Nassau boatyard to have in his room.'

'You mean money?'

'I mean what I say. Anything. OK?'

'OK.'

Castle replaced the telephone and sat for a long time smoking, but now the twenty-dollar cigar tasted like ash in his mouth.

Castle had grown up believing from boyhood that it was dangerous and disappointing, and sometimes possibly fatal, to trust anyone.

'We're all in this world for what we can get out of it,' Torrio had once told him. Despite Castle's Italian Catholic upbringing, he accepted that this was basically true. There might be another world, or again there might not. Priests believed, but that was their affair; the time to concern oneself with that was when one knew all the facts, and who did? He had not known even the basic facts about his wife and this stud on the ocean liner. He intended to find out at once. His future with Torrio depended on it, and without Torrio, he had no future.

Castle did not contact his wife from Nassau. He knew that Maria was at their apartment in New York because she had telephoned him to say how glad she was to be back, and how she was longing to see him. And he had believed her, then. But now he thought that her enthusiasm was false, overplayed. It was like seeing a show for the second time. On the first occasion, the actors seem to speak spontaneously, from the heart. On the second visit, you remembered how they walked upstage, downstage, turned left, right, smiled and said their lines. The make-believe was obvious. So it was here.

As he remembered his wife's voice, sugary as always, blowing kisses down the long-distance telephone, he felt a cold hatred for her. She had humiliated him. Not that he particularly minded her sexual betrayal; he was not interested in her in any way, but she had diminished him in the eyes of his boss, which was an altogether more serious matter.

She must have been a fool to carry on this shipboard infatuation so blatantly that others could see and report on it. Torrio had mentioned a steward. There were probably others, passengers and crew; Torrio had many unlikely contacts who reported to him on matters in which they thought he might be interested. Nothing was as it seemed, no one was one hundred per cent honest. But then he wasn't himself.

He took the next seaplane to Miami, then went on to New York, not telling Maria he was on his way, not waiting for what his men might find in Davey Moore's room.

A limousine picked him up at the station, took him to his apartment block. He told the driver to stop fifty yards up the road, just in case his wife was watching. She might then just have time to smuggle this lover – or maybe someone else – down the service stairs or by the service elevator. When you started distrusting people, analysing everything they said in case they were lying, you were on a road without any end.

The commissionaire bowed effusively to him. 'Mr Castle, sir. We haven't seen you for some time.'

'I've been away,' he said briefly. 'Nassau, Bahamas. Chicago. The Windy City. Everything all right here?'

'As far as I know, sir, perfect.'

Of course, this bastard wouldn't tell him. It was as much as his life was worth to tell Castle that his wife was two-timing him with someone else – and publicly. The elevator soared silently and swiftly to the twentieth floor. He walked along the corridor, paused briefly outside his own front door in case he could hear an alien voice, a lover's voice, but there was no sound whatever.

He opened the door with his two passkeys, went inside. From the hall, separated by double doors leading into the lounge, he could hear gramophone music. His wife was clearly copying Torrio in her love, or pretended love, of opera. Castle took off his coat, hung it carefully on the hanger in a cupboard. He had grown up without overcoats; now he had half a dozen of them, some fur-lined, others fur-collared. He took care of them.

He walked into the lounge. She was sitting in an easy chair, a martini at her elbow. The electric fire glowed in the fireplace. Blades of a hidden fan turned, projecting false red flames on a metal screen. Even the flames are goddamn phoney, Castle thought bitterly.

'Darling!' Maria said, jumping up and running towards him. She kissed him effusively on both cheeks. He could smell drink on her breath. He pushed her aside gently, suddenly feeling power. He could throttle her there, strangle her, kill her within seconds. And then what? The business of getting rid of the body. It wouldn't be worth it. Torrio would find out. He'd be in hock to Torrio for ever.

'You look tired,' Maria said sympathetically. 'A drink?'

'Yeah. Brandy and ginger,' Castle told her.

She went to the cocktail cabinet, mixed the drink, brought the glass back to him.

'How was Europe?' he asked her.

'Great,' she said. 'Very small compared to America, though. I was surprised. Of course, I was only a child when I left. I'd forgotten how narrow the streets are, how small the houses. Even the castles are nothing. And the food was all strange. I know we eat Italian food here, but it tasted sort of different there. And you don't get iced water. No fresh tossed salad. Just wine.'

'What was the boat trip like?'

'Wonderful.'

'Meet any friends?'

'Friends? No. Met a few nice people, of course. Had lunch, dinner in the restaurant and talked to guests at the next table or walking on the deck. That sort of thing. Stewards put out canvas chairs on the promenade deck and bring you hot soup while you sit there all wrapped up in rugs. Great.'

'So you met no one of interest?'

Maria looked at him sharply, eyes narrowing slightly, instantly wary. 'No. No one. Just other people travelling.'

'That's what I meant. What sort of people?'

'Well, I don't know, much older than me. One was vice-president of a company that made pots and pans in Michigan. There was a banker, a surgeon with heart trouble, people like that. All old and rich and retired.'

'No one young?'

'No way. I was the youngest.'

Castle put down his drink, took her by her arms, holding her, feeling her flesh, her small feminine bones beneath the silk sleeves.

'You're giving me crap,' he said thickly.

'What do you mean, crap?' Maria pulled away from him. 'Don't talk to me like that.'

'I'll talk to you as I like. You were a waitress till I picked you up, a hash slinger. Nothing.'

'What's got into you? What's wrong?'

'You know damn well what's wrong. You've had your ass screwed off by some Limey bastard you met on the boat.'

'Limey bastard? I don't know what you're talking about.'

'Don't waste my time. Or yours. If you do, you just might find you've got very little time left to waste.'

'What do you mean?'

'You know goddamn well what I mean. Where is the bastard?'

'There is no bastard, I assure you.'

Castle hit her then, across the face with the back of his hand. The ring scored her cheek. A tiny bead of blood grew in the cut and dropped like a tear. She staggered back, shocked and horrified, one hand to her face.

'You've gone mad,' she said hoarsely. 'Bill, what's the matter? What's happened?'

'Nothing to me. It's to you.' He hit her again. 'Now talk,' he said. 'Who was this bastard?'

'Oh, it was nothing. There was one fellow, a harmless Scot emigrating to Canada. I had a couple of drinks with him. That's all.'

'That's not what I hear. I hear he was screwing your ass off, every which way. Was he, or wasn't he?'

Castle hit her again before she could reply. Maria began to cry, slumped down in her seat, head in her hands.

'He's a nice boy. There was nothing in it, Bill, I swear to you. Nothing. As God is my judge.'

'He's not. I am. And I've witnesses. I don't care if you fool around with people, because I'm not interested in you and never have been. You know that. You bore me. But it was convenient for me to marry you, so I did. I don't care what you get up to with men, women, beasts, anything, but I don't want to be made a fool of publicly. Nor does Torrio.'

'Torrio? What's he got to do with it?'

'He told me.'

'How the hell did he know? He's making it up.'

'He doesn't make up things. He's got people all over the place who feed him news. Like the steward who brought you hot soup on the promenade deck. He pays informers well. What they tell him may mean nothing on their own, but put together, they're like a jigsaw. They build a picture. And this picture is that the whole outfit has been made to look cheap because you were seen openly whoring with some bum on a boat.'

Maria sat up now, hands in her lap. The cut was bleeding badly; blood dripped down onto her silk blouse. That cost me two hundred dollars, Castle remembered. Two hundred goddamn dollars and what gets blood out of silk? Nothing. When blood is spilled, that's it.

'All right,' she said dully. 'He kissed me. Once. Nothing in that. Just saying goodbye, like I was his sister.'

'Go on.'

'Why should I? You're not interested in me. I live like a bird in a golden cage. I try to make my own friends, my own amusements, because you're always away with Johnny Torrio or other terrible men. And then one day, one of them disappears altogether, he just doesn't come round here any more. And I ask you why and you won't say. You don't need to because you're off to a gangster's funeral. He crossed someone, so he's dead.

'I've got to have some life of my own, and here I've nothing, only clothes, chocolates and booze. I've got my own feelings. This boy was different from the people I meet through you. He was simple, if you like. Direct. He wasn't rich and I guess he never will be. But I'm fed up with you and your so-called friends, always talking about money and loyalty and revenge. How to cut into someone else's deal, how to bloodsuck some poor devil who's worked all his life to build up a business. You'll break his neck or his knees, and think nothing of it because that's your world and your life. This kid knew nothing of that, and I didn't tell him.'

'Where is he now?'

She paused. 'He's gone to Canada.'

'You're lying.'

'I'm not lying. Why should I lie? He had a letter of introduction to some company up in Toronto.'

'You're giving me crap again. He's in Nassau, working in Rafferty's boatyard. And he's been screwing you in Nassau, too. Hasn't he? Answer me, you bitch.'

Suddenly Maria's misery, the realisation of her totally wretched and indefensible position, fused with the alcohol in her veins to produce a compound of absolute despair. She began to weep noisily, her shoulders heaving.

'I'm telling you,' said Castle coldly. 'You see that bastard once more, and you're dead. So's he.'

'You wouldn't kill a boy for doing nothing.'

'I'm killing him for doing you too many times, too publicly, so others knew and passed on the news. You won't get another chance, either of you.' He turned, walked towards the door.

Maria glanced at him, saw his drink untouched. 'You've left your brandy,' she said suddenly, inconsequentially.

'I've left you,' he corrected her.

'What do you mean?'

'What I say.'

He walked out of the door. Maria heard the sound of his heavy footsteps diminish on the long, thick carpet in the corridor. Then she put her face in her hands and sat in silence, beyond tears, beyond grief, overcome by the horror of discovery.

Fourteen

For the next few weeks, Maria tried to pretend that everything was as it had been since her wedding. There had been a little argument, agreed, but nothing important. People talked about lovers' tiffs, and this had been no more than that. In every marriage there were bound to be some disagreements, and her husband was simply overwrought. He had a lot of strain in his job, that man Torrio to contend with; and probably he had other problems about which she knew nothing.

But although she tried to convince herself that nothing had changed between them, deep down she knew, and accepted with resignation, that everything had. This affair had been one too many. But for her it was much more than simply a casual romance. She really loved the guy. Or thought she did, which, to her, was much the same thing.

She did not know now where her husband was from one week to the next. She would telephone him in Chicago, and she wrote letters and sent telegrams to him in Nassau. But all her calls, like her letters and cables, went unanswered.

Sometimes Castle did come back briefly to their apartment in New York. When he did, he slept in the spare room. They might sit opposite each other for a short time at the table at breakfast or supper, but usually they ate separately. Their servants would wait on them as before, but he would not speak to her. It was as though she did not exist. She tried to make conversation, but the most he would reply was 'Yes' or 'No' or 'Really?' Sometimes he did not even speak when she spoke to him, but simply shrugged his shoulders dismissively.

Unable to bear this deliberate and wounding behaviour for days at a time, Maria began to drink too much in a vain attempt to dull the pain. Sometimes, on their own and half drunk, she would shout at him.

'I'm sorry,' she would cry miserably. 'I didn't *mean* it. You've got it all wrong. Can't we go back as we were?'

When Castle did not answer, she would scream, 'I love you! *I love you!*'

Then he would look at her as though he could not understand what she was saying, and still not reply. Or, worse, he would walk out of the room. She'd follow him, grab his jacket and shout at him beseechingly, 'Please! Please! Bill, I *beg* you.' He would shake her off roughly as though she was a tramp, a pan-handler wanting to cadge a coin.

Maria had no one in whom she could confide. She guessed that any telephone calls she made would be tapped, and that her husband was watching, waiting for her to make another mistake.

She desperately wanted to get in touch with Davey to tell him what had happened, but of course that was quite impossible. If she sent him a letter, although she could post it anywhere in New York, someone else might open it in Nassau. Was he even still in Nassau?

Her husband might have had Davey beaten up, or even killed. The thought made Maria feel physically sick. But she had no one she could ask, and no means of finding out. She felt like someone lost in a dark tunnel, walking forwards because she could not go back, and yet without any light at the far end to guide her and give her hope of escape. She was walking through darkness, into an even deeper dark.

Friends she had known as a girl, working in the ice-cream parlour, were not her friends now. She had moved above and beyond them socially and economically. She could not go back and admit the mess she had made of the life which doubtless they still envied. Similarly, she felt too proud to explain to her parents what had happened. And even if she could force herself to tell them, they would never understand how their daughter could ever have been so unbelievably foolish to put at risk a rich world totally beyond their dreams. She had to accept that she was on her own.

There was always plenty of drink in the apartment, and to sip steadily was a temptation she did not attempt to resist. She slept badly, and her doctor prescribed pills. At first, she took one every night as she went to bed. But they reacted unpleasantly with the alcohol; she would wake in the early hours and lie, mouth dry, heart beating too fast, a pulse throbbing in her ears like a drumbeat. Soon she was taking two pills every night, then three, and always with a large neat whisky to chase them down.

One evening, Maria went on her own to the theatre. Her husband was away somewhere, and when she was alone she always left lights burning in every room. She could not face returning to a dark apartment. She needed bright lights all around her in an attempt to compensate for the bleak emptiness within.

When she came home, she threw her coat over the nearest chair, went on into her bedroom. Then she caught sight of herself in the triple mirror above the dressing table. She had been crying, and her face was still puffy. She looked terrible and she felt worse. She opened the bedside cupboard, took out a bottle of whisky. She did not bother to pour any into a glass, but put the bottle to her mouth and gulped greedily.

That poor darling boy Davey. Would she ever see him again? Dare she? Torrio's informers seemed to be everywhere.

Maria put the bottle on the bedside table, kicked off her shoes, lay back thankfully on the bed. What could she do? She couldn't just let Davey go out of her life for ever. Yet what possible future could they have together, even if they eloped? She was married to Castle, and her religious beliefs meant that she could never divorce him and remarry. What grounds could she give for divorce anyway, even if she wished to do so? In law, she was the guilty party. She had transgressed, committed adultery, while her trusting husband had lavished gifts on her, even paid for a trip to Europe.

And if she and Davey simply lived together, what would they live on? Without any qualifications, it was unlikely that he would find a worthwhile job. Would her feelings for Davey survive if they were poor, and perhaps pursued by her husband's creatures? This was the most worrying prospect of all.

It wasn't just sex, this attraction she felt for Davey, she told herself. It was something much deeper. Davey appealed to her lost innocence. She did not realise until they met how much she regretted the loss, for she knew she would never find innocence again.

There might be other men, other lovers, but always she would remember Davey. And even when these other men of whatever cloudy future she might have lay with her, when they were in her, she would not be thinking of them, but of him.

The future held nothing for her now, Maria told herself

morosely, beginning to cry. She was on her own, no one to talk to, no one who cared.

She sat up, took another swig. As she did so, she saw on her bedside table the silver phial that contained her sleeping tablets. She'd have a good sleep at least, then she'd feel better. In the morning, when her head was clear, she could decide what to do. But even as she told herself this, she knew, deep down, there was really only one choice: she must stay with her husband. No one else would take her, and how else could she live? Slinging hash in a cafe, trotting round the tables carrying trays of coffee, gratefully picking up minuscule tips? Not after state rooms with iced champagne and hot lobsters, not after Cadillac cars with liveried drivers and closets packed with expensive clothes and jewels.

Maria's hands were shaking so much that she had difficulty in opening the top of the pill box. When she managed to do so, she counted the pills inside. Twenty. Years ago, she had never needed anything to make her sleep. But now she would, every night, for ever and ever – unless Davey came back. She tipped the pills out into the palm of her hand. How many would she need to take to send her off? One, two, three? Why not the lot, the whole damn frigging lot?

She scooped them up but spilled them. She picked up half a dozen, washed them down with whisky. The pills tasted bitter as bile on her tongue, and as she swallowed them she felt a brief burning sensation in her stomach. More pills and then more whisky soothed the pain. Soon she felt sleepy, pleasantly relaxed, at ease: no worries, no problems.

She was a young girl again, and her father and mother were hoping she'd get promotion at the ice-cream parlour.

'But I've *been* promoted,' she said aloud, and her voice was so dry and harsh she did not recognise it. She put the bottle up to her lips again, but before she could drink, sleep overcame her like a flood tide of oblivion.

Maria fell back, still holding the neck of the bottle. Whisky glug-glugged out over the pink satin sheets, but she was unaware of it. She snored in her sleep, and then her snoring grew fainter, her grip on the bottle neck relaxed, and she lay in silence and at peace.

Castle let himself in through the front door of their apartment, locked it behind him and stood for a moment in the heavily carpeted hall. All the lights were lit, so he guessed that Maria was home. But then he saw that her bedroom door was open, so perhaps she wasn't. She invariably locked it since his discovery of her affair with Davey Moore. She was afraid of him; he knew that. But then so many people were, just as he was afraid of Torrio, and other even more sinister figures struck alarm into Torrio's heart.

Castle took off his overcoat, hung it in the hall closet, walked on into his wife's room. To his surprise Maria was asleep on her bed, fully clothed, mouth open, face damp with sweat. The room stank of whisky. He wrinkled his face in distaste, picked up the half-empty bottle, put it on the bedside table. He could see pills scattered across the silk eiderdown. Maria was breathing steadily, and as he watched she wrinkled her face and groaned. She was dreaming.

Why should she ever wake up from her dreams, as no doubt she would wake at some hour of the night or morning, and then this ludicrous farce of their life together would continue? There was a very easy way out, and he might never again have such an opportunity to take it.

Castle crossed the room, picked up a silk cushion from one of the chairs, placed it over Maria's face, held it down firmly. He glanced around the room as he did so at the feminine knick-knacks – a satin doll with a crinoline skirt that covered the bedside telephone, bottles of face and hand cream, countless powder boxes, lip salves; the detritus of a woman losing her looks too soon.

He wondered how long he would have to hold the cushion over his wife's face. She moved slightly. He could feel her head turn, but feebly. Then she lay quite still, scarcely breathing. He picked up her wrist, felt her pulse. It was very weak. Soon, it stopped altogether.

Castle held the cushion, more firmly now, for another five minutes by the ormolu clock on the mantelpiece. Then he removed it from her face. Sweat from her skin had stained the silk, but that would dry. He put the cushion back on the chair, stained side downwards, returned to the bedside. This was the quietest, easiest killing he had ever accomplished. No risk. No fighting. No blood. Nothing.

He went out of the room. Force of habit made him turn off the light. Then he turned it on again, and wiped the switch with his handkerchief in case he'd left any fingerprints. The silk cushion wouldn't matter; they would never lift prints from that. He closed the door silently, holding the handle in his handkerchief, and went across the apartment to his own bedroom, turning out lights as he went.

There was something symbolic, almost religious, he thought, about the darkness all around, with the only lamp left burning in the room where his wife lay dead.

Johnny Torrio came down the gangway from his white motor yacht and stood for a moment on the Nassau quayside, savouring sun on his face and the scent of a nine-inch Havana cigar. He wore white pigskin shoes, white trousers, dark blue blazer, a yacht-club neckerchief. He was altogether pleased that he looked the part of a wealthy yachtsman.

'I wasn't expecting you, sir,' said Castle. He had not spoken to Torrio face to face since their meeting in Torrio's apartment. He did not feel any pleasure in seeing him now; only concern. Something must have gone wrong.

'That's the whole point of making a surprise visit. To see how things are going. And how are they going?'

'Pretty good, I think.'

'You think? You should know, not think. I read in the papers the sad news that your wife had passed away.'

'Yes. She was not very happy. The trip to Europe didn't do her much good. Unsettled her, I think.'

'I am sorry to hear that,' said Torrio with total insincerity. 'Trips like that, made on their own, meeting different people in strange cities, often unsettle young women.' Torrio drew on his cigar to let Castle digest this remark. 'And I hear unsettling news about matters here,' he added.

'Nothing wrong here, I assure you. I'm in Nassau all the time now.'

'Then maybe you ought to go away for a while. Get a fresh outlook. Put someone else in here.'

'What do you hear that is unsettling?' Castle asked him.

'That those schmucks, O'Grady and Shah and the Scottish girl Ballater, have bought a whisky distillery in Scotland.'

'Oh, yeah. I heard that too. Long Glen Distillery.'

'You didn't tell me.'

'I thought there was no need to.'

'*You* thought – again? Maybe you think too much and act too little, Castle. I do the thinking. Not you. Understand?

I judge if anything's important or not. And this is. Can't you see what they're going to do? They'll run the stuff in from Scotland themselves. Cut you out, cut *us* out. Don't you see that?'

'They wouldn't pay the extra bucks a case you wanted. But I hired some students who are down here on vacation. They paid gladly.'

'And they'll pay a hell of a price if they're caught. Ruin their careers if they go to jail.'

'That's their problem. They know the risks. And there's also what's going on in the States.'

'What's going on in the States is my affair. What's happening down here is yours. And I'm not happy about it. I want that Traders group broken up. The girl's the brain. O'Grady's the fighter. He's also a fag, so I'm told. That could be useful. Get him on that somehow, bring him down. Meantime, what about Shah?'

'I've made some enquiries round about. He's supposed to be the bastard son of some sultan of an island in the Indian Ocean.'

'What happened to the sultan?'

'Death. I've been working on Shah. Said we'd finance his return to Mamora to take over his rightful throne and all that crap. In return he'd help us if we decided to expand the coke trade. He said he'd accept our offer.'

Torrio grunted. This prospect was still well in the future. He wished Castle had not mentioned it. Still, it could work, but that would take time, and he wanted action fast.

'OK,' he said curtly. 'Just get him out of here. Maybe he's the one to go for first. Then pick off the others. Get 'em all out of our hair. And quickly. No messing around. Do I make myself clear to a thinker?'

'Perfectly.'

'I'm glad to hear it. I was beginning to feel you could be letting things slip. But I got to make allowances. Losing your wife must have been a big shock to you. Especially since you were so fond of each other.'

Anna returned to Nassau with a curious feeling of anti-climax and indecision. Making huge sums of money from smuggling had proved almost unbelievably easy, and now that she had bought the distillery an even greater fortune was assured. But this prospect, which she had imagined would fill her with excitement, seemed in some totally inexplicable way to have lost its lustre. Was making money so quickly and with so little effort what life was all about, or was there some more worthwhile and more satisfying aim that she had not yet discovered?

She felt she had reached a point of decision. She could go on as she was, or she could branch out – to do exactly what? She wondered whether O'Grady and Shah ever felt like this about the pattern of their lives. On the impulse, she telephoned them both and invited them over to her house.

When they arrived, Anna explained that they now owned Long Glen Distillery, and the first shipments of whisky were already on the way. She had expected congratulations, but although they appeared pleased, their enthusiasm was muted.

'What's been happening here while I've been away?' she asked, looking from one to the other. 'You seem a bit gloomy. Something gone wrong?'

'I think it's *going* wrong,' O'Grady corrected her. 'Your deal could either be kill or cure for us.'

'What do you mean exactly.'

'Castle has become increasingly unhappy that we didn't

trade with him. And with him, unhappiness takes the form of hostility.'

'He wanted too much money,' Anna pointed out. 'We all agreed on that.'

'I know. But he takes a different view and, more important, so do the people above him, in particular the gangster Johnny Torrio.'

'How does he show his hostility?'

'Very crudely,' said Shah. 'The bank manager Rettini was found dead in the sea last Friday.'

'Drowned?'

'No. Shot in the head. In the afternoon a typed anonymous note was delivered to his office. It simply said, "You talked too much". The local papers made a great play of this. Said it sounded like a warning to others.'

'He didn't talk to me too much,' said Anna. 'But he let me know Castle was behind the attempt to hijack our boat. Have either of you seen Castle since?'

'Yes. At Rettini's funeral. Said how sorry he was to hear of his death. But he made the point that Rettini could have prevented it – if the note was to be believed.'

'Since Castle probably wrote the note, just so the papers could print it, he knew what he was talking about.'

'I took it as a clear warning,' said Shah soberly. 'We either deal with Castle on his terms or we face the consequences. And I have to tell you that he has made me an unexpected offer he thinks I cannot refuse.' He explained Castle's proposal that he should return to Mamora, and why.

'What have you told him?' asked Anna.

'I said yes.'

'So you are going to take him up on it?'

Shah shrugged. 'I don't trust him,' he admitted, 'any

more than I know anyone I can trust back in Mamora. But I didn't want to give him no for an answer right away.'

'Very wise,' Anna agreed. But was it? she wondered. Castle was clearly not making the offer out of simple generosity, and his explanation about increasing the sale of drugs did not seem adequate. Mamora was not involved in growing opium or in shipping it. Anna suspected that Castle's offer could somehow be part of a deliberate attempt to ruin the partnership. If the partnership was to survive, he must be thwarted. But how?

'Anything else been happening?' she asked O'Grady.

'One thing. A young Scots fellow has been working at Rafferty's boatyard, doing well, a dab hand with engines. Then Castle heard some story he had been carrying on with his wife and had his lodgings searched. They found a card with Mrs Castle's New York phone number. So they beat him up and threw him out of the yard.'

'Where is he now?'

'Dossing down at my place till his bruises heal. Then I don't know what he'll do.'

'What's his name?'

'Davey Moore. Comes from some village near Perth – your neck of the woods, as it happens.'

'You're sure?'

'Well, that's what he told me. Why?'

'I think I knew his mother – slightly.'

'Then meet Davey and ask him. He could do with a friend now, I can tell you.'

When O'Grady and Shah had gone, Anna sat for nearly half an hour looking out at the sea. Was it really possible that Jeannie Moore's son, now grown up, was in Nassau, actually staying in her partner's house? What had happened to the job in Canada?

She decided to find out. She scribbled a note, sealed it in an envelope, told her chauffeur to deliver it personally to Mr Moore at Captain O'Grady's house and bring him back in the car.

She waited, feeling slightly nervous. What sort of person would he turn out to be? Some clodhopping hobbledehoy with a broad Scots accent and carroty hair like a wire brush? She was still wondering when she heard the crunch of tyres on the raked gravel drive. Her Bahamian butler came to the door of the patio.

'Mr Moore to see you, ma'am.'

A tall young man came out from the cool shadows of the main sitting room to the bright hard sunlight on the patio. Anna noticed with approval that his hair, though red, was not like wire, and it was smoothly brushed. He wore white duck trousers, a blue shirt. His face was badly bruised, his upper lip cut, one eye half closed. He looked at her, puzzled, wondering why she had sent for him.

'Come and sit down,' she said. 'In the sun or out of it?'

'Wherever you like, Miss Ballater.'

'A drink?'

'A beer, if you have one.'

'I have.' She ordered two beers, sat down on a canvas chair opposite him. 'You don't remember me?'

'I don't, ma'am. But I heard that a Miss Ballater from my home village, Long Glen, was in the Bahamas. I suppose you are that Miss Ballater.'

'You suppose rightly. And your mother was Jeannie Moore of Soldier's Wood?'

'Yes.'

'I met her, years ago, when you were small,' said Anna. 'You'd hurt your leg in a trap.'

'I remember that, Miss Ballater. My mother was very grateful to you for helping us then.'

'You know what some people said about your mother?'

'I've heard since, ma'am. They said she was a witch. But that wasn't so.'

'I always thought that in different circumstances she might have achieved all sorts of things. In Long Glen, however, there wasn't much chance to achieve anything out of the rut or station you were born into. I was a maid in the laird's castle, so I speak from experience.'

'You escaped, ma'am.'

'I was one of the few lucky ones. But even so, it wasn't easy.' She paused, remembering the strange vicissitudes of fortune that had brought her to this lovely house on the edge of the ocean. 'The laird thought that your mother had cast a spell on his son who drowned in a few inches of water,' she went on. 'Nonsense, of course. She just forecast what would happen, she didn't make it happen. Some people have that gift or somehow acquire it. Most people don't understand how or why so it's called magic. People like that are often called witches, and have been for hundreds of years – because they don't conform. My parents and I were put out of our cottage because the laird thought I was somehow an associate of your mother. Eventually, and very fortunately for me, I ended up here. What about yourself?'

'I was brought up by the laird, ma'am, oddly enough, when you tell me the opinion he held of my mother.'

'Perhaps that opinion was simply to cover up something else.'

'What do you mean?'

'It's a sort of hunch I have. Feminine intuition, if you like.'

'Well, he was very kind to me, ma'am. He was going to

send me to university. Then he died. Mr Macleod, the Writer to the Signet, brought the laird's will to the castle and asked me to be present while it was being read. But I wasn't mentioned in it, although Mr Macleod clearly thought I would be – or had been. And he should know. He drew up a will that couldn't be found. So all they had was an earlier one, in which, of course, I wasn't mentioned.

'Mrs MacTavish never liked me. She always resented me for some reason. They had no children, except for the little boy who drowned. And within days of the will being read she gave me a cheque for five hundred pounds and told me to make my own way, emigrate. Get out, in other words, as far away as possible.'

'Why did you choose the Bahamas?'

'I didn't, really. I was going to Canada. Mr Macleod kindly gave me an introduction to a relation in a chemical works in Toronto.'

'But you didn't take that up.'

'No.'

'Why not?'

'I'd really rather not say, ma'am.'

'Why ever not?'

'Some reasons are rather embarrassing to give.'

'Embarrass me,' said Anna, smiling.

'On the boat I met a woman who suggested I could work with engines in some shipping concern her husband ran in Nassau. So I came down here.'

'Mrs Castle?'

'You know her?'

'No, but I heard that Mr Castle was aggrieved that you were, shall I say, on intimate terms with his wife.'

'So I've found out.' Davey stroked his bruised face. 'I didn't know she was married to Mr Castle then.'

'When did you find out?'

'As our ship docked. I don't know why I'm telling you this, Miss Ballater, but we have the same background, the same home base. When I heard she was married, I wanted out. I didn't care to be involved with a married woman. There was no future in that for either of us.'

'And you wanted there to be a future?'

Davey shrugged. 'I didn't really think about that very much. I don't know if she did.'

'You know what happened to her?'

'She went back to New York.'

'You have an address for her?'

'She gave me a card. It was stolen from my lodgings just before I was beaten up.'

'Not difficult to find who the thief was, I think,' said Anna. 'I am sorry to have to tell you that Mrs Castle has died.'

'How do you mean? Killed?'

'No. She took her own life.'

Davey shook his head in amazement and disbelief. Why should Maria do such a thing when she seemed to have so very much to live for and enjoy? 'Are you sure? It seems so out of keeping. You think she did it – *if* she did it – because of me?' Davey asked her.

Anna shrugged. 'Perhaps that was an element. Perhaps not. I don't know. Maybe she just wanted to sleep and took too many pills by mistake. That can happen so easily.'

'An accident, then?' Davey asked hopefully.

'Possibly. Or maybe she was asleep and someone couldn't see any good reason why she should wake up.'

'You know that, Miss Ballater?'

'No. It's just a possibility, knowing what her husband is like. Now, what are your plans after all that's happened?'

'Go on to Canada, I suppose. See if that job is still open.'

'Did you write and tell them you didn't want it?'

'Yes. I said I'd found something else temporarily. Mr Macleod's relation was on a visit to Scotland. His secretary replied, and so he may not have seen my letter. It was kind of Mr Macleod to give me his name.'

'You might still find something permanent here.'

'Like what?'

'Working for me. Looking after the engines on Traders' boats.'

'But won't Mr Castle object? He told me to get out.'

'We don't work with Mr Castle any more, so his views don't come into it. With Captain O'Grady and Razadin Shah I ship whisky from Long Glen Distillery, which we've just bought, up into the States. When we first arrived, we worked with Castle, but he demanded too big a slice of the action so we decided to work for ourselves. He doesn't think much of this, but so far he's not been able to stop us. Though, no doubt, he will try. Now . . .'

She opened her purse.

'Here's a hundred dollars. Leave O'Grady's house, but thank him for helping you. He's got a kind heart. Not too many want to help anyone when they're down. Rent a place of your own. Then report to our sheds on the harbour, eight o'clock tomorrow morning.'

Davey hesitated. 'Do you think Castle's men will beat me up again if I take your job?'

'If they're wise they won't try. We can call on some strong muscle too, if we have to. But I think that Castle will only attack people who can't look after themselves. From now on, you are not in that category, Davey.'

They shook hands, and Anna watched him leave the patio. Once he was out of sight, she ran upstairs and stood well back from her bedroom window, because she wanted to see him walk down the drive without him seeing her.

Anna tried to analyse her feelings. He was younger than her by how many years she did not care to consider. And he attracted her. She felt drawn to him in a way she had never been drawn to anyone, which was absurd, of course, remembering the gap in their ages. Anna liked him, even after such a brief conversation. She wondered what he thought of her. She walked down the stairs. The butler was waiting for her in the hall.

'Mr Rosenblatt to see you, ma'am.'

'Who is he?'

The butler held out a silver tray with a small visiting card. Anna picked it up.

'Isaac A. Rosenblatt, Red-Rose Productions, Hollywood, California.'

'What does he want?'

'He said he would rather tell you personally, ma'am.'

'But I don't see strangers without appointments,' said Anna testily. 'You know that.'

'I'm sorry to butt in on you like this, ma'am,' said a voice from behind the butler's shoulder. 'The fault is mine. The name is Rosenblatt. Isaac A. Rosenblatt. A is for Aaron.'

'What do you want?' Anna asked him sharply.

'Only five minutes of your time, ma'am. And the chance to pay you some money.'

'I'd rather take you up on the second than the first,' said Anna, amused at his approach. 'I can give you five minutes. Come out on the patio. Would you like a drink?'

'That would be great. Can't get that anywhere in the States now. Legally, that is.'

'What'll you have?'

'Whisky sour.'

She nodded to the butler who disappeared, returned with a whisky sour on a tray.

Rosenblatt sat down. He was a heavy, short man, sweating in an alpaca suit and tight brown and white shoes. He had a cheerful face.

'I run Red-Rose Productions. Before that I was in the rag trade. I came west to Hollywood just after the first boys had got there and started making pictures.'

'I've seen your name, I'm sure,' said Anna. 'But down here we don't go to the cinema much.'

'You will. Soon everyone will, and several times every week. Believe me.'

'You didn't come here from California just to tell me that.'

'No, ma'am. I've a proposition to put to you. Finance is not too easy to come by, but we have the chance of money from the government for a production showing the Revenue boys in the cutters as heroes, fighting wicked pirates trying to smuggle in booze against the law of the land.'

'Which you like to drink here because you can't drink it in the States.'

'Check. But for us the important thing is we get government money to plug their theme, which you can imagine is not wildly popular back home. Usually, we make pictures in the studios. Any exteriors we shoot out of doors on the back lot. One tree or one rock looks much like another, and staying where we are cuts costs. You know why film-makers chose Hollywood in the first place? Because the sun's so bright, which means the light's nearly always good. If you're making pictures in New York, there's fog and soot, rain, clouds. California is sunshine land.

'It's much like that down here, too. So, as the government is paying, I'd like to hire a couple of your launches and film them leaving harbour, out at sea, with your crews on them. Adds a touch of truth – production value, we call it. Real boats, not just models in a studio pond. And it don't cost us a cent.'

'The crews could be identified.'

'Nah. They can put on beards, moustaches, what they like. For money, I reckon people will do anything. Well, almost.'

'Maybe it has to be a lot of money. These people don't come cheaply. They're not your usual sort of extras. They're all skilled seamen.'

'I'll look after that, Miss Ballater, if I have your permission to approach them.'

'Certainly, you have my permission to approach them. And as long as whatever you do doesn't interfere with our main business, you can hire whichever launches we're not using at the moment. Is that condition clearly understood?'

'Yes, ma'am.'

'Good. My colleague Mr Shah will deal with the financial side. Now, you're the first film producer I've met. Tell me how you go about things.'

'First, I always try to film a simple story everyone can understand. No complications that confuse audiences. You can hire actors and actresses easily enough, though top players think it's stepping down a rung to appear on the screen in a cinema rather than on the stage of a theatre, despite the fact that a hundred thousand times more people will see them. When they finally understand that, their prejudice will vanish overnight.

'Our hardest task is not getting a cast, but the money to finance productions. They take a lot, and we can never get enough, even though I haven't produced a picture yet that's lost money. It's against my religious convictions to lose money, and where that's concerned I've the strongest religious convictions.'

'So have I,' agreed Anna. 'I must come and see you at work.'

'My pleasure. Any time.' Rosenblatt stood up. 'Thanks for the whisky.'

Later that week, Anna walked down to the quayside, really to see what Davey Moore was doing but telling herself she wanted to watch the film being made. Davey was working on an engine that had been winched out of a launch and now stood on the edge of the harbour propped up by huge planks. She noted with approval that he was whistling.

'Happy?' she asked him.

'Very. I like anything to do with engines. I've been working on one of your boats for these film people. They tell me they have your permission.'

'As long as it doesn't interfere with your main duties.'

'This won't. The launch in question can just about keep afloat and make it to the harbour mouth. But Mr Shah says they're paying good money, hiring it by the day, and the boat's practically useless for any other purpose.'

'I leave all that to you, Davey.'

As she was speaking, Rosenblatt came up. He wore a green eye-shade, chewed an unlit cigar.

'Hi! Nice to see you again, Miss Ballater. I was coming to visit you, and you've saved me a journey. I'd like this young engineer to take a boat out for us. Has he your permission?'

'Of course.'

'Good. One of the crew hasn't shown up. It's not a long voyage. Just a matter of going into the bay and back again. We follow in another launch with the camera.'

Davey wiped his hands on a rag and followed Rosenblatt down the quay. He climbed into the cockpit of a motor launch, started the engine and took off towards the open sea. Behind him and to one side bobbed another boat with a camera crew aboard. One man, his cap turned back to front so that the peak shaded his neck from the rays of the sun, cranked the camera handle steadily as his boat came alongside Davey's launch, fell behind, then moved in front. This sequence was repeated three times. Anna grew tired of watching, and went home; making a film seemed to be a tedious, long-drawn-out business.

A week later, Rosenblatt again appeared in Anna's house, this time with a colleague, a tall thin American who chewed gum constantly.

'You've a problem?' Anna asked him.

'No. It may be a problem for you, Miss Ballater, but it's certainly not for us. I've brought a projectionist with me and a projector in the car. I'd like to show you what we call rushes of the scenes we shot down at the harbour when you were there. They've just come back from the laboratory this morning.'

'Whenever you're ready.'

Rosenblatt's assistant set up a folding screen in the lounge and carried in the projector. Anna's butler drew curtains over the windows.

'Take a seat,' said Rosenblatt. 'You're going to see something that will interest you.'

The screen glowed silver. A few hairs on the lens of the projector were magnified enormously, and then came a flickering film: 'Nassau Harbour. Bootleggers. Take 1.' Her old launch bobbed on the shining sea. She saw Davey take the wheel, wave to someone on shore, and then the launch sped out towards the horizon.

She saw the boat filmed from various angles and also Davey in close-up, eyes narrowed against reflections from the sunlit sea, bending down to make some adjustment to the controls. The strip of film ended within minutes.

'What do you think of that?' Rosenblatt asked her.

'Interesting, as far as it goes. But there's not much of it.'

'There's enough of it, Miss Ballater, to tell you something which, as a producer, I find remarkable. That young fellow at the controls, Davey Moore. He's a natural.'

'For what?'

'Films, that's what. I don't say he's a great actor. He doesn't have to be, for he's got bone structure in his face that photographs well. In our business we have a saying about the handful of people who become stars and make a million dollars a year – the camera loves them. And it adores him. You can see that. No argument whatever. When they showed that clip at the studios I'm told that everyone wanted to know who he was, who was his agent, was he signed up. I tell everyone he's working for me.'

'He's really working for me,' Anna corrected.

'Of course. But like with a piece of land, you own the head lease. I would like to take another lease on him. I'd like him to come back to Hollywood, give him a bit more to do in this picture, just so he gets his hand in, feels what it's like to act in front of a camera, not to look in the lens or at the lights, and so on.'

'And then?'

'Then we'll see how that goes. And I'll bet he's going to go right to the top. What do you say?'

'You'd better ask him,' said Anna.

'I brought him along, so you can do just that. He's in the car outside. He won't do anything without your agreement.'

Davey came in, obviously excited, but looking almost sheepish.

'I've just seen you on the screen,' said Anna. 'I'm told you could have a career acting in films. What do you think?'

'Well, you gave me a job, Miss Ballater, so my first allegiance is to you. As you said about Captain O'Grady, not too many people help you when you're down. You did.'

'There are no ties to your job,' Anna replied, pleased by what he said. 'We've no contract. It's not for a year, a month, just week by week.'

'Would I be letting you down if I had a go at this?'

'You might be letting yourself down if you don't,' Anna told him. 'When do they want you to start?'

'Not for two weeks. They say they'll do all the shots they can down here, with me in more of them. And then go back to Hollywood.'

'So you'll be here for two weeks more?'

'Certainly. I'm back working on the engines as it is.'

'If what Mr Rosenblatt says is true, you'll not need to do that much longer. In the meantime, come and have dinner with me here tonight. We'll talk about it.'

They ate dinner on the patio. Glass globes shielded the candles from the warm evening wind. Afterwards, they sat on settees, glasses of brandy by their side, lulled by the soft sound of breaking waves. Anna looked quizzically at Davey for a moment before she raised a question she had wanted to ask him since they first met.

'We discussed the rather extraordinary suggestion that your mother could have been a witch. Did anyone ever say that to you directly?'

'No. But often indirectly, for instance when she would take me with her calling at back doors of local houses to sell white heather. Some canny Scots housewives would buy, and some wouldn't. They'd say, "Be off with you. Dinna come to my door, a witch like you".'

'What did you think?'

'I couldn't believe it.'

'But your mother did have a gift for telling the future, which some superstitious folk might think was witchcraft.'

'Yes. She did. But then she believed anyone could cultivate that ability. I knew there were certain ingredients, or maybe just one ingredient, that she needed to exercise this gift. She would go out into Soldier's Wood very early in the morning to find whatever it was. Once or twice I followed her. She didn't like that. She wanted to go off on her own, where no one could see her.'

'What did she do?'

'She picked mushrooms.'

'What sort of mushrooms?'

'I don't know. I took care to keep out of her sight. She got angry when she saw me. Said I was following her, spying on her. What she did was her affair.'

'Did you eat the mushrooms?'

'No. That was the odd thing. I'd see her bring back perhaps half a dozen in her apron, but I have no idea what she did with them. We never had mushrooms to eat for breakfast on those days, though we did on other mornings.'

'Do you think they had some part in her ability to tell the future?'

He shrugged. 'I don't know, but I think it is possible, yes. She would often tell me that people are born with different gifts. One may have good looks, another be very witty, another clever with figures, or an athlete, and so on. She had a gift which didn't do her much good, of course, poor soul.'

'You mean she couldn't tell her own future?'

'Perhaps she could. But being able to tell your future doesn't mean you can escape it. That's what people don't realise. They don't want to be told bad things.'

'Did your mother ever tell them bad things?'

He shook his head. 'Never. If she saw troubles ahead for them, as sometimes she told me she had, she would never tell the person concerned. It would only make them worry. And maybe her vision was wrong. You see, it was never a full vision. She could see some things or parts of things. Then she had to try and work out in her own mind what they meant. When she told the laird that his baby son would drown, for instance, she told me she didn't know exactly where or how this would happen, only that it would, and when.'

'She gave me some dried stems,' said Anna. 'They could be mushroom stalks, sliced up.'

'You still have them?'

'Only one piece, which I keep as a sort of talisman.'

He smiled. 'The mushrooms she needed were always extremely hard to find. She could never collect more than a few. She probably gave you all she had. You had been kind to her. It was her way of saying thank you.'

They sat in silence for a moment, then Anna stood up and walked to the balustrade. She stood looking out at the silent sea. A liner was passing on the horizon; rows of lights so far away that sometimes a distant rolling wave would obscure them; then they rose again, like a constellation travelling across the dark water.

She was thinking of all that had happened since that evening when she heard a cry for help from within a wood that from childhood she had been told was haunted. She remembered images she had seen, never fully interpreted, and then events she could never have imagined in the safe homeliness of a Scots village.

She recalled diamonds spilling from Jan's waistcoat pocket; her dismissal when the troopship docked in Mamora; the heat and pain and indignity in the square; the seizing of the ship in mid-Atlantic, and all her experiences since then in the Bahamas. She thought of Jeannie Moore again and her sad, lonely end.

Then she heard a movement by her side. Davey had crossed the patio and was standing by her. Almost instinctively, as though it was the most natural thing in the world, he put an arm round her shoulder.

'I'm glad we've met,' he said softly. 'I know you're my employer, but from the moment we first met I thought of you as a friend.'

'Did you? Do you?' Anna turned, saw his face, so young, so unexpectedly handsome in the pale moonlight. For the first time she understood the effect his looks could have, magnified a hundred times on a giant screen in a darkened cinema. Not only would the camera love him, so would every woman in every audience. And, looking at him, Anna realised with a stab of astonishment, like a dagger to her heart, that she loved him herself.

This was absurd, of course. She was much older, and she didn't really know him. Yet of all the men she had met in Nassau, men she had danced with, dined with, whose passes she had resisted, none possessed a fraction of Davey's attraction. There was something different about him, gentleness combined with firmness the others all lacked.

She looked at him now as though seeing him for the first time. And he looked at her and smiled and kissed her. Not on the forehead, not on the cheek, but where no one had ever kissed Anna, on her lips.

As his arms went round her, she gripped him and they stood, locked in an embrace like two lost people who had suddenly and quite unexpectedly discovered each other. He was the first to draw apart.

'I'm sorry,' he said awkwardly. 'I shouldn't have done that.'

'But you should. And I'm so glad you did. I've been waiting for someone to do that for years. Not anyone. But – you.'

They kissed again. Then, hand in hand, they crossed the patio back to the house.

Fifteen

So began two weeks that Anna would always remember as a magical time. She felt as a traveller might feel who had crossed some arid lonely desert on their own and then suddenly reached an unexpected oasis, not marked on any map. Her own plans immediately fell into a position of secondary importance. What mattered, indeed all that mattered to her from now on, would be her relationship with Davey Moore.

At first, she felt embarrassed by the difference in their ages.

'You must be seven, eight, maybe ten years younger than me,' she said almost accusingly, as though this was his fault, something he had deliberately arranged.

Davey smiled at her concern, genuinely amused by it. 'If our ages were reversed, ten years would be an ideal gap between a man and a woman,' he pointed out.

'But they're not reversed,' she retorted. 'That's the problem.'

'It isn't a problem to me,' he assured her. 'It's still ideal – at least, to my way of thinking.' He took from his pocket a piece of paper torn from a newspaper article. 'I saw this quotation the other day,' he went on. 'It's by an American essayist – Emerson. Listen to his view. "A man only counts his years when he has nothing else to count." That goes for a woman, too.'

'So you also thought about the difference?'

'Of course. I *like* the difference. Now. You talk too much.' And he kissed her into silence.

The day came when Davey had to leave for New York and then take a train across the United States to Los Angeles and Hollywood. He had received a contract from Rosenblatt. To Davey it seemed almost deliberately and unnecessarily complex with its convoluted legal verbosity. Anna read it through with him. Although it was tough in that at first Davey would be paid very little, it seemed fair. On her advice, he signed.

When Davey set off for Hollywood, he did so with mixed feelings, sorrow at leaving Anna, yet delight at the prospect of a new challenge. Anna drove him down to the harbour. She wore dark glasses to help conceal the fact that she had been crying.

'You *will* come back?' she asked him, anxious for reassurance.

'Of course. I'll come back to you, and for you. Or maybe you should come out to Hollywood.'

'Of course, I could do that. Never thought of it before.'

'It could be a good idea to invest in what Rosenblatt is confident will be a growth industry. Prohibition must end one day. It would be wise to have something else planned well before it does. A lot of other people will be looking round then for opportunities, and Hollywood seems a safe bet to me.'

He kissed her lightly on the lips, and walked up the gangway. Anna stood on the quay, waving until the ship dwindled to a dot on the horizon. Then, head bowed, she walked back to her car. For a moment, she sat hunched behind the wheel, not seeing anyone or anything. All her thoughts were out on the shining sea with the only man she had ever felt she could love, who had exorcised all memory of the horror in Mamora, and so she did not notice another car pull away ahead of her. In the back of this car, Torrio turned to Castle.

'I assume the guy she's been seeing off is the guy who was screwing your wife,' he said conversationally. 'Seems like he's a charmer.'

'Maybe. Anyhow, I warned him off. He's taking my advice to get the hell off this island.'

'But not before he's added insult to what I would consider very considerable injury – screwing that woman, who is the prime mover of your greatest rival, Traders. And now he's off to Hollywood to become a star, so Rosenblatt is telling everyone. And what are you doing about that? Anything?'

'What do you want me to do about it?' asked Castle, trying to keep anger and irritation out of his voice. It was never safe to allow Torrio to imagine you were not in entire agreement with whatever he said, on any subject.

'Don't ask me. You're in charge down here. Or should be. I asked you some time ago – *told* you – to break up Traders. If you can't deal with the girl or O'Grady, go for the weakest man, Shah.'

'I've explained, I've already moved in on him and sold him the idea that we'd finance a revolution in Mamora and put him on top as the sultan. Once he's off this island, I'll make sure he never comes back.'

'You told me that long ago, and still nothing has happened. When I say I want action, Castle, I want action *fast*. Not weeks and months, even years ahead. Get him out of it. Break them up. I will not mention this again. You understand me? And that kid Moore. You missed a chance there that won't come again. If a bum like Rosenblatt can sign him up for peanuts and hope to make a fortune out of him, why didn't you sign him first, soon as you heard Rosenblatt thought he had potential? Then you could have rented him out to other producers, like he's bound to. You could have done that, easy as hell. And gotten us a foot in Hollywood. But you didn't. You let it slide – one more lost chance.' Torrio shook his head in disapproval. He enjoyed needling Castle, constantly bullying him. Torrio would push him until he broke – or until he lost interest in baiting him. It amused him that Castle simply didn't understand that he was expendable.

Late that evening, Shah was in the lounge of his house tuning a huge radio set that had just been delivered from New York. It required an aerial that stretched between two poles high above the house. He was delighted at the number of stations the set could pick up, and so clearly.

He was hoping he might hear a news broadcast from Mamora or, if their transmitter was too weak to reach across the world, from other transmitters in Zanzibar, Dar-es-Salaam, or even Aden.

Shah had not heard anything further from Castle about his offer to finance his return to Mamora, so he was in no hurry to leave until the groundwork for a coup had been prepared. Simply to travel to Mamora now would mean instant arrest and an early and painful death, for the sultan would be under no illusions as to the reason for Shah's arrival.

But how to find authentic, reliable information about what was happening in Mamora? Shah still had relations and friends living there, but he had to write to them by a circuitous route, and be most careful what he said. Those who replied were understandably reluctant to commit themselves in case their letters were opened by local censors. He hoped that this radio would provide news he desperately needed.

All the servants were off duty; a local celebration was being held in Nassau, and they had left work early to attend it. Shah had dined on his own, for it was easier to scan the airwaves after dark, when there was less atmospheric interference.

A bell chimed. At first, Shah thought that the sound was from one of the stations on his set. Then he realised that it was his own front door bell. He switched off the radio, irritated at the interruption, walked to the front door, turned on the outside lights. A man was standing in the storm porch, looking about him in an admiring way.

'What do you want?' Shah asked him brusquely.

The man bowed. He wore a lightweight suit and a hat with a snap brim. His eyes and most of his face were in shadow. Yet he seemed vaguely familiar.

'Is this the residence of Mr Razadin Shah?' he asked Shah politely.

'It is. Who wants him?'

'I would like to speak to him on an important matter.'

'You're speaking to him now. What is this important matter?'

'It concerns the island of Mamora, sir,' the visitor explained, suddenly obsequious.

'What about it?' asked Shah suspiciously. He was right. He had come across this man before. He recognised the voice, although the man was obviously trying to disguise it, just as he deliberately kept his face in shadow. But who the hell was he? Shah wished he had not answered the bell.

'I understand, sir, that you are thinking of returning,' said the man.

'What is that to you?'

The scent of bougainvillaea and frangipani and night-blooming flowers was almost overpowering. They reminded Shah of sweet-smelling cemetery flowers, what local papers invariably described as floral tributes. In the distance, he could hear the beat of goombay drums, like the pounding of a giant heart, as the party began in the town. Shah dredged his mind for clues as to this man's identity. Suddenly, he remembered. Pierre Montagne. The French pirate he had shot on the deck of the slaver long, long ago, who had tried to maroon his two partners. Somehow, he must have recovered and escaped, and now he was here.

'I have come to give you this, sir,' Pierre Montagne explained politely. He put a hand into an inner pocket of his jacket. Shah saw the glint of light on the barrel of a pistol.

'Wait!' he shouted, and ducked – too late.

Montagne fired twice. Shah fell forward down the steps. Montagne bent down, checked his pulse, then turned and walked away along the drive. He did not hurry. He savoured the sense of an injustice revenged, a debt repaid; he did not notice a deeper shadow behind a king palm. Then he saw the shadow move.

Pierre Montagne died as he reached for his revolver, two bullets in his heart. The other man bent over his body, removed his pistol, then melted away silently into the darkness.

Anna read of Shah's murder in the following afternoon's edition of the local newspaper. For a moment she could not assimilate the news; and when she finally did so, she felt a growing sense of loss: the first member of their partnership had gone. Who would be next?

Captain Razadin Shah, described as a shareholder in the 'successful company, Traders Incorporated', had been found shot in the doorway of what the reporter called 'his palatial ocean-side mansion'. And only feet away, a Frenchman, Pierre Montagne, had also been shot. It was suggested that possibly he had attempted to stop Captain Shah being killed and so had died himself.

The reporter claimed the local police believed that some disaffected persons from the Indian Ocean island of Mamora, from which Shah had fled on the accession of a new sultan, had followed him here. His death was a political murder, a revenge killing of a type quite new to Nassau. The police were treating the matter very seriously. Apparently, Captain Shah had been about to return to Mamora. This possibility had clearly alarmed some people in power on that island.

Anna put down the newspaper. She found this theory impossible to accept. How could a reporter on an insignificant newspaper in an unimportant British colony off the Atlantic coast of the United States know so much about the domestic politics of a tiny island in the Indian Ocean? Shah had never hinted to her that anyone from Mamora had followed him to Nassau. The idea seemed ridiculous, as was the suggestion that Montagne had died trying to save Shah. Somehow he had escaped from the island where she and O'Grady had left him. It seemed to her most likely that he had shot Shah on someone else's orders and had then been shot himself in case he talked.

Anna ordered up her car, and drove to see O'Grady. He had not read the paper. She handed him her copy.

'So now it's the two of us against the rest,' he said grimly. 'And we seem to have some tough opposition.'

'Have the police been in touch with you?' she asked him.

'No. Let's go to see them now.'

The chief of police was a retired army captain. In the Great War he had lost an eye, and now wore a black patch over the empty socket which gave him a curiously piratical appearance.

'Do you believe this?' Anna asked him, showing him the newspaper.

'I had detectives down there as soon as I heard the news of the double killing, Miss Ballater. Mr Shah's butler returned from a party and found the captain dead and this Frenchman also shot in the driveway. He called us at once. I can assure you, we'll do all we can to bring to justice whoever murdered Captain Shah and Pierre Montagne.'

'Have you any clues? Is there any way in which we can help?'

'I fear the answer as yet is no to both questions, Miss Ballater. But if you hear anything, please advise me personally. And if I make any progress, I'll be in touch with you.'

There was no progress, but then neither O'Grady nor Anna expected there would be.

O'Grady went to see the reporter to discover where he had got his information. The man was reluctant at first to talk. A hundred-dollar bill changed hands and instantly lubricated his reluctance.

He took out a piece of paper from his pocket. On this had been typed some basic facts about the island revolution and Shah's intention to return to Mamora.

'Who gave you this?' O'Grady asked him.

'I found it in my cubbyhole in the outer office. We get odd bits of information like that from time to time from people who don't want to give their names.'

'Do you always print anonymous information without making any attempt to check it first?'

The man shrugged and did not reply.

'I don't believe a word of his story about revolutionary

assassins and so on,' Anna told O'Grady when he reported this to her. 'Someone did it here for other reasons. Montagne was the killer and then someone killed him.'

'All this points in one direction. To the outfit. Castle,' O'Grady replied.

'We could deal with Castle on his own,' said Anna slowly. 'But there are people behind him who we don't even know. He's only an underling, out here on a limb. We can't deal with the men who sent him here, or whoever else is behind them. You know that as well as I do.'

'It's unlike you to be defeatist,' said O'Grady.

'I'm not being defeatist, but realistic. Whatever gangsters control Castle want us out. Then they'll have the field to themselves. They know Prohibition can't last for ever, and so they want to milk it for all they can, while they can. Why don't we give them that opportunity?'

'You mean quit?'

'I mean sell everything for the best price we can. And then go and start up another business.'

'Any ideas?'

'Yes. Take the weight off your feet and I'll tell you.'

Mr Rosenblatt, the president of Red-Rose Productions, sat in a leather chair opposite Mr Vandervell, vice-president of the Bank of World Indemnity, in his New York office.

Rosenblatt was accustomed to occupying a position of physical superiority, with his chair on a dais six inches above anyone he was interviewing, to give him physical as well as psychological domination. But now the banker sat in the higher chair, and Rosenblatt crossed and uncrossed his legs uncomfortably on a lower seat.

'I expect you know why I have asked you here,' said Vandervell. He was a tall, thin, bloodless man, who wore octagonal rimless spectacles, a butterfly collar, and a pearl pin in his tie.

'I assume to discuss financial matters,' Rosenblatt replied.

'You assume correctly. I am sure I do not need to go into all the details of the monies involved, for you will be aware that your company's indebtedness to the bank is considerable.'

'I am indeed aware of that,' Rosenblatt agreed. 'But equally I am sure you are also aware that the loan is adequately secured.'

'At the moment, yes, on several hundred acres of land on which you built your studios, and the buildings. Plus, of course, what you call intellectual copyright in the films you produce. But I detect a worrying shortfall in monies coming in against all outgoings.'

'It is not worrying me,' Rosenblatt replied shortly, irritated at the banker's apparent inability to understand the nature of his business. 'I have six pictures being made as we sit here. There's a lot of money tied up in them, agreed. The one we've just finished, shot largely in the Bahamas, and with government money, not bank backing, has been an instant success. The moment I saw the first rushes of the picture, I knew that the young man Davey Moore had that most elusive gift that somehow attracts women as a honey pot attracts wasps. He's going to be big as Rudolph Valentino. By the way, I hear Valentino is not in the best of health. I trust your bank is not backing any of his pictures?'

The banker shook his head. 'No such luck.'

'Soon you may say you've been lucky not to be involved. He's suffering from very bad stomach pains, apparently. Some say a woman poisoned him. The studio has put out that he has appendicitis. Either way, he's sick, but he has such a hell of a filming schedule ahead of him, he can't rest up as he should.'

'If Valentino died tomorrow, would that affect Davey Moore?'

'If Valentino died tomorrow, our man would go into pole position at once.'

'Well, despite your optimism, Mr Rosenblatt, your Davey Moore is not bringing in the sort of money you need to service your loan.'

'Give him a chance, Vandervell. He's only appeared in this one picture. We've got him in another already, and there's a third after that. I'm renting him out to Celestial Films.'

'On what basis?'

'I pay him two hundred dollars a week and hire him out to Celestial for two thousand a week. For five weeks. Then it goes up to six thousand a week – a very considerable profit on my original investment. He's a marketable commodity, this Mr Moore.'

'Even so, the figures your accountants have supplied show no sign that you can repay the considerable amount of capital that under our agreement falls due in the very near future. In that case, I have to remind you that the bank could take over all your assets.' Vandervell paused. 'On the other hand . . .' he hesitated.

'Well?'

'I have heard from other parties that they could be interested in buying your studios – outright.'

'Really? What parties?'

'Businessmen in Chicago.'

'Gangsters?'

Vandervell frowned at the crudity of the question. 'I

cannot comment on that, Mr Rosenblatt,' he replied coldly. 'These gentlemen have built up considerable holdings in trucking corporations, warehouse properties, and bottling plants – only for soft drinks, of course. Their money is the same as anyone else's.'

'Not if they are part of the outfit. Then their money comes from extortion, rackets and murder.'

'That's as may be. The fact is, I feel you would be well advised to meet them, and allow them to take, if not complete control of your studio at first, at least a majority holding.'

'That would amount to the same thing,' Rosenblatt retorted.

'If you cannot meet your financial commitments to the bank, you might be forced into a shotgun marriage with them or even lose your company altogether.'

'When my pictures are finished and on release, you'll see a healthy upturn in my finances,' Rosenblatt replied confidently.

'Provided, of course, that they finish on time and within their budgets.'

'Why shouldn't they? They always have done up to now.'

'Up to now, agreed. But times change, Mr Rosenblatt. You might suddenly have labour troubles – strikes – or law suits over contracts. Or fire could damage your studios and throw your schedules to the wind.'

Rosenblatt understood the drift of the conversation. This cadaverous bastard was clearly warning him that the outfit could easily put him out of business.

'And if I found another backer?' he asked.

'Before they could take over, you might still have labour disputes. Or this new star of yours, Davey Moore, could be injured in a motor accident, say. His face must represent a good part of his fortune, and yours. If he went through the windscreen of his car, he could be permanently scarred. In any of a dozen unfortunate situations, the value of your enterprise could diminish sharply.'

'You speak as though there is a likelihood that such troubles are going to happen, although I've never experienced any of them in years in the business.'

'Not so. You misunderstand me, Mr Rosenblatt. I am simply giving you the worst possible scenario, which in all the circumstances is wise. Indeed, as your banker, it is my duty to point out the problems you may encounter.'

'So you're on the side of these guys in Chicago?'

Vandervell pursed his lips and shook his head gravely as though personally hurt by such a suggestion. 'I'm on your side, Mr Rosenblatt,' he replied. 'I'm also on the side of the bank's stockholders, and of our staff. As a bank, we cannot afford to lose.'

'You're not losing.'

'Not yet, Mr Rosenblatt. But we could, so very easily. And so could you. Please do think things over carefully. And let me know your decision by this time next week.'

Orpheus in the Underworld died to a whisper as Castle came into the apartment. Torrio frowned at the interruption and turned off the gramophone.

'I thought I'd report to you personally,' Castle told him. 'First, Shah isn't with us any more. Nor is a man who's given me grief in the past and could talk too much. Name of Pierre Montagne.'

'I heard about that from other sources. I take it there'll be no investigation down there into either death?'

'No. I put out a cover story to a reporter who owes me

a favour. And the police are friendly to us. I subscribe to their charities.'

'Don't we all?' said Torrio drily, opening a cigar box. 'Smoke?'

'Thank you.' Castle felt relieved; they were on good terms again – for the moment.

'So that's the first thing. What's the second?' Torrio snipped the end from a cigar and lit it.

'Traders. There are only two partners left now, the woman and O'Grady. He came to see me and said they had decided to sell up. He said that Shah's death had disturbed them both very badly.'

'He wanted out? He was yellow?' asked Torrio, frowning. This reaction somehow seemed out of character; he suspected a trap.

'You could say that, or maybe he's showing sense. Anyway, either way, I've bought them out.'

'How much?'

'Two million dollars. Half paid now, half over two years.'

'He accepted that?'

'It was either that or nothing. No one else would pay that money.'

'What do we get for it?'

'Some very fast boats and liens on others. Most important, there's no one else in competition with us now in Nassau. We control all the boats, all the booze.'

'Good. But I must remind you, you brought these people in yourself. Without your initial offer to them to run one boatload of whisky, they'd never have been involved in the first place. Now we have to pay two million bucks to get them off our backs.'

'It was different when we were starting. We needed a

boat in a hurry, and theirs was the only one available.'

'Excuses, always excuses,' said Torrio. 'What are the two remaining partners going to do?'

'They're going to New York, I think, to spend their money.'

'You *think*,' Torrio scoffed. 'From what I *know* from a number of sources, they're too smart just to do that. They know that money is for making as well as spending. Whatever they plan, we might do business with them again, but strictly on our terms. You follow me?'

'Yes,' said Castle.

Anna and O'Grady booked into the Gladstone Hotel in New York on the evening of their arrival. Next morning, they had breakfast together.

O'Grady had been up early, walking through the strange streets trying to get the feel of the city. Anna was experiencing a strong sense of reaction after Nassau. Despite her denial to O'Grady, she felt they had retreated, and she was not a person to retreat. But she admitted that sometimes one had to take a single step back in order to take two forward. She kept telling herself this was one of those times, but she was still not entirely convinced. O'Grady watched her closely across the table.

'Sleep badly?' he asked her.

'Not when I did sleep, no. But I read until about three o'clock.'

'What were you reading?'

'Books I had ordered. They were waiting here for me.'

'About what?'

'The film business.'

'So you're still keen we go into that? When we discussed this in Nassau, I pointed out we know nothing about it.'

'We knew nothing about running booze when we started, but it didn't take long to learn.'

'This'll take a hell of a lot longer.'

'Not necessarily. We can buy talent easily enough. Directors, writers, stars. Rosenblatt will help us.'

'What about those books?'

'I wanted to read about the influence of films now and their potential in the future.'

'And?'

'The figures are remarkable. Eighty-five million Americans go to the pictures every week.'

'How does anyone know that?' asked O'Grady suspiciously.

'From box-office receipts. Ticket tabs. And when you realise that quite a percentage of cinemas will be faking their receipts for tax reasons, the number could be as high as ninety million. And every week, remember.'

'It's a hell of a lot of people.'

'There are already seventeen thousand cinemas in the States, in nine thousand towns. In fact, it's very difficult to find a town without at least one. Three thousand very small towns, which only have a few hundred people in each, no more than villages really, still have cinemas. The average for the whole country works out at one seat in a cinema for every twelve people. Going to the cinema appears to be addictive. Women make up the largest part of the audiences. They can go in the afternoons when the men are working, and according to psychologists they go to escape from dull housebound lives. They want something to take them out of themselves before they have to go back to reality – an unsuccessful husband, a dreary home, crying children.'

'I've always heard that there are two bedrock businesses

to be in,' said O'Grady. 'One is food, for people have to eat. The other is undertakers, for people have to die. But on what you say, this seems to beat them both.'

'It does. If you're making food, you have to keep your factory turning out packets of cornflakes or tins of peas or whatever else. But when a film is made, it just goes round and round on circuit. Sometimes it brings in money for years.'

'So what you need,' said O'Grady, 'is something that pulls them in *every* week.'

'You can't make new films every week.'

'No? I've an idea about that. While you've been reading up on this, I've been out on the hoof, walking the streets. And I've found a man with a little cinema tucked away in a back street who shows nothing but serials. Like a serial in a newspaper, the punters get one short episode every week. The hero or the heroine is always left in some terrible situation – strapped across railway tracks with a train racing towards them, imprisoned down a well with weights round their feet and water rising. The question is, how will they escape? So the punters go next week to find out – and then there's another equally impossible situation. So they go the week after that and so on, week after week. This man doesn't just show one serial a week, as most places do, he'll show four, one after the other, every day.'

'I want a word with him,' said Anna firmly.

'We'll go and see him now.'

They walked from the residential area into a section of seedy shops. One sold secondhand clothes – odd jackets and trousers hung from metal hangers around the door. Another dealt in Italian cheeses; a third, cheap magazines. Then they saw a small arcade of garishly painted machines. Behind small, brightly lit windows, folded dollar bills lay enticingly on beds of yellow and red sweets. Above them hovered the jaws of tiny cranes, operated by turning a wheel at the side of the machine. But the grabs never came closer than half an inch to the dollar bills.

In the back of this modest arcade stood a short, thickset man, chewing gum. O'Grady introduced Anna.

'This is Sam Axner,' he explained. 'I've told him you are interested in pictures.'

'Glad to hear it,' said Axner, moving the gum from one side of his mouth to the other. 'What can I do for you?'

'You show serials?'

'All the time,' he said. 'We have this crap outside here to get the punters in. Once in a thousand years maybe someone will get a dollar with the grabs, but I've never seen it. I set the machines up, so I know. But people are optimists.'

'Why do they keep coming to see serials? Surely they see the same stars in much the same situations every week? Don't they want anything new?'

Axner shook his head. 'No way. They get to know the characters, maybe identify with them. The man in the white mask, whose face you never see; the beautiful girl who can tote a gun with the best. Serial fans like to get out of their own dim, dull, boring world, but not too far out. They don't want to feel they're entire strangers. They don't want to adjust to seeing new people on the screen every week. They find safety in familiarity. Rather like people who go to a foreign country, it's not entirely foreign to them if they speak a few words of the language – French, Italian, German, whatever.'

'You're the only house showing serials?'

'No. But maybe I'm the only one showing so many.'

'You plan to open another?'

'I would if I had enough money. But what I'd do then is first go to Hollywood and make them myself. I think I know what the punters want to see.'

'How much would you take for your enterprise here?'

'It's not for sale, but five thousand dollars, cash, could make me change my mind.'

'If you go to Hollywood, who would run this?'

'My kid brother. He's sharp. Full of good ideas.'

'I'll give you four thousand.'

'Five is the price.'

'Four is the offer. Take it or leave it.'

'You serious?'

'She's always serious about money,' said O'Grady solemnly.

'OK. Four it is. For a quick deal.'

They shook hands.

'I'll need an attorney to handle the sale,' Anna told O'Grady.

'Try along the road,' said Axner. 'Jackson and Hogan. Two young guys. They've got merits.'

'What are they?'

'They're cheap, and they're quick.'

Anna walked along the road past other shops until she saw gold lettering on a black painted window: 'Jackson and Hogan, Attorneys'. She went inside. Two young men were sitting at identical rolltop desks reading magazines. Trade obviously was not too brisk.

'I want to hire you,' she told them. 'My name is Anna Ballater. Sam Axner has just sold me his amusement arcade for four thousand dollars. How long will it take you to check everything so I can take possession?'

'A week if we move, lady.'

'What if you move faster? For double fees.'

'Like how much faster?'

'Like tomorrow,' she said.

'You're in a hurry,' said Jackson, impressed.

'I always am,' agreed Anna.

'What are you going to do with that little show?' O'Grady asked her when the deal had been concluded. 'Have you any idea at all?'

'Of course. I'll let his brother run it.'

'He may be no good. You haven't even met him.'

'I don't think it matters too much who runs it, if you've the right product. That's the important thing. Thank you for introducing me.'

'I take it,' said O'Grady, 'we're now going west to make films?'

'As soon as possible. When I've seen what can be done, I'll keep this little cinema to try out new films. If the punters like them we can make more of the same. If not, we'll try other ideas.'

'You're getting into a very expensive business, Anna. We could lose everything.'

'We won't. Isaac Rosenblatt told us down in Nassau there was no trouble getting the stars or the stories. Raising the money is the difficulty. And we have the money.'

'I know,' said O'Grady irritably.

'Rosenblatt rang me last night.'

'What about?'

'Buying a majority share in Red-Rose Productions. He's here in New York, and invited me out to dinner. I accepted. I wanted to hear how Davey Moore is getting on. I told Rosenblatt we'd bought this enterprise from Sam Axner. He said he had heard about that, which was why he'd rung me. He came straight to the point. "Would you like to buy into a studio yourself?" he asked me. "Whose?" I asked him. "Mine," he said.

'He explained that the bank was leaning heavily on him to sell to some people in Chicago – he thought on the orders of Johnny Torrio, the gangster. Rosenblatt doesn't want to sell to him, but with the bank on his back he has no option – unless someone else makes a bid. If he doesn't sell, his life could become hard – labour troubles, fires, failure of equipment, all kinds of hassle. He gave me the figures, and explained the potential. It excited me.

'If you won't come in with me as a partner, Sean, then I'll go on my own. But I'd be sorry to do that. There were three of us in the beginning, now there's only us two.'

'All right,' said O'Grady, but without enthusiasm. 'I'll come in with you. Fifty-fifty, down the middle?'

'Not quite. I suggest forty-forty each, and we give Rosenblatt twenty. After all, at the start, he'll have to make the pictures we mean to show.'

As the needle dipped, the gramophone record began to turn. Both men heard a faint hiss and then the whole room was filled with sound. Torrio turned to Castle, nodding approvingly.

'A new machine,' he explained proudly. 'Picks up all the notes, high, low, middle. Cost a fortune, of course, but it's the best in the world. What do you think of it?'

'Very good indeed. Very clear,' said Castle hastily. 'Just like being in the middle of the orchestra.'

'Yes. Just like that.' Torrio glanced at his polished fingernails, blew on them, rubbed them against the lapel of his jacket. 'I didn't get you here just to talk about music,' he said. 'Business comes first. The outfit is going into the movie business. That's where the future lies.'

413

'I think you're right,' said Castle, eager to please.

'Of course I'm right. Every town now has a cinema, many have several. People want to get out of the rut, away from their own miseries. They flock to the cinemas every week, sometimes every night. Soon, they'll have sound pictures, talkies.

'On radio or the gramophone, you just hear the words and music. But with talking pictures, you won't simply hear actors like in a radio play, you'll see *and* hear them. And it will be far better than the theatre, much more realistic. You're actually out there in the desert, in the hills, at sea, anywhere. And, more important, cinema tickets cost much less than theatre tickets, and there are a hell of a lot more of them all over the country.'

'A great idea,' said Castle enthusiastically. 'Are we buying a studio to make the pictures?'

'Of course. Vandervell at the bank is looking after that side of things. He's leaning on this fellow Rosenblatt of Red-Rose, to persuade him to sell. He was down in Nassau, you remember.'

'Yes. He hired one of Traders' launches to make a film.'

'I've told Vandervell to move his butt because I hear that the crafty Rosenblatt is trying to do a deal with Traders. However, I don't want to step on Vandervell's toes. He controls the bank that controls Rosenblatt. We'll let him get on with it. Our priority now is not to buy a studio but to buy cinemas. Not one, not a dozen, but hundreds. Then we can show anyone's films – ours included, of course, when we make them. There's a Greek, Andropolous, I've heard of, who personally owns five hundred cinemas coast to coast, north to south. Get him to sell to us.'

'Does he want to sell?'

'Make him want to. It shouldn't be too difficult. He's got

two sons, bums. He built up his cinema chain just to hand it over to them, but they haven't the brains of a louse between them. They want to spend money. What we want is to make it. Get Andropolous to sell.'

'Where does he live?'

'In New York, mostly. But like all people in show business, when they strike it big they suddenly get the bug for the good life in Hollywood. He has a house there overlooking the ocean.' Torrio held up his hand to forestall Castle's reply. The orchestra had reached a delicate part of the music. He did not wish an underling to come in with some damn fool, crap-house question and spoil the moment. There were so few moments of real enjoyment in life, he thought, he did not wish even one to be sullied.

Sixteen

The first thing Anna did on arriving in Hollywood was to rent a large house for herself. She selected an imposing Spanish-style house because she knew that, in a society where success was all, producers and stars and studio heads would be curious about her as a newcomer. She felt she needed to impress them immediately, to prove in the simplest, quickest and most convincing way that she was not short of money.

The second item was to check production facilities at Red-Rose. The third was what she had wanted to do first of all, and most of all: visit Davey Moore.

She had sent him a telegram to say she was arriving, and was surprised that no answer was waiting for her at Red-Rose. Maybe he had not received her cable, or perhaps his reply had somehow been mislaid. The only way to find out was to ask him. She telephoned Rosenblatt and then drove over to Celestial, where he had hired out Davey Moore to make his first film as a star.

Rosenblatt was waiting for her at the ornate entrance gates and took her through to the studio where Davey was working.

A red light glowed outside the small door that led into the hangar-like building. This meant that a rehearsal was in progress, and no visitors were allowed. They waited. After some time, a messenger came out. Rosenblatt asked him how long it would be until they could enter. The man shrugged his shoulders; long delays and even longer waits were an accepted part of filming.

'They haven't started yet,' he explained. 'They're still getting the scene set up, Mr Rosenblatt.' He looked at Anna. 'Are you by any chance Miss Ballater?' he asked her.

'I am. Why?'

'I have a message here from Mr Moore for you, ma'am. I was going to leave it for you at the front gate.'

He handed a sealed envelope to Anna. She ripped it open – and suddenly realised she had never seen Davey Moore's handwriting before. It was as she would have imagined: round, bold, at an angle, words joined together, the writing of a young man in a hurry, impatient of any delay.

'Dear Anna,' she read. 'Mr Rosenblatt told me you'd be coming to see me today. I tried to telephone you to put you off, because I'm stuck in here until they get this scene right, and so most unfortunately I can't see any visitors at all, not even you. We've had trouble with the scenery, the lights, the actors, stuntmen, everyone and everything, except me. But maybe that's only because I haven't been on yet. I'll ring you as soon as I'm free. Love.'

'Is there any reply, ma'am?'

'No reply,' Anna said brusquely.

She folded up the letter, put it back in the envelope and in her handbag. She felt unreasonably disappointed. She did not know much about the process of film-making but she had assumed that Davey Moore could leave the studio if he wasn't actually working. Perhaps he didn't want to leave.

'Trouble?' Rosenblatt asked her sympathetically, seeing dejection on her face.

'No, nothing. He's just too busy and can't come out. I'll see him later.'

She drove back to Traders' studios.

'Any calls or callers?' she asked her secretary.

'Nothing at all. Your telephone hasn't rung, Miss Ballater. Were you expecting anything?'

'Yes. I was rather expecting a call from Davey Moore.'

As soon as Anna said this, she regretted the admission. She did not want to appear hurt or disappointed in front of another woman – and an employee.

'No, he hasn't rung, Miss Ballater. I hear he's doing very well. I've a boy friend at Celestial who's seen the rushes of his new picture. He says there's something about his face which just sends women wild.'

'A great asset for a male star, I'm sure,' Anna said, trying to sound impersonal, as though she and Davey had never been lovers and her interest in him was purely business.

She waited for a couple of days and telephoned Davey on his direct line inside Celestial. She did not give her name, but said she was a close friend.

'Sorry, ma'am,' a woman operator explained. 'No calls are being accepted for Mr Moore.'

'Why's that?'

'I cannot say, ma'am. But Mr Moore has left strict instructions that he will not speak on the telephone to anyone.'

Anna put down the receiver, scribbled a note to Davey, sent it round by hand.

'Sorry we couldn't meet the other day. I have tried to telephone you but without success. Please give me a ring this evening when you finish work. Don't worry about the time. I'll be waiting.'

She hated herself for admitting this; her mother would

say she was making herself cheap. But she would be waiting. She knew this, and so did he. There was no point in denying it. That night she waited until the dawn came up, but the telephone by her bed did not ring.

Anna felt lonely, tired, depressed. The pleasure of being part owner of a studio diminished without Davey to share in this good fortune. She kept telling herself that he would be in touch; if not immediately, then just as soon as he was able. No doubt he would telephone later that day. Or if not that evening, then tomorrow morning, tomorrow afternoon. But he did not telephone. She tried to ring him again, but always came the same reply: Mr Moore was not accepting any outside calls.

Anna was alone in her house when a special-delivery messenger brought her a letter. She looked at the heading first. Who could be writing to her from Celestial Film Productions? Only one person, surely. She turned over the page. Yes, she was right. At the bottom she made out a scrawled signature, Davey. But why on earth was he sending her a formal, typed letter instead of a handwritten note? She sat down, began to read.

'My dear Anna,

This is a difficult letter to write and I feel I am being a coward by not coming to see you. But after long consideration this seems the best and, in all the circumstances, perhaps the kindest way of putting into words thoughts that have been concerning me for some time.

When we were in Nassau, I felt that in you I had found someone for whom I'd been searching, if unconsciously, probably all my life. I had never met a woman like you. I will probably never meet another. Being with you, knowing you, was a wonderful experience that for me enriched every hour of every day and night.

Here in Hollywood, however, I have been forced to examine realities which have nothing to do with dreams and personal happiness. My contract at a low wage for Rosenblatt is about to be completed. You will have heard of the death of Rudolph Valentino. With his passing, I am now being projected by the studios as the "screen's greatest lover". This is not a title of my choice, but then this career was not of my choosing either, although I am grateful – and amazed – by the results. Films are simply a matter of selling something or someone. At the moment, I happen to be the person on sale.

There is a clause in my contract now that will not allow me to marry, either for a period of three years or until Celestial Pictures goes into liquidation, which does not seem very likely. There is also a strict morality subclause insisted on by Celestial. If any scandal whatever can be proved against me, such as having a serious affair, my contract can be instantly cancelled, with a heavy fine due to Celestial to be paid out of my previous earnings. The studio is very scared of anything which they feel could adversely damage the market value of their product – me.

I am therefore writing to say that until I have honoured my contract, I will not be able to ask you to be my wife, as I had hoped to do. Since having an affair or living together is out of the question, I think it is possibly fairest if we end our relationship now, painful as this is to both of us.

I will always remember you, Anna, not as a special person but as the special person. If things had been different, our futures would also have been different. But it is better to end cleanly and both be hurt for a time than to drag on with even more pain and sadness. Every wound heals in time, although the heart may be scarred. Believe me, I loved you. Davey.

Anna sat back and closed her eyes. She thought at first that she would faint; she felt dizzy and weak. But the mood passed, and she read the letter for a second time. Davey was right, of course. He had his life, and she had hers, and between them loomed an age gap in the wrong ratio. She could not altogether believe this story of the contract, but told herself that Davey meant it as a kindness to let her down gently. It was not impossible he had met another, younger woman: Hollywood seemed full of them, all hoping to make a screen career or find a rich husband.

She sat looking at the letter, not reading the print because her eyes were filled with tears. She had loved Davey. She believed he was telling the truth when he said he had loved her.

She remembered the first time she had chewed one of the stems Davey's mother had given her and the voice she had heard, 'You will be rich. You will be rich.' And then . . . And then . . . What then?

This, now, was then. The future had become the present. She had to live with the knowledge and keep on living with it.

Looking round the room with its white leather chairs, its white carpet, the Picassos and Paul Klees on the walls, Anna knew that it did not really matter if you gained the whole world if in so doing you lost what was beyond any price: love.

However, she must be realistic not nostalgic. Everything that began must also have an end, although she found it difficult to accept that this was indeed the end of her so very brief affair with Davey Moore. She had no one with whom she could discuss the matter. O'Grady would not understand. Or if he did understand, she did not wish to admit defeat to him. This was a pain she had to bear on her own. She decided she must put all thought of Davey Moore and what was and what might have been out of her mind.

This proved impossible. She would see him at another table in a restaurant, and despite her determination to ignore him she would surreptitiously try to catch his eye. He would deliberately look right through her, as though he did not know her, had not even noticed her. At a premiere they might be sitting within a few seats of each other. But again, although he might glance in her direction and smile pleasantly and vaguely as though at someone he thought he knew, or ought to know, his eyes would always flick past her. He never made contact. She might not have been there. He could have been looking at an empty seat.

And at night she would dream of him. She would be held in his arms, while beyond the open windows of her Nassau house the sea pounded on a bone-white beach and the moon laid its silver path to the horizon. Time and again she would open the little box Jeannie Moore had given her and wonder whether she dare risk using the last piece of stem it contained. If she did and saw a vision of the future, would she understand what she saw? Would it – could it – tell her whether Davey was out of her life for ever, or only for a time? Did she really want to know what the future held if Davey played no part in it?

She could not doubt now that Davey would go his own way, and she would go hers. They had met, love had lit a brief flame between them, and now all that remained was the memory of what had been.

The business side of her life was also worrying her. She had followed her own judgement in two instances over studio matters, and now she felt she might have decided wrongly in both cases.

One decision concerned an actor whose contract with the studio was ending. She let him go, largely because he was a difficult man with a history of drinking and spells of being dried out, and in any case Traders did not have any film scheduled which would have a suitable part for him. Now another studio had taken up his contract with a great deal of publicity, proclaiming they had discovered a huge new star.

The second possibly wrong decision involved a technical matter about which, for some reason, she had not asked anyone's advice. The studio had three major silent films due for imminent release, all finished by Rosenblatt before Traders took control. Each featured popular stars and seemed set to produce easy profits. Then Warners announced that they were going to issue a film in which for the first time the actors and actresses spoke; there would be music and laughter. Sound pictures had arrived.

Anna could hold back her three films to allow sound effects to be hastily added to the last few reels, and so cash in on this new departure, or she could let them go as they were, silent, but possibly the best in their class. Thereafter, Traders would make pictures from the outset specifically designed for sound.

She decided on the latter course, but cinemas were now reluctant to promote silent films. They felt they were in the same position as the sellers of gaslights after Edison invented the electric bulb. Overnight, silent films, no matter how well made, were old-fashioned. Anna knew now she would probably lose on these three pictures, and she hated the prospect. If the studio had owned its own chain of cinemas, they could have shown the films, discounting seat prices if need be. But since they were forced to rely on the whims of other cinema owners, they had to accept their decisions.

Worst of all, she wondered whether she had been wise to sink all Traders' profits into a studio. O'Grady had been quite right in warning her that they knew nothing about making films, and so had to rely on the expertise of others, at least initially. And she had been wrong to think it would be an easy business to master. Could this last remaining piece of the substance Jeannie Moore had given her give her any clue about her future professional life as well as her private concerns?

She sat down behind her desk, unlocked the drawer where she kept the box. It seemed impossible to find what particular root or herb or tuber the sliver came from, but perhaps she could try and discover what specifics or chemicals it contained that might conceivably possess the rare quality that could help people to foresee events. Such an examination would have to be carried out very discreetly. She could not afford to let word get around that the co-director of Traders studios relied on what could be termed fortune-telling when making important executive decisions.

Anna put the box on one side, pressed the button on her intercom, and at the same time released the electric lock on the door to her office. Her personal secretary, Miss Jones, came in. She was in her mid-thirties, hair brushed back tightly into a bun. Miss Jones hoped, as did many female employees, that one day she would somehow become a star. Unconsciously, she played this part in her real life. She was not just a competent secretary; she was a famous film actress pretending to be one.

'I want to see Dr Hausmann,' Anna told her. 'Ask him to come here as soon as he can.'

'Very good, Miss Ballater. The playwright you asked to come from New York is in his hotel waiting for you to call him, and the Hungarian director whose last picture you liked is here in the outer office. You have an appointment with him for ten o'clock.'

'They can both wait. They want us more than we need them. I will see the doctor first.'

Dr Hausmann was an Austrian. He had arrived in the United States before the Great War and originally practised in Los Angeles where his cousin was an accountant with a film studio. When the company that was now Traders was first being formed, Hausmann's cousin suggested him as its resident doctor. This post had many advantages for him, and for the studio. Hours were regular, and a monthly pay cheque was infinitely preferable to chasing debts from defaulting patients. At the studio, Dr Hausmann soon found that his duties were not always ones that would have found favour with Hippocrates or Aesculapius, but he did not allow such abstract ethical considerations to concern him.

Every studio maintained strict control of their stars and contract players, but in case of any lapses of good behaviour, most subscribed generously to various funds involving the local constabulary. This was in the nature of an insurance, so that if a star was found drunk at the wheel of an expensive car after an accident in which perhaps others had died, he or she would not necessarily face charges of drunken driving. The excuse could be that through overwork, or after a charity function (where, it would be stressed, the star had been appearing totally free of charge), the driver had simply dozed for an instant at the wheel.

A woman star, finding herself pregnant and with her picture still two months away from completion, would enter a local clinic under Dr Hausmann's care to undergo an operation for acute appendicitis. Even such unfashionable afflictions as crabs or syphilis assumed happier names when treated by the studio doctor. Hausmann therefore wielded power and influence quite unimagined by the general public.

He had not yet met Anna. There had been no reason for them to meet, but as an immigrant and still surprisingly insecure, he could not help wondering uneasily now why he should suddenly receive such an urgent and unexpected summons. For Dr Hausmann, the repository of many murky secrets concerning stars idolised by millions around the world, possessed a dark secret of his own. He was a very heavy drinker.

'Do take a seat, Doctor,' Anna told him, mentally comparing him with Dr Bailey in Long Glen. Without Bailey's kindness she would not be sitting here now. And in remembering Bailey, she also remembered Drummond in Mamora. He had not been a qualified doctor, but he had saved her life. With an almost conscious effort, she brought her mind back to the present.

'I am sorry I have not yet had the chance to meet you socially or professionally,' she went on. 'Fortunately for me, my health has always been good.'

'I am glad to hear that, Miss Ballater,' Hausmann replied, smiling effusively.

'Since taking over the studios, I have been involved with producers and directors actively engaged in making the pictures on which all our livelihoods depend. This has most unfortunately meant that I have not yet been able to meet others whose contribution is equally important, and this has been a matter of regret to me.

'Now I am meeting all heads of departments not directly concerned with the actual production of films, and you are the first. I am told you have a well-equipped laboratory.'

'Very well equipped indeed, ma'am.'

'And while your speciality is general practice, am I right in thinking that your own inclinations are towards research?'

Anna had done her homework. In the drawer of her desk she had a folder containing every newspaper cutting that mentioned Dr Hausmann since his arrival in the States, and all references to him in medical journals.

'In Vienna I took a research degree,' Hausmann told her. 'But there's little money in research unless you are fortunate enough to be employed by a large pharmaceutical company. Also, I like dealing with people, hearing their problems, trying to help them when I can. So research went into second place.'

'I hear the highest opinions of you from many patients, but now I would like to ask you to rekindle your interest in research.' She opened Jeannie Moore's box, passed it across the black leather top of her desk. 'What do you think this is, Dr Hausmann?'

Hausmann picked up the box, put on his glasses, peered at the single sliver of stem, sniffed at it cautiously.

'It appears to be dried vegetable matter of some kind,' he said.

'You know what?'

'It is impossible to say accurately without proper analysis.'

'Could you carry out such an analysis in your laboratory?'

'Of course. If you wish it.'

'I do wish it. But I must make two points clear. This piece of vegetable matter, as you describe it, is the only one I have. I do not know where it came from, or what it is, or its constitution. So, in any experiments, please remember this is the only specimen there is.'

'I understand, Miss Ballater. What is the second proviso?'

'That you tell no one what you are doing. Take no one else into your confidence. No assistant, no secretary. This is strictly between you and me.'

'I understand, Miss Ballater.'

'Good. Whatever you may need in terms of funds or new equipment, let me know and I will sanction the expense at once. I look forward to having your report in due course.'

Anna picked up a large envelope, placed the box inside it and handed it to the doctor.

'I will be in touch, Miss Ballater, as soon as I have something to report,' Dr Hausmann told her. He walked out of the executive block, climbed into his Dodge, sat for a moment behind the wheel. He had half expected a reprimand, although as far as he knew he had not done anything to warrant one, but he was a nervous man, concerned about his fragile hold on prosperity.

He opened the glove compartment on his dashboard, took out a glass bottle marked 'Cough Mixture', opened it and gulped down neat whisky thankfully. At once, his racing heart slowed. He felt more confident. He replaced the empty flask in the glove compartment, glanced at his reflection in the rearview mirror, and then drove on to his laboratory.

Two days later he telephoned Anna on her private line. 'Dr Hausmann here, Miss Ballater,' he said, and paused.

'What have you discovered?'

'I would rather not say on the telephone. You never know who may be listening. Some lines are tapped all the time.'

'And you think mine is?'

'I have no reason to believe that, Miss Ballater. But I would rather see you in person, and deliver my report and answer any questions you might have.'

'Right. Have you told anyone else about your research?'

'Of course not. All the notes are in my own hand. I have not made a copy.'

'Have you any of the original substance left?'

'No. There was very little to start with, and I needed it all for my experiments.'

'Then be here as soon as you can,' said Anna. 'Come straight through to me. I will be waiting for you.'

Ten minutes passed. Fifteen. Twenty. Half an hour. Where the hell was the man? His laboratory and surgery were a short distance from the studio. Where could he have got to? Had an emergency case come in unexpectedly, perhaps one of the studio's stars? If so, why hadn't he telephoned to say so?

Anna pressed the intercom button.

'I am expecting Dr Hausmann,' she told Miss Jones. 'He should have been here half an hour ago. Please find out what has delayed him. It is not like him to be unpunctual.'

'I was coming in to see you, Miss Ballater. I have just had a telephone call from the police.'

'What about?'

'Dr Hausmann. On the way from his surgery, there was an accident. A truck struck his car at an intersection. According to the police, Dr Hausmann was in a hurry and tried to beat the red light.'

'How is he?'

'I am sorry to have to tell you he was killed instantly.'

'I see. And his car? Is that badly damaged? He was bringing me some papers, the result of research he was doing.'

'The police say his car caught fire. It is completely burnt out. Only the metal shell is left.'

'You are sure the accident was his fault? The police are usually friendly to us.'

'I know that, Miss Ballater, and I specifically asked the officer about this. I don't like to say so, seeing the doctor is dead, but the police say he had a reputation. For drinking. On his own.'

'I didn't know that.'

'Not many people did. The police knew because there have been one or two incidents before this, but they were always, shall I say, understanding. Apparently the doctor kept a full flask in his car.'

'I see. Has he left any family?'

'None at all. He was a widower.'

'Then you had better make arrangements for his funeral. It must be on a scale matching his standing in Hollywood. He is a great loss, not only for this studio, but for everyone.'

As Anna spoke, she thought of herself. She felt a sudden enormous sense of regret. She had lost more than an able and pliable physician who could help to protect her investment. She had lost her only opportunity to discover the secret of the shavings Jeannie Moore had given her. Presumably Dr Hausmann had discovered the secret, but now his discovery had died with him.

From now on, Anna was on her own. Probably she always had been, but Jeannie Moore's gift had provided her with the comforting thought that she was not entirely alone. Now she felt totally and unexpectedly vulnerable.

* * *

When Celestial Film Productions realised just how much money Davey Moore pictures were going to make for them, they allowed him the use of a white Chrysler convertible to drive to the studio from his one-room apartment. This was not his car, of course; he simply had the use of it. Celestial was controlled by shrewd accountants; they appreciated the benefits of publicity but not the need to pay unnecessarily for it or, indeed, for anything else.

O'Grady parked his own car outside Celestial and when he saw the white convertible leave with Davey at the wheel he tucked in behind it. He parked two cars up from Davey in the parking lot and followed him to his front door.

'Hi, there!' he said as Davey took out his key.

'Why, Captain O'Grady! Didn't expect to see you here.'

'I don't know why not. Anna Ballater and I bought Red-Rose. We're in the movie business ourselves now. As Traders.'

'I know.'

'So don't look surprised to see me. Are you going to invite me in?'

Davey shrugged. 'Please do come and have a drink,' he said without enthusiasm.

He showed O'Grady into the apartment. They sat down.

'You're up here permanently then, Captain?' Davey asked him.

'For the time being, yes. I'm glad to see your pictures are doing so well. Because after this we want to buy you back.'

'Is that what you've come to see me about?'

'No. Not entirely. But it's good to know we'll be working

together. And with rather different roles for you than just piloting a beat-up motor launch out of Nassau harbour and back again.'

'Yes, that was lucky.'

'Lucky?' repeated O'Grady. 'I think it was fated. The harder you work, the better your luck becomes. That's my motto.'

'A good one in all circumstances, I'm sure,' Davey agreed.

'Well, I didn't come here to swap aphorisms,' said O'Grady. 'I want to know why you're keeping out of Anna's way. She doesn't know I'm here, by the way. But I understood back in Nassau, from what I heard – nothing she told me, of course – that you were, shall we say, fairly close.'

Davey's face tightened. 'We were,' he admitted.

'So what loosened you?'

Davey took a sip of his drink. 'I really can't say,' he said.

'Can't or won't?'

'Possibly a bit of both. What seemed wonderful in Nassau, Captain, somehow seemed different here.'

'Because you're going to make a lot of money?'

Davey shrugged. 'Not only that. It's a different life style. I've a morality clause in my contract. Everything's different. And maybe I'm more mature.'

'I wouldn't necessarily say that,' O'Grady replied. 'You're a bit older. But that's all. Now why are you ducking out from her? You got someone else?'

Davey shook his head. 'No.'

'Then the only reason is you just feel you've grown apart?'

Again, Davey sipped his drink before replying. 'I don't want to hurt her,' he said. 'I have tried to let her down gently. I've asked the studio to admit no callers and I take no telephone calls.'

'She could, however, come over here and see you. Like I've done.'

'She could. But I don't think she will.'

'I agree. She's too proud. And maybe she's got too much sense. She thought you were a nice young guy from her home town in Scotland. Instead of that, you seem to be becoming a jumped-up jerk. You may not want to go to bed with the woman any more, but at least you can see her. You can be civil.'

'I agree,' said Davey. 'But there's more to it than that. I can't go into it. Please don't press me. I cannot give you a satisfactory answer.'

'Maybe you're not trying.'

Davey shrugged his shoulders. 'Please. This is a personal matter. I'm very sorry for her, and I'm sorry for me.'

'She picked you up when you were down on the deck. She could have bitched you up by not allowing you to come to Hollywood, but she wanted to help you. She liked you. Maybe she loved you. But as soon as you get a sniff of the big money, you throw her over. All right. That's your business. But I've lived longer than you, so I'll tell you something you may not have discovered yet. Life is like a turning wheel, the sort you see in a fairground. And while you're at the top now, Davey Moore, maybe one day you'll go down and see what the view is like from the bottom. That's when you'll want good friends. That's when you'll need them, badly. And if you treat them like you're treating Anna, that's when you may find you don't have too many. Thanks for the drink, and goodbye.'

Not long after Dr Hausmann died, Anna was cheered by an

unexpected letter from Dr Bailey.

He wrote that Tam Douglas had discovered something interesting from his researches in Soldier's Wood. Was there any likelihood of Anna coming back to Scotland to hear this or should he forward Douglas's report to her? He hoped that she would return, since it would be much more satisfactory to explain everything to her face to face than in a letter.

Anna's immediate response was to book a passage home by the next liner.

She went with Dr Bailey to meet Douglas in his laboratory.

'I'm very glad indeed you could come, Miss Ballater,' he said as they shook hands. 'I think I have found something that will interest you and may help to answer your questions about the wood.'

They sat down in his office. He took a large file from his desk, opened it.

'I thought it might be helpful, Miss Ballater, if I first described a few of the more common plants in Scotland that have medicinal powers, and then come on to what I have found in Soldier's Wood.

'First of all, herbs are the basis of all medicines. In the early days, however, herbalists were not held in very high repute. For instance, Aesculapius, generally known as the father of medicine, was scathingly described by a contemporary as a "root digger and a wandering crank". Herbalists therefore tried to give their calling exclusivity and dignity by fencing in their work with all kinds of ridiculous stories.

'For instance, it was discovered that the root of the peony plant can help patients suffering from epilepsy, rheumatism and glandular ailments. But if this fact became generally known, people could dig up these roots themselves

435

without consulting herbalists. To prevent this, herbalists claimed that peonies could only be dug up at night, because if a woodpecker happened to see anyone doing this during daylight hours it would peck out the eyes of the digger. Rubbish, of course, but the professionals felt they should attach some mystery to their remedies.

'The names of plants often reflect their original medical uses. For example, the little blue flower of the eyebright, with its yellow centre, not only resembles the human eye, the extract from its petals is efficacious for tired eyes – the French call it *casse lunettes*. People with lung complaints were prescribed the plant lungworth, which has spotted leaves, like a diseased lung.

'Red clover and scarlet pimpernel were popular for purifying the blood. The flower of the scullcap, which can produce a sleeping draught without any unpleasant side effects, has a strong resemblance to the shape of a human skull. Nettles stimulate the circulation, because they have a sharp sting. Willow bark cures rheumatism, which is brought on by damp, and of course the willow grows in very damp places. Herbalists treat jaundice with yellow flowers – dandelion, celandine, marigold. The seed of the viper's buglass, which is an antidote for snake bite, looks just like a serpent's head.'

Anna interrupted what she felt was becoming a lecture. 'But what have you found in Soldier's Wood?' she asked.

'First, traces of baneberry, which is poisonous and also useful because its strong smell drives off vermin. Then we found hollyhocks which, when heated in wine, can sometimes avert a threatened miscarriage.

'Herb Robert is fairly abundant. Made into a syrup, it can help people suffering from kidney and bladder troubles. We found foxgloves, which contain digitalis, prescribed for heart problems. Then we found henbane, which the Greeks preferred to opium. This is useful as a general sedative. Early surgeons used it to sedate patients before the discovery of anaesthetics.

'Finally, we discovered several sorts of mushrooms. Some were edible and some were not. The most interesting contains a hallucinatory drug, which I believe holds the answer to many of the rumours about this wood.'

'Have you any samples?'

Douglas nodded. He crossed the room, unlocked a white metal cupboard and took out a small glass phial. Inside, Anna could see slices of stem, similar to the ones Jeannie Moore had given her.

'It contains a dangerous drug,' he explained, 'which I don't recommend anyone using. This is present with traces of mescaline, a specific that possesses very strong hallucinatory qualities and is found in dried slices of the American peyote cactus. We're not really sure yet how the combination works, for it seems to produce different results in different people, but clearly it has a powerful effect on the central nervous system and parts of the brain.

'The human body can absorb it either by eating it dried or by burning it and eating the ash plain or mixed with water or milk. According to its reaction, you may become soporific or experience wonderful dreams of the kind that opium smokers enjoy. You may have the illusion that you can fly, walk on water, walk right through a brick wall. On the other hand, these hallucinations can produce astonishing visions.

'In a controlled case, a young man was asked to describe what he saw after eating a slice of the mushroom. He described seeing a room full of strangers of his own age, seated at small desks, all apparently writing busily. Then he saw an older man who became very angry. Then, another room, and this time people in it were celebrating. All this was mixed up with a motorcycle in a shop window, letters being posted and others arriving.'

'What did it all mean?'

'Nothing to any of us at the time. But afterwards it made some sort of sense. This young man was about to sit an important public examination, hence all the desks. He failed. His father was furious, because he believed his son should have passed easily. The young man tried again, and received by letter the news that he had passed. Before he sat the exam the first time, his father had promised him a motorcycle if he achieved certain grades. He didn't, so he didn't get the motorcycle. All the parts of the picture were there, the problem was fitting them together, rather like doing a complicated jigsaw puzzle, not knowing what the finished picture is.'

'So really he was seeing the future?'

'In a sense, yes. I think myself it depends on the blood group of the person who takes these stems. But that needs a lot more research before I could be sure. Why are you specially interested in this, Miss Ballater?'

'I once knew a woman who lived in Soldier's Wood. She was said to have the gift of foretelling the future. When she was dying, she gave me some pieces of stem which she said could help me to do the same.'

'And did they?'

'To a degree, as with the case you have just told me. But, like that young man, I could not plan future decisions on what I saw. I tried to, but I could not make sense of what I had seen until after the events had taken place.

'One night, before I left home, my father and another

man went to consult this woman, who had the local reputation of being a witch. The other man, a neighbour, had recently lost his wife and hoped that the woman could somehow contact her. But they saw – or thought they saw – a great goat the size of a man and a pack of large wild cats. Then one of the cats literally flew through the air at my father.

'Had they taken this drug too?'

'My father mentioned that before they went to the wood his friend had cooked a simple supper of eggs and bacon and fried mushrooms, gathered in Soldier's Wood. Could that account for it, this vision of the flying cat, if one of the mushrooms had the power you describe?'

Tam Douglas looked at Dr Bailey. 'What do you think?' he asked him. 'I must say it seems very possible to me that your father was hallucinating.'

'And to me,' Bailey agreed.

Douglas put the phial back in the cupboard, locked it.

'So that is the secret of Soldier's Wood?' said Anna.

'Well, one of them. But there are others we can exploit. I mean the wide variety of herbs growing there. And this is what I would like to do, with your permission. More and more people – patients and doctors alike – are becoming aware of the serious side effects that certain drugs can produce. The so-called wonder drugs that the lay press hail from time to time indeed achieve remarkable results. But sometimes their side effects may be almost as serious as the complaint for which the drug was originally prescribed. Here, in this temperate climate, it is possible to find all manner of plants and herbs from which we can extract natural drugs. I would like to do this and pay you a royalty on what we extract from Soldier's Wood. Would you be agreeable to this?'

'I think that is an excellent idea. Do you share that view, Dr Bailey?'

'Entirely.'

'Then I shall draw up an agreement between the three of us,' said Douglas. 'I think that a three-way split would be fair. We could incorporate some part of the name, Soldier's Wood, in our advertising. Something on the lines that while soldiers guard our nation, Soldier's remedies can guard our health.'

'Go ahead,' Anna told him. 'I leave all the details to you.'

'In the meantime, I suggest we all have lunch to celebrate the fact that perhaps we have answered what appeared to be a puzzling question.'

Seventeen

Andropolous the Greek stretched out in his white leather armchair, drew on his huge Havana, and regarded O'Grady quizzically through the smoke.

Andropolous, O'Grady knew, was one of the richest men in the film business. Yet he had never made a film. This, some said, was one reason why he was so wealthy. He had never backed a film, and he never bought a film. He simply rented films that others had made and showed them in his chain of cinemas which extended from New York in the east to San Francisco and Los Angeles in the west, up north to the Canadian border and down south to the Mexican frontier.

He personally owned five hundred cinemas, five hundred darkened temples dedicated to fantasy, where audiences could sit in softly cushioned chairs, surrounded by imitation Byzantine splendour, and briefly escape from the dreariness and frequently squalid drudgery of their real lives into a make-believe world of wealth and wonder.

O'Grady had never met Andropolous before and he had been surprised as well as flattered to receive an invitation – not by a telephone call but in a handwritten letter – asking him to dine at Mr Andropolous's private house overlooking the ocean. O'Grady had been so flattered indeed that he had not mentioned the invitation to Anna on her return from Scotland. He felt that this was a private and personal invitation, and so nothing to do with her.

'I have followed your career with interest, Mr O'Grady,' Andropolous told him in a thick, accented voice. 'In fact, the late Mr Shah and I had a mutual acquaintance.'

'Who was that, sir?'

'A Scotsman named Drummond. When I met him, years ago, Drummond was a sick-bay attendant aboard a British cruiser that put into Athens on some state visit. I was suffering from a complaint which I did not wish my family to know about. I was a young man then, and you know what young men are like. We indulge our natures and our passions too freely. I met Drummond in a bar. He treated me, and he cured me. I heard you mention his name once at a reception in this strange city, and I knew he had settled in Mamora. Do you ever hear from him?'

'No, sir. Unfortunately, like Shah, he is dead.' O'Grady explained briefly how Drummond had died. Andropolous nodded sagely.

'I had heard vague rumours to that effect,' he admitted sorrowfully. 'But it was not to discuss the past that I asked you here tonight. I know about you, Mr O'Grady – Captain O'Grady, I should say. But what do you know about me?'

'Only what I've read in magazine articles. According to them, you came here as a poor immigrant, having left Greece to seek your fortune. You did what all immigrants seemed to do in such classic stories. You shone shoes, ran errands, took bets. When you had saved enough money, you bought a small corner shop with a one-room apartment above it. Using this as collateral, you then bought another, and so on. As your business grew, you bought corner sites in large cities or growing towns. You felt you might build shops or offices there. And then, suddenly, films became popular, and you had your answer. A chain of cinemas.'

'Correct. You've done your homework, Mr O'Grady. I admire you for that.'

'I admire you for what you've done, sir.'

'Since we're paying each other compliments,' said Andropolous, drawing on his cigar, 'I might say you have succeeded in your own line of business just as well. But praise apart, I understand you are one of the partners in Traders, are you not?'

O'Grady nodded. 'I am,' he agreed.

'I want to put a proposition to you and your partner. I want to sell my cinema chain. I think you both would be wise to buy it.'

'What price are you asking?'

Andropolous named a figure.

O'Grady shook his head sadly. 'That is beyond our resources,' he said at once.

'In cash, it may be. But I believe your company has had dealings with the Bank of World Indemnity in Nassau. I can introduce you to the vice-president, Mr Vandervell, with whom I am on close terms. I think he would be willing to help in this transaction. You could repay the loan out of your takings, which would be considerable, because you would be feeding your own five hundred cinemas with your own films. You would have no middle men creaming off fifty per cent of the profits. Your return would be much greater than it is with me. As you know, I do not make films. I simply rent them.'

'That is a very interesting proposition, sir. But let me ask you one thing. Since it appears so lucrative, why do you wish to sell?'

'A fair question. And I'll give you the truth, although truth is sometimes hard to accept. You are a bachelor and so may not quite understand the stresses of parenthood. I have two sons, and from their boyhood it has been my wish to pass on my business to them. With that end in view I built one tiny cinema into a chain of five hundred. But they show no interest whatever in my enterprise. They spend their time with chorus girls. They run fancy cars, live in big apartments, play about in expensive sailing boats. Perhaps I am partly to blame. I had a harsh upbringing and did not want them to endure the same. But I now think it might have been better if they had. Children, especially sons, are like young animals. They need to fight against the bridle and the bit, otherwise they go soft. Mine have never had anything to fight against. Everything was given to them. They had only to ask.

'I have built up one of the largest cinema chains in the world and had thought to branch out into other similar investments in Britain, on the continent of Europe, anywhere. But if I do so, I know that on my death my sons could not conceivably handle business on that scale. Within months, all would be in ruin, borrowed against, divided up, sold off or gambled away.

'I could not endure that to happen. I could not bear to know that what I had built with my own hands – the terrible gambles, the risks, lying awake at night for hours on end wondering if my whole venture would crash – would vanish like snow in sunshine. You understand me, Captain?'

'I have no children,' O'Grady replied. 'But I understand your views perfectly, and I accept your reason for wishing to sell. I would like to discuss this offer with my partner.'

'Please do so. And when you have reached a decision, telephone me. Not at my office, but here. But do not be too tardy in reaching a conclusion. Others are also interested. I do not wish to sell to them. They would pay me with dirty money. But sell I must, and I very much hope it will be to you.'

Andropolous took out a card on which was printed a telephone number, but without any name or address.

'This is my private number. Memorise it and then destroy the card. I would not like it to fall into the wrong hands. Ring me at any time. Now, shall we dine?'

O'Grady sat at the head of the big horse-shoe table in the main conference room of Traders' film studios. Around him sat the studio's salaried producers and directors.

'I've called you here for two reasons,' he began. 'First, you will be pleased to hear that our studio has taken over a chain of five hundred cinemas – the Andropolous group. We are renaming it Mamora, a name that has associations for Miss Ballater and for me, as it had for our third partner, Mr Shah, who died some time ago before we arrived here in Hollywood. This purchase means that we have five hundred guaranteed outlets for our films.'

O'Grady opened a folder, took out a sheaf of press cuttings.

'Second, as you know, Hollywood has in the past few years faced a barrage of attacks from the press and some sections of the public. They claim our films deliberately debase people's morals. These attacks are increasing – and if we do not take care, they can overwhelm us. They are based on various unfortunate incidents in our recent past which have nothing whatever to do with us, but for which we are blamed. Let me give you the ones most often quoted against us.

'The first scandal concerned Olive Thomas, a former *Vogue* model who became a Ziegfeld girl, then a star of Selznick Pictures. At the time in question she had just married Jack Pickford, Mary Pickford's brother, so The World's Sweetheart was her sister-in-law.

'Olive was one of the most photographed girls in the world. Then, on her honeymoon in Paris, everything went wrong. She was found on the floor of her hotel room – the Royal Suite of the Crillon, no less – stark naked and dead, clutching a bottle of bichloride of mercury granules. For lovely Olive, The World's Sweetheart's sister-in-law, had been a drug addict for years. Now she was dead, aged twenty. Jack, her husband, immediately went into a clinic – said to be suffering from grief – but in fact to treat *his* addiction to cocaine.

'The next newspaper cutting I have here refers to Mr Roscoe Arbuckle, "Fatty" Arbuckle. He started his working life clearing blocked drains. He cleared one in Mack Sennett's home, and Sennett thought he was a funny-looking fellow, and hired him on the basis that if he thought this, so would millions of others. And Sennett was right.

'Arbuckle worked his way up from playing in Keystone Cops films and finally signed a three-year contract with Paramount for three million dollars. That's how big he was. There was no one in Hollywood then with a contract that valuable, and only one or two now.

'Just one year after Olive's death, Arbuckle, a heavy drinker, hired three suites in the Hotel St Francis in San Francisco to give a party to celebrate his new contract. Some time during his stay, Fatty took one girl, a virtually unknown actress called Virginia Rappe, into his bedroom. Instead of going to bed with this creature, Fatty, drunk as a skunk, and quite incapable of any sexual activity, stuck the neck of a champagne bottle into her vagina. She died in hospital. Fatty stood trial for murder, and Virginia became far better known dead than she had ever been alive.

'After deliberating for forty-three hours, the trial jury were divided. The judge declared a mistrial. At the second trial, the jury could not agree, so Fatty faced a third trial. This time he was acquitted. At last he was free – so he thought.

'Now one of Virginia Rappe's former lovers decided he could make a few quick bucks by declaring that in Hollywood the stars indulged in orgies which surpassed all the decadent goings-on of degenerate Rome. So while Arbuckle was free – he was only free to starve. Which he damn nearly did.

'His three-million-dollar contract was cancelled. When his films were shown, women rampaged through the cinemas and tore down the screens. In Wyoming, a crowd of cowboys came in and drew their guns and shot the cinema to pieces. No other studio would hire him. He was finished – at the very moment he had reached stardom. End of story.

'There are half a dozen more examples in this folder of what can happen when some young man or woman from a humble background suddenly becomes world famous and rich beyond their dreams. They just can't handle what this means, and Hollywood takes the blame.

'The campaign against Hollywood has grown so big and so dangerous, politically, that the leaders of the motion-picture business have appointed Will Hays who, as chairman of the Republican National Committee, helped nominate Harding for President, to become Hollywood's clean-up man. The word is he's looking for a studio to make an example of. He has to do something for his salary of a hundred thousand dollars a year, and as one of the newest studios we could be first in the firing line.

'We have therefore all got to watch our step, not only in how we behave personally, but in our pictures. We can't risk making anything controversial. Happy endings are to be the rule. The good guys must always win before the final fade-out. We cannot afford anything less – or more – than simple, undemanding family entertainment.

'And from now on, all new contracts will have a special morality clause. If anyone – and I mean *anyone* – is caught breaking it, they're out. No appeals. And if you're out over this with us, the way things are, you'll be out everywhere in Hollywood. Is that absolutely understood?'

The producers and directors nodded gravely.

'Right,' said O'Grady. 'Now I want you all to sign these forms to that effect, and I will declare the meeting over.'

Castle had just tipped the carver, who sliced roast beef from the trolley, thick and rare as Castle always liked it, when the head waiter of the San Francisco restaurant approached him and bowed obsequiously.

'Excuse me, sir,' he said nervously. 'Someone outside in an automobile wishes to speak to you. Urgently, he says, sir.'

'You can see I'm having dinner,' Castle replied shortly. 'Who is he?'

'A dark-haired gentleman in a Cadillac with a driver and another man up front. He gave me this envelope for you, sir.'

Castle nodded, put down his knife and fork and opened the envelope. Inside was a plain card and two letters, 'J.T.', printed on it.

Johnny Torrio. My God, he'd found him even here. Who could you trust? The answer was no one, no one at all. This cringing waiter, or the carver, was probably in his pay.

'I'll see him,' said Castle, wiping his mouth with his table napkin and standing up.

'Shall I keep this dish warm for you, sir, or would you like to order again?'

'I'll decide when I come back.'

Castle walked out between the tables. At the far end of the room an orchestra began to play a waltz. He looked at the diners as he passed them, men in tuxedos, women in evening dresses, and he wondered how many of them were secretly as worried as he was. He had cause to worry. That Greek bastard Andropolous had sold his cinema chain right over his head, and to Anna Ballater and that fag O'Grady of all people.

He walked past the reception desk, through the foyer. The commissionaire opened the huge front doors, and Castle went down the steps. Torrio's Cadillac was parked in the no parking zone, but Torrio was above laws. He made his own. As Castle reached the car, a bodyguard opened the rear door. Castle climbed in. The man closed the door carefully, jumped in beside the driver. The car accelerated away.

Torrio and Castle sat encapsuled in the back compartment, with a thick bullet-proof glass division between them and the driver and bodyguard.

'You wanted to see me, sir?' asked Castle nervously.

'I sure did. You've bitched up that deal with Andropolous. The one with Rosenblatt also got away although the goddamn bank was backing us both times.'

'You told me that the bank would handle Rosenblatt,' Castle replied defensively. 'And Andropolous had already decided to sell elsewhere before I got to him, sir.'

'Is that a fact? So why aren't you in Hollywood now, making him change his mind instead of eating here? You got a woman with you?'

'No, sir, I'm on my own.'

'After your wife's death I shouldn't think you'd want to get involved with other women.'

Castle said nothing. He was conscious that his heart was beating very fast and very heavily. His throat seemed to have constricted.

'Don't just sit there,' Torrio continued in his harsh, nasal voice. 'What are you going to do about this deal? I gotta have those cinemas. The outfit needs them. There's money waiting to buy the whole damn lot. And this pipsqueak company, Traders, goes in right under our nose – *your* nose, Castle – and gets them. Now they're changing the name to Mamora, another kick in the crotch, I'm sure just to let us know they think we rubbed out that guy Shah.

'I remember Traders in Nassau when they first got out from under you. You let them go then, and tried to use students who just didn't know where they were at. Now they've screwed us a second time. You're not trying to be smart behind my back, by any chance, are you?'

'I would never do that, sir. You know me.'

'Too damn right I know you. And maybe I've put too much faith in you. You're like so many guys, OK in small deals. It's the big ones you can't handle. This is a big one. And I need it handled quickly. I don't want any more excuses from you. Not one, ever again. Never. For the last time, do I make myself clear?'

'Perfectly, sir.'

Torrio smiled a wintry smile. 'I hope this hasn't spoiled your dinner,' he said sarcastically. 'That seems more important to you than doing a deal, apparently. But they do nice roast beef there, even warmed up a second time.' Torrio lit a cigar; he did not offer Castle one from his case.

Castle sat in silence, drained of speech, of coherent thought. He wished to hell he could get away from Torrio.

But there was no way out. He knew far too much, so he had to stay in until the end. But the end of what? Castle did not wish to address himself to the question. He believed he already knew the answer.

Since selling his New York amusement arcade to Anna, Sam Axner had been living in Hollywood for nearly two years. He would have preferred to describe himself as working there, but that would not have been strictly true.

When he first arrived, he confidently anticipated that, with his own abilities, about which he held a high opinion, he would have an easy time financing, making and marketing his own films.

He had heard how others did this on borrowed money, or even, if some accounts were to be believed, on almost no money at all by persuading a writer, a director and the cast to take a share of any future profits instead of expecting money up front. This arrangement was thought to appeal to gambling instincts inherent in many creative people, but somehow Sam Axner was unable to persuade anyone to work for him on these terms. Maybe he tried too hard; maybe people just did not believe he had the touch to produce films others wanted to see.

He did not own a studio, indeed, he did not even have an office, and so his suggestions that directors and actors should work for nothing until a serial he hoped to make was in profit invariably produced the unanswerable question: 'What serial?' He lacked sufficient money to back his own ideas, and after several false starts no one else appeared willing to back him.

Recently, Axner had been reduced to peddling ideas to various studios. Some of his ideas had been lifted or adapted; others were discarded. None was paid for. Studio executives assured him earnestly that they would be in touch with him directly, but his telephone did not ring.

At first, he rented a small apartment. Then, as his capital dwindled, he moved to a much smaller one. Now he was living in an upstairs room in an apartment house on Vermont Avenue. The room did not have its own telephone, only an extension from the main reception hall. He was certain he had not missed any calls because he promised a five-dollar tip to the telephone operator if she took any messages for him when he was out. There were never any messages, so the five-dollar bill stayed in Sam Axner's back pocket.

There were not many five-dollar bills to keep it company. He felt depressed, like so many other hopefuls who had come west, certain they would find fame and fortune in pictures, only to end up working as waiters or gas-station attendants.

As Sam Axner sat, brooding on this melancholy downturn in his fortunes, the extension telephone rang. He picked it up, thinking someone must have been put through to the wrong room. But, no, the call, at last, was for him.

'Mr Axner?' a man's voice asked him.

'Yes. Who is that?'

'My name is Castle. Bill Castle. I'd like to see you over a business deal.'

'A film?' asked Axner hopefully.

'Involving films, yes. I hear high praise for your abilities both as a businessman and a creative person.'

'That's very kind of you,' said Axner, warming to the caller. 'Have we met?'

'No. That's why I want to meet you now. Are you free for half an hour?'

'I could make myself available,' said Axner carefully. It was never wise to admit too readily that you had no commitments, no work.

'I'll be right over.'

The phone went dead. Axner tidied up the room as best he could. He put the one bottle of bootleg gin he could afford under the bed coverlet, brushed his hair, then stood by the window.

A black Duesenberg with a uniformed driver approached the house and stopped. A man sitting next to the driver jumped out and opened the rear door for a heavily built passenger. He did not look to right or left, but walked straight through the front porch of the rooming house.

Usually, visitors spoke to the clerk at the desk. He would then telephone to enquire whether it was convenient for the client to receive a guest. Not infrequently, the visitors were debt collectors the client might not wish to see. This man ignored the clerk and came right up the stairs. Axner could hear his firm footsteps along the corridor. He opened the door to him.

As soon as he saw Castle, Axner sensed instantly he was bad news. Castle had the look of a successful gangster. His suit was too obviously expensive; creases in his trousers were sharp as knives; his brown and white shoes too highly polished. And Castle's cold eyes regarded Axner with all the compassion of olive stones.

'Come in,' said Axner, trying to keep out of his voice the alarm he felt. As Castle passed him, he could smell a faint scent of expensive aftershave. Castle sat down in the only chair, took out a cigar case, offered it to Axner. Axner shook his head; he did not smoke. Castle lit a cigar, flicked the match over his shoulder onto the threadbare carpet. He made no attempt to pick it up.

'I'll get to the point right away,' he said. 'I understand you ran some kind of house in New York that showed serials.'

'Yes.'

'Then someone bought you out and you moved here, hoping to make your own films. But you haven't had too much luck since. That so?'

'Correct,' Sam agreed. There was no point in denying it. The truth must be obvious; he wouldn't be living in this rooming house if he was successful.

'Right,' said Castle. 'I'm going to put a proposition to you. I want you to be front man in a film deal that will make you a lot of money. When I say a lot of money, I mean maybe a hundred thousand bucks. Cash. In your hand. Thereafter, with that capital, you should be able to borrow money from banks or anywhere else to make any pictures you want.'

'That's very generous of you. But why me?'

'Because I've done my homework. You're the sort of guy I think would appreciate this offer. You'd also make good use of the money. And, most important, you can carry out what I want done.'

'What is that, exactly?'

'I want to buy a chain of cinema theatres. Five hundred. In your name. With my money.'

'That's a big chain,' said Axner, greatly impressed.

'Mamora is a very big chain,' Castle agreed. 'Five hundred cinemas, some seating at least a thousand people, some maybe twice that number. And you are the man to get it for us.'

'Who owns it now?' Axner could not afford to buy any trade papers and was therefore ignorant of Hollywood news and gossip.

'An Irishman is involved. Name of O'Grady. With a woman, Anna Ballater.'

'O'Grady?' repeated Axner. He remembered O'Grady coming to look at his amusement arcade, first on his own and then with that Scots woman, but this wasn't the moment to say so. He did not want to say anything that could conceivably compromise Castle's astonishing offer. With this money he'd have no worries, none. So he said nothing, but nodded enthusiastically.

'He calls himself Captain O'Grady,' Castle continued. 'I offered a lot of money to the previous owner, a Greek, for that chain only a few months ago. O'Grady screwed me and got the deal.' Castle paused, drew on his cigar until its tip glowed red like a tiny neon sign.

'So how can I help you?' Axner asked him politely.

'By doing exactly what I tell you. When I give you the word, I want you to put in a bid yourself for that chain.'

'But I've no money, Mr Castle.'

'Don't tell me what I know. Like I said, you'll buy the chain with my money. For reasons I need not explain, you will unexpectedly be able to buy this chain from them at a very low price. You will sell it on to my consortium at the same price. Your fee, your commission, is the hundred thousand bucks.'

'Is that all I have to do?'

'That's all you have to do, yes.'

'But I don't understand it. Why pick on me?'

'Mr Axner,' said Castle seriously. 'I have already told you. If you must delve into the background of everything, we just haven't got a future together. You have an interest in show business, and you want to get ahead in show business. This is your chance to do so. Are you on or are you off?'

'I'm on, Mr Castle. My God, I'm on,' said Axner fervently.

Castle sat in a hotel room in Los Angeles, jacket off, tie loosened, a glass of whisky in his hand. In one corner, a tape machine spewed out a long white sheet. He pulled out one page, read the headlines aloud.

'New Hollywood boss Sean O'Grady pledges support for family pix. No more controversy. No more sex scenes. All to be one hundred per cent wholesome from now on. Every pic to have happy ending.'

Sitting in a circle round Castle eleven young men nodded their approval. They were all fresh-faced, with blond hair, blue eyes. In contrast to Castle's heavy jowls, his thick body, they seemed innocent and naive.

'You see, gentlemen,' he said, looking at each one in turn. 'At last, but too late, the filth merchants, the purveyors from Europe of foul pornography cry "Enough". But we know these men of old. We have heard too many weasel-words from them. We have had to endure too many broken promises to change their evil ways. So now we take the war into the enemy camp. For make no mistake, this is war, the ultimate battle, right against wrong. Many studios pollute our young with their films, but Traders is the worst, for this man O'Grady is a total hypocrite. Not only is he a secret homosexual, he lectures his producers on the need to reinforce moral standards. As cynical an exercise as I have ever seen. Our campaign therefore must first be against him and his company. Beat them, and the others will fall quickly and meekly into line.

'You will be the shock troops who will destroy this vile man. I believe that millions in this country are eager to take a stand against this torrent of filth, immorality and depravity that pours from the sewer called Hollywood, but they lack a lead. This, gentlemen, you will provide.

'Out of my own money I have formed what I call the March of Morality to embrace the basic, enduring American virtues of honesty, integrity, chastity. Now is our chance to fight for what we believe. It may be our last chance. Therefore we must not – we dare not – fail.

'Each of you will have a specific city or large town where you will operate. You will go there, rent accommodation, and then from your address you will write to the local newspapers along the lines of sample letters I will give you. These will say how you – perhaps a high-school teacher, a Sunday-school teacher or maybe just a regular churchgoer – want to take your stand against this rising tide of evil, which is corroding and corrupting the youth of our once great nation.

'If the papers won't publish your letters on their merit, pay editors to do so. If that fails, buy advertising space. However you do it, keep up the crusade until you receive a telephone call from me or from a colleague. The message will be simple and unequivocal: "The time is ripe. Praise the Lord."

'When you hear this, go at once to your local cinema. In the middle of the main feature film – whatever it is, but hopefully one of Traders' productions – you will stand up and shout that you've endured enough of Hollywood's filth. You ask all right-thinking, clean-living, red-blooded Americans to join you in the fight against it.

'Of course, you will have confidentially informed local newspaper editors and radio stations of your intention in advance, so your intervention will secure maximum publicity. I found each of you through advertisements in religious publications, so I know you are wholeheartedly with me on this matter. I also know you will not fail, for we are doing the Lord's work.

'I will now give each of you five hundred dollars cash. In addition, I will meet all your hotel bills, all advertising costs and any other out-of-pocket expenses. As soon as I receive details from you, I will cable the money to your local bank. Now, any questions?'

They shook their heads. Everything was quite clear.

'Right, gentlemen. Now, here are what I might call your action packs. First, the money. Next, drafts of three different types of letter for you to write. Use them all, using different names and addresses. We must hit Hollywood where it hurts most. They are very good at publicity, so we must be even better. And here for each of you is a return railroad ticket to the city or town allotted to you. You're sure you have nothing to say?'

One man spoke up.

'Yes, sir,' he said warmly. 'I have this to say. It is wonderful to think that at last we have the chance to do something positive for the faith and the values in which we all believe so strongly. I'd like to thank you, Mr Castle, sir, from the bottom of my heart for financing this. I am sure you'll have rich blessings in the next world.'

'Hear, hear,' others murmured approvingly.

Castle inclined his head gravely at the compliment. 'You are very kind,' he said. 'I appreciate what you say.' Castle did not add that what he really wanted were rich blessings in this world – very rich and very soon.

Eighteen

O'Grady and Anna were in the rear seat of the studio limousine driving along Sunset Boulevard. He closed the glass division that separated them from their chauffeur. What he had to say was not for other ears.

'This morning I had an odd memo from the manager of the Mamora cinema in Des Moines,' he said. 'Another in almost exactly the same terms came from Denver, a third from Atlanta, all enclosing virtually identical letters that had appeared in local papers, each signed by different people in that particular locality. And all attacking our pictures on moral grounds. No other studio has been picked on so far, only ours.'

'Show me.'

O'Grady passed over to Anna three letters cut from newspapers. All were violently critical of Traders films. The writers called them lewd, disgusting, perverted, anti-American.

'As you say, they are basically the same, except for a bit of topping and tailing,' Anna agreed. 'One's supposedly from a Sunday-school teacher. Another is signed by a Bible reader, the third from a lay preacher – so they say. They're attacking everything we show in our cinemas. In Des Moines we had a cowboy picture. In Denver, a knock-about comedy, both inherited from Red-Rose. You can criticise them on their quality as films, for they're pretty routine stuff. But you cannot conceivably fault them on moral grounds.'

'I know that. Someone's behind this. It's a deliberate campaign.'

'You may be right,' Anna said slowly. 'But why?'

'To break us. That's why. And then buy us out.'

'This smells of Castle to me. The outfit. What's our biggest house?'

'The New York Mamora. Seats more than two thousand, and for almost every show it's ninety per cent full,' O'Grady replied.

'I suggest you catch the next train to New York. Be on the spot in case similar letters appear in papers there. You can then reply at once, point out that these criticisms and allegations are totally untrue. You might pay the writers a visit and see whether they're actually living at the addresses they give. Make sure editors all know about our policy of making nothing but happy-ending family films and more and more serials intended for family audiences. And if need be, pass a few presents to them or their families to show them where their interests lie.'

Rudolph Valentino leaned across the screen and flung the woman from him into the sand of a studio desert. His oiled hair glittered like a raven's wing. A great sigh – an amalgam of envy, surprise, wonder and sadness that such a great artiste was dead – rose from two thousand people seated in the New York Mamora for the afternoon show as they watched him turn away with a scornful sneer.

At that exact climactic moment, a real scream cut the air in the huge cinema like an Arabian scimitar.

'Get off me! Get *away*!' shrieked a girl hoarsely from one end of the upper circle. 'Help! Rape! *Help!*'

And then came a long wordless cry of pain and anguish.

Every face turned from the flickering screen towards the girl. Actors dressed as sheiks, bedouins, travellers of the desert were instantly forgotten. That was only one-dimensional fiction; this was reality, flesh, blood, and terror. Instantly, house lights came on. The projectionist switched off the projector. The film faded and died.

All over the huge cinema, people stood up. Some clambered onto their seats to gain a better view of whatever was happening. They saw a girl standing outside a door that appeared to open into an office. Her shoulders shook as she sobbed uncontrollably. She looked pathetic, a slightly built waif-like creature. Her light cotton dress had been ripped. She spread her hands modestly across her breasts, and bowed her head, convulsed with tears. Behind her in the doorway stood a thickset man in his shirtsleeves. He was staring at her in amazement and disbelief.

'What the hell is going on?' he shouted furiously.

The girl turned towards him, and in a clear voice everyone could hear, cried: 'You know, you bastard! You tried to rape me! Get the police!'

'I'm a police officer,' shouted a man from a seat in the circle. He rushed towards them, treading on other people's shoes in his haste to reach the side aisle.

'This woman came into my office unasked, tore off her clothes, and now claims I tried to rape her,' explained the man in his shirtsleeves. 'I've never seen her before in my life. This is a total frame-up, officer.'

'Who are you?' the policeman asked him sharply, relishing his unexpected moment of importance, knowing that everyone in the cinema was watching him, wondering what he would do next.

'I'm Sean O'Grady. A director of the company that owns this cinema.'

'Your trousers are undone,' said the officer flatly.

O'Grady looked down. His flies had been ripped open.

'The damned woman did it,' he said angrily, buttoning them up. 'She's mad.'

'He's the mad one!' shouted the girl. 'Look at him! Hasn't even bothered to do himself up. I beg you, help me, officer!'

'I'll have to take both of you down to the station,' said the policeman. He glanced around at people sitting in the gallery. 'Anyone witness this assault?' he asked.

'There was no assault, officer,' said O'Grady stonily before anyone could reply. 'This is a totally put-up affair.'

At that moment, exactly ten past three in the afternoon by Castle's watch, telephones rang in hotel rooms across the United States. The message to each occupant was the same: 'The time is ripe. Praise the Lord.'

Within minutes, in Mamora cinemas in towns and cities, young men stood up in the aisles to declaim against the films being shown. As Mr Castle had instructed them, they had previously alerted local newspapers and radio stations to ensure prominent coverage of what to the audiences would seem spontaneous and totally unconnected outbursts against what they called the 'ever-rising and encroaching tide of filth poured out by the evil, godless people in Hollywood'.

'This is a city of sin, a modern Babylon,' they cried passionately. 'A fount of iniquity, to be compared with the wickedness of Sodom and Gomorrah in the Bible, which for centuries personified every foul and evil lust and perversion.'

This was good strong stuff, of which great headlines are made. Editors did not neglect such an unexpected opportunity to use their largest type.

New York newspapers carried smaller news items about these outbursts, but on their front page they printed more astounding news. Captain Sean O'Grady, who had only recently declared that his company would produce nothing but wholesome serials and films for all the family, was accused of attempting to rape a woman in their most important cinema, the New York Mamora. They published interviews with members of the audience, the projectionist, the policeman. On inside pages, articles described O'Grady's background.

Most of the details had been provided by the publicity department of Traders Films with a view to stressing his sterling character. No mention was made of his years as a slaver captain, or his activities in Nassau. The writers claimed that O'Grady had been a distinguished naval captain, following a long family tradition of service in the British Royal Navy. During the war he had served at Jutland, in the Dardanelles and in the Atlantic Squadron. He had been decorated by King George V for various, if unspecified, acts of valour. He had then inherited a fortune from a distant relative who, being childless, was so impressed by O'Grady's personal courage that he had left him his wealth when he died.

None of this was true, of course. But as Anna read the account she remembered Pilate's words: 'What is truth?' Anna was more interested in reading about the girl than about her partner's fictitious past. She was a Miss Priscilla Hartley who, as a debutante in London, had become engaged to a young South African millionaire. Arriving in Cape Town, Priscilla made the tragic discovery that her fiancé had died in a riding accident only days before her ship docked. Overcome with shock and sorrow at his death, she could not bear to land, but sailed on to the United States where she booked a suite in the Waldorf Astoria, in New York. Miss Hartley appeared to be of impeccable social background. So what had taken her up into the circle, to one of the cheaper seats in the cinema, on that particular afternoon?

She explained how, having enjoyed a life where lavish expenditure was the norm, she decided, after the tragedy of her fiancé's death, to live in what she described as a more sober and worthwhile way. Just as some rich people might occasionally ride on the top of a bus in preference to the family limousine, she now wanted to be one of the crowd and so had bought a ticket for a seat at the end of the circle.

As she sat down, she saw a door open, and a strange man, whom she now recognised as Captain O'Grady, beckoned to her urgently. Surprised but intrigued, she followed him into a room, which apparently was his office. Immediately, he had shut the door, ripped away her clothes, opened his trousers and attempted to rape her in a most vicious and brutal fashion.

Fortunately (and no doubt maddened by the heat of his insatiable animal lust), he had neglected to lock the door and so she was able to escape, screaming for help.

Curiously, while photographs of others involved appeared in the papers, there was no photograph of Miss Hartley. It was explained that she felt so shocked and ashamed that she did not wish to be recognised.

Women columnists at once took up her case. They were grateful for any topic that would run for days or, hopefully, even weeks. Their theme was that the filth being spewed out by Hollywood studios and the attendant and ever-increasing risk to young and innocent girls in the sensuous atmosphere of these huge, dark and cavernous cinemas were matters of most serious social concern. They quoted eminent physicians who, in the early days of the cinema, had forecast that films would inflame men's grossest and darkest passions. All manner of crimes and acts of violence could stem from watching degrading scenes on a vast screen in surroundings of Babylonian opulence.

American laws of libel were lax, so Captain O'Grady was now regularly referred to in many tabloid newspapers as the 'Beast from Babylon'. While awaiting trial, he was released on bail of a hundred thousand dollars. He immediately travelled across the States to Hollywood to explain to Anna what had happened.

'It was a frame-up,' he said bluntly as they sat in her private office.

'By whom?'

'I've no firm proof, but this smacks of Castle's work. I hear that he wanted to buy Andropolous's chain, but we beat them. If this rap sticks, Mamora's value will plummet. He could then buy the whole batch of cinemas from the bank for a fraction of our real worth.'

'Did you know this girl Hartley?'

'Never seen her before in my life. Never heard of her. As you know, girls don't interest me. They never have. But if she's a socialite, born with a silver spoon in her mouth, then I'm the Caliph of Baghdad. Her biography, printed in papers I read in the train coming west, is probably as accurate as the rubbish they wrote about me. She's been put up to this. No question of that. It ties in with those letters in provincial newspapers all viciously attacking our films.' O'Grady paused as they both digested this fact. 'Have you read the financial sections of the papers this morning, by the way?' he asked Anna.

'Not yet. What's in them about us?'

'Bad news. Interviews with World Indemnity, who bank-rolled our deal. They're worried. They wish to join the campaign to stamp out this filth, so they say. Their directors are all family men, apparently, regular church-goers, desperate to show they are whiter than white.'

'But how does that affect us? We're not producing filth.'

'Of course we're not. But we've borrowed millions of dollars from that bank on the value of these cinemas, their development potential and our products. The bank isn't going to be too happy if these attacks force down their value.'

'But one girl saying you tried to rape her won't cause all that, surely?'

O'Grady was about to reply when the buzzer sounded on Anna's desk. She pressed the switch.

'Mr Vandervell, senior vice-president of the Bank of World Indemnity, is in the outer office,' Miss Jones told her.

'Show him in.' Anna flipped off the switch. 'Talk of the devil,' she said.

O'Grady shrugged philosophically.

Mr Vandervell wore a Harvard tie and a worried expression. 'I'm glad you could see me at such short notice, Miss Ballater,' he began hesitantly. Then he noticed O'Grady, and his manner changed abruptly. 'Hullo, O'Grady,' he said without any pleasure. 'I thought you would be in New York. Didn't expect to find you here.'

'I could say the same about you,' O'Grady replied. 'But here we both are.'

The banker sat down. 'You've seen the newspapers?' he asked, looking from one to the other.

'All of them,' said O'Grady. 'I wanted to see how they handled this ludicrous farce.'

'You call it ludicrous, Captain? Have you read the reports of spontaneous outbursts of criticism in Mamora cinemas right across the country? The value of our investment has dropped disastrously as a result of this girl's claims and these newspaper accounts.'

'How can you reach that conclusion so quickly?' Anna asked him.

'By a simple arithmetical sum. The takings. The drastic fall in audiences. That's how. The value of each cinema, as an entity on its own, can only be calculated from the takings each week. And your loan from World Indemnity is based on their value before this calamitous downturn.'

'There's the value of the buildings, too,' Anna pointed out.

'Agreed. But the value of each building as a cinema is what concerns us.'

'Takings will recover, I assure you. Audiences will come back, Mr Vandervell. This is only a temporary fall. Going to the cinema has become a way of life. People won't give that up overnight.'

'There are now very strong pressures on them to do so right across the country.'

'We have a loan for three years. A temporary fall in ticket sales does not affect that, Mr Vandervell.'

'Agreed. But without going into the small print, Miss Ballater, you will recall that your company's loan has to be serviced regularly, every quarter, by an agreed date. I hear that in synagogues, churches, chapels and cathedrals, preachers of every religious denomination will be hammering at the need to stem what is now generally called the tide of vice from Hollywood or, more specifically, from your studio, although I expect the attack will broaden to include other studios as well. Newspapers will run more and more editorials on the same theme. People will stop going to the cinema; they'll be urged to stay away almost as a moral duty.'

'I repeat, this decline in audience numbers will not be permanent. It is a purely hysterical reaction to a deliberate campaign.'

'How can you be sure? And who could conceivably orchestrate a campaign that appears to be totally spontaneous?'

'We intend to find that out.'

'You'll have to work fast, because this crusade – it is nothing less – gathers steam every day. Remember, a ban for only a few weeks can tilt the balance between profit and ruin for you. Without people in the seats, there is no money in the tills. That's the basic situation.'

'I hear everything you say, Mr Vandervell, but we will weather this,' Anna assured him calmly. 'We need a little time, that's all. When Captain O'Grady's case comes up, it'll be thrown out. The newspapers and the preachers can then attack people who give false witness, and all this will be forgotten.'

'I wouldn't be too sure the case will be flung out, Captain.'

'Why not?' asked O'Grady sharply. 'I'm innocent.'

'So you say, and I personally do not doubt you. But with all the hostile press comment every day, your innocence becomes more difficult to prove. Also, you have several factors against you. One, you're rich. Two, you're not American. Three, you're in a business which arouses the fiercest envy on every side among all classes of people. People in Hollywood are believed to have wonderful lives in the sun with beautiful young girls and handsome young men, and this assumption brings with it the hint of immorality, even if there isn't any.'

'This is rubbish,' said O'Grady contemptuously.

'Maybe. But most people believe it. And the jury may well believe this girl Hartley. I must warn you that the term for statutory rape is up to fifty years in prison. If you go down, your whole company will go down, too. The speech the captain made to your producers and directors has been quoted in several newspapers, especially his remarks about the comic, Fatty Arbuckle. Remember, he faced *three* trials before he was cleared. So by then bad publicity had ruined him. However, on a more positive note, I have already received an offer to buy your stock, just in case you feel it prudent to get out before the roof falls in.'

'So soon?'

'Yes. From a consortium of businessmen in what we call the Bible Belt. They want to make and show nothing but religious films, each with a high moral purpose. They wish eventually to buy a studio, but first they want their own cinemas so that they can guarantee their films will be shown.'

'They'll lose their shirts,' said O'Grady dismissively. 'Audiences in cinemas want to be entertained, not preached at.'

'Maybe. But without your Mamora cinema chain, your studio is useless if the case goes against you. No other cinemas will book your films. You'll be out in the cold for ever.'

'Who are these people who want to buy our cinemas?'

'They are led by a New Yorker, Sam Axner, who has had long experience in the entertainment industry. His associates have been involved with other business activities. They wish to keep their names out of negotiations until they are more advanced.'

'What are they offering?'

'Two-thirds of the sum you borrowed from us.'

'You told them the sum?' Anna asked coldly.

'Of course not, Miss Ballater. That is a confidential matter between us. But they discovered it somehow, I must admit.'

'And what do your directors think?'

'They are seriously considering the offer.'

'Under the terms of our agreement, Mr Vandervell, the bank cannot sell us out unless we default on interest payments.'

'That is so. But as I have reminded you, these payments have to be paid on the nose, every quarter. One day late, even one hour late, and your loan can be called in immediately. And if it is called in, I do not think you could repay it out of present takings.'

'That is your opinion, Mr Vandervell. I will not comment on that. But this I will say. Your bank's interest will be paid the moment it is due. If we do decide to sell, that will be our decision, taken in our own time.'

'In the present economic climate, and with all the bad publicity, you will not get a better offer.'

'Again, that is your opinion. We have already had dealings with Sam Axner. He owned a small cinema in New York that showed only serials. He told us he was coming out here to make them, but since then I've heard nothing more about him.'

'You will now, Miss Ballater.'

'It strikes me as very odd that an anonymous consortium, sheltering behind this man, should suddenly try to buy us and that your directors are apparently not unwilling to help them.'

'It is not odd at all. Simply businessmen wishing to buy

470

when the price is down. I thought I should come and personally explain the situation that is developing as a result of this most unfortunate business in New York.'

'We appreciate your interest, Mr Vandervell, and thank you for calling. But please tell Mr Axner that neither the studio nor our cinemas are for sale. Make that point very clear. And should, by chance, one of these businessmen be a Mr Castle, please make sure that you tell him this personally. Do I make myself clear?'

'Perfectly, Miss Ballater. Perfectly.'

They stood at the window and watched Vandervell being driven away in his limousine.

'Axner,' said Anna. 'Where did he get money to make a bid like this?'

'He didn't,' said O'Grady. 'He'll only be the front man. The rest are up behind him. The outfit. Castle. I'll put a private dick on to Axner and see where that leads us.'

Shortly after midnight, O'Grady drove over to Anna's house. She was waiting for him.

'Well?' she asked.

'I've had a full report. But to save time I'll only give you the gist of it. It's as I thought. Castle is behind it. He's in trouble with the gangster Torrio. And my understanding is that Torrio's also got a few unhappy colleagues after him. They're all desperate for more profits. They're making millions out of Prohibition, but they're also paying out millions, bribing judges, juries, senators. Everyone's got too greedy.'

'If Castle can break us here, we're out,' said Anna grimly. 'We've got to keep one step ahead of him.' She glanced at her watch. 'I don't trust anyone in this film city. It's early in New York, but I'm going to phone those lawyers, Jackson and Hogan, who acted for us when we bought out Axner. They couldn't be further away from Hollywood or they'd be in the sea, so they're unlikely to be bought by Castle or anyone else.'

'What are you going to tell them?'

'The less I can, the better. Then, if my plan succeeds, we can congratulate each other. If it fails, you can blame me.'

Anna was in her bath when the telephone rang. She wrapped a towel dressing-gown round her, picked up the receiver. Jackson was on the line from New York.

'I thought I'd better ring you at once,' he said. 'To get right to the point, this woman Priscilla Hartley is not here any longer. She's moved to Hollywood.'

'Why?'

'She says she wants to make a public statement from there. Thinks it would have more impact if it came right from the heart of Sin City. My guess is she's desperate. This is a last throw. She hopes you'll buy her off. If not, then she'll rely on a jury's sympathy, which she'll probably get. Anyway, she's rented a room in the Moonlight Cove guesthouse in Hollywood.'

'Alone?'

'There's a man with her, but he's booked in separately. I don't know his name or what name she's using — presumably not Priscilla Hartley until she's ready to do so. I understand he's advising her about selling her story to the newspapers.'

'Surely if she's a socialite she doesn't need that sort of money?'

'*If* she's a socialite, no. But that is open to doubt. I checked she did book into the Waldorf, though. But for one night only. And a very small room. She did it so that if anyone checked she'd been there, she'd be covered. That's about it. You want me to fly over?'

'Please do. If this case goes to trial, I want you to be here.'

That morning, Anna drove out towards Moonlight Cove. She had passed it often enough, a cluster of white-walled buildings in pseudo-Spanish style with green fluted tiles and palm trees. A small pond, scummy and stagnant, stood in the centre of a courtyard. She parked a hundred yards past the complex and walked back.

A man sat at the reception desk reading *Thrilling Detective*.

'I'd like to see Miss Hartley,' Anna told him.

'No one of that name here,' he replied, without looking up at her.

'Maybe she's registered under another name.'

'Maybe.'

'She has an English accent. She could be here with an Englishman.'

'No one like that here. I've told you.'

Anna took out a ten-dollar bill, put it on the table. 'Think again, buster,' she told him sharply. 'If your memory returns, this ten-dollar bill's yours. If not, it's mine, and I'll wait out here till she comes out. Make up your mind.'

Now the man looked up at Anna. His eyes were close together, foxy, flecked with matter in the corners.

'Bungalow on the left,' he said briefly. 'Red door. Woman of that description's rented two rooms downstairs. Name of Browne with an "e". Man's name is Smith.'

'How original.' Anna pushed the note towards him. 'She's in now?'

He nodded, went back to his magazine.

Anna crossed the patio and knocked on the red door. A girl's voice answered.

'Who's there?' she asked in an American accent.

'Room service,' Anna replied, also with an American accent. 'Special delivery.'

'Push it under the door.'

'It won't go. Want to accept it or not?'

'OK.'

The door opened a couple of inches. Anna rammed her foot against it, pushed it back.

The room felt very hot and stale with cigarette smoke.

'*You!*' cried Lucy in amazement. 'I didn't expect to see you!'

'I could say the same to you,' replied Anna, equally surprised. 'But I'm not looking for you. I've come to see a Miss Hartley, an English socialite whose South African fiancé was killed in an accident and who now claims to have been raped by a Captain O'Grady. I'm told she booked in here under the name of Browne.'

'That's me,' said Lucy nervously. 'But I didn't know you were the Anna Ballater involved with O'Grady. If I'd known, I wouldn't have got involved with this at all. I don't want to hurt you, Anna. I've nothing against you. As I say, I had no idea you had anything to do with O'Grady. I never thought you were the Anna Ballater on that troopship.'

'You should read the trade papers. There's been enough in them about me.'

'I can't drop the charge against the captain now,' said Lucy. 'I would if I could. Believe me, I would. But I can't.'

'Who put you up to it?'

'I can't say here. It's all too risky. You remember Piet, the South African I went off with in Cape Town?'

Anna nodded.

'Well, he dropped me. Now I'm with his friend, the one who took you out – Jan. He's in the next room. As Mr Smith.'

'You've got yourself in a mess here, whoever you're with.'

Lucy shrugged. 'I know. But you don't understand what it's like to be here without money. Someone makes you an offer, and you think, if I take it I could use the money to get out of this rut – for ever.'

'So it's all a put-up job?'

Before Lucy could reply, a man's voice called from the next room. 'Who've you got out there? If it's room service, tell them I'll have another cold beer.'

Jan came through the door, smoking a cheroot. 'Why,' he said raising an eyebrow in surprise. 'The little English nursemaid who ran away to get back to her ship on time. Remember that?'

'Very well.'

'How did you find out who we are?'

'Because Lucy is claiming that my partner, Captain O'Grady, tried to rape her in one of our cinemas.'

Jan shook his head gravely. 'A terrible offence,' he said. 'He faces fifty years in the slammer, so the lawyers tell me. And quite right, too. Unless he, or you, come to terms.'

'What sort of terms?'

'A hundred thousand dollars. In cash. No cheques, no bankers' drafts, no credit. Cash.'

'That's blackmail.'

'No way, English nursemaid. That's not blackmail. It's simply a way to buy your partner his freedom. Look at it like that. Two thousand dollars a year for fifty years. It's nothing – over such a long time. If he goes on, he'll pay more than that to lawyers who won't get him off – because he's guilty as hell.'

Anna turned to Lucy. 'What did you two do in Cape Town?'

'We ran a bar. It wasn't very successful. We tried various other ventures. None of them worked out.'

'We had the cards stacked against us,' Jan explained. 'You know how it is. People didn't like us.'

'I can imagine they mightn't. And you think your best chance to make them like you now is to pretend someone raped Lucy? You want that sort of publicity?'

'We've had several offers already from newspapers and true-confessions magazines for the inside story,' Jan retorted defensively.

'And presumably whoever's put you up to this will also pay you something? And would I be right in thinking that man's name is Castle?'

Jan did not reply. He drew on his cheroot, but his face flushed. 'If those are your last words, a hundred thousand dollars, my last words are that you won't get a penny from me or from Captain O'Grady,' Anna told him. 'But I do have this to give you.' She put a hand in her pocket and took out a small washleather bag, opened it. The diamonds that had fallen from Jan's waistcoat pocket under the trees outside Cape Town scattered like tiny stars across the table top.

'They helped me build up a business. I wouldn't want to think it was founded on any kind of false pretences.'

'You're giving them back to me *now*?' asked Jan, amazed.

'That's right.'

'You're a soft touch,' he said, scooping up the stones quickly. 'But this doesn't make me change my mind. A hundred thousand is the price. Take it or leave it.'

'I'll leave it.' Anna turned and walked out across the patio to her car.

Years later, whenever she read newspaper reports of other

trials, she would remember every detail of Sean O'Grady's.

To her surprise, as the date for the hearing drew near, O'Grady became increasingly nervous. He admitted he was on edge, taking sleeping pills each night and then different pills each morning to pep him up. His face was grey; his hair looked thin and brittle and dry.

'You've nothing to fear,' Anna told him repeatedly. 'We'll get you off. Jackson's a first-rate lawyer. It's a try-on, as you've said from the start. And he'll prove it to the jury beyond a shadow of doubt.'

'Maybe,' O'Grady replied. 'But I don't trust the law. All those smooth-tongued bastards up there. Remember what happened to Fatty Arbuckle? Now it's a young girl against a rich older man, and a former slave captain. They'll kill me over that. And there's my own background: boys.'

'Jackson's dug out facts about Lucy's background we didn't have before,' Anna said, trying to restore his confidence. 'She's not the grieving bride-to-be or the simple virgin she's claiming to be. We'll have medical evidence on that, and juries are always impressed by doctors. She's been living with this man Jan for years. Jackson hired a private detective in Cape Town. She was up on a charge of prostitution over there, and Jan was charged with living on immoral earnings. Then they were caught working the three-card trick on tourists off cruise liners.'

'Did they do time?'

'No. They got off in each case. People came forward with fake alibis, said it was all mistaken identity.'

'That's what I mean about the law. It's a load of crap. I'll go down over this.'

'If you do, you won't be on your own. I'll go down with you. So put that right out of your mind. We're not going down. We're going to win.'

'I wish I knew the hell how,' said O'Grady miserably.

'By telling the truth, that's how.'

'What is the truth?'

'That this is a frame-up.'

'Who's going to believe that? If we claim unknown people have set me up – and I can't very well name Castle – the jury will think it's all movie talk, made up. They will only believe what sounds feasible to them.'

And so, unfortunately, it proved. O'Grady was right. Anna, more trusting, less worldly-wise, was wrong. First, Lucy explained tearfully what she claimed had happened. She appeared so distressed by having to recall it, she broke down twice. A chair was brought so that she could continue giving her evidence seated, since she appeared too faint to stand. An usher handed her a glass of water. Lucy's hand trembled so much that she dropped the glass.

Members of the audience in the cinema came forward to have their say. One described seeing Miss Hartley in tears and hysterical with terror. Two women swore they had seen that Captain O'Grady's fly buttons were undone. They could see his private parts clearly, in a state of intense sexual excitement.

A nurse in the audience claimed that Miss Hartley was so distraught she seemed on the point of suicide. A doctor described how he had been called to sedate her. A woman, claiming to be the fiancée of a Frenchman, the late Pierre Montagne, explained to a hushed and astonished court that O'Grady had thrown him off his ship and left him to die on an uninhabited atoll. Worse, Montagne had later been murdered in Nassau – and the accused had been in that town at the same time, apparently involved in bootlegging.

Two Negroes claimed they had actually been slaves in one of Captain O'Grady's ships. They had been shackled together and denied food and water for days. O'Grady was not a man, he was a monster.

Sitting in the public gallery, Anna watched each of the jurors in turn to see how they reacted to these statements. They were dumpy and middle-aged, easily shocked and obviously gullible. Some had been film extras; one or two worked in local stores; others were clerks or housewives. They clearly relished this unexpected moment of power and importance.

Newspaper columnists and radio commentators stressed the vital nature of this trial, and the jurors believed what they read and heard. Was it fair or just that one of these human beasts, these despoilers of American women, a deliberate corrupter of national morals in Hollywood, should be allowed to continue with this odious life?

There was no doubt in Anna's mind that O'Grady had lost the case even before his defence began. This was not a fair trial; it was a charade. She watched the jurors lick their lips and glance meaningfully at each other and then at O'Grady, anticipating the moment when they could tell the judge they had found the prisoner guilty.

O'Grady did not make a good impression on the court. He appeared nervous and ill at ease. He was sweating, and kept dabbing his forehead with his handkerchief, adjusting the knot of his tie, smoothing down his jacket. His attorney did his best to take him through events easily and clearly, step by step, but O'Grady could not deny he had been a captain of a slaver, or that he and a colleague had abandoned Pierre Montagne on an uninhabited island. His explanation that Montagne had first tried to kidnap them seemed quite unbelievable. Such an event was totally out of the limited experience of the jurors, and so without any credibility.

Newspaper reporters describing the scene day by day made the most of this apparent unreality. Jurors, reading the accounts each morning before they arrived in court, had their own prejudices heavily underlined. O'Grady was guilty, of course. He was a beast, a rapist. Worse, he had made a lot of money. He must therefore go down as a stern example to others that there was no escape for evildoers, however rich they might be.

O'Grady spent the evening before the final defence speeches on his own. Anna and his attorney offered to stay with him, but he said he had matters he wanted to work out alone. He sat on his patio, overlooking the ocean, considering his past and his probable future. He remembered boys and men he had known, some of whom he had loved. He recalled the religious beliefs of his father, and he could find no comfort in his thoughts.

The charge against him was preposterous. So was the offer to drop the case for a hundred thousand dollars. No less preposterous was the strong possibility that he would be sentenced to years in an American penitentiary for a crime he had not committed; indeed, was incapable of committing.

Turning the problem over and over in his mind, he suddenly, and quite unexpectedly, reached a solution. It was so obvious that he marvelled he had not thought of it before. And having found it, he felt at peace. This would set him free.

His mind made up, he went to bed early and slept as he had not slept since the trial began.

On the following day, as O'Grady's attorney stood up to make his final defending speech, O'Grady waved his hand at him. The attorney sat down, perplexed. O'Grady stood up and addressed the judge.

'Your honour, may I have the opportunity of speaking in my own defence rather than having my learned attorney do this?'

A buzz of interest and surprise rustled round the court.

'You may,' the judge replied. 'If your attorney agrees.'

'I do so agree, your honour.'

O'Grady put his hands on the rail in front of the box, looked at each of the jurors in turn, and then at the judge.

'Ladies and gentlemen of the jury,' he began in a quiet voice. 'I stand indicted of a very grave offence, possibly the gravest offence this side of unjustifiable homicide. I am accused of attempting to rape a young girl in a public place, a crime that fills me with horror and revulsion, as I am sure it is equally repugnant to you all.

'You have already heard medical and other evidence that the woman who accuses me is by no means as innocent as she would have you believe. Nor is her name Priscilla Hartley, as she claims. And she is not a member of the English nobility, or indeed of any other nobility.

'Her real name is Lucy Graddon and she was once, very briefly, an unqualified nursemaid. She is now living in Hollywood in one room using the name of Browne. She has been co-habiting with a man for a number of years. He is living in an adjoining room, using the name of Smith. During their time together she has faced charges of prostitution in South Africa. He has been accused of living off immoral earnings and taking part in confidence tricks and other unsavoury deals.

'None of these charges, of course, approaches in gravity the charge she has brought against me, which, as you have heard, she would drop if I paid her and her companion the sum of one hundred thousand dollars.

'Ladies and gentlemen of the jury, I am totally innocent of the crime with which I am charged and I am not willing to be blackmailed.

'You have heard evidence that I was captain of a ship which carried slaves. That is quite true. But I am not being charged for that. And in many parts of the world the barter of human beings is a regularly accepted part of business life. I could give the court the names of some of the oldest, most distinguished, most liberal-minded families in the Social Register in this country, who have bought slaves very recently. They don't call them slaves, of course. They call them indentured servants. And so they are, but not for one year or even for ten. They are indentured for life. That is simply slavery under another name.

'You have also heard people give what I will prove is totally false witness. Two women have solemnly declared, on oath, that they saw me sexually aroused by the sight of this woman Lucy Graddon. I will prove to you all beyond any argument, any allegation by such so-called witnesses, that I was not aroused for the simple reason that I *could not* be aroused by her, or by any other woman.

'I am going to admit now something I have never spoken of before, something that in this country is never mentioned in public.

'I want to speak of what the great English writer Oscar Wilde called the "love that dare not speak its name". Ladies and gentlemen of the jury, you see before you a man accused of a terrible crime. He is innocent, totally innocent, because he carries what many would agree is an even more terrible stigma, and he will do so until death releases him.

'I declare to you that I am not as most other men. I find no satisfaction in women. I am not interested in women. I never have been. Women as sexual partners do not arouse me. Instead, they have a totally opposite effect. They *disgust* me. I have never been attracted to women and I never will be. I am only interested sexually in people of my own gender – other men. I am a homosexual.

'The idea that I could attempt or even contemplate raping an unknown woman in an office with a door opening on to the audience in the middle of a cinema performance is not only ludicrous. It is impossible.

'My defence is that I am totally incapable, physically, mentally and morally, of this crime of which I stand accused. I am willing to undergo any test or examination, psychiatric or medical, so that the court may accept this basic if unfortunate fact to their own satisfaction. The accusation of attempted rape is as false as the other lies so many people have glibly and shamefully told this court on oath.

'I did not do this deed. I am as incapable of perpetrating it as a blind man is of seeing this court. That is my defence. Your honour, ladies and gentlemen of the jury, I rest my case.'

After O'Grady ceased speaking, the court was silent for a moment. Then reporters sprinted from the press benches to their telephones. The judge rapped the table with his gavel.

'Has the prosecution anything further to say?' he asked.

'Nothing, your honour.'

'I will adjourn the case till ten o'clock tomorrow morning,' said the judge. 'By that time the jury may have reached a conclusion in their deliberations.'

Outside the courthouse, a crowd of reporters surrounded O'Grady, besieging him with questions. Anna pushed her way through them, pulling O'Grady along with her.

'Don't say anything to anyone,' she warned him. 'Not a word.'

She bundled him into her car. They drove to the studios. O'Grady did not speak on the way, but sat, hands folded in his lap, his face downcast. When they were in her office, she closed both the inner and the outer doors and poured him a double whisky. O'Grady drank it neat, held out the glass to be refilled. Then he sat down.

'What did you do that for?' she asked him gently.

'The case was going against me. I knew I wasn't guilty, because I couldn't be guilty. It was physically impossible, mentally impossible. Maybe, Anna, I was just tired, not only of this ridiculous charge, but of the sham my life has been. I have been living a lie, keeping in the shadows all the time, always afraid in case one day the truth should come out. Suddenly, I wanted to say who I am, what I am.

'There are a lot of fags here in Hollywood. I know many of them. Writers, actors, technicians, designers, set decorators, hairdressers. They're all pretending to be something or someone they aren't. Just like me.

'What I was didn't matter a damn when I was captaining a slaver. I could either find amenable members of the crew or a boy in the next port. It was the same in Nassau. But here, to be accused of something I could not do, this was somehow just too much to bear.'

'You were your own man,' said Anna. 'I admire you for that. You didn't trim your sails.'

O'Grady smiled bleakly. 'No. I put on full sails for a strong wind. I think I'll go back home now, and wait until the court reassembles tomorrow.'

'You'll be all right? Not too depressed?'

He shook his head. 'I know now that for years I've been depressed, like a man wearing shoes that didn't quite fit and always trying to pretend they did. Now I'm beyond all pretence. I'm relaxed, at ease. I'll see you tomorrow.'

'I'll come home with you. We can have dinner together.'

O'Grady shook his head. 'No,' he said. 'Please don't. Thank you for the idea, but I would rather be on my own. When you were first brought aboard my ship, I thought I could make a few pounds out of you by selling you to a whorehouse, or as a housekeeper, a mistress. I didn't care where or to whom. And then everything went wrong. Or maybe it went right. You've helped me make a lot of money, and perhaps that has given me the courage to be myself at long, long last. Anyhow, I'll be on my way now.'

O'Grady walked out of her office. He left the studio by a side door, and hailed a passing cab.

After his confession, his outburst, his declaration – each newspaper gave his words a different description – it was clear that O'Grady could not work again in Hollywood. He was finished as totally as if he had admitted to murder or leprosy, or both. Anna guessed O'Grady knew that and accepted it. But he had gone out on a high note, like a doomed ship going down with all guns blazing. They weren't guns she would have chosen herself. They weren't even guns she particularly admired. But she admired him for firing them.

The telephone call she was half expecting came at seven o'clock in the morning. O'Grady's housekeeper was on the line.

'I have to tell you, ma'am,' she said in a voice tight with emotion, 'the captain took his own life in the night. I found him when I came on duty.'

'How did he do it?'

'With a pistol.'

'I see.' A pistol. Anna remembered O'Grady ripping up

the floorboards in his cabin aboard the slaver. He had handed pistols to Shah and to her, and kept two himself. Had he, even then, a presage that one day he might need one for just such a purpose?

When the court reconvened, the case was dismissed. How could a dead man be tried? Later that morning, Anna received a telephone call on her private line. She expected that it would be one of the many reporters who sought her opinion, her impressions, her experiences of working with Sean O'Grady. But this was from Lucy. She sounded nervous.

'Is that Anna?'

'Yes.'

'I feel very badly about things. I had to ring you.'

'Because O'Grady killed himself? Or because you gave false evidence?'

'For both reasons. I feel a heel. But I tell you, I had to do it.'

'Castle?'

Lucy did not reply. For a moment, Anna thought she had rung off. Then she spoke.

'Most of all,' she said, 'I feel badly that you gave those diamonds back to Jan. He didn't know you'd even got them. You could have kept them – or given them to me.'

'You had no more right to them than I had. I kept them until my company was up and running. Without them, I wouldn't have built anything. I've carried them in my handbag for years, as though I sensed that one day I would be able to return them. I had no address for him and didn't even know his surname, or I'd have sent them back long ago. It was only right he got them back.'

'I don't know anybody else who'd have given them back.

I wouldn't have done. Nor would he.'

'That's only two people,' said Anna.

'Anyway, I wanted to tell you I was sorry. And thank you again. We've made some money out of it. Sold my story to a Sunday newspaper. We're leaving the States now, going back to South Africa. I hear that the man you mentioned, Castle, isn't too pleased the way things turned out. We think it best to go as soon as we can. While we can, is what Jan says.'

'Goodbye,' said Anna and replaced the receiver.

She never heard from either of them again.

Nineteen

The steward bowed Davey Moore into his state room aboard the *Benares Castle*, bound for Liverpool from New York, then hesitated for a moment at the door. Davey thought he recognised the signs, put his hand in his back pocket for a five-dollar bill.

'No, sir,' said the steward, shaking his head. From his jacket pocket he produced a small book covered in cheap red rexine.

'I was just going to ask you, sir, if you would be kind enough to sign this autograph book for my young daughter.'

'Of course. What's her name?'

'Kathleen, sir. Kathleen MacNamara.'

Davey took out a gold fountain pen which the studio had supplied for such encounters, scribbled his name, added best wishes, handed back the book. How odd, he thought, that people never asked for an autograph for themselves, always for someone else.

'Thank you very much indeed, sir,' said the steward gratefully, peering at the signature as though doubting it was genuine. 'Is this the first time you've travelled with us?'

'No, the second.'

'I don't remember having the pleasure of attending you before, sir.'

'I don't think you had that pleasure,' Davey agreed. 'I was travelling steerage then with several other emigrants.'

'Oh, really, sir? I think you'll find this more pleasant than steerage.'

'It should be, with what the shipping company charges,' replied Davey with a smile.

When the man had gone, Davey sat down thankfully on the sofa. He felt tired. He had held a press conference just before he boarded, to publicise his latest film, and he always found those occasions wearing. Although the studio had provided each reporter with a handout listing the salient points in Davey's life and career, still the same questions had to be fielded. How old are you? Do you have any hobbies/girl friends/secret ambitions?

Davey had signed a contract of a size that aroused enormous interest: three million dollars, to star in three films. This was remarkable enough for a newcomer, but what was even more newsworthy was that he had been paid this huge sum in advance. The last star to warrant such a fee had been the unfortunate Fatty Arbuckle, and he would only have been paid when he had completed the films.

Davey took no credit for his altogether better arrangement. He had left the details to the Scottish lawyer James Macdonald, whose only previous association with Hollywood had been as a member of the audience in the local Perth cinema. There had been some comment in some of the more serious newspapers that Celestial must have put themselves heavily in hock to the banks to provide such a huge sum up front, before even a camera started to turn. Well, that was their affair, thought Davey. They must have thought him worth the money or they wouldn't have paid it. And maybe they also wanted to keep him out of Traders' hands; there was a lot of jealousy between some studios.

Davey's state room was packed with flowers from fans,

well-wishers, and Celestial Studio. Their smell was heavy and unnaturally cloying in the autumn afternoon air; he'd get rid of them as soon as he could. The ship trembled as her engines took up the strain from the tugs, and the faint movement recalled his first hours aboard the *Benares Castle* on that outward journey long ago. How many voyages had the ship made since then?

For want of anything better to do, he picked up a little booklet that the steamship line presented to every first-class passenger. It contained the name of everyone travelling first class. If they were of any public note, a brief description was added: a senator's widow, a member of parliament, the director of a public company. He turned over the pages until he came to 'M', and read 'Davey Moore, screen star'.

He glanced through the booklet, turning back to the As. No one he knew there. Then, under B, he saw a name that still caused his heart to contract: 'Anna Ballater, co-founder, Traders Film Corporation'.

So she was on the boat too. That was bloody bad luck. He had not expected her to be here. It was odd to think that at this very same moment she could be in her cabin looking through her copy of this booklet. If she did so, she was almost certain to see his name, and, even if she didn't look through the booklet, it was inconceivable they would not run into each other on a five-day voyage. He must avoid this at all costs. He felt it absolutely imperative that he did so.

If only he had known she was booked on this ship he could so easily have gone on another liner. If only. What short, sad words they were!

He crossed to the drinks cabinet, mixed himself a Long Glen whisky and water. As he sat down to drink it, the ticker-tape machine in the corner of the state room began to chatter excitedly. A long stream of paper whirled out, then the machine stopped.

Davey stood up, pulled the paper ribbon from the machine's glass mouth, carried it back to the sofa. He'd never used one of these machines before, but the studio had insisted that one was installed in his state room. They said it was quicker than using the radio telephone which was so dependent on atmospheric conditions that frequently ship-to-shore communication was impossible. Also, there could be no doubt as to what was said in any message, because there it was, on paper. He began to read a general digest of financial news.

The first item dealt with fluctuations in the American stock market. A statistician named Roger Babson, of whom Davey Moore had never heard, had been speaking at a national business conference. The ticker tape quoted him: 'A great crash is coming and it may be terrific stop Factories will shut down stop Men will be thrown out of work stop The vicious circle will get in full swing stop More to come stop'.

Well, there was nothing in that for him. He did not own any stocks or shares. He read on. A news flash from Wall Street reported that five and a half million shares had been traded in one day. It seemed that an astonishing rush to sell had begun.

Davey read on.

'Chicago stop 7.30 p.m. stop A shooting in the Windy City's gangland is causing many known mobsters to leave town stop First, William Castle, originally Giuseppe Castiglione, was found shot at the wheel of his Packard sedan in the underground garage of his luxury apartment stop Castle was a close associate of Johnny Torrio, who started life as a hit man in New York and was brought to Chicago by Big Jim Colisimo stop

'Bill Castle is believed to have carried out many contract killings either himself or on the orders of others in the outfit but witnesses were always afraid to testify against him stop He is known to have been involved in bootlegging, running rum and whisky up from the Bahamas to Florida and New York stop Recently there have been reports of disagreements between him and Johnny Torrio stop'

Davey read the item for a second time to make certain he had not somehow imagined that Castle was dead. But no. The facts were clear and beyond dispute. The ticker-tape machine chattered again. He read the message as it came out.

'Flash stop Further gangster killing stop One man, name unknown, held on charge of shooting Castle stop He admits he shot him three times at close range, said he shot in self-defence stop More follows stop'

So Castle was dead at last. Davey felt an immense surge of relief to his spirit. He felt free, something he had not felt since he had left Nassau. He finished his drink in a kind of toast to the future. Then he picked up the passenger list, checked Anna Ballater's internal telephone number and asked the operator to connect him.

Anna let the telephone ring, hoping it would stop if she did not answer it. She knew no one aboard the ship. The caller would probably only be the purser or some other ship's officer inviting her to a routine social engagement aboard ship, like the captain's cocktail party before dinner on the first night out.

The telephone kept on ringing. Frowning, she picked up the receiver.

'Is that Miss Ballater?' a voice asked before she could speak.

Anna recognised Davey's voice and her mouth went dry. She put out one hand to steady herself.

'Yes,' she said slowly. 'Who is that?'

The question was pointless. She knew who it was. Davey Moore was telephoning her after all this time, after so many unacknowledged letters and unanswered telephone calls.

'Davey Moore here,' he said easily. 'I wonder if I could come and see you.'

'You're aboard the ship?'

'Well, obviously. If I weren't, by now I'd be drowning.'

'What do you want to see me about?' Anna asked him. She had been deeply hurt by his behaviour. She was in no mood to capitulate too quickly without a satisfactory explanation. But how could he explain his conduct if she didn't meet him? And, after all, she had been longing to talk to him from the moment she arrived in Hollywood. She made up her mind.

'Give me ten minutes,' she said, surprising herself.

She was sitting, face freshly made up, hair brushed, reading the passenger list when Davey knocked at the door. She opened it to him.

'You must wonder why I'm coming to see you now,' he began awkwardly. 'Why I deliberately haven't spoken to you since you came to Hollywood, and why I now call on you the moment the ship leaves port.'

'The thought had crossed my mind, yes,' Anna admitted coldly. 'But no doubt you have a reason. A good one, I hope.'

'The best. The very best, believe me. Have you seen the ticker tape?'

'No. I haven't a machine here. I have enough of it in the

office every day. I enjoy being where people can't reach me.'

'The ticker tape can. Castle's dead.'

'Dead?'

'There's been a news flash about it. He was shot three times in the garage under his apartment block. Some man's just been arrested for it.'

'The judge or jury will be fixed. The outfit is involved. He'll get off.'

'Maybe. The important thing is, Castle didn't.'

'When I was a girl and used to go to the kirk on Sundays, the text I remember best was this: "He who lives by the sword shall die by the sword." The same goes for those who live by the bullet, I suppose.'

'In this case, yes.'

'But what has that got to do with you suddenly coming to call, not having replied to any of my messages or answering even one of my letters? The only letter I ever received from you was to say you didn't want to see me again.'

'Ask me inside your suite and I'll tell you.'

'You're inside. Tell me.'

Anna closed the door behind Davey. They sat down on easy chairs, on either side of a coffee table.

'When I first went to Hollywood with Rosenblatt I finished the picture he had been shooting on location in Nassau,' Davey began. 'He gave me a few lines to say and a bit more to do. Not much, but making that film I learned a lot. There was an old actor playing a heavy. He had taken to the bottle and was on the way down. He latched on to me and helped me, largely because he thought that in return I might help him get a part in my next film, which I did.

'He gave me all sorts of good advice. Never to look at the

Klieg lights, or at the camera. Never to move too fast, because movements on the screen are magnified a hundred times. You walk quickly and it looks as though you're running to attack someone. Move slowly. Keep your head still, don't gesticulate with your hands. All basic things, but I didn't know them. The most important thing he taught me was to find out which is the best side of my face to be photographed. Now I don't let anyone photograph the other side.'

'And it worked,' said Anna.

'Yes, it worked. I finished that picture and was beginning the next when I had a visit from Castle on the set. I was surprised to see him, and alarmed. He'd already had me beaten up in Nassau for being too friendly with his wife. I thought he was checking where I was so that his men could pay me another visit. As you know, his wife killed herself in New York, or, as the rumours went in Hollywood, Castle killed her. Either way, I felt very uneasy when he showed up.

'He said he could make my life very hard if he put it about she'd killed herself because of me. The studios were all running scared of any scandal. They still are, for there has been so much – suicides, murder, sex, drugs, everything. If Castle put the word about, Celestial would at once invoke the morality clause in my contract and drop me like a red-hot coal. But that would only happen if he talked.

'He wouldn't, as long as I agreed to his terms. I asked him what they were. I was never to get in touch with you. If I did, I was finished. And worse than that, the outfit would deal with you. Permanently. There would be no arguments, Castle said, and no excuses. I could write one letter to you saying our affair was over, and that was it. No more. Ever.

496

'He knew that you and I were close, and he guessed I'd find it difficult not to contact you. I don't know if he would have had you killed, I think maybe the beating he gave me didn't satisfy his need for revenge, particularly when I started to make a name for myself, and he wanted to make me suffer. But I couldn't risk calling his bluff, if it was bluff. He was quite capable of killing you if I didn't do as he said.

'I told him that, without you, I wouldn't be in Hollywood at all. He just said, "Listen to what I say. If you think I'm fooling, you go see her. Give her a ring. Tell her you want to meet some secret place. But remember, there is no secret place. The outfit's everywhere. There's too much money involved not to have scouts and spies all round. Lay off, or she dies and you're finished." That was the deal.'

'So that's why you didn't get in touch with me, wouldn't answer my calls, wouldn't see me?'

'That's why. It hurt terribly to have you think badly of me. But it would have been infinitely worse the other way. That could have been fatal.'

They stood looking at each other, six feet of space between them. Through the curtained window, the Atlantic horizon rose and dipped slowly.

'I wanted to tell you as soon as I knew Castle was dead,' Davey went on. 'Now I have, I feel better.' He turned. 'I'll be on my way, then.'

'Wait,' said Anna. 'You've certainly saved us both embarrassment, if we'd seen each other on the promenade deck, say, or sat next to each other in the restaurant.'

Davey smiled ironically. 'Embarrassment? Is that all? As far as I'm concerned, explaining everything now has saved me a lot more than that. All the misery of desperately wanting to speak to you, see you, love you, but never being able to. I kept all your letters and would reread them, wondering where you'd written them, what you were wearing when you wrote, whether you still even thought of me. I love you, Anna. I wouldn't have done what I did if I hadn't. Please believe me, if it's the last thing about me you do believe.'

Anna looked at Davey closely. His young, now famous face was pale and tense, the mirror of his mind, she thought. It displayed all his emotions, his despair. For women audiences, Davey Moore would be more than a star. He would be the man they should have loved, the man they should have married. And for her, who was he? Just this, or more?

'I do believe you,' she said slowly.

Davey took a step closer to her, and then, suddenly, they were in each other's arms, and it was as though the long period of parting, the pain, the secret tears were all over. Not just for the moment, but for ever. They kissed long and lingeringly.

'Come to bed,' he said urgently.

'Yes,' she agreed. 'But first, I must get used to having you back, to being with you, to knowing we're together. We've all our lives to go to bed.'

'The way I feel, one life is far too short,' said Davey.

As he spoke, a voice interrupted them through a concealed loudspeaker in the ceiling.

'This is the ship's first officer, speaking from the bridge. Owing to exceptional demand on the telephone system in New York, apparently because of nationwide calls to stockbrokers jamming the exchanges, all ship-to-shore radio-telephone links are suspended indefinitely.

'I regret I cannot give any indication when the service will be resumed. I am sorry to have to pass on this news, but I thought it best that anyone desirous of contacting telephone numbers on mainland USA should be aware of this unprecedented situation. That is the end of the announcement. Thank you.' The voice ended on the click of a switch.

'Why is that?' asked Anna, puzzled. 'We're only a few miles out at sea.'

'I told you that I got news of Castle's death from the ticker tape. There was other news I didn't bother to pass on. A great rush on the stock market.'

'Let's go and see what the latest is,' said Anna.

Hand in hand, they went back to Davey's room. In the brief time he had been away, a huge white serpent of tape paper had spewed from the ticker machine, which chattered on busily. Davey ripped out the paper and began to read.

'It's the biggest slump since the stock exchange started,' he said in amazement.

'Let me see,' Anna asked him. He handed the long screed of paper to her.

She began to read it out loud.

'Banks attempt to stem worst ever stock crash stop Thirteen million shares sold in one day stop Market swamped unable to cope stop Political leaders confer urgently stop'

Click click click went the machine.

'Stock prices slump by fourteen million dollars in nationwide stampede to unload stop Banks fight desperately to support plummeting share values stop Shares worth ten dollars each yesterday now cannot find buyer at ten cents stop Thirty bankers commit suicide overnight rather than face ruin stop Dealers die of heart attacks stop Celestial Films Hollywood's biggest studio out of business stop Other film makers likely to follow stop Industry spokesman prophesies cutbacks lay-offs bankruptcies more more'

'Lucky for me I took my money up front,' said Davey.

Anna read on. Companies were closing down across the country; they had literally no money left to pay their employees, and the banks had none to lend them. Clients besieged bank buildings which locked their doors to keep them out. Crowds of investors flooded into Wall Street. Everyone was desperate to sell, no one wanted to buy, at any price. More stockbroking firms were going out of business by the hour.

'What went wrong?' asked Davey, bemused. 'Only a few months ago, everyone was predicting that the boom would go on for ever.'

'Ever heard of the South Sea Bubble?'

'Tell me.'

'I remember hearing about it in history lessons at school. Roughly two hundred years ago, the South Sea Company was formed in Britain to trade with Spanish America. It did so well for the first few years that it actually took over responsibility for the National Debt.

'Everyone thought that investing in this company was like printing their own money, just as earlier this year I read an article in the *Ladies Home Journal*, by the chairman of the National Democratic Committee, who claimed that anyone who invested only fifteen dollars a month in ordinary stocks would make eighty thousand dollars in twenty years. Guaranteed.

'More and more money poured into the South Sea Company and the directors indulged in increasingly speculative ventures, all guaranteed to make a quick and certain profit. So they thought. And then suddenly, inexplicably, the whole thing went down. It crashed in the greatest financial catastrophe that had ever involved Britain, France and Holland. What's happening now in Wall Street sounds even worse.'

As she spoke, she was skimming through another long tape.

'Ah, a familiar name. Mr Vandervell, vice-president of the Bank of World Indemnity. He's been found shot at his house in Connecticut, leaving a note for the police. The bank's ruined. You know what that means for me?'

'You didn't invest in it?'

'The other way round. I first used them in Nassau. Then O'Grady and I bought Red-Rose Productions, using them again, and changed the name to Traders. We went into serious debt with the bank when we borrowed money to buy up five hundred cinemas from the Greek, Andropolous.

'We beat Castle to that deal by days. He tried to ruin us so the outfit could pick up the chain cheaply. We staved him off, and now the bank's broke. That makes me broke as well. All that effort, all that risk, Shah and O'Grady gone, and for nothing. Nothing at all.'

Anna caught sight of her face in the mirror. She realised that with this terrible news she should look distraught, pale, desperate. And yet somehow she did not feel as though any of this really involved her personally. Almost incredibly, she felt above the catastrophe, beyond its reach.

It was as though the money she had made in Nassau, in films and through the cinemas was not real money. Real money was what she had earned working for Mrs MacTavish in Scotland, or what Mrs Johnson paid her for looking after her children. These other huge sums had come too easily to be dignified with the description of being earned, and now they had gone just as quickly.

She had never really expected to make so much, and now that she had lost a fortune, the loss seemed unimportant, as though she was not affected. It was all happening to other people, not to her. She remembered the voice she had heard so long ago, prophesying that one day she would be rich. And then . . . And then . . . So it had all been forecast. Perhaps the reason she felt so calm about what had happened was because she had been subconsciously expecting it.

'You think the bank's creditors will sell off Traders' studio and the cinemas?' Davey asked her.

'They'll probably have to. If they can find a buyer. There will be great bargains going now. New fortunes to be made by anyone who has any spare cash.'

'I suppose so. Well, this is the moment when I declare my interest – in you and in Traders. In that order. First, I'm asking you to marry me, Anna.'

'But you told me long ago your contract with Celestial ruled out marriage.'

'It did, until Celestial went out of business. Now it's out of business. So I'm free to propose, and I'm proposing.'

'In that case, I'm accepting.'

As they kissed, more ticker tape poured unheeded from the machine.

Slowly, they drew apart.

'I am delighted about your interest in me,' said Anna softly. 'But what about Traders?'

'That is what we will be from now on.'

'But all I've built up is finished. I'm not rich any more.'

'And a very good thing, too, for now you can advise me on the price I should pay to buy back the company. That can be my wedding present to you. Then we will be more than traders, we'll be partners. And from then on, I'll pay the bills. I was always led to believe a husband should support his wife. You wouldn't argue about that, now, would you?'

'Right now I'm not arguing about anything,' Anna replied meekly. 'As you say, we're not only traders. We're partners.'

More Enchanting Fiction from Headline:

JANET MACLEOD TROTTER

Shortlisted for *The Sunday Times* Young Writer of the Year Award

The Darkening Skies

A moving saga of
the North East in
wartime

Though by nature an optimist, when Sara Pallister arrives in
the mining town of Whitton Grange she cannot help but be
appalled by the welcome she receives. Her father having died
leaving their farm bankrupt, Weardale-born Sara is now the
poor cousin, reluctantly taken into the household of her
officious, narrow-minded Uncle Alfred whose wife Aunt Ida
does little but spoil their unbearable seven-year-old, agree with
her opinionated husband and attend endless W. I. socials.

Determined to make Sara pay her way, Uncle Alfred hires her
out to work in Dolly Sergeant's grocer's shop where she meets
funny, bashful young Raymond Kirkup and his warm-hearted
aunt, Louie. And it is through Raymond that Sara encounters
the family that is to change her life: the Dimarcos, exotic,
extrovert and Italian, the owners of Whitton Grange's popular
ice-cream parlour. Even as the shadows of the Second World
War grow more menacing and hostility increases towards the
foreign Dimarcos, Sara finds herself irresistibly drawn to
leather-jacketed, motorbike-riding Joe Dimarco...

Don't miss Janet MacLeod Trotter's first saga, *The Hungry
Hills*, also available from Headline: 'Full of warmth and
courage' *Sunderland Echo*; 'Wonderful...if you don't mind
losing sleep as you read by torchlight into the night, do get this
book' *The Miscarriage Association Newsletter*; 'Truly a novel
for saga lovers, weaving together the lives of many characters
with compassion and affection' *Northern Echo*;'You'll believe
you are there!' Denise Robertson

FICTION/SAGA 0 7472 4359 X

A selection of bestsellers from Headline

THE CHANGING ROOM	Margaret Bard	£5.99 ☐
BACKSTREET CHILD	Harry Bowling	£5.99 ☐
A HIDDEN BEAUTY	Tessa Barclay	£5.99 ☐
A HANDFUL OF HAPPINESS	Evelyn Hood	£5.99 ☐
THE SCENT OF MAY	Sue Sully	£5.99 ☐
HEARTSEASE	T R Wilson	£5.99 ☐
NOBODY'S DARLING	Josephine Cox	£5.99 ☐
A CHILD OF SECRETS	Mary Mackie	£5.99 ☐
WHITECHAPEL GIRL	Gilda O'Neill	£5.99 ☐
BID TIME RETURN	Donna Baker	£5.99 ☐
THE LADIES OF BEVERLEY HILLS	Sharleen Cooper Cohen	£5.99 ☐
THE OLD GIRL NETWORK	Catherine Alliott	£4.99 ☐

All Headline books are available at your local bookshop or newsagent, or can be ordered direct from the publisher. Just tick the titles you want and fill in the form below. Prices and availability subject to change without notice.

Headline Book Publishing, Cash Sales Department, Bookpoint, 39 Milton Park, Abingdon, OXON, OX14 4TD, UK. If you have a credit card you may order by telephone – 0235 400400.

Please enclose a cheque or postal order made payable to Bookpoint Ltd to the value of the cover price and allow the following for postage and packing:
UK & BFPO: £1.00 for the first book, 50p for the second book and 30p for each additional book ordered up to a maximum charge of £3.00.
OVERSEAS & EIRE: £2.00 for the first book, £1.00 for the second book and 50p for each additional book.

Name ....

Address ....

....

....

If you would prefer to pay by credit card, please complete:
Please debit my Visa/Access/Diner's Card/American Express (delete as applicable) card no:

Signature .... Expiry Date ....